Mirage/Dream

S.E. Van Meter

This book is dedicated to Mom and Dad, Eric Troyer, and Brian Paone. Without all of these wonderful people, this project may have never been made.

Editor: Brian Paone
Cover art & interior graphics: Amy Hunter
Formatter: Kari Holloway

ISBNs
Paperback: 978-1-7344523-0-3
eBook: 978-1-7344523-1-0

Chapter
One

The time displayed 5:25 a.m. in bright crimson red digits. Nik Vanelli stared at the red digits as he awoke from a dreamless sleep. He shifted his glance from the alarm clock to the adjacent bathroom entrance at the foot of his bed. The light was still on, and both entrances were open. It was strange the light above the medicine cabinet was left on. Nik always preferred to sleep in absolute darkness except for the alarm clock light. He was puzzled he forgot to turn off the light. He blinked hard and rubbed his eyes, straining to break the sleep. He steadied himself with his left elbow. Still lying on his side, he reviewed the order of events from the previous night. Drowsily, he remembered he performed with his band, Lapis Lazuli, at Jeanelle's Bar in Gibbswood. He slowly massaged his forehead, gaining memories. He was glad today was the Sunday morning of Memorial Day weekend and could take the day to rest.

Last night, his partner and lead guitarist, Alex Cahoon, had been feeling apprehensive and had wrestled with a bout of stage fright, but Nik did not have to carry Alex or the rest of the band. Everyone had brought their *A*-game. Kenny Elnor, the drummer, had kept precision time; Andy Wardley, a disciplined self-taught musician, played well on rhythm guitar. Nik's pumping basslines and keyboard work had been top of his game. He had played with pride, knowing his performance was showcasing his classical training and vocal work. He had blinked hard, exhibiting quiet gratitude toward Penny, his piano teacher, enriching him with music theory and chord structure. He had also extended gratitude toward his father who taught him how to play the bass guitar.

No longer wishing to focus on his memories of musical education, he separated his mind from reminiscing on the set.

The band opened with a cover of Rush's "YYZ." It was Nik's idea to begin the set with the song, to impress the crowd. Gibbswood's audience was a refined group of affluent people. He executed the roster of songs until they ended with "Josie" by Steely Dan. Employing a fusion of progressive rock and jazz resonated well.

Still lying in bed, he recalled how a tall shapely sandy-blonde woman wearing a sapphire-blue spaghetti-strap tank top and tight blue jean cut-off shorts had approached him. He exchanged glances with her as he panned the crowd. He first noticed her sitting leisurely, sipping a mixed drink—possibly a Washington Apple or a vodka and cranberry. As the night

progressed, she approached the stage. As each song ended, she grew closer until she stood at the front of the stage. The performance finished, and he introduced the band members then finally introduced himself.

At the end of the introduction, she disappeared. He scanned the crowd and faced his bandmates, nodding. The crowd dispersed off the dance floor. Nik and Lapis Lazuli started the teardown process. Once they had stowed their instruments and amplifiers to be loaded, Jeanelle and Charlie Spaulding approached them.

Charlie, a rotund bald man, stood in front of them, excited. His arm was locked with Jeanelle's. "You guys were fantastic. I can't believe four guys could display such musicianship."

Jeanelle, resembling an old hair-band groupie, smiled at the band, sizing up Nik. The bleached-blonde cougar enjoyed more than the band's performance. "I think you guys sounded hot tonight."

Charlie faced her, darting a look of disapproval. After surveying Nik with tunneled vision, he tightened his grip on her arm, shaking her from her trance.

"Oh, oh, and of course my Charlie really contributed projecting you guys with his light and sound work."

Charlie's wide face lightened with the compliment. "You boys know you're the first band we've had perform here since we bought the bar." Charlie then bragged how he had purchased the bar for his wife to run.

Jeanelle shifted the subject to the band's payment. "You guys definitely earned your paycheck. You guys should come back and play for us again. I think it's good for Charlie to get back out there and run sound and lights." She reached into her red vinyl purse and distributed four one hundred-dollar bills to each band member.

Nik grabbed his hundred-dollar bill, thanking her. Alex followed by expressing gratitude; Kenny followed employing humbled reserve.

When Andy received his payment, he swiftly grabbed the bill. "Yoink! Thanks for the bread, Jeanelle."

Everyone laughed as Andy commented how he would spend the money on vices of the flesh and women of loose virtue. After the band and the Spauldings finished their laugh, they carried out their equipment. Charlie cleaned the bar floor, and Jeanelle tallied the cash drawer and tended to the bar counters. The band walked out the rear exit as the owners bid them a good rest of their evening and invited them to play again. Charlie added that it was Memorial Day weekend and only the beginning of the summer. Nik and the rest of the band gleamed with excitement.

As Nik and the others loaded their gear into their own vehicles, a woman approached him in the back alley. He had just loaded his Ampeg amplifier, Roland keyboard, and sunburst-red Rickenbacker bass into his Dodge Dakota's bed when he felt a tap on his shoulder. Nik startled, not expecting the touch. When he turned, he saw the shapely sandy-blonde staring face to face with him. She glistened with an attractive shine in the sultry night heat.

Nik felt instantly drawn to her as he sized her up, attempting to not be noticed. He scanned her from top to bottom as she tilted back her head and arms to remove her hair tie. Her movements appeared deliberate to gain attention. She shut her eyes and arched her back, protruding her chest. Nik tactfully beheld her body. He was attracted to her beautifully sculpted shoulders and enticing cleavage that shined with perfect sheen. Continuing to look farther down, he was drawn to her tanned shapely thighs that looked silky to the touch.

Nik's confidence broke him free from the trance. After all, she was the one who had approached him. The comic relief of the band always lived and swore by one fundamental rule he often shared. "If a man must chase the woman, then he must do all the work. However, if she chases him, then you know it's in the bag." Andy would say this often in hope he would be at the receiving end. Being overly thin, gawky, and gangly, this would not come to be reality. He would boldly defy his own advice, chasing after anyone he found attractive. Usually Andy would be shot down, watching the other guys approach.

As confident as Nik was with his musical talents and abilities, he was also confident with his looks. At the age of twenty-seven, he was muscular, toned, and had a handsomely shaped jawline, with large blue eyes. He enjoyed his newfound looks and body. Four years ago, he had lost seventy-five pounds and began a rigid workout regimen, changing from a quiet loner into a charismatic band leader. His thoughts culminated on all his attributes with pride. He regarded Andy's words of wisdom. The woman had been transfixed on him throughout the entire performance. He watched her let her hair fall; he was armed with a seductive smile to greet her as she opened her eyes.

She had a momentary look of shock then returned a smile. She straightened herself, gaining composure as she wanted to play it confident. "Hi, I'm Samantha, and I wanted to talk to you after the show."

Nik attentively regarded her. He returned the introduction as he closed his truck's tailgate. "Hi. I'm Nik Vanelli."

She followed him as he walked along the driver's side. "Yeah, I already know who you are. I saw you guys play last weekend at the Cabana Bay Bar in Sandousten."

Nik remembered playing at the Cabana Bay Bar but did not remember seeing her. Along with being blessed with good looks and musical talent, he was also blessed with an uncanny memory. He would have remembered seeing someone like Samantha. If he mentioned that, the control of the conversation would be shifted to her court.

He employed good verbal judgment and decided to talk about the venue. "Yeah. In the spring and summertime, we really enjoy playing the coastal area. People know how to party there, and the crowds are always lively. I also like the lake during this time of year." He stood by his truck and waited to see what Samantha would say next. He wondered whether she would bid him a goodnight and leave or if she would further the conversation.

She leaned her back against the side of the truck and bent her left knee upward, pressing her foot against the side. She reached into the left pocket of her shorts and checked the time on her cellphone. She returned her phone into her pocket and removed a pack of Marlboro Light 100s.

She rubbed her legs in circular motions with her palms then placed a cigarette to her lips. "I don't think I have a lighter. Do you have one I could use?"

Nik retrieved his cigarettes and lighter from the pocket of his khaki shorts. He placed a cigarette into his mouth and lit it, then he lit Samantha's cigarette. As he extended his arm to light her cigarette, she grabbed his hand, guiding it to her lips.

She took a deep drag, tilted back her head and stretched her arms upward and spread them along the length of the truck's bed, smiling seductively. "I saw you looking at me from across the stage earlier."

Nik looked at her and said nothing. He did not want to respond by competing with her ego. He waited to see if she would add more to the statement.

"It is okay. I was looking too, and I was looking last weekend." She raised an eyebrow.

She thoroughly intrigued Nik. He knew the conversation was now gainfully in his favor and wanted to ask how she found herself in Gibbswood, as Sandousten was more than an hour away. He took a moment to tactfully find the right words. He took a drag from his cigarette, giving him a chance to smoothly allocate the question. "Sandousten to Gibbswood is over an hour drive. What brings you to this small-town hamlet?" He laughed by employing the word *hamlet*.

"My baby sister Miranda lives here, and she just had her first baby—a little girl. She and her boyfriend, Troy, live on Sattler Street—the next street over. I visited for the weekend to see the baby. I also realized your band was playing tonight, so I figured it just might be an added bonus."

He smiled at her finishing his cigarette. He finished his cigarette and reached into his pocket to check the time on his cellphone—11:20 p.m.—and he was in the mood for some cold beer. He knew if he hurried, he could make it to Trixey's drive-thru before they closed.

Still wanting to maintain his cool, confident stature, he wished her a goodnight. "Well, I hate to cut this short, but I want to get some cold beer and relax. The drive-thru where I get my beer closes soon, so I have to hit the road."

Samantha's eyes widened with excitement. "I think a few cold beers sound like a great idea! I also lost my lighter, so I was wondering if I could ride with you to the drive-thru and pick up a new one."

Nik was surprised at Samantha's boldness, asking him for a ride. He regarded her shapely body and threw caution to the wind, concealing his reservations. "Why not? Go ahead and hop in."

Nik fastened his seatbelt, started the truck and drove down the alley, cautiously turning onto Main Street, which became Gibbswood Road once outside of the village limits. Trixey's drive-thru was located on Gibbswood Road, which ran between Gibbswood and Pemkey, where Nik lived.

An awkward silence crept into the truck's cab, and Nik felt obligated to break and gain levity. "I just live in the next town to the west in Pemkey. I've been there for around four years now. It's kind of a tradition for me after a show to pick up some beer and toss back a few."

Samantha turned her gaze from out the passenger window and smiled. "So, you usually drink alone after you finish a show?"

He nodded nervously. A quiet moment passed before Trixey's drive-thru's sign emerged on the right. Nik entered the drive-thru through the rear.

By the time Nik had rolled down the window, the drive-thru attendant stood at the window. "Hey, Nik. What are you having tonight, buddy? You want the usual—a case of Busch Light?"

Nik smiled, realizing he had become a predictable patron. He acknowledged a case of Busch Light would be fine and requested a cigarette lighter for his companion.

The attendant peeked into Nik's truck. When he noticed Samantha's vibrant smile, he felt a glimpse of joy for his regular patron. Even though the attendant was much later in his years, he knew the combination of beer and a stunning woman would be a formula for an interesting evening. The attendant handed the case of beer and change to Nik, smiling at both.

Nik wished the attendant a good evening and pulled through. As they exited the drive-thru, Nik pivoted his head left and right, checking the traffic. He smiled at Samantha as he activated his left-turn signal.

She observed Nik as he prepared to make the left turn. She realized he had activated the left-turn indicator and placed her hand on his thigh. "Wait a minute. Where are you going?"

Nik explained he was driving her to Gibbswood, to her sister's house.

Samantha curled her bottom lip under her front teeth, drawing attention to her mouth, and shook her head. "No, no, no, boy. You said you were drinking beer alone tonight, and we both decided that would simply not do."

"Look, I'm glad you enjoyed the show, and it has been fun talking with you, but I don't think we really have been all together acquainted."

Samantha laughed in an unnerving manner. "How far is your home from here?"

"Around eight to ten minutes."

Samantha gestured toward Pemkey with an insisting motion. "That's just great. That's more than enough time for us to talk and get acquainted. Sometimes the best way to get to know someone is to take a ride with them."

Nik reluctantly agreed and retrieved a cigarette and his lighter from his pocket. He felt that smoking another cigarette might relax and help him to question the woman. He cracked his window, cancelled his left-turn signal and proceeded toward Pemkey.

As they headed toward Pemkey, he felt the timing was right for his onslaught of questions. Nik finished taking his final drag from his cigarette and flicked it out the window. "You know, I really don't know much about you other than your name is Samantha and you live in Sandousten. I think I'd feel better if I knew more."

Samantha finished smoking her cigarette and flicked it out the window. She rolled up the passenger side window, placed her palm on his thigh and made circular motions. "Well, my full name is Samantha Moore. I am twenty-three, single and have never been married nor do I have any children."

Nik nodded in acknowledgment.

As she spoke, she seemed more intent studying his leg. In a playfully sardonic manner, she indulged other information about herself, hoping to divert his reservations. "I was born in January. My favorite color is blue. I enjoy attending live shows, and my favorite type of underwear is thong panties." She grabbed deeper into his thigh and ran her pinky finger alongside his right testicle.

Nik reared back in the driver seat with shock and arousal as she tickled him.

Samantha laughed as she finished grazing him.

Nik grew embarrassed as she caused his testicle to jump.

She turned her gaze from his thigh to look at him.

He shifted his gaze from the road ahead to her. He glanced quickly into her eyes and saw she was full of desire. He stifled a small cough and returned his attention to the road.

She leaned toward his right ear. "Oh, baby, you have nothing to be afraid of. I like the way you feel, and, by the looks of it, I think you do too."

The hairs on the back of his neck stood upward as she softly bit the side of his neck. She reached for his right hand and placed it on top of her shapely thigh.

She turned to him again as they approached Pemkey's skyline. "It's okay. I want whatever happens tonight to happen." She pressed his hand deeper into her thigh, manipulating his hand as they passed Pemkey's village limit sign.

Nik realized he was speeding within the village limits. He did not know if he was speeding due to anticipation or sheer nervousness. Regardless, he knew he would have to employ mature judgment and slow down. He had beer in the truck and could not face the embarrassment of a deputy pulling him over and issuing him a ticket.

They entered Pemkey's village limits, and the road changed its name to Main Street. He passed through downtown, vigilantly watching the street signs. He passed Donaldson Road, followed by Lytle Street, Lamb Street, and then Broadway before stopping at the four-way stop at the intersection of Main and Caulenberg Street then making a left. After passing a few houses, he turned into the driveway of his single-story midnight-blue vinyl-sided house at 615 Caulenberg Street.

He stopped the truck and noticed she was humming to herself, entranced in self ecstasy. Nik was reluctant to interrupt her. He cleared his throat and faced her. "We're here. I might need my hand back to put the truck into Park and grab my stuff."

Samantha gracefully broke from her trance. "Oh, we're here already? That's awesome."

Nik told her to go onto the porch and wait for him; he had to carry his equipment into the garage.

She smiled and stepped from the truck. "That's okay. I think I might text my sister and let her know I'm all right. I'll grab the beer and watch you carry your stuff with those sexy arms." Samantha snatched the beer and exited the truck.

Nik approached the truck's rear, feeling his movements examined under close observation. Nik's strategy was to carry the heaviest piece of equipment into the garage first. He placed the amplifier on the sidewalk and grabbed his keys from his pocket. He excitedly rattled the keys, trying to guide them into the keyhole. He found a sturdy grip and plunged in the key. After placing the amplifier in the garage, he dashed to the open tailgate to grab his Rickenbacker guitar case and his Roland case then speed walked to the garage. He knew Samantha intently watched him, anticipating for him to join her on the porch.

He crested the porch's third step and saw Samantha had opened the case of beer and helped herself. She was fast to begin the night, and she wanted him to be aware of that. After she finished a large gulp of beer, she bent over from her seated position and reached into the case, retrieving and delicately handing a beer to Nik. "I couldn't wait, so I started without you. I think you have some catching up to do."

Nik was surprised how quickly she consumed the beer. He popped the tab, standing over her and staring at her with sharp interest. He studied her as she fanned her knees back and forth. He knew the motion was intentional.

She still glistened from the night heat, the streetlight from across the way amplifying and accenting the tone of her flesh— bright and vibrant. Her body called to him with full invitation as she shined.

Nik grew eager as he raised the bottom of his beer skyward. He was unsure of what the remainder of the night would bring, but he was anxious to get Samantha into the house. He finished his beer, set the empty can on the porch next to the post and asked if she wanted to come in and see the rest of the house.

Samantha spent no time as she raised both arms and dipped her fingertips to offer her hands.

He reached to grab her and pull her up gracefully.

When she was standing on both feet, she pulled her hands from his grip and wrapped her arms around his neck, pressing against his body and gently thrusting and gyrating. She locked her eyes with his in an inescapable gridlock. "Wow, you feel good," she whispered enticingly as she pressed. She leaned her face into his neck and ran her nose and lips under his Adam's apple through the side of his neck under his ear.

Nik felt his member take bulk gaining girth.

"Ooh, I think I just felt something," she said with excitement. "I think it's time to take this beer into the house and you give me the first-class tour."

Nik gained his composure, ushering her to the front door.

She gestured for him to not forget the case of beer and stepped through the doorway as he grabbed the case.

He flipped on the living room light and scurried to place his keys into his pocket.

Samantha surveyed the living room, looking impressed that a bachelor could keep an organized home. "I think the beer is going through me. Could you tell me where the bathroom is?"

Nik told her it was down the hallway and to the right before the master bedroom, across from his music room.

She thanked him and walked through the living room. She turned to him before she entered the bathroom.

Nik carried the case of beer to the kitchen on the right of the living room, placed it in the refrigerator and walked down the hallway, turning into his music room. He turned on the light and approached his Baldwin piano. He pulled the duet bench from underneath his piano and sat, inspecting to ensure he did not have embarrassing contraband lying around.

As he sat on the duet bench, he heard Samantha attempting to whisper. However, he understood every word. He assumed Samantha was on the phone with her sister.

"Hey, listen. I just wanted to call and let you know I'm here, and I think things will get pretty interesting tonight. I'll have him take me home tomorrow morning or maybe in the early afternoon, depending on just how interesting things get."

Nik heard a muffled voice ask Samantha if she was with the band member she had seen the other weekend and tonight. Samantha confirmed that Nik was indeed the person. Nik heard the faint voice question Samantha if she would have sex with him.

Without a doubt, Nik heard Samantha say, "Well, I will tell you this, when he helped me stand up, I felt it grow and swell, so I think the evening is off to a good start. Look, I got to go, because I've been in here long enough. Sometime, when Troy is out doing errands, I'll fill you in on what happened. I've got to go now. Goodbye."

Nik knew Samantha's intentions were absolute and she would be coming from the bathroom any second. He broke from eavesdropping and turned to his piano.

The bathroom door opened, and the light switch clicked off. He was in haste to find a piece of sheet music to place on the music rest. He grabbed a piece at random from the shelf where he kept his collection. He placed "Caroline, No" by The Beach Boys on the rest. He felt luck was tremendously on his side due to the romantic nature of the song. Most songs written in D-flat major create a romantic atmosphere. Brought back to his music theory memories, he recalled his introduction to the D-flat major key signature with "Clare de Lune." He strategically placed his hands on the piano keys, positioning his left hand's thumb and pinky on the A-flat octaves to bring broad range to the bassline. He placed his right hand on the keys to form a second inversion of the F-minor chord as he sang and played while Samantha entered.

Upon entering, Nik arrived at the song's bridge, raising his vocal pitch. He pretended he did not notice she was standing atop of him. Adding more to the illusion, he pretended that she had startled him. He faced her, feigning embarrassment she had caught him entangled in the music. Nik raised his hands from the weighted piano keys.

She approached him through the threshold and sat next to him, straddling the duet bench. "Wow, you play really well. You should do that song during one of your shows."

Nik smiled with reluctance. He slightly tilted his head and shook *no*. He agreed that "Caroline, No" was a beautiful song, but it did not have the appropriate presence. He commented further that it was a personal song he played to keep acclimated to his own personal musical theory training. Feeling his comments might cause him imminent danger of sounding pretentious, he broke from the rigors of musical knowledge.

She regarded him with enthralled interest.

He shifted quickly and added that some theory was quite easy to learn, and that anyone could apply the knowledge. He showed her as he asked her to sit facing the piano.

Samantha swiveled her right leg from her straddled position.

He instructed her to sit upright with shoulders high.

She arched her back, sitting up.

He grabbed her hand and showed her how to form a basic C-major chord triad. He explained it was as simple as hitting a note, skipping a note, hitting a note, skipping a note and finally hitting a note in unison to achieve a chord. He further explained the positioning of a chord and lowering the third position would achieve a minor chord, lowering the third and fifth position would diminish the chord, and raising the fifth would augment the chord while returning the third position to natural.

She recited what she did as she played the different variations. She spoke the type of chords—natural, minor, diminished, and augmented—as she played.

Nik was surprised she retained her first lesson.

She faced him with pride, feeling accomplished.

He identified something peculiar about Samantha he had not noticed earlier. From the overhead light's glow, he found she exhibited a unique feature—two different colored eyes. Her right eye was a shocking and beautiful sapphire blue, and her left eye was a calming emerald green. Her beautifully shaped, different colored eyes enticed Nik, and he thought her distinctive characteristic added to Samantha's aesthetic.

He did not comment on the two different colors of her eyes—a condition he remembered being called heterochromia or something like that. He sat on the duet bench, studying her with greater interest.

She asked if she had played well.

He agreed, solidifying her ability.

She leaned toward Nik.

Before he realized it, her tongue was in his mouth, whirling dreamily. His body became light-stricken with dreamlike fuzz encompassing his head and body. The kiss was inevitable. He gained reality of the circumstance, matching her tongue movements.

After Samantha and Nik finished their kiss, Samantha removed her hands from the piano and sat on the duet bench, surveying the room. She looked at his shelves of sheet music and his racks that held vinyl records, .45 rpms, cassette tapes, and compact discs. When she finished panning, she scanned his desk, taking notice of a manila envelope. Samantha stood from the duet bench, approached the desk and picked up the manila envelope.

Nik broke free from his spell. "No, don't touch that."

Samantha startled and faced him.

"Look, I'm sorry I made you jump, but that is important to me and private."

Samantha's look of shock and embarrassment dissipated. She apologized for being forward, inspecting the items on his desk. She could not help her curiosity on the label scrolled on the envelope stating LIFE'S WORK. She questioned him about the contents.

Nik felt a sense of shame when she brought the subject to question. He did not want to divulge the sad truth of the envelope's contents. He decided to amend the saddest details. "It's true it's my life's work, but it's not finished yet, and it's not ready to be exposed."

She looked at the envelope again and placed it on the desk. She stood waiting for him to indulge her in the history of its contents.

Nik blew a quiet sigh. "It started seven years ago when I was twenty. I had a painful break up from a relationship. I made some bad decisions that led me to the hospital. I was unconscious for a day. I felt, having such a close brush with death, I should try to accomplish something with my life, so I bought that envelope to keep the album you see in front of you. However, it's more than just an album. It's a concept album detailing life and romance."

Samantha stood, staring at Nik. "So, besides being good looking, you're pretty deep too. That is hot." As she spoke, he felt relief he did not have to indulge the vivid details.

He remembered the true origin. He had been an overweight loner viewed by others as undesirable. During this time, he had luck twice with the opposite sex. He recollected the night of his first kiss at the Amsdale summer fest the July after his sixteenth birthday and his first and only girlfriend—a petite elfin girl with tight curly brown hair, Kara Anderson—who broke his heart and left him for a privileged clean-cut prep.

He reacted with the sobs of a broken heart, knowing what he had felt proved true. Kara had always loved her first love,

Derrick Connly, and felt nothing for Nik. His hatred for Derrick ran deeply, continuing to loathe him and Kara with totality with what they drove him to do. It was on the day he overdosed on the full bottle of Vicodin the dentist had prescribed him from his wisdom teeth removal. It was the twenty-second anniversary of John Lennon's death. He regained consciousness in the hospital to his mother pleading for him to wake up. He awoke in fear, strapped to the hospital bed. The resident psychiatrist told him the county sheriff's department mandated him to spend three nights in the hospital's psychiatric ward or spend time in jail. Nik opted for the three nights in the psychiatric ward.

Shortly after he had returned home, he questioned his station in life. After spending three more years at home, he had dedicated and played music intensely while losing weight. Shortly after he had celebrated his twenty-third birthday, he moved through the ranks at Moline Medical Warehousing, promoting to the position of straight truck driver from warehouse associate. As he studied for his class-B commercial driver license, he lost more weight, becoming inspired to perform. During that time, he traded his Chevrolet Corsica for his truck and left his hometown Amsdale to move to Pemkey, as he was at optimum physical condition and began his partnership with his bandmates of Lapis Lazuli. Despite playing music and tightening his musical abilities with his band, he enjoyed the single life and the conquest of one-night stands. Such a conquest was only a few feet from him. He knew the evening would be exciting.

Nik stood from the duet bench, stretching his arms. His motivations lay with entertaining his company. He knew he needed to regain control of the mood. "Say, don't we have some beer chilling in the fridge?"

Before they left the music room, she gestured at his music collection. "If I'm drinking with you, why don't we spin some music?"

Nik thought that would be an excellent idea. He grabbed his favorite romantic mixed disc from the racks. He had copied this disc the day he had moved into his house, and it contained his favorite slow-dance song. Employing this strategy meant he could be drunk, close to her, and pressed against her. Nik lead Samantha to the kitchen table.

Samantha sat while Nik went into the living room and turned on the stereo.

Nik rejoining Samantha in the kitchen as Billy Squier's "My Kinda Lover" played from the adjacent room. He grabbed four beers from the refrigerator. The compact disc stereo played while they spoke and flirted as sobriety escaped. She asked him how he came to live in Pemkey, and he responded it was his job that originally led him here. She asked how he came into playing music, and he told her music was always in his family. His father had been in a performing band called Music Works, and they were playing at a local dive bar when his mother approached him, requesting a song. He concluded the rest was history.

He also told her that he was in the school concert band, and, during his time in junior high school, he took initiative in expanding his talents by learning to play piano while his father taught him how to play bass guitar.

The music played from the other room, and they continued to drink. She asked Nik more questions on how he had met his bandmates. He explained how he had met them at work, and they used to be on the same shift before he became a delivery driver. It was not instantaneous that they all became acclimated to playing together; it took a considerable amount of time and motivation for them to find their tightness. Alex

Cahoon was the up-and-coming lead guitarist; Kenny Elnor was the quiet and reserved drummer, and Andy Wardley was the class clown rhythm guitarist looking to become famous and get laid. Samantha said it was impressive Nik was not only the lead vocalist but a multi-instrumentalist playing the keyboard and the bass guitar. Nik felt esteemed.

Nik felt virile as Samantha quested for knowledge. All he had to do was answer questions, not having to go through extreme measures to impress. They were both feeling the effects of the beer as time pressed.

While the disc approached the end, Eric Troyer's "Mirage" played. As the intro started, Samantha stood from the chair, alluringly swaying her hips. "Oh my god, this song sounds amazing." She sashayed to Nik's side of the table, dancing seductively. She straddled his lap, dancing above him. She grabbed his open beer and poured the liquid into her mouth. She grabbed the collar of his Union Jack tank top, pulling his body to her and forcing the beer into his mouth.

Nik drank from Samantha's mouth, falling to full intoxication. He swayed his head back, and the last thing he remembered seeing was the overhead light.

Running through the order of events, he felt the immense urge to urinate. He lifted the covers from his naked body; he felt a tug of weight from his private regions as he sat up. He was wearing a condom, and it was generously full. He reached, feeling the tip of the reservoir through the shaft and realized he had released a hefty load. He remained sitting, thinking he had not been able to produce so much since he was a horny teenager. He silently laughed, thinking it was not as much of a desire to have sex but more of a necessity.

As he straightened his legs, he glanced to the other side of the bed and saw Samantha lying on top of the covers. Her naked body was in full glory as she slept. He sat with his mouth agape as he studied her beautiful full pert breast with ripe pink pierced nipples. He looked farther down, taking notice of her core. She had a flat, toned stomach adorned with a naval ring. Her bare, shapely hips and her shaved, manicured pubic region mesmerized him. Her bikini line displayed a tattoo of a unicorn's profile with a windswept mane. Nik placed his bare feet on the hardwood floor, lamenting he'd had the most amazing sex and could not remember it.

Nik stood from his bed as his head felt heavy from the aftermath of drinking. His footsteps were strategic, as he did not want to awaken the beautiful vixen. He was quietly grateful to whomever had left on the bathroom light. The light was his beacon through the dark terrain. He employed stealth, ensuring his movements would not jostle Samantha. When he arrived to the bathroom, he gently closed the door. He stood above the toilet, leaned forward and extended his arm from his body against the wall. As he readied to urinate, he panicked, realizing he still donned the condom. He awkwardly removed it; once removed, he raised it to eyelevel, to confirm the fullness of his previous night's endeavors.

The amount of fluid he had purged captivated him. It appeared as if he hadn't had sex for years. The last time he'd had a conquest was in March at a Saint Patrick's Day party, playing Beep's and Lisa's Bar—a small venue in Blanchard Mill. After the show, Lisa had introduced Nik to her younger sister, Tonya. Tonya had taken him to her apartment above the bar, and they had an unsatisfactory one-night stand. He had wanted to flee Tonya's place, feeling unfulfilled, while she was already planning their wedding. He had cringed when Beep called to request the band play at his bar. Beep further attempted to entice the deal, mentioning that Tonya would be there. He had shuttered from Beep's uncomfortable invitations. Not wanting to relish on the unpleasant memory, Nik was about to drop the condom in the waste basket until he noticed something unusual.

After close examination, what he saw appalled him. Reddish-brown spots spattered its exterior. He adjusted the sleep residue from his eyes and identified the substance as dried blood. He felt uneasy fright take over, wondering what had transpired from the night before. He dropped the condom in the waste basket and washed his hands with scalding water. He scrubbed deeply, adding abundant amounts of soap. The hot water on his hands became agonizing, driving his urge to urinate to painful measures. Nik raced to the toilet without drying his hands and released his bladder. He stood over the toilet, urinating loudly and wishing the stream would be less audible.

He slowly flipped off the light to avoid the following click from waking Samantha. He exited the bathroom, gingerly closed the door and set his footsteps to memory. Nik lay awake in bed for an hour, wondering what would befall him when Samantha awoke. He was a bundle of nerves, running the scenarios through his mind. He feared she would wake and claim he had violated her. His mind dwelled in dark thoughts. He shivered from uneasiness as he stared at the alarm clock. He watched the time perpetuate as the minutes climbed. He had no strategy how to wake Samantha, as he did not truly know what had transpired. He did not know whether to tactfully wake her with a passionate kiss or pat her lightly while speaking her name. He only wished she would wake up and detail him on what had happened. All he could do was lay and wait for the hands of time to reveal the truth. Nik pulled the covers closer to his face, shielding him.

The alarm clock displayed 6:35 a.m. Nik succumbed to the wind of exhaustion. As his eyes became heavy, he felt a shifting movement behind him inch closer and remove the covers from his back. Exposing the entirety of his backside, he felt fingertips graze him through the top of his shoulders. The movement increased in intensity, and warm breath tickled the back of his neck. His body relaxed with relief. He turned slowly to face Samantha.

Her bright eyes shone through the morning light. Her body was inviting to him. She wrapped her right arm and leg around him and drew him closer. She smiled deeply at Nik, displaying her satisfied mood.

Nik mustered, "Good morning."

"Oh my god, it certainly is, especially after what happened last night."

Nik smiled, not remembering the events.

"What was that face about?" she asked him with playful contradiction.

Nik confessed he had no memory of the events, so he was unable to critique what had happened.

Samantha smirked with deviance and rolled on top of him. She leaned toward Nik, vibrantly eager to disclose the events. She passionately kissed him, aggressively whirling her tongue.

Nik felt the back of his head press against the pillow while reciprocating her excited kiss. Enjoying the moment, he still yearned to know what had happened.

She rose from kissing Nik and placed her hands on his shoulders, tilting her head to one side. "You really have no memory of what happened?"

Nik sadly shook his head.

"Oh my god, baby. You must not be able to hold your alcohol. You were intense last night. I have never experienced an orgasm like that in my whole life."

Nik became eager to hear more.

"What is the last thing you remember?"

Nik strained his memories, telling her the last thing he remembered was sitting at the kitchen table and receiving a mouthful of beer from her.

Samantha straddled him. "Really? That's too bad, because after that was when things got intense. After I gave you the beer kiss, you leaned backward, but, when you came forward, you became a fucking animal. You stood up and wrapped my legs around you, kissing me as you carried me to the bedroom. You threw me on the bed, and, in a flash, you were erect. I could only try to remove my clothes by the time you got onto the bed. You opened your nightstand and had slipped on a Magnum in no time, then you got inside me just as quick. You grabbed the back of my legs, pinned me down and plowed me deeply. At first, you hurt me, but then it felt good. You went at me for a what felt like a good thirty minutes. I arrived one last time with you before you passed out. You were so good and long that I came four times last night. You even caused me to bleed a little bit. I've never had a guy with that much girth to cause me to bleed. You left me sore and throbbing in all the right ways."

Nik beheld Samantha with indulged satisfaction. Regardless of not being able to remember the events, he was pleased to discover the sexiest woman he'd had told him that he was the best.

She straightened her back, sitting on her knees while straddling him. She leaned to the left to reach for her pack of cigarettes and lighter.

Nik grabbed an amber glass ashtray from the nightstand and placed it to his side.

Samantha lit her cigarette, arching her back to expose her bare breast. She tilted her head in an elegant manner while taking a drag from the cigarette then offered Nik a drag. Once finished with the cigarette, she set the ashtray and her cigarettes on the nightstand. She returned to her natural position, locking her fingers behind her head and stretched her arms to the ceiling. She reached her hands behind her back and massaged his penis.

Her hands felt amazing as she grazed him, bringing him to arousal. He was impressed she could accurately massage him from that position.

She pulled on him, rocking with enticing rhythm. Once he was fully erect, she retrieved a condom from the nightstand and tore out the contents with her teeth. She looked down on Nik with desire, telling him it was his turn to have something to remember. She grabbed his shaft and unfurled the condom as she gyrated. Once the condom encompassed Nik, she positioned herself on top and guided his penis inside her.

He felt the walls of her vagina slide over him and expand as he penetrated her. He grabbed her hips, pulling her to him. Her hips quivered as he went deeper. He bottomed out inside her, and she yelped with concurrent pain and pleasure.

She writhed for a moment with pain and resumed riding, increasing her speed. She placed her hand on his chest, clawing as she entered the apex of orgasm. She cooed softly, and he felt her contract and flex as she looked down.

"I think that I could get used to riding you," she said, panting. "I'm feeling good, babe. If you're ready for your turn, go ahead."

Nik told her no. He wanted to take this as far as he could and make up for lost memories. He grabbed her shoulders, forcing her down and driving deeper.

As she rode, she sweat on him through increased motions.

Nik lay while Samantha's sweat rained on him as he smelled her perfume—intoxicating and evocative—and he concentrated the scent as a means of a deterrent to prevent premature arrival. He wanted to impress Samantha with his sexual prowess. He wanted to solidify his grasp on her and secure a return visit.

She regarded him, flushed near exhaustion.

Nik felt self-assured knowing it was his time to release. Nik pulsed and throbbed as he felt his own orgasm coming; Samantha achieved a strong and flushing orgasm. As he arrived, he felt his head swirl to the point of being clouded with haze.

Samantha bent down after they finished and smothered him with heated kisses. "You are fucking amazing," she said, winded. Samantha kissed Nik then climbed off him and lay spread out in a starfish position next to him.

Nik and Samantha lay in bed gasping and panting, collectively attempting to catch their breath. His thoughts swelled as he looked at her. He could not believe he had shared a kiss with this woman let alone acquire her sexually. He despondently recalled his last sexual experience with Tonya— mediocre—and remembered his birthday resolution. He thought of the unpleasant braying sounds she had made as she achieved orgasm. Upon completion with Tonya, he wanted to get as far away from her as possible. He now felt the other end of the spectrum for Samantha. He did not want to put distance between her. He enjoyed watching her pant as she lay next to him.

The night of his twenty-seventh birthday on May 6, he would no longer settle for average or below average. On that night, he had drank in his music room, holding the Life's Work envelope. He knew with absolute resolve that if he would derive inspiration for his labor of love, he would have to fuel himself with beauty and passion. He hoped with Samantha that his creative muses would overflow. She had given Nik something he had never experienced. She far exceeded his expectations of his resolution. He knew the memory of Samantha Moore would be cemented with him for the rest of his days. He also was taken with a sensation of great fear. While true he was pleased with his resolve, he feared he may be falling in love with her. The fear compounded him knowing she was an endeavor from a previous night's conquest. He took conviction over his unpleasant thought, reassuring it was *she* who had approached him. After running through the thoughts, he stood and stretched his arms.

Samantha looked at him, still catching her breath.

"I'm going to hop in the shower and get cleaned up," he said. "I was wondering if you'd like to join me."

Samantha pried herself up from her starfish position and reached for Nik.

He carefully grabbed her hand and lead her into the bathroom. He found two of his softest towels from the linen closet, placed them on the closed toilet lid and stepped into the shower. He turned on the water and felt the beads hit him with a feeling of renewal. Nik watched Samantha as she became soaked. He thought nothing was more attractive than a wet woman. The water seemed to accentuate the details of her features, bringing attention to her curves and shapeliness. Nik was being polite by inviting her to take a shower, but it was for his own pleasure to watch her soaking wet. He may not be able to remember the previous night's events, but he was definitely going to enjoy the pleasure of watching her.

They finished the shower, and Nik stepped out first and offered Samantha a towel.

She smiled at him, regarding how thoughtful he was.

He gently raised his towel to dry her face. They finished and entered the bedroom with their towels wrapped around them. As they arrived at the foot of the bed, Nik drew her toward him and kissed her.

His actions surprised her, and she enjoyed returning the kiss. "You must have really enjoyed your shower. Hold on a second. Let's get dressed." She collected her clothes from her side of the bed.

Nik followed suit from his side.

While they got dressed, she pulled her phone from her pocket and swiped it on.

Nik pulled his shirt over his head and saw Samantha's face had become forlorn—the light on her face faded.

She looked at Nik, frightening him with her expression. "Look, we got to go right now. I need to get back to Gibbswood."

Panic swooped over him. It was his natural instinct to question her if something was wrong, but that only fueled her urgency. Nik hurried to locate his shoes by the side of the bed and slipped them on without tying them.

"We have to go now. I need to get back to Gibbswood."

Nik's heart raced with fear as Samantha barked at him with need. Nik did not question her; he complied and rushed out the door with her racing to his truck.

Once they were both seated inside the truck, Samantha's mood shifted more. She became urgent, commanding him to hurry.

Nik, flustered and nervous with Samantha's tone, sped through Pemkey, heading east on Main Street where it became Gibbswood Road. As they drove, he glanced at Samantha nervously typing on her phone. Nik decided to concentrate on the road and not question her.

In-between texting, she asked if he could go faster.

Nik did not reply. He increased his speed, but he employed caution, knowing today was Memorial Day weekend, and the police would be patrolling with heightened vigilance.

Arriving in Gibbswood, Samantha burst with anticipation. "Drop me off at Jeanelle's, please."

Nik looked at her and asked if she would rather be taken to her sister's house.

She faced Nik and darted him a hateful look. "No, I don't want to be taken to my sister's. Take me to Jeanelle's. Now."

Nik did not respond. He followed Samantha's wishes, stopping in front of Jeanelle's and throwing the truck into Park.

Samantha surprised him gripping his right hand. She drew his hand to her mouth, squeezing the circulation from his fingers and pressing her lips hard against the back of his hand.

"You're scaring me, Samantha. Did I do something wrong?"

She told Nik that he had not done anything wrong. She assured him that he, in fact, had done everything right. She leaned over quickly and pecked him dryly on the lips.

"Can I get your number at least before you go? Is there a chance I'll ever see you again?"

She studied Nik's face. Her eyes became glossy and reddened with tears, the contrast between her blue eye and green eye brightening. "Whether it's here or in another town, I *will* see you play again, and I promise I'll give you my number. But I must go now." Samantha sprung from Nik's truck.

As he pulled away, she flashed him the *I-love-you* gesture as he drove by. Nik returned the gesture and turned to see her running in desperation toward Sattler Street. He headed toward Pemkey, alone.

Quietly pondering the strange events and Samantha's peculiar shift in mood, he shouted, "What the fuck just happened?" Nik's emotions were a hypervigilant roller coaster as he pondered the previous night and this morning. His thoughts shifted toward fear and anger as he passed Trixey's drive-thru. He realized he had just met Samantha, and it was not his place to pry, but he felt apprehension on her urgency to return.

As he entered Pemkey, he calmed his fear. He took solace in his thoughts about Samantha's last action. He recounted the kiss on his hand, the firm pressed kiss against his lips, and how she became glossy-eyed. Her words felt true to him when she told him that she wanted to see him again. The sadness and desperation of her tone seemed heartfelt. When he approached the four-way stop before his turn to go home, he thought about the *I-love-you* gesture she had flashed him. The gesture seemed premature, but Nik thought how adamant she had been to display to him.

Once he made the turn, he felt calmness embrace his mind. He was grounded when he pulled into the driveway. He exited the truck, sure of the events. He firmly closed the truck door behind him and approached the porch. He climbed the steps and sat leisurely on the porch glider. He grabbed his pack of cigarettes and lighter from his pocket and enjoyed his morning cigarette. Through the chaos earlier, he did not have time to enjoy his first cigarette of the day and felt it was a wonderful treat to enjoy it at that moment. He sat with pleasure, looking upon the front lawn glazed with morning dew. He panned the other houses and their lawns on the city block, and they were coated glistening with the sparkles of morning light.

As he observed the morning dew on the lawns through the sunlight, he realized he was reclusive. While he was grateful his neighbors respected his privacy, as he did theirs, he wondered if they had been privy to him bringing a strange woman into his house last night and if they had watched Samantha and him leave the house with unpleasant haste. Regardless, he knew the neighbors would not approach him and question him about the matter, as the neighbors would have in his hometown.

He thought of his next-door neighbor at his parents' house. Brian Smalls, who lived with his parents and ten years to Nik's senior, would usually be found on Nik's front porch after Nik would bid a guest farewell. Brian mooched cigarettes from him and would ask about his guest. Brian and the other neighbors would peak through their windows at Nik and his girlfriend as they kissed goodbye. As soon as Nik became aware of his neighbors' voyeurism, they would remove their fingers from the blinds. Nik thought Brian would be at his front porch right now if he still lived in Amsdale, making crude comments about Samantha's body. Nik laughed as he thought of Brian Smalls still living with his parents in that monochromatic town. Nik felt great joy to be in his new hamlet away from Amsdale and Bateson School District.

As he stood from the glider, he saw the two beer cans from the previous night. He flicked the cigarette into the coffee can he used as an ashtray and grabbed the two empty cans. "I think it'll be a long time before I have another evening like last night's."

Nik unlocked and opened his front door. He turned and glanced at the dew-covered lawn again.

Chapter Two

His living room drew golden rays of light beaming through the windows. The beams of light were fixed and appeared tangible, as if they were solid bars of gold. The fleeting residual unpleasantness of Samantha's hasted urgency had dissipated. Still feeling some minute apprehension reside within him, he strolled with motivation toward the kitchen to fetch a cold beer and begin the remainder of his Memorial Day weekend. When he entered the kitchen, Samantha's lingering scent greeted him. He stood puzzled, challenging his memories of the smell. He knew Samantha's scent was evocative in a manner he could not piece together, but he pressed on knowing the mystery would be revealed. He concentrated further, and the memories embodied him with a flutter. He spoke aloud with an uncontrollable pitch. "Freesia."

After pinpointing the fragrance, he attached the timeframe when an event had first introduced him to the smell. It was shortly after he had lost his weight and discussed starting a band with some of his acquaintances. Once Nik had achieved an ideal weight, he explored local bars and clubs to acclimate himself to crowds. He would quietly explore the layout of local bars and eventually encourage self-bravery and stage presence by participating in karaoke. One weekend in late April before his twenty-third birthday; Nik found himself at the Light House Bar and Grill in Hiedel, the next county over. As he entered the bar, he realized it was not a typical watering-hole bar but a club that catered to dance music over live music and karaoke. He was reluctant to enter and part with an eight-dollar cover charge, but he relented and entered regardless.

Being thrust into an element unfamiliar to him, he approached the bar, skillfully bobbing and weaving between the patrons. He arrived at the bar counter ready with cash in hand and ordered a shot of Jack Daniel's and a Washington Apple. As the bartender placed the shot of Jack Daniel's and the Washington Apple in front of him, he grabbed both and consumed it before the liquid could settle. After he drank the shot with a single gulp, he nursed the Washington Apple until ice remained. The alcohol took hold as he cut across the bar, edging to the dance floor. He observed the crowd before finding his body inching toward the dancing area. As his courage increased, he realized he was on the dance floor, swaying loosely.

A slender, curly haired brunette wearing glasses, a white silk blouse, and a red plaid school girl skirt inched toward him. Before Nik could react, she turned her back to him, pressing against him. She moved rhythmically to the pulsing club music. As she gyrated, she ushered his movements to her's.

Nik smelled her perfume, and it enthralled him. They danced for two songs before she grabbed his wrist and pulled him toward the pool tables in the back, smiling. Nik observed her slender athletic build. As he panned up, he saw her smiling at him with large teeth.

"Hi, I'm Christine. What's your name? Are you from around here? You moved pretty hot out there on the dance floor."

Nik reciprocated with gratitude and introduced himself. Christine had an attractive build, but her face illustrated an innocent nerdlike expression that was not all together unattractive but slightly different. Nik asked if she was from Hiedel, and she told him that she lived in town and attended Croghan Community College, majoring in accounting and early childhood development. Her pride for her double major made her appear more nerdlike as she manipulated her facial expressions. Nik tried to remove his concentration from her expressions and told her where he works and lives before he inquired about her perfume.

"Oh, do you like it? It's something new I wanted to try called Freesia. I think it smells like spring coming into bloom. Don't you think so?"

Nik agreed and noticed her necklace adorned with a blue teardrop stone. "That's a pretty curious necklace."

Christine chortled. "Do you like it? It's lapis lazuli. I wear it for its properties in bringing good luck and good dreams. I know it sounds kind of crazy, but I've always been a person in tune with nature and the supernatural elements."

Nik conversed with Christine until the bar was closing.

Christine's boisterous, overweight friend, Abby, approached them. "It's time to go home, Christine. Besides, I'm not getting any fish to bite."

Nik thought it was obvious why no one would accept.

Christine glared at Abby then regarded Nick with softer eyes. "I'm sorry, but she's right. It's time to go."

Nik agreed as he wished her a good evening and turned away.

She grabbed his wrist and pulled him toward her, tightening her hold. "Before you go, why don't you walk Abby and me to our car? It's late, and two young girls shouldn't be walking to their car alone."

Nik shifted his view from Abby pouting from a night of failed conquest then back to Christine and nodded in agreeance.

Abby took the lead, trudging through the pool room and across the bar as Christine pulled Nik. They walked along the buildings while Abby continued to complain. "I just don't get it. I have big breasts, and I'm willing to do anything and everything to make a guy happy."

Christine turned to Nik and smiled at him with attraction and uneasiness masking her embarrassment. They arrived to the rear parking lot; Abby ferociously swung open the Ford Probe's door and slammed it shut behind her. Christine and Nik shared a quiet moment on the passenger side before Christine craned her defined arms around his neck and kissed him goodbye. Nik felt overwhelmed; this was his first kiss in a long time.

After the kiss concluded, he opened the door for Christine, giving her a cheerful wave before taking one last look at her lapis lazuli necklace.

Abby shifted the car into gear with grinding force, rattling the exhaust as she sped off.

He stood behind the car, watching the taillights fade into the night horizon as he continued waving and wondering if she was watching him. He said "lapis lazuli" aloud to commit it to memory …

Nik rattled himself from deep concentration of the memory. He stood reflecting on the importance of the memory of freesia. It was not just a scent shared between two attractive women, but it was also the introduction to the words *lapis lazuli*. He opened the refrigerator, grabbed two beers, and guzzled them to achieve a buzz. He placed the empty cans in the waste basket and continued his trek of memories. He thought about the formation and evolution of his band and their show's success from the previous night. However, a sense of dismay took over as he left the kitchen, walking toward his music room.

He peered at the manila envelope that had been a topic of discussion on the previous night. He grabbed the envelope and closed his eyes with disappointment. He had described its contents being of the utmost importance and a great and timeless opus pertaining to life and romance. He opened the envelope and looked at the blank staff devoid of notation, key signature, time signature, and dynamic values. His intentions toward writing such a masterpiece were meaningful, but he felt a great sense of block and lack of a true musing. The motivations of great love were simply absent. He thought perhaps that his experience with Christine awakening his inner charisma would become the genesis of the project, or his fiery experience with Samantha would summon the motivation, but all he felt was an empty void. Through his shame, he felt his worth was only resigned to being a cover musician lacking originality. With this sense of dread sickening him, he placed the blank sheet music into the manila envelope, pulled out his duet bench and sat down.

As he sat staring blankly at the wood finish of his piano, he leaned toward his sheet music shelf with great resolve, deciding to enrich his morning by selecting a fitting song to enjoy purging his feelings of failure. He selected "Time" by the Alan Parson's Project. He sat observing the sheet music, noting its four/four time signature, E-flat major-key signature, and the dynamic value mezzo forte. He had played the piece on numerous occasions, entertaining his mother and father in the parlor room, but was stuck reading the front page's top right corner: *Words and Music by Eric Woolfson and Alan Parsons*. He daydreamed, wondering about his Life's Work. Fighting his urge to dwell and become miserable, he placed the sheet music on the stand and played from beginning to end without vocal accompaniment. In his inner thoughts, he knew he did not require the sheet music, as this song was one he had set to muscle memory. He simply wanted the sheet music in sight to add to the ambiance. After concluding and wallowing in a moment of unnerving silence, he walked away from his piano and left his music room without turning back.

The day ebbed forward, and Nik lounged around the house. With a small glimmer of anticipation for the following day, he began his daily workout regimen in his living room. Nik looked forward to Memorial Day, as that was when he would load his gear and rehearse with his band in Alex's pull barn. He opened the kitchen's sliding door and entered the side yard. He drew a deep cleansing breath in watching the stillness of his yard. He stepped onto his cement patio and sat on his canopy swing, beholding the modest view of his side and back yard, and glanced down the alleyway through the cracks in the shadow block fence. He shifted his thoughts toward the scheduled rehearsal and cringed knowing what was coming. He was not looking forward to the prodding questions, but mostly, he did not want to deal with seeing Alex's girlfriend, Desiree.

Nik shuttered at the thought. None of the band members could stand the sight of her, let alone being in her presence. The sight of Desiree Trieter was not only appalling but disgusting. She was as rude as she was physically unattractive. Nik rocked in his canopy swing, thinking about her features. He thought of her thinning, fried, light brown hair that exposed the top of her forehead with imbedded flakes of dandruff, her wide hardboiled face with bulging eyes encased in sagging eyelids magnified by her thick eyeglasses, along with her bulged neck laced with boils and thick five-o'clock shadow. He envisioned her morbidly obese figure and her beer-keg-shaped calves smothered in varicose veins and purple scales. He thought of the Crocs-style shoes she wore year round, feeling pity toward them as they appeared they would split at the sides from supporting her weight.

He knew she would greet him and his fellow bandmates with condescending tones, feeling threatened they would encourage Alex to rid himself of her. Kenny and Andy knew Desiree longer than he did and told him horror stories of how she treated Alex before they began their relationship.

Kenny and Andy told him that prior to Nik starting at the facility she would single out Alex, demanding he restack her pallets as she sat on the lift and berated him in front of everyone. They also mentioned how Alex's equally obese mother, Linda, and his older sister, Megan, worked in the front office and had forced Alex into the courtship. Andy and Kenny included that, shortly before Nik started working there, management had promoted her to the welcome center position, as she could not maintain a three-point stance entering and exiting the forklift. Her time as a floor associate before promotion was the shortest length of time any associate had to endure. They felt it was the obvious support from Linda and Megan that aided her to move up.

Nik felt great remorse toward Alex. He also heard from Kenny and Andy that Alex's father had abandoned the family during Alex's younger years. His father could not stand his wife or his older daughter. Andy often made crude comments that Alex's father could no longer contend with it and left Alex the charge of tending to the hog farm. After Andy made these comments, he was met with Kenny's dark eyes glaring at him, stating he had crossed the line. Kenny would stare bitterly at Andy; Kenny's father and mother had been killed in an automobile accident shortly after he moved out from home after graduating high school. Andy would stare back at Kenny, offering him heartfelt apologies. Kenny appeared to have the facial features of a hardened criminal accompanied with coal-black hair, but his looks were more than deceiving, as he was extremely sensitive and compassionate.

Nik and the rest of the band felt a large amount of guilt toward their bandmate. While it is true they all validated Alex's ability as an up-and-coming lead guitarist, they also realized they were using their friend. Alex's home facilitated them with an ideal place to practice, as Nik's garage was far too small and unaccommodating to house their equipment, while Kenny and Andy both lived at the modest Liberty Apartment Complex at the north end of town. It was also a selling point to the band that Alex housed a PA system in his pull barn.

While it was true that they exploited their friend's amenities, they genuinely liked him and enjoyed his cheery mood and love of playing. Alex lacked good looks, with his deep red hair and his freckle-covered body, but Nik and the others felt he could truly acquire a better quality of woman than he had settled for. Nik diverted his thoughts from his bandmates' inner drama and spent the day making trips from the refrigerator to retrieve beer. The evening approached more quickly than desired, and he went back into his house to prepare a simple TV dinner before retiring for the evening.

The morning light of Memorial Day peeked through the curtains as the ring of Nik's cellphone jarred him awake. He answered the phone, observing the alarm clock display—9:00 a.m. He was met with Alex's excited tone.

"Hey, buddy. I was just calling to wake you up and remind you that today's jam day."

Nik sat up from bed, sniffing and coughing as he climbed out.

"Are you okay, bro? Are you still up to jam today?"

Nik reassured Alex that he would still attend.

"Okay, great. Sounds good to me, partner. I'll call the others and let them know it's time to rise, shine, and rock out."

Nik chuckled at Alex's enthusiasm and placed his cellphone on the nightstand, wishing the phone call had been from Samantha. He realized that would not be a possibility, as Samantha never exchanged phone numbers with him. Still, he secretly hoped she had obtained his number and would place the call; however, he knew logically she couldn't have acquired his number.

Nik quickly showered, employing endurance, as he did not wait for hot water. Motivation guided him to get dressed and assemble his gear. He surveyed the side of his bed, realizing that, in his laziness, he was wearing the same clothes from the previous night. He scrambled to gather his clothes and empty the contents of his pocket onto the bed. He selected a clean pair of khaki shorts, a red tank top, and a clean pair of socks from the dresser. As he dressed, he collected his dirty clothes, bringing them to his face to sniff them in hopes of taking one last smell of Samantha's scent. Once dressed, he sprang to the front door and locked it behind him, preparing the service door key to his garage. He collected his amplifier first, carrying it to his truck, followed by his bass guitar and keyboard. After loading his equipment, he inspected the truck bed cover, ensuring it was not ripped or torn. Satisfied with his truck's state, he headed downtown.

When he arrived, he perceived the town as festive with the American flag displays and bunting as he passed the Pemkey Public Library, post office, Huntington Bank, and the Frazier local IGA. Passing Pisanello's Pizza Parlor, he activated his left turn signal and headed north on Donaldson Road. He concentrated on the wealthier district. He retained a quiet wish that he could afford a house in this area the locals called Liberty Heights. Traversing the town, he looked toward Liberty Apartment Complex on his left. Andy's faded red Ford Focus and Kenny's rusted white GMC Jimmy were nowhere to be found. Nik knew Alex must have called both, shaking them from bed. He thought it was foolish that Andy and Kenny drove separately. It was likely due to Kenny being unable to tolerate Andy's constant rambling.

Upon leaving the village limits, he smelled the eve of summer hanging free and clean in the air. He rolled down his window after lighting a cigarette to allow the refreshing air into the truck's cab. Traveling two miles out of town, he looked at Liberty School's centralized campus—the school his bandmembers attended. Going through school, they had only been mildly acquainted despite being in the same graduating class. Nik was the odd man out, as he attended Bateson School District.

The marquee displayed a message wishing the students a happy Memorial Day weekend and a reminder that graduation would be held June 3. Nik traveled a few more miles until he reached the intersection of Donaldson and Hollow Ridge Road. He turned right onto Hollow Ridge Road, looking at Alex's confederate-gray-colored house with matching pull barn. Traveling a half mile, he turned left into Alex's driveway lined with flowing weeping willow trees on both sides. The driveway curved, and he spotted Kenny and Andy carrying their equipment from their vehicles to the front of the pull barn. Alex's red Kia Sportage along with Desiree's white Kia Sportage was present. He pounded his fist against the steering wheel, cursing that Desiree was here. He was sure his fellow bandmates cursed to themselves as well. Regarding them as he crept along the driveway; they turned to him, sharing their dismay.

He decided to gain levity with his disgruntled companions by demonstrating a pleasant attitude. "Hello, boys. Are you ready to get down to business?"

Kenny shook his head, speaking softly with purpose. "Yes, I am. We do have another show to plan for next weekend at Roen's Bar."

Andy studied Kenny's mannerisms, attempting to match his tone. "Yes, Nik. It's time to get down to business, just as you got down to business with that sexy vixen the other night." Andy, unable to contain his serious and stoic act, broke into laughter and then returned to his nasally pitched voice. "Yeah, seriously. I want to know all the deranged and deviant details. It's okay, bud. I assure you that I can handle the details blow by beautiful, beautiful blow. Hey, did I happen to mention *blow*?" Andy cackled.

Kenny backhanded Andy without inflicting a sting but made his point to stop. "Andy, you need to secure that shit right fucking now. You know Desiree has got a pair of ears on her."

After the three made multiple trips carrying their equipment to the pull barn's service door and setting it down inside, they walked along the curved sidewalk to the front porch. Kenny rang the doorbell only once, grabbing Andy's hand to prevent him from continuously ringing the doorbell.

The door flung open with a fury. Desiree stood before them. She huffed annoyed as she drew her gaze on them. "Well, well, well. If it isn't the goth, the geek, and the *pretty boy*." She jeered at Kenny then turned to Andy with sharpened hate before facing Nik with a furrowed brow. She hated Nik the most of her boyfriend's bandmates, detesting him for taking Alex from her control, accompanied with fear that Nik would entice other females to take notice of Alex. "You guys all look weird. You have Kenny wearing his typical unwashed Ramones shirt and dirty black jeans, then you have Andy wearing his Sonic the Hedgehog shirt like a first grader, and finally, you have pretty boy trying to impress everyone with his tight tank tops. News flash—we're not impressed."

Nik smiled at Desiree, knowing she was afraid of him.

Kenny turned away; he could not tolerate her insults and demeaning comments.

Andy wildly smiled at her, clearing his throat and speaking with a poor impersonation of James Mason. "Well now, Desi, I apologize for my current and lacking wardrobe selection, but you must understand I was in great haste to arrive at your stately manor and indulge in the act of practicing our instruments with your betrothed. I was wondering, dear woman, if the gentleman of the house is ready to join us uncouth lads, or does he require that you powder his bottom before he is to be released?" Andy batted his eyebrows at her, nudging Kenny on the side.

Kenny remained silent, fuming as Andy further agitated.

"You know, stupid shit like that, Andy, is why you're still single."

Andy widened his eyes in a false manner. "Well, we can't all be as lucky as Alex and have a dream-barge—I mean, dreamboat—as soft, delicate, and dainty as you, Miss Desi."

Nik anticipated Desiree's disgust would move to anger and decided to interject to keep the peace. "Hey, look, Desiree. Sorry about all this. Could you let Alex know we're here waiting by the service door?"

Desiree huffed and used the doorway to support her morbidly obese body. "Don't be trying to kiss my ass, pretty boy. I know what you're all about."

Alex heard Desiree speak from the dining room next to the living room and dashed toward the front entrance, hoping none of his bandmates had agitated her to the point of him needing to employ damage control. He greeted them flushed and out of breath. He handed Desiree a glass of lemonade she had requested before they had arrived. She smugly leaned toward Alex, closing her eyes and demanding a kiss. He kissed her on the side of her wide and flabby cheek; Nik and the others knew it was not a desire of affection but a demonstration of her dominion over him.

Together they walked off the porch while she gulped her lemonade and boisterously yelled to Alex, "I hope you have your phone on you, babe, just in case I might need something."

Alex patted his pocket to demonstrate he had his phone.

She sneered and smiled at them as they approached the curved sidewalk.

Kenny stormed along first, wanting to trudge through his heightened temperament and create distance from Desiree. Andy proceeded employing mature judgment to not irritate Kenny further. The two partners distanced themselves from Kenny and Andy.

Alex sauntered with his head down, watching his steps, before turning his attention toward Nik. "Look, man. I'm sorry about Desiree's attitude earlier. She's dealing with a lot, and this whole band thing makes her feel threatened. I appreciate that you didn't further upset her, like Andy did."

Nik placed his hand on Alex's shoulder, feeling him tense. "Bro, she has nothing to worry about, and I wish she could see that. We're all in this to make our mark and showcase what we have as musicians. I know she has a strong dislike toward the others, and she has a deep hatred of me, but she really has nothing to worry about."

Alex looked at Nik and tightened his lips, giving a stiff nod, then he straightened his head as they approached the pull barn.

"I don't want to offend you, but I have to say, it was pretty nice that she did not show up at the show at Jeanelle's. It's embarrassing when she bulldozes her way to the front of the stage, pretending to like our music."

Alex shrugged and dipped his head, like a defeated dog. "Hey, I know she's a bigger girl, but did you really have to say that she *bulldozes* her way to the front?"

Nik stared at Alex as they stopped walking, feeling agitated. "I know she's controlling and possessive, but the others have brought this to my attention, and I agree with them. Before you say she's just having a good time and enjoying herself, stop right there. We know she hates our music and us. When she dances, she's mocking us and making a fool out of herself and the band."

Alex glared at Nik through squinted pale green eyes. "So, you guys are having private meetings behind my back?" He puffed his weak chest, attempting to intimidate Nik.

Nik knew Alex would back down from a challenge, whether it physical or verbal. "No. We are not having private meetings. We take what we are doing seriously and want to project that. She needs to realize there is nothing to worry about. Look at reason, man. During intermissions, Kenny sits quietly at the bar, reading the newspaper; you spend all the breaktime reassuring her. If I talk to any women, it's because they approached me. I'm not out there trying to bring groupies to us."

Alex relaxed his demeanor, regarding Nik curiously. "You forgot to mention what Andy does." Alex stifled a laugh, as he knew what Nik would say.

"Come on, man. We all know what Andy does. If he can't land a chick, he goes to the men's room and takes a gamble with the most trustworthy glory hole he can find."

Nik and Alex laughed before Alex spoke cautiously, looking toward his house. "You know, you're right. You're lucky, never having to chase the ladies. I don't want to say this too loud where Desiree hears this, but the one you caught the attention of the other night looked pretty intense."

"I can't get into that now, but, as soon as I have the chance, I'll fill you in on as much as you can stand to hear."

Alex grinned to Nik's conquest while hiding jealousy. The two stopped talking and caught up with Kenny and Andy.

Kenny stared at the door, appearing antsy while waiting for Alex to unlock it, so he could inspect his drum kit. He knew Alex's apartment was too small to accommodate his drum kit, and it would be a taxing labor to disassemble and reassemble it before and after practices.

Andy darted his gaze between Nik and Alex, making a derisive statement. He placed his hands on their shoulders, giving a look of concern. "Is everything all right, you two, or were you having a lover's spat? I hope you can put it aside for a while, because we have some motherfucking music to practice. *Woohoo!*"

They shook off Andy's hands in unison.

Kenny stared at the service door eagerly. "Can we just get in there and start, please?"

Alex fumbled for the keys then unlocked the door.

The band entered the pull barn, walking carefully not to trip over the raised floor. Kenny sat behind his drum kit while the rest followed, setting down their equipment and plugging into the power source and Alex's PA system. When they finished getting ready, they took their positions, looking toward Nik for guidance.

"Okay, guys," Nik started. "We're playing in Westor Rapids this Saturday, and it's the first time we've played this venue. I say we make things simple for ourselves and practice the set we played the other night. Besides, we're playing after Hexed, so I think that set will impress the crowd tremendously."

All the members smiled except Andy. As he was tuning his guitar, he paused. "For real? We're headlining after Hexed? Those guys are a fucking joke. I mean, where do I start? The drummer looks like a bus station hobo who learned how to play in a bathroom stall. The guitar player and co-lead singer is discordant with a galaxy of cold sores. The bass player needs an intervention for his meth addiction, and don't get me started on that woman lead singer. That fat beachball smells like spoiled cat food and rotting carp. She's probably the reason Mr. Cold Sores has his flawless complexion. I sure hope they don't want to exchange high-fives and handshakes." Andy turned his head, shooting Kenny a menacing look.

Kenny clutched his drumsticks with concern. "I hope they don't touch any of my equipment."

Alex did not reply; he stood, tuning his guitar.

Nik directed the band to begin with Rush's "YYZ."

During the practice session, Nik looked at Alex as he removed his chord hand from the guitar neck and reached into his pocket to silence his phone. As the guys arrived at rehearsing "Josie," Alex called out abruptly, causing the band to cease. "Woah, woah, woah, guys. I'm being lit up here. Give me a minute."

Nik crept closer to observe that Alex had fifteen missed text messages from Desiree, complaining she was hungry.

"Guys, Desiree is blowing up my phone. She's hungry and wants to order lunch."

Nik and the rest shook their heads, silently communicating about how typical it was that she would bother them and that the demands would reside in food.

"Desiree wants to have a few pizzas delivered. Besides, we know the set pretty well. I think we're at a good stopping point for the day." Alex stood with fear, anticipating their insulting comments. "Well, I did promise I'd buy you guys lunch today, and, when Desiree craves pizza, she likes to eat it throughout the week, so she doesn't have to plan for dinner."

Nik watched Alex nervously advocate for his girlfriend, exchanging a look at him, pleading him to interject. Nik acknowledged Alex's silently pleas.

Kenny shook his head with disgust, mouthing, *It fucking figures.*

Andy appeared he would explode with an onslaught of fat jokes without the ability to contain his words.

"You know something?" Nik said. "Pizza sounds like an excellent idea. Don't bother having it delivered. The guys and I will pick it up, so we don't have to wait for the delivery boy to take his sweet-ass time. Besides, it'll give you time to spend with Desiree."

Alex placed his guitar on his stand and raced out the pull barn.

Nik and the rest followed a distance behind.

Alex arrived on his front porch, calling out to his bandmates inquiring what they wanted on the pizzas. They agreed pepperoni and whatever Desiree decided would be fine. Alex entered the house, telling Desiree to order the pizzas.

Nik and the rest stood on the curved sidewalk, listening to Desiree shout at him for making her wait.

Alex charged out the front door and slapped the cash into Nik's hand, telling him the pizzas were under Desiree's name, while Nik and the others knew Alex was paying.

Nik, Kenny, and Andy jumped into Nik's truck and pulled away. Kenny sat quietly in the rear while Andy called shotgun.

As Nik turned onto Donaldson Road, Andy burst out loudly, "Of course she wants a week's worth of pizza. A week's worth of pizza to us would last her ten minutes."

Kenny remained fuming while Nik laughed, agreeing. Nik felt Kenny's mood growing with frustration and shifted the subject. "So, Kenny, I wonder if Savannah is working today at Pisanello's. You know every time we walk in there, she stares at you with starry eyes."

Everyone knew Kenny was infatuated with the Pisanello's manager. Savannah was pale-skinned with raven-black hair, shapely, and usually wore short-shorts, exposing a tribal-band tattoo around her right upper thigh.

Andy shifted his tone, offering friendly encouragement. Nik and his companions bantered as they arrived at Pisanello's Pizza. The smell of the pizzeria hanging heavy in the air met them. Nik opened the front door while Andy and Kenny entered through the rear. The door's chiming sound—alerting the associates that customers had entered—greeted them. No associates were in sight. They stood scanning the black-and-white-checkered floor, at the unisex restroom's opened door, and to the game room that held two arcade cabinets and a pinball machine.

Nik recognized the machines, as they were popular machines he had played as a child. The two arcade cabinets were Sega games—Outrun and Space Harrier. He knew the pinball machine was The Machine Bride of Pinbot. Nostalgia encumbered him as he reminisced playing the classic cabinets. Concluding his survey of the black-and-white-checkered pizzeria, he rang the bell on the counter. Kenny smelled the air, quickly perking up his head as they smelled patchouli when Savannah entered from the rear to greet them.

She stood in front of them wearing a red bandana with her long black hair hanging behind, a tight black Motorhead t-shirt that brought attention to the shapeliness of her breast, and faded denim shorts high on her legs. They beheld her with amazement as she asked if they were dining in or picking up.

Nik told her they were picking up an order for Treiter.

Savannah casually acknowledged Nik, looking past him to focus on Kenny through her smoky eye makeup. "Hi Kenny. Are you guys doing your Sunday usual and practicing at Alex's place?"

Kenny fumbled responding with an intrapersonal tone. "Yes. Alex and Desiree sent us out for pizza."

Nik looked down, shaking his head with disappointment.

"I heard you guys played at Jeanelle's the other night. I bet you were phenomenal. I heard you can really rock out."

"The show went rather well, and we all played decently." Kenny maintained a steady tone.

"You're so adorably modest, you know that? The next time you play locally, I want to check you out."

Kenny smiled stiffly at Savannah as she told Nik the total for the pizza.

Nik gave her the cash, and Savannah turned from them to retrieve the pizzas from the back counter.

Nik, Andy, and Kenny studied her shape as she intentionally showcased her body. She turned to face the group and handed the pizzas to Kenny.

Kenny grasped the pizzas as she deliberately grazed the top of his hands.

Andy stood shocked and childish while Nik smiled with genuine pride toward his friend.

"I hope you enjoy the pizzas, and I hope to see you perform soon." She winked at Kenny as she returned to the kitchen area.

Kenny thanked her and pushed the door open with his back. The three remained silent until they climbed into Nik's truck.

"What the fuck is wrong with you, dude?" Andy asked. "That heavy-metal hottie was practically prostituting her body onto you, and you were as cold as an Eskimo's asshole. Hell, I would have taken her in the back and fucked her on top of the pizza dough. At least you could have seen if she had some other tattoos located in other sexy areas."

Nik drove, thinking about Samantha and her exposed body and remembering the tattoo on her bikini line. Nik looked in his rearview mirror at Kenny furrowing his brow. Nik wanted to avoid fueling the fire Andy was stoking. "You know, I hate to agree with Andy on this one, but she really was throwing out some major signals to you, bud."

Kenny's brow relaxed and he spoke softly. "I don't know. Maybe you're right."

Nik employed caution, encouraging tact with his statements. "You should look at reason, bud. She ignored Andy and me. She spoke directly to you with fuck-me eyes, and, when she handed you the pizzas, she made an obvious attempt to touch you. I think it's safe to say you're guaranteed to have a good time with her."

Kenny caught Nik's gaze through the rearview mirror and gave a bashful smile. "I think I'll go for it. If she's at our next show, I'll go for it."

They passed Pemkey toward Alex's, feeling joy and good nature. Upon arrival, they cleared their smiles, employing caution of Desiree questioning them over the reason of their smiles. They knew she would assume they'd be making crude jokes about her. To ensure they maintained peace, they strolled up the sidewalk with clear expressions.

Nik opened the door, followed by Andy and Kenny holding the pizzas, and saw Desiree sitting on her recliner in the front room with Alex knelt, rubbing her fat bearpaw feet. It was a disgusting display to see their friend in a submissive position. Each hoped Alex would wash his hands before touching the pizza.

Alex pinned at Desiree as obedient as a mongrel dog yearning for praise. "Does that feel better, honey?"

The display sickened Andy. "Yeah, Alex, maybe you should try sucking on those toes to make them feel better."

Desiree shot Andy a look of raw hatred. "You're just jealous because you have no one in your life."

Andy felt fierce and could not endure the display or her comment. "Oh yeah. I crave nothing more than having someone in my life to rub their smelly and sweaty feet. I just yearn for that type of completion."

Nik harshly tapped Andy with the front of his hand, striking him to stop.

Kenny placed the pizzas on the coffee table in front of Desiree and Alex's recliner, and the three sat on the adjacent couch.

Alex feared confrontation from both sides and stood to face his girlfriend and friends. "I'm sorry, everyone. Desiree had some cramps in her feet, and I did not get plates and drinks ready." Alex asked his bandmates what they wanted to drink, and they all agreed water would be fine. He asked Desiree the same, and she demanded a Diet Coke.

Andy nudged Nik in the ribs, conveying a joke they shared about obese people. Nik knew he was suggesting that she would binge eat the pizza and then comment about having a Diet Coke to avoid the extra sugar. Nik returned the nudge discreetly, acknowledging.

They heard the kitchen sink faucet running and hoped Alex was washing his hands before filling their glasses. When Alex returned, they observed residual wetness on his hands and felt relieved they could maintain their individual appetites.

Alex appeared as a dedicated servant, distributing the plates and drinks. He served everyone before approaching his place next to Desiree. Before he could sit, Desiree commanded him to serve her more slices before he could have his first serving.

Nik, Andy, and Kenny only allowed themselves two pieces each, as watching Desiree devour her slices diminished their appetites.

Alex sprung from his recliner and collected everyone's empty glasses and plates.

Desiree leaned forward, slowly prying her back from the recliner. She panned the couch, deciding amongst her boyfriend's friends who to insult. She lightened her expression as she stared at Kenny with cruelty. "So, was that boney little hippy slut working today, Kenny? I know you like that little skinny bitch. You both lack any sort of a sense of fashion. I don't know why either of you can't dress like normal people."

Kenny's blood boiled. "Well, Desiree, I guess it's just a matter of taste, just like Alex has a taste for fat girls."

Desiree's eyes widened as she did not expect Kenny to go for the kill. Still feeling the need to insult her boyfriend's bandmates, she turned her attention toward Nik. "I don't understand you either, Nik. Alex told me about the little hoochy slut you hooked up with the other night." As she insulted Samantha, she raised her robust arms over her head, gyrating in a mocking manner.

"She might be a slutty hoochie girl, but at least she can move without breaking a sweat from a seated position."

Andy laughed out loud, clapping his hands and raising his knees to his chest.

Desiree blew a strong-winded harrumph at all of them, jammed her palms on the recliner arms and slowly rose, beaming at them. "I'm going to the bathroom. I don't have to take this shit. By the time I get back. I want all of you out of this house." Desiree trotted out, screaming at Alex.

Nik looked to the others, suggesting now was the time to collect their gear and leave. They swiftly exited through the front door.

As they were disassembling their equipment, Alex interrupted them, trembling with fury. "What is wrong with you, assholes? How could you talk to Desi like that?"

Kenny and Andy did not speak; they only returned Alex with an equally hateful look.

Nik raised his hand to motion to the others not to speak. "We didn't start anything. It was Desiree. As soon as you left the room, she insulted all of us with no provocation."

Alex maintained his anger, trembling. "I'm glad we already know the setlist pretty well, because practice is officially over. You guys need to get out right now, because now I have some serious fucking damage control to do. You all know how sensitive she is about her weight."

Nik's rage matched Alex's with great self-control and patience. "We're all sorry about what went down in there, but listen to reason, man. It's a two-way street, and she drew first blood."

Alex, the perpetual submissive, suppressed his rage as he feared that if he angered his fellow bandmates, he might be expelled from the band.

Nik felt the anxiety radiate from Alex and anticipated fighting a two-front war, so se employed compassion. "It's all cool. Things got a little out of hand from her side and our side, but I think you're right anyway. We know the set material pretty well, and I think we should rest and pack it up for the day. Go spend time with Desiree. Relax, and enjoy yourselves."

Alex regarded everyone and lightened his mood. He was relieved his bandmates did not appear angry, and he offered them assistance with packing their gear. He dreaded having to soothe Desiree's anger once he returned to the house, but he felt relief seeing his friends not appear angry with him.

They knew Alex was in turmoil. His two passions were his girlfriend and his position in the band. Nik and the rest thanked him for paying for their lunch and offered him reassurance.

Alex displayed relief and told his friends goodbye, racing to the porch.

Nik wished them a good rest of the day before they entered their vehicles. Nik anticipated that his friends would be in great haste to leave, so he sat in his truck, patiently allowing them to leave. After the dust from their vehicles settled, he reached into the armrest and grabbed his Steely Dan *Aja* CD. He advanced the tracks until "Deacon Blues." He would unwind and relax as he drove home to the calming track. Numerous thoughts reeled through his mind as he embarked on the country drive. He contemplated his verbal confrontation with Desiree. He wondered why he did not remain silent when she insulted Samantha.

He thought for a moment longer and realized he could not stand her words and actions any longer. He felt justified as he remained silent on previous occasions before. He knew it was bizarre to defend the honor of a woman he only briefly knew, but, when Desiree raised her arms and moved in a mocking manner, he knew it was more than just insulting Samantha—it was her way of taking dominance not only over Alex but over him and the others. She would rush to the front of the stage, barricading audience members from approaching them, and dance foolishly to say to the band and the audience, "I am here to make you look ridiculous, and I'll take control with whatever means I see fit."

He was proud he had made a stand against Desiree and that patronizing words and actions had motivated said stance. He was fearful that feelings of love with Samantha drove his motivation—feelings he did not want to consider.

Kenny's and Andy's cars were parked in the apartment complex's lot and appeared to have been sitting there for a while. Nik shifted his focus toward the wealthier subdivision of Liberty

Heights. He thought about how good it would be if he could afford a house there. The size of the houses, with the attached garages, would be able to facilitate the practices at his house instead. He felt guilt take over, thinking the band's situation may be more enjoyable without Alex. He did not wish to think of Liberty Heights or Alex anymore.

Instead, he diverted his thoughts toward being happy. He was making it on his own in a town he enjoyed living in. He turned into his driveway, unloaded his equipment, approached his porch then entered through the front door. Once settled comfortably in his house, he went to the kitchen to fill a glass of water and sat on his couch. He slid off his shoes and placed his glass of water on a coaster on the coffee table. He reached for his Diazepam then thumbed through his favorite novel—*Yours Truly, 2095* by Brian Paone.

After he opened the pill bottle, he placed a pill on his tongue and swallowed harshly, as he did not easily take pills. He chased it with a smooth sip of water. He felt the pill clear from his throat and placed his water on the coaster. After reading a few pages, he felt the Diazepam take effect as relaxation flowed through him. He smiled each time he progressed through the pages, finding new Electric Light Orchestra references the author had included in his book Nik had not noticed before.

He found time had accelerated as the afternoon shifted into the early hours of the evening. He placed his book on the coffee table to start his evening ritual of working out before retiring for the evening. As he prepared for bed, he plugged his cellphone into the charger on his nightstand, undressed and jumped into bed face first. His eyelids felt heavy when he set his alarm clock for five o'clock, knowing his sleep would be unsatisfying before starting the work week. While closing his eyes, he heard his cellphone chime alerting him of a call. He scrambled for the phone, adjusting his gaze onto the display identifying the caller as Jeanelle.

"Hi, Nik," Jeanelle's husky voice greeted. "I hope I'm not calling you too late. I know you and the rest of the guys work day shift."

Nik reassured her that it was not an inconvenience and that he had not yet fallen asleep.

"That's good, because I wanted to talk with you before the others regarding playing at my bar again."

Nik informed her the band was playing at Roen's Tavern in Westor Rapids next weekend, but they were available to play at her bar the weekend after. Jeanelle was excited by the news that they were available and asked if the same payment would be satisfactory. Nik assured her that they would make the appearance.

Hope of seeing Samantha again overtook Nik. He knew with what had happened at Alex's place with Desiree, he wanted to keep the offer between only her and himself without letting Alex or the others know. He knew if Desiree learned about the show, she would be out for vengeance, ruining the venue. Jeanelle offered understanding with Alex's belligerent girlfriend's behavior, explaining Nik was the only member she had called. She employed tact over the situation, offering to schedule the show on a Friday night at 9:00 instead of a Saturday night so the band could relax for the weekend. Nik knew he had acquired borrowed time to tell the band about the upcoming show in hopes that Desiree would not be present.

Bidding Jeanelle a good night, he ended the call and rolled onto his back, looking at the ceiling and anticipating the chance to see Samantha again.

Chapter
Three

The alarm clocked blared, rousting Nik from his sleep. It was time to begin the week. Relieved to know it would be a short week, he climbed from bed and dashed to the shower. His urge to get dressed and arrive at work to tell his friends about the previous night's phone conversation rushed him along. He left the bathroom and grabbed the closest work uniform he could find in his closet. He rapidly brushed his teeth, turned off the water, grabbed his keys and locked the door behind him. He drove through Pemkey, making a fast turn onto Donaldson Road heading south toward Moline Medical Warehouse.

Arriving at the lonesome brick building, he drove through the gate of the chain-link fence, satisfied to see Alex, Andy, and Kenny's cars. He was also delighted that the driver's parking space lot was empty, providing him ample parking. He grabbed his lanyard containing his facility photo identification from his rearview mirror and walked briskly past the guard station. The security guard buzzed him in the door. He made his way to the break room.

Taking his place at the table, he heard Andy complain about the work week and morning meeting.

Andy discussed the general manager, Jim Whitman, would make them feel like dirt for allowing them to have the holiday weekend off. Andy detested old man Whitman coining him with a nickname that preceded him. "I wonder what kind of guilt trip Old Droopy Drawers will employ today for his generosity. Aside from walking around like he has a full shit in his pants, he probably also has a burr up his ass."

Nik and the rest laughed as Andy made colorful comments toward Jim Whitman. Andy often remarked that it was a sizable shit he did not have time to make it to the toilet to squeeze out, a giant purple studded dildo, or possibly an alien probe. The time was 5:45 a.m. when he made the announcement to his bandmembers about Jeanelle's phone call. But first. He wanted to test the waters with Alex and find out how damage control went with Desiree.

The best strategy to approach the situation was to appear apologetic. "I'm sorry to revisit a sensitive situation, but how did things go with Desiree after we left?"

Alex's smile disappeared. "Well, it went as best as it could, I suppose. She rambled for nearly an hour spouting pure hatred, but she also felt heartbroken that you guys feel she's trying to make a mockery of our shows."

Kenny and Andy looked at each other, rolling their eyes. Nik, hoping to gain information, did not express the same expression. Alex felt his other bandmates were making gestures between themselves, conveying disbelief.

"I think you guys will be pleased to hear the next show, and from here on out, she'll be spending time with Mallory and Roberta, going out to eat, shop, or to the movies."

Kenny and Andy perked up. They were overjoyed to hear good news. Nik rejoiced inside the confines of his own mind but kept solid composure.

Desiree, by herself, was more than enough to contend with, but, when she was paired with her other abrasive friends, it was a recipe for disaster. Nik had only met Mallory Groff and Roberta Rath a few times and was not satisfied with the time spent. Mallory Groff felt she was the beautiful one of the trio, wearing an overabundance of makeup to hide her acne scars, and Roberta thought she was the comic relief but fell short to arouse a laugh. The only thing Roberta could arouse was body odor.

Kenny and Andy had the displeasure of going to school with Desiree, Mallory, and Roberta ever since kindergarten age and often referred to the trio as the Bovine Triplets. They told Nik, in the absence of Alex, they were as rude and insulting as they were fat and ugly. Nevertheless, they were overjoyed to hear the good news.

Nik felt confident telling his bandmates about the invitation to play at Jeanelle's on the following Friday evening.

The good news heightened their moods, as each member had their own ulterior motive for playing the bar. Andy was excited with the pay from Jeanelle. Charlie anticipated the added exposure for the band. Alex enjoyed the general ambiance of the bar. Kenny smiled, knowing Savannah would likely make an appearance. Nik knew Jeanelle and Charlie would advertise the event on the bar's front marquee, and Samantha's sister might take notice and inform her they would be playing soon.

Finishing the celebration, they looked toward the clock illustrating five minutes until 6:00 a.m.—time to gather for the shift meeting on the warehouse floor. While they did not relish what Jim Whitman will say, they were still in high spirits toward the prospect of playing at Jeanelle's Bar.

As they approached the dock office, they took notice of the sizable crowd of associates congregating. Jim Whitman stood in the center of the circle, raising his aged-spotted hand toward the ceiling and commanding the associates to become silent. "I hope you all had a restful and relaxing extended weekend. I can tell you all this, we must have a productive week to recuperate from having Monday off. Before we begin, I think it's time to stretch it out before receiving work tasks."

The associates grumbled as Jim led them in pre-shift stretches. Everyone thought it was Jim's way of creating false camaraderie amongst his subordinates. As the associates mimicked Jim's attempt to perform the stretches, Andy whispered insults to his friends regarding how this was the only physical activity Jim's sagging ass could withstand. Completing their stretches, Jim groaned and huffed out of breath.

Jim went through the roster of associates, taking attendance and assigning tasks while informing them management has mandated that they increase their units per hour by double the normal workload.

Nik's friends separated to start their work assignments. He wished them good luck before he walked off to enter the dock office for his driving assignments. Nik's bandmates headed to their assigned areas with zombielike fashion as Nik turned to enter the dock office.

Andy ran back to Nik before he opened the door and tapped his shoulder. "Barber shop pole."

Nik regarded Andy strangely as he stood in front of him, snickering. "What the fuck are you talking about, man?"

Andy chuckled. "You know what I mean. That is what is causing Old Droopy Drawer's pants to sag today."

Nik laughed and shook his head as Andy ran to catch up with his other crewmembers.

Jim stood behind the ring of transportation dispatchers as the other drivers stood at the far side of the dock office. He gained composure joining the others, straightening his face. "Okay, people. We have a sizable amount of freight to move this week, but I know you all can do it right, do it on time, and do it safe. Collect your paperwork from your dispatcher and make sure that once you have it, you perform a proper pre-trip vehicle inspection. I don't want DOT pulling you guys over and fining you." He snapped his suspenders and lifted his gut.

Nik and the other drivers watched Jim walk to his office and close the door behind. Nik approached his dispatcher, Darcy Glenn, and grazed the back of her neck with his fingertips.

Darcy straightened her back, curling like a housecat as Nik finished. She spun toward Nik in her office chair and smiled with her frail, thin face, looking infatuated. Darcy knew she stood no chance of acquiring a relationship with Nik, as she was too thin and plain looking, but she enjoyed the physical contact. She also enjoyed the privilege of using pet names with him, such as babe, honey, and sugar. She knew he would dismiss the names as just being playful, but she was esteemed she could use the names with him regardless. She felt it was a comforting release she could say such things to him without being judged. She studied Nik, dreaming his frame made his uniform cling to his body. She wished she could see him wearing other attire—or, better for her, no attire at all.

With a snap, she broke from her own induced spell and reached for his daily paperwork. "I have some good news for you, babe. You get to do your hospital deliveries at the beginning of the week, which leaves you the doctors' offices and the urgent care clinics toward the end of the week. I know you and the guys like to have your practices on Fridays before your Saturday night shows."

Nik smiled brightly at her, collecting his paperwork and returning a playful pet name as he walked out the driver's exit. He located his Freightliner straight truck unit number five and began his exterior pre-trip inspection. He inspected the lights and the glass windows, along with inspecting exterior compartments, checking under the hood, and the physical components of the air brake systems.

Once seated into the cab, he checked his gauges and administered his in-cab air brake tests. Once completed with the pre-trip inspection, he scanned his paperwork and logged his inspection. He also took notice that he was to dock to door number three, pleased to know that was Kenny's assigned outbound door; he knew he would be loaded with precision to start his hospital deliveries.

He realized it took little time before he saw the dock light in his left panel mirror turn green and heard the electric dock lock release. Kenny couldn't see him, but he still gave a friendly nod and wave as he released his spring break and pulled away.

The work week ended just as quickly as it began. Friday afternoon had arrived with great welcome. Nik enjoyed weeks such as these. Once he pulled into the truck lot and set the park brake, he ceased to feel like just a number and regained his individuality.

Nik performed his post-trip inspection with record time, pulling the key from the ignition and racing toward the dock office. As he closed in on the exterior entrance, he removed his cellphone to see the time—1:54 p.m. If he hurried, he could meet his bandmates in the associate parking lot and have time to discuss the plans for the upcoming show in Westor Rapids. He hoped Darcy would not impede him with lengthy flirtations.

He entered the dock office, adjusting his eyes from the bright sunlight to the artificial light. Darcy greeted him with a smile, asking if he'd had pleasant deliveries. Nik was cordial and brief as he handed her his truck keys and daily logs.

Darcy, disappointed by Nik's hurried manner, illustrated understanding that he was driven to leave the facility. "I know you have an upcoming show, hon, so I'll sign you off for the day." Darcy was content that Nik appreciated her accommodating his expedited leave

He offered a polite wave, wishing her a pleasant weekend.

The forklift traffic had ended for the shift as he walked across the floor. Alex, Andy, and Kenny waited at the front of the time clock line, looking worn, as the heat of the day had taken them. He made a noticeable effort to pass them, exerting his presence. Once they looked at Nik, they acknowledged him. The associates waiting to clock out for the day murmured loud enough to express their discontent that he could leave the facility before them. He did not want to perpetuate their grouchy mindsets; he carefully weaved through them, ambling through the main entrance. Outside the facility, he raised his arms skyward, reacquiring his identity as he strutted to his truck. When the associates exited the building, he waved to his bandmates, signaling them to come.

They diverted from their own vehicles, approaching Nik with curiosity to hear what he had to say.

"Well guys, here we stand with another work week done and over with and another show on the brink."

The band expressed their eagerness to strip themselves from the mundane warehouse life and re-establish their rock-star fantasies.

"I just wanted to remind you all that a week from today we'll be playing at Jeanelle's, and it's time to alter the set a bit. We'd be fine playing the same set as last week, but I think it's time to up our game at Jeanelle's so we don't appear stale."

They looked curious to what Nik had in mind.

"I think that with the show at Jeanelle's Bar we should embrace a sexier appeal."

Alex and Andy looked at each other puzzled as Nik spoke. Kenny looked to Nik, agreeing with him. Kenny knew Nik's motivation and proposed idea was meant for him as well. They understood Nik's intended concept. Desiree's absence, allowing more people on the dance floor, motived Nik.

Alex swallowed his guilt, realizing his girlfriend was guilty of acting like a buffoon. He felt a sense of infidelity that he would rather see a better quality of women dancing to their music than his own girlfriend.

The bandmembers often assigned names to their sets. Last weekend's set was referred to as the "Progressive Rock/Jazz Fusion set." They knew Nik wanted to employ the "Slow Dance on the Bar Floor set." They played this set previously at the Cabana Bay Bar, knowing it began with "One of These Nights" by The Eagles and concluded with "Satisfaction Guaranteed" by The Firm. It was a set they knew the crowd enjoyed and one they enjoyed themselves, allowing the attractive women of the crowd to visually stimulate them. With Nik's announcement, they agreed with him.

Nik bid his friends farewell while they dispersed toward their vehicles, leaving the crowded parking lot. Nik allowed his fellow associates time to leave, providing the parking lot traffic to thin and granting ease of access to exit. After the congestion had cleared, he headed downtown in his truck.

As he drove, his stomach rumbled with hunger pangs. It was time to stop and eat something. Being vigilante of his weight, he allowed himself to eat once a day and trusted his body's physical signals to inform him when that time would be. He stopped in front of Frazier's IGA, hearing the growling increase. Knowing he did not want to overeat, he entered the IGA and approached the deli in the rear. He requested a pound container of ham salad along with pasta salad. He felt uninspired this weekend, figuring a pound of each would last and would negate him having to make challenging decisions on what to eat. He added a loaf of store-brand bread and headed toward the checkout.

After paying for his items, he drove home anxious to make a plate and shed his work uniform. He parked his truck, strode up the porch steps, unlocked the door and headed toward the kitchen to grab a paper plate from his cupboard and a spreading knife and fork from the kitchen drawer. He stood in the kitchen eating a single ham salad sandwich and a small portion of pasta salad. Once he finished eating, he strolled down the hallway into his bedroom and stripped from his uniform, flinging it into his laundry basket, then changed into a pair of red jogging shorts and a white cotton tank top.

Looking into the laundry basket, he felt it was exceedingly full and he should do his weekly laundry. He collected his basket and walked down the hallway and into the kitchen and tossed his laundry into the washing machine.

A ritual Nik often enjoyed on Friday evenings was to stroll around town after his work week. This was a time usually after he had eaten his meal and completed his workout. As soon as he folded and put away his laundry, he worked out for forty-five minutes then dropped his cellphone and keys into his jogging shorts pocket.

He left through the front door, locking it behind him and beginning his evening walk. He enjoyed his body releasing the day's tension and cooling down. His senses were immersed in pleasure with the physical stimuli of the clean village. He derived absolute satisfaction from his Friday evening walks, feeling freedom and calmness as he traversed the community. He felt quiet gratitude toward the community, as they did not stare at him as a misfit.

In Amsdale, he had felt like a pariah as the neighbors regarded him with prejudice eyes. Since his childhood, so-called family friends had considered him an odd child, and the looks continued throughout his adulthood until he left town. Nik often found that he had to self-assure himself that Amsdale's residents were only small-minded town folk.

Knowing these citizens would not glance at him with prejudice, he greeted the ones sitting on their front porches with friendliness. After walking for an hour and a half, he returned home feeling his mind and body had achieved satisfaction.

He sat on his couch and turned on his television and Blu-ray player to end his evening with a movie. He approached his entertainment center and scanned his massive Blu-ray collection and selected *House*. He was in a mood to indulge in both horror and comedy. *House* would be the optimum selection to appease his appetite. He figured, if he could stay awake long enough, he may watch *House 2: The Second Story* and have a small movie marathon before lying down. Saturday would be saturated with preparing for a show and motivating the others in time for the drive and set up at Roen's. Westor Rapids was a forty-minute drive from his home, and he would have to drive through the county seat of Rawling Springs, which proved to be a speed trap.

He inserted the Blu-ray disc into the player and returned to his couch, ready to indulge in the story. After he finished watching *House*, he found he had enough energy to indulge in the sequel. After part two had concluded, he powered off his television and Blu-ray player without removing the disc. He set his alarm clock for 8:00 a.m.

The following morning, Nik awoke before the alarm. He sprang to his feet and raced into the shower. He sifted through his drawers for his Union Jack tank top and his tan khaki shorts. He located his black and white tuxedo oxford shoes and prepared for his day.

At 8:30, he made a trip to the bank to withdrawal some money for gas expenses to Westor Rapids along with cash for other items. The bank tellers greeted him by his first name and wished him a good morning. Nik returned the greetings as Aileena—his favorite teller with her method of service and attractive looks—invited him to step forward for assistance. Nik was thrilled that Aileena was tending to his banking needs. Nik enjoyed looking at her on Saturday morning bank visits. Aileena's physique was ideal. Aileena was close to 5'7" and shapely, curvy, and busty. Regardless if it was intentional or by sheer accident, she always donned a wardrobe that exposed the shape and perfect symmetry of her ample breasts.

After idle greetings, she asked him if he wanted to make a withdrawal or deposit. He told her that he wished to withdrawal one hundred dollars. She smiled after he presented her with his bank card and counted the money back to him in twenty-dollar increments. She asked him if she could help him with anything further then wished him a good weekend and asked if he was playing another show.

Nik turned from her as he told her about playing at Roen's. She smiled pleasantly and wished him good luck. While walking through the glass entryway, he turned back to take one last glance at her before leaving. He thought her body resembled Samantha's and wished that he could get to know her intimately.

He placed his cash and bank receipt into his wallet, started his truck and returned home. Pulling into the driveway, he activated his phone to call his bandmates. He started with Alex, followed by Kenny and then Andy. He told them to be at his house at 7:00, allowing them time to discuss their method of performing before arriving at the venue. Nik spent most of the day dedicated to his music room. He sat on his duet bench playing the piano and singing aloud through the setlist, having a private practice session.

Confident he could flawlessly perform tonight's set, he rose and pushed the duet bench under his piano. He walked outside and opened the service door to his garage. He loaded his equipment into his truck bed, returned to his front porch and sent out a group text, telling his band he was loaded and ready. Nik sat on his porch glider, rocking and relaxing and wondering how the evening would pan out and how the new crowd would feel toward their performance. He felt apprehension about the crowds' critique, but he did not feel apprehension on Lapis Lazuli's performance.

As 7:00 p.m. rapidly loomed, Nik saw Kenny's rusted GMC Jimmy approach, followed by Alex's Kia Sportage and Andy's Ford Focus. When they arrived, they looked at Nik sitting on his porch glider.

"Well guys, it's Roen's Bar tonight. We've all heard the horror stories of how much of a dump this place is, but let's hold strong and play like it was a top-tier place."

"Do you know who's running sound and lights for us tonight, and will this place be difficult to find?" Kenny asked.

Nik told Kenny that it was Don Valentine, who Doug Roen had used before with karaoke nights, dance parties, and birthday parties. Nik also informed him that Don would be volunteering his services for free to them and Hexed. Don genuinely enjoyed providing the service, and, from what Nik could infer from Doug, it was a means to look at local bar women and escape his wife's company.

Andy blurted out with laughter and nudged Alex on his side. "Does that sound familiar?"

Nik stood from the glider. "You need to secure that shit right now, Andy. We don't need your shit-talking. We need to organize and plan for tonight." Nik noticed he had frazzled Andy. "Look. There is a time and a place for shit-talking, and that time is when those dicks and that cunt from Hexed are on stage, braying and squealing." Nik smiled, hoping to arouse laughter.

Nik and his bandmates spoke for an hour before he asked if anyone needed to use the bathroom before they made their sojourn. They heeded Nik's advice and took turns using the bathroom. Nik led the pack, followed by Andy, Kenny, and Alex holding back the rear. As they approached downtown, they turned south on Donaldson Road, leaving Pemkey behind.

Nik looked toward Moline Medical Warehousing. It was empty, and the parking lot was vacant. He checked his rearview mirrors to ensure his bandmates were still behind him. He observed Andy extending his left arm and raising his middle finger in exaggerated manners. Nik laughed as he could only imagine the string of colorful profanities that flowed from Andy's mouth.

They eventually approached State Route 14, where they headed west toward Rawling Springs. Nik activated his turn single early, hoping to instill safer driving habits and communicating to drive by the letter of the law once they arrived in Rawling Springs. Nik enjoyed the solitude inside the cab of his truck. The evening air was pleasantly cool.

Crossing Rawling Springs city limits, he jabbed his breaks to slow his truck and the other's vehicles to the precise speed of the posted limit. He admired the town's architecture and the overall aesthetic of the community, such as the college girls walking the sidewalks and entering and exiting the coffee shops and new-age restaurants. He blew a sad sigh, wishing he could have attended Rawling Springs State University and majored in music education or English. He would have made an excellent music teacher or English teacher. He deliberately narrowed his vision.

Passing the university, he resigned himself to the sad realization that with his work schedule, performing in a band, and purchasing a house he would never attend university. He was eager to increase his speed as he cleared the city limits. The sweet smells of rural country air inhabited his cab once again. He looked for certain visual landmarks as he drove westbound. He passed a row of houses recently unincorporated and once called Burton. He looked at a road sign stating McHutchen was ten miles to the left.

In his youth during Halloween time, he heard stories about a mentally challenged man in his early twenties named Brant Perryman who was riding his bike when a drunk driver struck him. The stories involved seeing his ghost traveling homeward at night. Driving farther past Burton, he saw the shady adult bookstore on the left. He cringed as he'd heard horror stories of the establishment; it was plagued with armed robberies, resulting in a few murders of some of its cashiers. Passing the building, he saw the neon marquee had blown-out lights. The lights intended to illustrate XXX-Ray's Adult Books and Novelties; however, every other letter was burnt out. The lighting's poor quality further solidified his assessment of the place.

He refocused as he looked for Apache Road. Doug had told him a house would be on his right side with a strange building that resembled an old-time dancing pavilion.

Perceiving the strange looking structure, he activated his right turn signal and passed the house. Eventually, they entered the town limits of Westor Rapids. Apache Road ended, and he turned left onto the narrow main drag. He drove slowly with his band creeping behind him, trying to locate Roen's Bar. An accessible parking lot sat to the side of the building. It was 8:40, and the band had arrived within a comfortable time. The establishment proved not as difficult to find as he had expected. Everyone joined Nik at the rear of his truck.

"Okay, guys. Time is on our side, so let's get the gear in and meet with Doug."

Don Valentine granted them access through the rear fire. "Hey, are you guys Lapis Lazuli?"

Nik and the others acknowledged him.

Don stood to the side as the bandmembers entered, appearing dry and somber. He offered the band assistance with their gear, but they declined in fear that the tired man might accidentally drop their equipment.

"I'll let Doug know you guys are here. Hexed will begin in fifteen minutes."

Andy made a snide comment about Don's voice sounding like a burned-out, aging hippy.

Nik urged him to stop making comments as Doug Roen entered the room.

Doug appeared equally aged and withered as he sized them up with disbelief. "So, you guys are Lapis Lazuli? You don't look like musicians, at least no one I've ever hosted."

Doug's comments stupefied Nik and the others. Nik thought they may not share the appearance of the others who have played here, but they were sure to be the most talented musicians who have ever graced his stage.

To everyone's surprise, Alex challenged Doug. "That may be the case, but I can assure you that we'll bring something entertaining to your bar—the likes you've never heard before."

Nik stood with pride that Alex exhibited confidence.

"That is yet to be seen. Go ahead and drop your gear. You'll be on after Hexed," Doug grumbled.

The bar looked drab, and a film of residue and degradation coated the interior. They stood for a moment before Hexed took the stage. The crowd reaction and reception was surprising. Lapis Lazuli felt Hexed was a basic and puerile band at best.

Mike Balmer, the lead guitarist and co-lead singer, introduced the band.

Andy made the same comments he had made in Alex's pull barn.

Nik and the others tried to suppress their laughter as they could identify each member's physical appearance by what Andy had assigned them.

Mike Balmer introduced the drummer, Byron Whelton; the bass player, Matt Shephard; lead vocals, Tawny Baker, and then introduced himself simply as Balmer on lead guitar and co-lead vocals. He raised his hands and threw the devil-horn symbol at the crowd before introducing the band name.

Andy surveyed his bandmembers as the introduction concluded. "Oh my God. This guy is a fucking douchebag. I mean, seriously, who just introduces themselves by their last name? Look at this guy. He looks like the product of an eighties glam rocker and a crackhead Poison groupie had grudge fucked and conceived him next to a rear dumpster by a local 7-11."

They nearly erupted with explosive laughter, holding back to not draw attention to their conversation.

Hexed began with a cover of Seven Mary Three's "Cumbersome." Mike Balmer sounded strained as he sang, and Tawny Baker shrilled as she sang along. They followed up with a cover of some Nickelback, along with some Creed covers, concluding their show with a cover of Evanescence's "Bring Me to Life."

Andy mocked her voice, mimicking a crow being torn to death. Andy assessed the band's discordant sound and lacking vocal abilities as they reentered the utility room. "Jesus Christ, I thought that would never end. The whole time they were up there, I felt like Beaker from *The Muppets* was sodomizing my ears. I think Balmer needs to pass the constipated shit before he sings, and Tawny's vocal talents are those of a female alley cat in heat yowling into the night."

Nik and the others agreed with Andy's statements.

Conversing amongst each other, Hexed passed them while carrying out their gear. Balmer extended his hand, attempting to shake with Nik and the others. "Hey, you guys are up next. Don't worry though. I think we warmed up the crowd for you pretty well."

Nik crinkled his face and looked amongst his bandmembers with disgust over Balmer's ego and foul body odor. The others illustrated the same disgust as they carried their equipment onto the stage.

Once on stage, the foul stench of clove cigarettes and body odor struck them. They coughed and strained to hold back demonstrating their awareness of the pungent odor. Eventually collecting themselves over the wave of imposing odors, they set up with the assistance from Don Valentine. When they finished setting up, Hexed had returned to the bar.

"Let's show these assholes what accomplished musicians can do."

The rest of the band smiled brightly at Nik's confidence. They began their set with "YYZ." As the band played their first song, the audience fell silent and attentive to Lapis Lazuli. They were stunned as they watched Nik and the others showcase their talent. The crowd at Roen's Bar was not used to the band's complexity and precision musicianship.

As they arrived at the end of their set playing "Josie," the crowd populated the dance floor. It was also a bonus that Hexed looked defeated and microscopic. Nik introduced his bandmembers then bid the audience a good night. Nik urged his bandmembers to begin the tear-down process and make their leave.

While disassembling their equipment, Don Valentine rushed the stage flushed and sweating. "Man, I can't believe you guys pulled off that kind of show tonight. You guys know your stuff and are one hell of a tight band."

Nik and the others remained cavalier with Don, exhibiting a fair amount of gratitude. His compliments were minuscule at best. They were aware of their musical capabilities and did not require a leathery drunkard's praise. Don continued with his own personal conquest of other bands he provided lights and sound for. He droned on about acts from years back.

Eager to dismiss Don from rambling about his prior glory days, they insisted to meet with Doug regarding their payment.

Once they finished dismantling their gear, they carried it to the utility room, leaving Don standing at the front of the stage. They sat sown their equipment and watched Don leave to locate Doug.

Andy was in his usual state, ready to make his assessments on Don's comments. "Who the fuck does that pickled livered drunk think he is?"

Nik and the others looked at Andy, wondering what sparked his comments.

"Hey, come on," Alex said. "He wasn't that bad. Granted he is a drunken buffoon, but he did run sound decently."

Nik shrugged off both their comments, ready to hit the bar floor and collect their pay.

"You're right about one thing, Alex," Andy said. "He did do his job surprisingly well, but you could just tell by listening to him that he's one of those generic stock assholes you find at every roadhouse dive, demanding the band to 'play some Skynard, man.'" Once Andy finished his imitation of Don, they all snickered.

Surprisingly, Kenny laughed at Andy's comments. He agreed with Andy and complimented him on his accurate imitation.

They collected themselves and wiped the laughter from their faces as they returned to the bar floor. Before they could locate Doug Roen to collect their pay, they were met with the members of Hexed.

Mike Balmer approached Nik with his bandmembers following. The stench of clove cigarettes and body odor wafted through the air. An undecipherable fetor added another component to their foul odor, a stench that hung heavy smelling like feet, cheese, and sloppy menstruating sex. The members of

Lapis Lazuli stifled their sickening expressions as Hexed stood in front of them.

"Hey, bros. You guys played pretty good tonight," Mike Balmer said patronizingly.

Nik and his band showed mild gratitude, wishing they could dismiss his company.

Mike Balmer did not notice them trying to escape his company and continued to speak, flipping his greasy hair. "This is a good opportunity to make you guys a great offer. I think your band and my band could be a force to be reckoned with, and we should form an allied touring schedule."

Nik could feel the heat of anger growing from his bandmembers, and he fanned his hand behind his back, urging them to not strike out.

Balmer reached into his chain wallet and removed two business cards scrolled with the Hexed band logo and handed one to Nik and the other to Alex. Mike Balmer fist-bumped Nik and failed to gain the same gesture from the rest of the band as he left the bar floor with his bandmembers following, the chains of his trip pants rattling. The rest of Hexed followed, with Tawny Baker bringing up the rear. As she passed, she smiled at Nik and flashed her smoky eyes.

Nik beheld her with disgust as he looked at her folds and rolls protruding through her Joan Jett and the Blackhearts t-shirt and her fat hips bubbling through her leather skirt and fishnet pantyhose. She had new developing cold sores budding at the corners of her mouth. Nik, marred with disgust, wondered which strain of herpes afflicted her face.

The urge to collect his pay and leave the bar increased. Once Hexed left the building, Nik dropped the business card and kicked it to the side.

Doug Roen approached them. "I guess you guys did prove to be an alright act after all." Doug removed his wallet from his pocket, reluctantly rifling through with nimble movements. He gave Nik and each of his fellow bandmembers twenty-five dollars, smiling at them with brown wooden-colored teeth. "If you guys want to be regulars, just give me a holler, and we can book you for future events." He laughed, boastfully hacking dry, broken phlegm.

They dashed to the rear utility room and scooped up their equipment, swiftly loading it.

Alex burst out with frustration as he finished loading his equipment. "If that grubby sonofabitch thinks we'll ever play his shitty little bar again, he has got another think coming. His lousy pay wasn't worth the gas of coming out here. Plus, the audacity of those dirty fuckers from Hexed thinking we would join them for future shows is not only an insult but ridiculous too."

Nik agreed with Alex's outburst, sharing his frustrations.

They stood for a moment outside, cooling down from resentment and disappointment from the pay, before Andy spoke. "Yeah, fuck that noise joining forces with those assholes. Hell, just playing on the same stage with those dirty bastards makes me want to go to the nearest VD clinic and get a penicillin shot."

Nik and the others laughed.

"They need to crawl back to whatever cesspool or Hot Topic they crawled from and leave the real entertaining to us."

The members laughed as Andy closed with his last insult, cementing their decision to never return to the venue and decline future invitations to perform with Hexed.

Nik thought about his music room and setlists he kept stored on the shelves. He labeled the arrangements of his setlists by a category that he referred to as his "Various Tunes." He thought about what he had said earlier to his fellow bandmates about changing it up at Jeanelle's Bar, playing the Slow Dance on the Bar Floor set. He had this arrangement of songs committed to memory, but he was unsure on whether the others were as sharp on the setlist. "Well, guys. There's a light at the end of the tunnel. You know the next show is at a friendlier and cleaner venue."

They perked up with a new sense of life.

"I just want to remind you that we're playing the Slow Dance on the Bar Floor set, the one that gets all the girls on the floor. Is everyone familiar with the order of the song list?"

Andy and Alex both told Nik they remembered it began with "One of These Nights" and concluded with "Satisfaction Guaranteed." Kenny stepped forward, reciting the list with perfect linear order, surprising Alex and Andy but not surprising Nik. Nik knew Kenny was endowed with the capability to remember information almost as good as he could. Kenny also held high hopes that Savannah would be present at the show. Nik and Kenny shared a non-verbal moment of communication. Kenny expressed gratitude toward Nik, as he knew this decision was for his benefit as well. Nik suggested that after work during the coming week they should assemble at Alex's pull barn to reestablish themselves with the songs' finetuning. He wanted the show played with ease.

Andy grumbled and moaned once he realized what was transpiring between Nik and Kenny. "Dammit! I hate this setlist. I think it's sappy, and it's just a way for you guys to impress the ladies and try to get laid. This shit never works for me."

Nik glanced at Alex as Andy looked to the ground, feeling defeated. Alex nudged Andy on the side, knowing what he had to say. "Hey, bud. I'll tell you what. During this show, I think

I'll take a back seat on lead guitar and play rhythm while you play the lead parts. Besides, let's face it, 'Come Again' by Damn Yankees was your idea you brought to the table, so you should be the one out there showcasing it. I don't want to come off as showboating anyways."

Andy looked up renewed as Alex offered him the opportunity to step up. Playing the lead parts would get him some much deserved attention, providing the opportunity to get laid.

The conversation on the upcoming show concluded. Nik bid his fellow bandmates a good night. He called out to them one last time, asking if they remembered the way back. They were a little unsure how to get back precisely. Nik assured them he would not drive too far ahead. Kenny had a good working knowledge of the directions home, so he offered to pick up the rear. Once everybody was sure of the vehicle formation, Nik pulled out and led his pack.

He led them out of town on Apache Road in the direction of State Route 14 and had an epiphany and a pleasant self-realization. He thought he was blessed to work with such talented musicians. He looked in his rearview mirror, nodding with gratitude toward the shine of their trailing headlights, knowing they couldn't see this gesture but hoped they would feel his expression. He signaled left as he approached the intersection of Apache Road and State Route 14.

The drive home seemed to take less time than it did to get there. Nik led the others on Donaldson Road, passing Moline Medical Warehousing once again and knowing Andy would be exploding with insults. Arriving on Main Street, he turned left, heading home. His bandmates blared their car horns as they continued north toward Alex's house to drop off Kenny's drum set and their gear, so they would be set up for the upcoming practices.

He felt guilt that they would have to take the time to set up in Alex's pull barn, but he was sure Kenny and Andy would be flying high on their own private hopes and expectations toward the upcoming show. It may give the others time to vent and complain about him, if they felt the need to decompress over his leadership. Nik dismissed the thought about the possible scenario and drove home.

He was exhausted when he carried his gear to his garage. It was a fraught duty to fulfill. It was a task he had taken on numerous times before, but tonight he felt physically exhausted. His motivations lay with going through the front door, racing down the hallway and laying his head to rest for the night.

Chapter
Four

The following morning greeted Nik with large overcast and distant rumbles of thunder from the northwest. He glanced at the alarm clock and was appalled the time displayed 9:55. He feared he had overslept and missed a large portion of the morning. He rolled from his left side onto his back, rubbing his eyes. The rumble of northwestern thunder increased in volume and elongated. He thought he must have been more exhausted than he realized to fall asleep in last night's clothes.

While gaining his posture, he walked to the bathroom. His urge to urinate pounded with each step. Before he lifted the toilet seat and lid, he pulled the front of his shirt to his face to sniff the fabric and sighed in relief that no smell was present on his clothes. He feared the smell that had permeated from Hexed was communicable.

As he urinated, he pondered their strange wardrobe—their shabbily dressed gothic appearance. He remembered the bass player's and drummer's unwashed faded Pantera and Anthrax shirts along with their ripped and tattered jeans. He thought about Tawny's tight and constricting outfit that lacked appeal, exposing her rolls, and the trip pants with the rattling chains and multiple sweet stains—he recalled counting seventeen—on Balmer's white wife-beater tank top.

Nik reflected on his band and his appearance, beginning with Kenny's attire. He usually employed a black t-shirt adorned with a punk band's album cover or a horror movie picture while wearing black jeans and combat boots. Andy would don a t-shirt that illustrated a videogame cover or a game distributor company, with jean shorts and Chuck Taylor shoes. Alex chose a clean-cut approach, selecting polo shirts and dress pants, wearing shoes with a high-mirrored shine. Finally, he arrived at his own wardrobe, which displayed a various style of Union Jack flags on shirts and khaki shorts and black and white oxford shoes. He contemplated the Union Jack's significance; his father had been the central motivation to become a musician, but he had other influences—the British bands from the 1970s and the 1980s. Nik concluded it was his way of paying homage honoring his heroes.

After flushing the toilet, he placed down the seat and lid, realizing what had provoked these thoughts—Doug Roen on the previous night had commented about how they did not appear to look like a band he hosted in his establishment.

Arrogance swept over as he dived deeper. Lapis Lazuli may not dress the part of the archetypal roadhouse dive-bar musicians, but they could entertain and immerse a crowd like no other act. Substance far outweighed physical appearance. Completing his self-praising, he washed his hands and stepped into the hallway. Cool air enveloped him, and a chill crawled over him. He walked down the hallway to the front of his house, noticing the sky neared blackness and the wind gained momentum.

Nik became joyous with the oncoming thunderstorm and ran into the kitchen to fetch his tea kettle; his father had instilled this pleasure in him at an early age. As a small child, he had felt fear and apprehension toward the thunder and lightning until his father encouraged him to think of them as firework shows. Bringing his water to a boil, he readied a tea mug and a bag of Earl Grey tea.

Carrying his mug of steeping tea, he stepped onto the porch and sat on his porch glider. He sipped his first drink as the storm came into full glory with its cooling winds, flashing lightning, and guttural rumbles of thunder. The storm lasted for close to an hour before ending and passing through the south. He wanted to be prepared for the following day and arrive at work early to discuss the setlist and practice session with his bandmates. He dressed in his comfortable clothes and approached his music room.

He selected the Various Tunes folder and flipped through the different setlists until he arrived at the Slow Dance on the Bar Floor sheet. He panned it carefully, reviewing the songs, "One of These Nights" by The Eagles, "Faithfully" by Journey, "Change" by John Waite, "Don't Answer Me" by Alan Parson's Project, "Without You" by Harry Nilson, "Strange Magic" by Electric Light Orchestra, "Come Again and High Enough" by Damn Yankees, "Endless Summer Nights" by Richard Marx, "Don't Let It End" by Styx, "Pamela" by Toto, "Follow You, Follow Me" by Genesis, "Broken Wings" by Mr. Mister, and "Satisfaction Guaranteed" by The Firm." Nik looked with pride, feeling the arrangement of songs presented a good atmosphere and transitions between songs.

He carried the setlist to his bedroom and placed it under his cellphone charger and his alarm clock, so he could show it to his bandmates. He was confident they could still play those songs but wanted to ensure they remembered the song order. The day carried on, and he ate a modest dinner of vegetable beef soup and two slices of buttered bread. Finishing his dinner, he returned to the living room to read his Brian Paone novel before the evening became night. Before retiring, he set his alarm for 5:00 a.m.

As morning arrived, he awoke before the alarm clock. He sprung from his bed with urgency to get ready and leave his house. He grabbed his setlist and cellular phone. He directed his thoughts toward the show at Gibbswood, along with seeing Samantha. Upon arriving at work, he saw that the guys were already parked. He had plenty of time to discuss their practice plans for the coming week. The week seemed off to an exceptional start.

He flashed his employee ID badge to security, and the officer casually nodded and waved him through. Nik's bandmates were isolated at their own break table. He retrieved the setlist, placing it on the table.

"That won't be necessary, Nik." Alex spoke through his laughter.

Nik appeared puzzled at Alex's behavior.

"You're not the only one here who has a steel-cage memory. Kenny already wrote down the setlist, and it is in exactly the same order that you have."

Kenny leaned back in his seat, folding his arms.

Nik endowed Kenny with a satisfied smile.

"I got you covered, bro. Like I said before, I had it memorized."

Nik and his band spoke amongst themselves, watching the clock in the break room. Andy made obscene comments toward the facility general manager while leaving the break room.

The typical stock crowd congregated in the morning meeting—a crowd Nik was pleased not to endure any longer but felt remorse for his fellow bandmates as they still had to. They were a basic crowd of people who encompass a typical drama-ridden warehouse. He privately categorized them by genres. He never shared his assessment with anyone in the facility. He had labeled the other warehouse workers as being white trash, Monday-morning quarterbacks, NASCAR nitwits, or gossiping church hens. The women were the absolute worst to endure. They would sit parked, blocking him from his work and subjugating the meek associates and accusing them of being lazy while they did nothing. They would complain when the associates they were gossiping about would make rate and they would not. Aside from his bandmates, Nik never committed the others' names to memory. He only assessed them by the foulness of their faces.

Jim Whitman exited the dock office and stood in the center of the associates. He appeared in rare form, trying to generate respect through his poor attempts of taking a commanding stance and using a booming voice. "Well, everybody, we have a busy work week, and we must move some serious products here."

Nik and the others rolled their eyes.

Jim berated everyone that their performances have been under expectation. Concluding the meeting, the associates broke the circle and headed to their departments. Andy did not approach Nik with any opinions toward the contents of Jim's pants. Nik walked through the dock office door to collect his paperwork and keys. All the dispatchers and other dock office associates were somber. Darcy appeared upset, making minimal eye contact with Nik.

He knew that as hard as Jim came down on the warehouse associates, he must have come down harder on the dock office personnel. Nik collected his paperwork from Darcy and patted her shoulder, wishing her a good day. She grabbed his hands and gave a gentle squeeze, demonstrating gratitude. Nik made haste to leave the dock office.

In the driver's lot, he performed a less-than-thorough pre-trip. He was assigned Kenny's dock door, knowing he would gain extra time. After loaded, he embarked on his workday. The week was long, as everyday Jim Whitman became sharper urging the associates and dock office personnel. After work was when Nik felt at his best. Despite the work week being grueling, Nik and the others would reconvene at Alex's for practice. It was a wonderful way for Nik to decompress while the others sharpened their abilities to commit the set to muscle memory. All Nik could think about was the upcoming show at Jeanelle's Bar, hoping for another opportunity to get Samantha back at his house.

Time itself seem to creep backward as he reported to work. When Friday eventually arrived, time accelerated, and his routes were quick, along with the facilities unloading his truck. On Friday afternoon, he returned to the driver lot early at 1:30. Once the park break was set, he ran around the truck, inspecting it before heading toward the dock office. As he entered the dock office, he hung his keys and set his paperwork on Darcy's desk, but she was not present.

Nik was in his truck's cab in no time. As he left the facility and glanced in his rearview mirror, he noticed it got smaller, creating distance. He detoured to the bank to withdraw some cash and then went to Frazier's IGA for a quick grocery pickup.

He dashed home, parked his truck in the driveway then charged through the door, anxious to peel off his work uniform. Feeling greasy and scummy from sitting in the straight truck's hot cab, he jumped into the shower. Once he stepped out of the shower, he felt cleansed and refreshed. He carefully shaved his face with tact, as he wanted to appear his best for the evening. He selected his best-fitting khaki shorts and most form-fitting Union Jack tank top from his dresser drawers.

Nik practiced his piano for a few hours before realizing the time was 7:30. He left his house, locking the door behind him and loading his truck with his equipment to drive to Gibbswood.

Nik sped despite having plenty of time. He felt compelled to arrive early, so he may mentally play through the events of the night. He wanted to be set up and relaxed, so he could watch the entrance for Samantha. He did not want to take any chances of an unforeseen hiccup spoiling his evening before it began.

Arriving in Gibbswood, he spotted Jeanelle's Bar and spun the steering wheel, pulling to the building's rear. Once parked, he eagerly unloaded his equipment. In his haste, he felt embarrassment realizing he did not get a hold of his bandmates, and they would be unaware that he was already there. He fumbled his cellphone from his side pocket and dialed Alex.

Alex's phone rang only once before he answered. "Hi, Nik. What's going on, buddy? Is something wrong?"

Nik paused. "Everything's okay. I just forgot to tell you that I'm at the bar."

Alex chuckled once. "Wow, dude. You must be in a real hurry to get things going tonight."

Nik agreed that he was feeling eager.

Alex's voice relented, knowing he had to deliver less-than-good news. "I'm glad you're excited about the show, bro, but I have some news that will not please you or the others."

Nik knew what Alex was about to say but wanted to hear it from Alex's mouth just the same.

"I know you guys are not her biggest fan, but Desiree is coming to the show."

Nik mouthed silent curse words as Alex paused.

"I also have to tell you that Mallory and Roberta will be at the show as well." Alex then informed him that he would be at Jeanelle's with the others around 8:30.

Nik winced, bit his bottom lip in frustration then said goodbye and thanked Alex for letting him know. He slammed his fists against the steering wheel, shouting with frustration. Regardless, he would stay strong and not let Desiree or the others spoil his evening. Nik exited the truck, closed the door firmly, approached the rear of Jeanelle's Bar and rang the doorbell.

Charlie flung open the rear door, surprised to see Nik early. "Jeez, Nik. The early bird really does get the worm. I wasn't expecting you until eight thirty, along with the others." Appreciating Nik's punctuality, Charlie assisted with carrying in his equipment.

Entering Jeanelle's Bar, Nik beheld its aesthetics. It felt good to be playing at a clean place once again. He placed his equipment on the stage as Charlie connected it to the PA system.

Nik approached the bar, greeting Jeanelle and asking for a Washington apple cocktail to calm his nerves. She flirted as she mixed the drink. The drink was on the house, and she wished him good luck.

Nik's bandmates arrived after 8:30 p.m. Nik greeted them, and they expressed the same pleased look to be back at Jeanelle's Bar. At 8:50, the crowd filed in, and Lapis Lazuli began at 9:00.

After the band played the second song, Desiree and her friends arrived and sat down. The three women appeared to ooze from their seats. After the fourth song, Nik watched

Savannah enter excited for Kenny to see she had made well on her intentions. The crowd was enjoying the show. Nik and the others were glad to see everyone on the dance floor. A full-figured redhead with shoulder-length hair gave Andy a starry-eyed look. Happy for his fellow bandmate, Nik still watched the entrance, vigilantly hoping Samantha would walk through the door.

As the band played on, the entrance door flung open with force. Samantha stood motionless with an eerie expression. His heart fluttered as he looked at her. He realized that something was amiss; she did not appear with the same light as she did the night they were together. She was dressed plainly with longer shorts and a baggy orange t-shirt with DELBERT'S TREE REMOVAL SERVICE scrolled with black letters. She stepped into the bar, looking guilty and defeated. A short, moderately obese man in his early-to-mid forties followed her, with a full bushy mustache and wearing a Cummins Diesel hat along with the same color t-shirt with the same words scrolled on it. Nik felt his heart sink as everything made sense to him. He realized why Samantha was desperate to return to Gibbswood. He knew she was an involved woman, and this was her man.

Controlling his shock and gaining his composure, he knew the show must go on, and he would have to deal with the repercussions of his actions. He avoided glances with her as she appeared as a shamed dog with her tail between her legs.

Her male companion beamed stares of hatred toward Nik. The short, fat man approached Desiree, questioning her. Of all people in the bar, he approached Desiree. Nik's luck was becoming lousier as the show progressed.

Desiree's eyes widened, and she cupped her mouth with her meaty hands. She blatantly pointed to Nik.

Samantha shot out the entrance door with a burst.

The fat man followed her, storming out.

Nik did not see Samantha or the fat man for the rest of the set, relieved as the band finished the show.

Savannah approached the stage to greet Kenny. They spoke while the short, full-figured redhead approached the stage and introduced herself to Andy, telling him that her name was Rebecca. Andy had finally gained the attraction of an audience member. Andy burst with joy with this newfound attention. Nik did not want to dampen the moment for his fellow bandmates, but he felt a sense of urgency to collect his payment and leave. Kenny and Andy told their female companions that they would be back to talk with them soon, but they had to settle some business with management.

Alex walked across the floor first to Jeanelle to collect payment, followed by Kenny then Andy with Nik in the rear. Jeanelle stood behind the counter as she handed each member a one-hundred-dollar bill.

Desiree grab Nik by the wrist, shaking him. "Looks like you've been fucking around with the wrong girl."

Nik shot Desiree a glare of raw hatred, shaking her grasp from his wrist, then noticed the look of surprise on Jeanelle's face. He tried his best to shake the scowl, reassuring Jeanelle that he was fine but must leave immediately.

She handed him his payment and wished him a good night.

Nik thanked her and turned away. His bandmates had left the building; they must be loading their vehicles with their equipment.

Nik approached the stage to collect his equipment, and a hand grabbed his shoulder. He rose up, jerking away and stepping backward.

Charlie stood in front of him with an equally shocked face. "Jesus, man. You scared the shit out of me. What's got you so jumpy tonight, Nik?"

Controlling his apprehension, he apologized to Charlie.

Charlie assisted Nik with carrying his equipment. While both exited the rear entrance, they saw Kenny and Savannah conversing by his white GMC Jimmy, and Andy chatting with his new companion by his Ford Focus. Alex's Kia Sportage was nowhere to be found.

Charlie wished Nik and the other remaining bandmembers a good night and asked them if they needed anything before he closed the back door. They did not, so he secured the door.

Nik closed his truck's tailgate, feeling a different hand firmly grab his shoulder. He knew it was not Charlie or one of his bandmates. Nik knew exactly who it was, anticipating the coming events.

Spun around with great force, Nik faced the fat mustached man. He snorted with red fury, breathing through his mouth and nose, like an angry bull. He raised his right hand to Nik's face. "Do you know who the fuck I am, boy? Well, do you, goddammit?"

Samantha stood behind, staring at the ground.

"I'm Ross Delbert, the man whose wife *you fucked* the other weekend, you sonofabitch!"

Nik no longer felt fear; his fear had oscillated into a rage directed toward multiple fronts—Samantha and Ross, along with Desiree and Alex, as if they had a part of this transgression. His suspicion heightened, knowing Desiree had identified him as the man who had slept with Ross's wife. Alex had been the first to receive payment from the show and leave.

Nik glared at Ross with boiling fury, tightening his body and readying himself for an ensuing fight. "Really? That's a funny story, Ross, and I'll tell you why. She didn't introduce herself as Samantha Delbert. She told me that her name was Samantha Moore, and I didn't see any *fucking ring* on her finger!"

Kenny and Savannah's conversation fell silent, along with Andy and Rebecca's. They watched the events unfolding in front of them in shock.

Ross turned to Samantha, screaming and questioning her about how she could do this to him.

She sobbed, pleading with apologies.

Ross hoped to catch Nik off guard and delivered a heavy right hook.

Nik skillfully swayed backward, dodging the attack and throwing a solid right jab centered at Ross's nose, followed by a solid uppercut, knocking Ross to the ground. He felt Ross's jaw and teeth clatter and crack as he struck him.

Samantha looked up from the ground, shrieking at Nik, with her hands clawed toward his face and scratching him across his right cheek.

Nik grabbed her wrists defensively, shaking her away.

She screamed at Nik that she hated him for all he'd done as she kneeled beside Ross. Accusations flew at Nik for ruining her marriage. Samantha helped Ross to his feet.

He wobbled to gain his footing, holding his jaw with one hand and his nose with the other. Ross knew he was a defeated man, and, if he approached Nik, what would happen next would result in permanent injury. He turned away from Nik hunched over and wrapping his arm around Samantha.

Samantha helped to sturdy him and turned to Nik one last time, bursting with tears and mouthing, *I'm sorry*, before flashing the *I love you* gesture as she walked down the alley.

He could only look at her with hatred. His dreamy feelings of budding love and passion were absent.

When Ross and Samantha were no longer in sight, Kenny and Andy, along with their companions, approached Nik, shaken with the events. Kenny placed his hand on Nik's shoulder before

Nik jolted away Kenny's hand. Kenny respectfully stood back, realizing his friend was still in fighting mode.

Andy, unable to contain his words, spoke with amazement. "Holy fucking shit, dude! You just took fat ass apart!" Then Andy asked him if he was all right.

Nik glanced back and forth at everyone around him, assuring them that he was fine. Nik apologized to Kenny for jerking away and also to his friend's lady companions.

Everyone assured Nik that apologies were unnecessary. They told Nik that if that man decided to call the police and press charges over the fistfight, they would make statements that Ross had started the fight.

Nik articulated gratitude toward all of them and reached into his pocket for his cigarettes and lighter. Nik calmed himself while smoking his cigarette. "Hey look, guys, I appreciate you all checking on me, but you should get out of here and enjoy your night. If the police get involved, I hope your offers to make a statement will still be on the table."

Everyone nodded.

Nik bid them a goodnight, hoping he had not spoiled their evening. He walked to the driver side of his truck and climbed in. He pulled out of the parking lot behind Jeanelle's Bar with shredding speed.

Nik stopped at the intersection of the alley and Main Street. He pounded his steering wheel three times, and an orange full-size truck raced by. His chest tightened as he grasped the steering wheel, knowing the orange truck was Ross's. He heard the occupants screaming at each other. He could not decipher their exact words but could understand the jest; Delbert yelled about what she had done and the pain caused, Samantha cried that she was sorry about her moment of weakness. Nik remained stationery watching the truck turn toward Sattler

Street, disappearing. Through his violent rage, he felt sickened knowing a cheating whore had used and played him for a fool.

He recounted the chronological order of the events—their first night together and her dazzling him, to his feelings of contempt and disgust. Concluding his thoughts, he fisted his steering wheel once, rattling it before he grabbed it and turned onto Main Street. With tunneled vision, he drove, fuming. He cleared the town limits and decided he must gain control of his emotions. He felt that if he continued to drive in a reckless manner, he may find himself on the receiving end of a speeding citation—or worse, involved in a traffic crash. He calmed himself knowing an accident or a ticket would further exacerbate the failed evening.

Achieving calmness, he examined certain events of the evening. Two key points resonated in his mind—Desiree grabbing his wrist and commenting about sleeping with the wrong woman and Alex's Kia Sportage was gone before Nik reached the parking lot. He pondered if Alex and Desiree were involved in the setup or if it was just a strange coincidence that Alex had left early due to Desiree demanding his company and that of all the people Ross could approach, it happened to be a person who hated him and would have no reserve outing him. He purged the thoughts from his mind. If he continued to dwell, he would tailspin deeper. In the past, he had often wondered if Alex's jealousy toward his talents and abilities fueled Desiree's hatred for him. He remembered earlier in the band's formation how Alex had commented regarding his own leadership deserving to be more prominent due to him hosting the rehearsals. Despite his own self protest, he could not shake the thoughts and realized he was doing what he had adamantly fought against. Now was not the time to search for more reasons to entice rage. The silent drive caused him to brood, gaining distance from Gibbswood.

He turned on the radio in hopes of finding some music to deter his mind. He fumbled through the dial and landed on 100.5 WXBV—a classic rock and pop station. He was surprised to hear the station playing "Advice for the Young at Heart" by Tears for Fears. It was strange that they were playing a deep cut. On most occasions, if a radio station played a Tears for Fears song, it would be "Shout," "Everybody Wants to Rule the World," or "Head Over Heels." However, Nik felt this was their best song, and it did not share the typical obnoxious sound the band exhibited. He continued to listen to the song as he entered Pemkey.

Once Nik finished the drive and parked his truck, he felt the heat and sting from the right side of his face. He perched up toward his rearview mirror and saw he had a small superficial scratch, only mildly breaking the skin. He was fortunate the scratch was the only mark on him in comparison to Ross. He wondered if he had broken the fat man's nose, jaw, or teeth from the strikes. With a prideful mind, he had won the physical confrontation, easily devastating his opponent. Nik did not relish the thought of what Ross was enduring on his drive home, contending with defeat and a broken heart. He felt sympathy for the man and how he had contributed in his anguish. He buried his emotions, remembering that Ross had attempted to catch him off guard with a surprise right hook.

Samantha had shattered both the man's pride and heart, but Nik remembered how Ross had attempted to cheat with a sucker punch. Ross would not have won naturally, and his only means of gaining control would be to catch him off guard. He wondered if Ross's defeat would result with further attempts of violence. He thought that if his rage and desperation became overbearing, he would approach him with the intent to kill. Samantha knew where Nik lived, and, if Ross gained this knowledge, he could come to his house for revenge another time.

Nik felt uneasy and exited his truck with haste. He readied his garage door key and collected his equipment from the truck bed. He fumbled with the equipment, nearly tripping as he made trips to his garage. He placed down his equipment, closed the garage door and checked the door rigorously to ensure it was locked.

Satisfied that the door was secure, he bound up his porch steps to make sure that the state of his home was still intact. No tooling marks or other indication that someone had tampered with his door were visible. He dashed toward his bedroom and reached under his bed for his overnight backpack. He stuffed two days' worth of clothes into his bag, along with his cellular phone charger. He ran to the bathroom, flipped the light switch with a snap and collected his toiletries from the medicine cabinet. He looked at his reflection in the mirror with disgust and shame that he had been foolish to participate in those actions a few weeks ago with Samantha and had developed feelings for someone who was not real and not worthy. The mark on his right cheek was not as large as it had appeared earlier in the rearview mirror; he was relieved he could dismiss it as being a small shaving nick.

Once he had finished packing his backpack, he glanced at the time—10:43 p.m. It was still early in the night; time to place a call to his parents. They were both night owls due to his father's second-shift work schedule. His mother would be awake, catching up on her soap operas she had acquired through the week. His father would be getting off from work at Lakota Wire at 11:00 p.m.

He retrieved his phone from his pocket while entering his bedroom and flipping off the light switch in the bathroom. He dialed his mother's phone number, straightening his back and clearing his throat.

His mother answered after only two rings. "Hey, kid. How are things going?"

Nik zipped his backpack closed. "I'm doing all right, Mom. I just wanted to call and say hi and see how you and Dad were doing."

"Everything's okay over here. I'm just finishing *The Young and the Restless* before Dad gets home from work. What's up? I'm surprised to hear from you this late. Did you have a show tonight?

Nik explained he had just finished a show a little earlier and wanted to call and see how they were doing. His mother agreed that it had been a long time since they had spoken. Nik asked what she and his father were doing this weekend. She said they had nothing planned. He told her that he wanted to see them and stay with them during the weekend.

"Well, I can tell you that your old room, the newly converted guest, room is ready for you, but I need to know something. Is something wrong? Are you in some kind of trouble?"

Nik swallowed his fear, knowing he and his mother shared a bond. She could read Nik like a book, just as he could read her. He realized he had appeared too eager. He needed to remedy her suspicion.

"Oh, no, Mom. Nothing's wrong. I just realized that it has been a couple of weeks since I had called, plus living on my own gets a little lonely sometimes. You must have heard that in my voice. Everything is okay over here, just lonely."

The suspicion had broken from her, and she told him it would be great if he came over, and his father would be pleased to see him too. Nik told her that he would have to pack a bag, and he would be over promptly. He did not want to confess that he had already packed his bag. She would know something was truly wrong.

"Well, Mom, I'll collect my things and see you in around a half an hour."

His mother told him to drive carefully and watch out for drunk drivers. After his mother told him that she loved him, Nik returned the same and ended the phone call.

He traversed his house, committing everything in sight to memory. Still feeling hyper-vigilance from the events earlier, he wanted to create a mental map of his house if Delbert decided to pay him a visit during his absence. After his thorough scan, he checked the power outlets behind his furniture and reset the timer adapters, offsetting the times his lights in his living room and music room turned on. If Delbert had been previously casing his house, employing a different strategy of the lights' activation might detour him from breaking in or vandalizing.

Nik finished his sweep of the house and stepped onto the porch with stealth, closing the door firmly and tugging on it with repetition. He crossed the porch and lawn with delicate footfalls. The truck did not start loudly, as it had been running from earlier. He placed his backpack on the passenger seat and fastened his seatbelt before leaving.

Chapter
Five

Nik drove through Pemkey, creeping with tact. He glanced at everything he could take notice of—vehicles, buildings, and people walking the streets and sidewalks of the community. Not seeing anything suspicious, he increased his speed as he approached downtown. The buildings were dark and quiet with only the security lights activated as they stood sleeping. He passed by the Pemkey Public Library, followed by the post office, bank, and the IGA.

He looked to his side and studied the park's lot for Delbert's truck. No unusual activity was happening in the park. The only sights were the cars driven by the local teenagers who hung out at Pisanello's before taking their dates to the park for rushed teenage coitus. Nik saw one car rocking in the parking lot. As he passed, his headlights shined through its windows, and two heads popped up cautiously from the horizon of the back seat.

Nik chuckled as he knew they were two horny teenagers in fear of someone catching them in the act.

Nik turned his attention across the street to Pisanello's, thinking about Kenny and Savannah sitting quietly at his place before Savannah could take the stillness no longer and pounced. Nik shifted his thoughts toward Andy and Rebecca. He would most likely ejaculate prematurely from a few rapidly placed thrusts then explain that usually does not happen to him and how it must be due to how attractive she is, before attempting the act again.

Turning down Donaldson Road, he regarded his backpack in the passenger seat. It should have been Samantha sitting there after the show, not be his loaded backpack. In his mind's eye, he saw the evening concluding with her riding with him to his house to engage in the activities they had engaged in the other weekend.

Nik spoke aloud, shocking himself as the volume of his voice was louder than expected. "Shit, everyone is getting some but me." After he spoke, he suppressed the thought. Getting some the other weekend is what has caused him his current grief.

He cleared the town limits and glanced at Moline Medical Warehousing with added dread and the foreboding thought of Desiree spreading the drama and rumors throughout the facility once the weekend ended. Nik dwelled on the thought that Alex would willfully participate in the storytelling, running his name through the mud. Nik could no longer stand the anticipation of the impending drama waiting for him; he turned his head forward, concentrating on the dark, winding rural road.

He was in dire need to calm his thoughts, so he rolled down his window, placed a cigarette in his mouth and lit it, inhaling a deep drag. Before he realized it, he was at the intersection of Donaldson Road and State Route 14. He smoked his cigarette down to the top of the filter, feeling the heat of the cherry approaching his fingertips. He sat at the intersection, watching the floating headlights of passing cars drive from both directions. As the rows of cars cleared, he blasted the accelerator.

He continued down Donaldson Road, feeling the road narrow and riding rough underneath. He knew as the road jogged and bumped from side to side that he was approaching the intersection of Donaldson Road and Paulding Pike. He could drive blind as he felt the condition of Donaldson Road worsen. Arriving at the intersection, he looked left in the direction of Bradford, residing in Graham School District, then looked right toward the village of Hoyle, located in the farthest corner of Bateson School District. Nik turned right toward Hoyle. His mind and body took on coldness as he grew closer to the district where he grew up. Gaining speed, he passed the small Friendship Marathon gas station on his left that stood as the divider between Bateson and Graham School districts.

During his senior year of high school, he often made several sojourns to that gas station after Friday night football games to purchase bottles of MD 20/20 for his fellow marching band mates and various members of the football team. Nik recalled how, with his long hair and early developing beard, the clerks did not card him. He made some side money for his troubles and would buy the members of the football team the most terrible flavors he could find, such as banana red or kiwi lemon. He smiled as he remembered telling the football players that the store only had those flavors available. He purchased the tolerable flavors for his marching band mates.

Entering Hoyle, he saw the town's accolades proudly displayed on the village limit sign. Hoyle boasted that it was the hometown of Kenny Bahrenson, Evan Feassey, Amanda Rennholds, and Josh Chapnan, for their athletic performances.

The last-name society were illustrious and regarded highly throughout the halls of the Bateson School District, from elementary throughout high school. These last names became synonymous with each other, and the sound of them alone sickened Nik. The sight of Josh Chapnan's name especially sickened him. Josh was the most pompous and arrogant of the lot and a constant agitator and rival. He winced hatefully at the signs as he followed Paulding Pike to the four-way stop at Main Street then forked to the right and continued through Hoyle.

Growing up in the Bateson School District was a hardship for him, but when he eventually integrated from Amsdale Elementary into the junior high school in Schwin was where he found the trouble and segregation from his peers take flight. The last-name societies from Hoyle were far worse to Nik than their Amsdale relatives. If a child did not grow up in the villages of Hoyle, Gary Town, or Schwin, then the residents regarded them largely as the filth of the district, unless the birthright of their name had graced them.

Driving through Hoyle, he felt his coldness grow into a dull sickness by the nauseating layout of the once-proud, now-depreciating town. He panned the houses as he drove and thought their positionings were off putting. Instead of the houses sitting parallel to the street, they appeared at an unappealing angle. Nik felt grateful that he was not under the influence of alcohol or any other substance, as the appearance of the housing structures might cause him to erupt with physical illness. Following Main Street through Hoyle, the road branched off again to the left, becoming Paulding Pike once more entering the rural area. Feeling relief as he passed the limits of Hoyle, he knew he had arrived only at the tip of the iceberg regarding his sad journey through his childhood memories. He would pass other landmarks that held deeper, sadder memories as he made the trek.

Driving in the rural area with Hoyle to his rear, he maintained precise focus, knowing that if he did not give full attention to the road ahead, he would miss the severe right curve of Paulding Pike and land on Hattoon Road—an unpaved single-lane road where teenagers often rolled their vehicles due to overcorrecting. He slowed his truck appropriately to commit to the maneuver. A half of a mile away, he arrived at the intersection of Paulding Pike and State Route 181. With his foot placed firmly on the brake, he made a complete stop and rubbed his forehead and the bridge of his nose. State Route 181 was vacant, quiet, and unpopulated with traffic. As he checked both directions for potential oncoming traffic, he crept slowly as he drove.

He dedicated strong attention to the small, nearly unreadable road signs in the dark country night. He passed Prairie View Road—an abandoned road that lead to the left and dead-ended—and then passed Lawson Road, accessible in both directions, before arriving at the intersection of Babcock Road, where he decided to turn left. He based his decision on the geographical fact that from Paulding Pike, Amsdale Road is surrounded on both sides with wooded areas known for inhabiting an abundance of deer. After the evening Nik had endured, he did not want to take the chance of a possible collision with a deer. He also knew the wooded area would end once he arrived at the intersection of Gary Town Road and Amsdale Road. He did not wish to pass his old high school but figured it may be for the best to sour his sight instead of taking a gamble potentially striking a deer. He pressed forward on Babcock Road, paying vigilante attention to the steep crevices on both sides.

After traveling a mile, he arrived at the intersection of Babcock and Bay's Road, coming to an abrupt four-way stop. On the left corner stood the Zion non-denominational church. Passing through the intersection. he examined the church and the cemetery located to the rear, a single light illuminating it. Nik had always derived a morbid pleasure from viewing the cemetery. The cemetery headstones were those of the patriarchs of the Bateson School District elite. The names on the headstones were proudly displayed at the cemetery, as they were displayed in Hoyle. He drew a sizable pleasure to see their names etched in cold and weathering stones. He crackled a smile as he passed, knowing one day those he had grown up with would be there along with their decomposing ancestors. He reached into his pocket for his pack of cigarettes and lighter as he drove.

Nik continued down the road until it became a dead end at the intersection of Babcock and Gary Town Road. He stopped his truck, looked in both directions then turned right on Gary Town Road. Once on Gary Town Road, he saw the old Bateson High School on his right, realizing the town had converted the building to the district transportation offices, with school buses parked in what used to be the senior parking lot. As he passed the bus lot, he glanced to his right at the new Bateson centralized campus.

The building appeared unwelcoming as it entered his line of vision. To Nik, the facility bore a strong resemblance to a reformatory or a prison. He felt patronized as he drove by the reduced speed limit sign to see another sign colored in the blue and white district schematic, stating, *Bateson School District— An Excellent Rated School District*. He scoffed, and, with a lapse of maturity, he made the same gesture Andy had toward Moline. Feeling modestly vindicated, he diverted his attention from the campus.

Arriving at the intersection of Gary Town Road and Amsdale Road, he made an eager left onto Amsdale Road. His mood deepened into a darker state as he pressed on. He knew in a few miles he would approach the last landmark that caused him despondency. He felt his chest and mind tighten. He did not relish the impending thoughts and memories. He tried to rebuke and submerge his thoughts; however his resolve faltered, and his mind fully enveloped Kara Anderson and Derrick Connley. He sat at the intersection for a time, sadly reminiscing on what they had drove him to do, but he only thought of them briefly, as anger and contempt from the physical altercation he'd had earlier with Ross Delbert, along with reliving painful memories from his peers growing up at Bateson School District, infiltrated the scope of his mind.

Nik was flustered from his lengthy concentration as flashing lights in his rearview mirror and the sound of a knocking diesel engine from a Ford F-150 shook him back to reality. The Ford truck's driver blasted its horn with long frustrated bursts before Nik proceeded through. As the rear of his vehicle cleared the intersection, he heard the driver scream obscenities at him. Nik looked in his rearview mirror, smiling and flipping him off as he increased speed. Nik knew the driver couldn't see his gesture but felt a small sense of satisfaction nonetheless. Along with feeling annoyed from the driver's impatience, he could not help but carry a small manner of gratitude toward the driver for breaking him from his entranced spell.

The F-150 followed closely behind with its bright lights shining in view of his mirrors. It continued to follow him until it turned right onto Tank Center Road. Nik felt great relief as he noticed the truck was red and did not feature any Delbert Landscaping insignia.

Nik achieved a higher state of calmness as he crested Eagle Trail Road's raised intersection and saw the distant buildings of Amsdale. Tranquil thoughts entered as he looked forward to spending time with his parents. He believed the only two redeemable aspects of his hometown would be waiting and excited to see him. Nik crossed the intersection of Lafferty Road, soon to be followed by Amsdale's village limit sign, where Amsdale Road becomes Main Street.

The smell of sewer gas and hog farms greeted him. He gagged and coughed loudly, realizing the stench of the community had increased since the last time he was in town. He looked left and found the mausoleum's condition was far worse since his prior visit. A considerable amount of the roof had caved in, and vegetation grew from its top.

While pressing passed a row of houses, he arrived at the three-way stop at Main and Vine Street; the street's state had worsened. His truck rumbled and rocked. The side of Elmbury Street had become torn up, rutted with wear from excessive semi-truck traffic.

Nik spoke aloud approaching the intersection of Main and Cherry Street. "Jesus Christ, this town is turning to worse shit than it was before I left."

Making his right turn from Cherry to Garfield Street, the smell of sewer gas grew. He looked left and saw the yellow house that he called his childhood home and took an immediate right into the church parking lot.

Chapter
Six

Nik collected his thoughts while exiting his truck. He self-reassured that he was in a calm and friendly place amongst people who would offer him kind and welcoming arms. He sighed with relief before collecting his backpack from the passenger seat and exiting the truck, slipping a single arm through the strap. His mother sat on the porch glider next to a vacant rocking chair in the corner. She waved at him then shot him a look of annoyance to communicate that Brian Smalls was patronizing her as he stood to the side of the porch, visibly intoxicated and holding a can of Steele Reserve.

At first, Nik did not notice Brian Smalls standing to the side of the porch; his vision was tunneled. Nik waved at his mother, stifling a small giggle and communicating to her that he understood why she was annoyed. Nik looked down the street in both directions; it was devoid of traffic.

After he strolled across the street and reached the sidewalk, he heard the nonsensical ramblings of his parents' neighbor. "Yeah, so I had been fighting with my ex, Crystal, over visitation of my two youngest sons, Dylan and Carter, and she says to me that I can't see them till I pay my back child support. Then her new husband gets on the phone and says to me that I am an unfit father, so I say to him that he needs to mind his own business or I will knock him the fuck out." Brian concluded his failed attempt to impress Kayla with his macho attitude.

She diverted her half-hearted attention from Brian toward Nik, wishing Brian would stumble across the alley to his house.

Instead, Brian turned to Nik, engaging him in conversation—a conversation Nik did not want. Nik regarded Brian with reluctance, knowing he would spew nonsense. Brian's eyes were bloodshot, and the whites of his eyes appeared yellow. Nik thought Brian was a low-level excuse for a human being, with his white stained Tap Out sleeveless t-shirt that permeated body odor and torn cut-off jean shorts and lack of shoes. Nik focused on the structure and shape of Brian's skull as he rambled incoherently about his personal misfortunes with his ex-wife. His head appeared disproportionate to his body with its hexagonal shape, along with his hooked nose that protruded along his Neanderthal forehead and lack of his two front teeth.

Brian babbled about his bum rap, raw deals, and previous fighting conquest; Nik found he was distancing himself further from Brian's idiotic blithering, wondering if the shape of his skull was the result of fetal alcohol syndrome or from generations of compounded incest.

Unknown to Brian, Kayla shot Nik a look of comical annoyance.

Brian questioned Nik regarding where he currently lived and worked.

Employing tact, Nik contemplated methods to get his obnoxious neighbor to vacate. He thought the sure-fire way to remove his neighbor would be to inform him of his raise and promotion to straight truck driver after acquiring his commercial driver license.

Once Nik told Brian of his current increase in position, Brian's drunken mood became colder and grim. Brian mustered a small amount of pride through his intoxication after a moment of silence and spoke. "Yeah, well, I've been thinking about going to truck driving school myself next month and getting my class-A CDL. I think I can make a lot of money and get the fuck out of this town."

Nik knew he had Brian where he wanted him in the verbal exchange. "Yeah, a person can make a pretty penny having a CDL, but quite a bit of responsibility comes with it, like accountability. People with a regular operator's license are allowed a minimum of point-oh-eight alcohol content, but once you get your CDL, a person is only allowed point-oh-four." Nik smiled at Brian snidely. "It is fun and rewarding to drive a truck but a lot of self-discipline."

Brian huffed loudly and licked the sides of his dry mouth then spit on the ground. "It's getting late, and I think I'll call it a night and crash out."

Nik and Kayla watched him stagger across the alley before he stumbled one last time entering his house.

Kayla's silent snickers turned into a soft cackle. "You little asshole. You knew exactly how to get his goat and make him leave."

Nik and his mother laughed over what had transpired. He rested his backpack beside the rocking chair, sat down and placed a cigarette into his mouth. When Nik finished his cigarette, he flicked the butt into the alley looking toward

Cherry Street. He saw the shine of headlights approaching the intersection, knowing the vehicle was his father's red single-cab Dodge Dakota Sport. Nik wondered if his father would notice his Dakota in the church parking lot or if he would just park out of routine and pay no mind—either way, Nik knew his father would be surprised to see him.

As Terrence exited his truck, he accidentally slammed the door, and the truck rattled rust. He shook his head with annoyance and proceeded toward the porch.

Nik realized his father had not seen his truck in the church lot as he strolled oblivious. Nik studied his father and noticed dirt and sweat saturated his dark blue work pants and his white-and-blue striped work shirt. Despite his father's exhausted appearance, Nik noticed the strong resemblance between his father and himself.

"I would have been home about seven minutes ago, but a goddamn train blocked me at the south end of town. I can tell the shit barn and town stink are in true form tonight." Terrence spoke to Kayla with fatigue.

Nik stood from the rocking chair and entered his father's line of sight. "Well, despite your eyesight not being what it used to be, I'm glad your sense of smell is still working."

Terrence's eyes widened, bewildered, as he did not realize his son had been sitting on the porch. "Hey! It's the kid. When the hell did you get here?"

Nik smiled at his father and told him that he had arrived shortly before he did and wanted to spend the weekend with them. Nik also included that the next-door neighbor had just been here, drunk and blithering.

Terrence cringed at hearing he had just missed Brian. "I'm glad I didn't have to see that stupid fucking bastard."

Nik laughed at his father's response and decided to fuel the fire. "Get this too, Dad. He just got done telling me that he wants to get his CDL."

Terrence looked at his son, shaking his head. "I suppose we should watch the news more closely now, because if that dumb drunken sonofabitch gets his CDL, there will probably be a pile-up crash on the highway making headlines. I think on that note, I'm going inside to hop into the shower."

Nik laughed as he watched his mother and father walk through the front door. He sat on the rocking chair, deciding to have a cigarette before entering the house. He panned the settled street of his childhood home, realizing how calm and at ease he felt.

Nik stood from the rocking chair and entered his parents' house. He glanced around and thought how the place had remained the same yet changed equally. Besides the displayed professional pictures of him from infancy and toddlerhood, he noticed only residual remnants of his life from when he had resided there. Regardless, he still felt a sense of belonging and a minute relief of a place he could still call home. He looked where his mother sat on the couch, watching a late-night comedy show while waiting for Terrence to finish his shower. Nik and his mother heard his father complaining to himself through the thin walls and the bathroom door about the events from the work night.

Nik regarded his mother, and she rolled her eyes as she heard Terrence complain. "He is always bitching to himself every night when he comes home from work. He still has a ways to go, but I think he's getting ready to retire."

Nik sat on the recliner next to his mother and surveyed the living room. The room appeared empty and barren without his piano against the corner, but he realized he was the one who had taken it when he had moved.

A few quiet minutes passed before his father opened the bathroom door and walked out. He joined Nik and his mother from the adjacent dining room and entered the living room. He looked at Nik, still surprised to see him, as he sat down. "It is really something to see you here tonight, kid. I was just telling Mom earlier today that it has been a while since we heard from you."

Nik looked at his mother and father and asked them how the redecoration of his former bedroom went. They told him that the project took no time and that they were proud of him for making it on his own, but they were glad he would be the first person to utilize it.

Nik and his parents conversed for nearly an hour, asking him about his job, how he liked living in Pemkey, and how his band faired. When they arrived at the subject of his band, his parents made crude jokes regarding him hooking up with bar girls and not knocking someone up. Nik laughed at their crudeness but felt a nervous sickness engulf him as he reminisced about what had transpired with Samantha and the imposing trouble. He gained control of conveying outward emotion and resumed laughing. To deflect the subject, he included that if it was not for bandmembers hooking up with audience members that he would not exist.

After laughing with his parents, his mother noticed the scratch on his face. Nik thought his mother's eyes must be really keen in the dimly lit living room.

Kayla approached her son to exam the cut.

Nik had to think quickly and fib to not worry his parents. He told her that he might have scrapped his face on his truck's hood-mounted mirror while performing the pre-trip inspection or maybe while he was shaving due to rushing to get to the performance.

After she concluded her motherly inspection of the abrasion, she felt satisfied with his explanation. They sat quietly for the next fifteen minutes before they bid him a good night and retired up the stairs.

Nik remained on the recliner until they were out of sight. He left the living room and headed for the bathroom. He stared at his face in the mirror for what seemed to be an eternity, inspecting the scratch. He was beside himself, wondering how his mom would notice such a superficial scratch. He relieved his bladder in the toilet, flushed and turned off the light.

He traversed the house to familiarize himself with being home. He walked through the dining room and into the kitchen and then the utility room. He was pleased to see that his parents had not changed the house's arrangement. When he concluded his self-guided tour, he realized he had left his backpack by the rocking chair on the porch.

The night air had cooled, and a blustery wind broke the quietness of Garfield Street. Nik thought the breeze smelled as if a rain might be approaching. He welcomed the aspect of the possibility of an incoming storm; after being the target of one hell of a proverbial storm earlier, he figured an actual rainfall might cleanse the strain of previous events.

After taking a few deep breaths, he felt exhaustion seize his tired body, and he welcomed the aspect of turning in. He walked through the front door and toted his bag upstairs through the dark staircase. Once he reached the top of the stairs, he turned on the air conditioner, closed the door behind him, removed his clothes off and dove into the guest bed.

He lay on his back, feeling the cool refreshing breeze from the air conditioner. Lying silently, he quietly prayed to any deity who could hear him and would answer the call for a well-rested, dreamless sleep. He also prayed for said deity to purge his mind of thoughts of Samantha, Ross, his bandmembers and the impending drama that would await him at work. His body felt fuzzy and dreamlike, and consciousness became fleeting. While drifting into slumber, he heard the distant sound of thunder and the approaching storm. Nik used to resent that he usually slept through thunderstorms and would miss experiencing them, but he appreciated how they became a drug-free sleeping aid. He readjusted his body one last time before he achieved an ideal position for rest. The sandman's realm was now imminently upon him, and he reached a state of rewarding blissful sleep.

The following morning arrived greeting Nik with vibrant light. He was satisfied that his deity had answered his prayers of a dreamless sleep. He awoke in the morning in the same position in which he had fallen asleep. He had not tossed, turned, nor stirred during slumber. He glanced at the ceiling, refreshed. After relaxing and allowing his body and mind to coincide with his state of consciousness, he faced the nightstand. It was 8:10 a.m., he had not overslept or missed the ample time of the morning.

Nik sprung from the bed, dressed quickly in his clothes from the night before and grabbed his backpack. He eased open the door, as he was not sure whether his parents were awake, and crept down the narrow staircase. Once he reached the landing, he ambled through the front door and sat on the porch rocking chair. He dazed at the residual moisture on the street from last night. He was met with the cleansing smell of the lingering moisture.

Time escaped Nik, and he grabbed his backpack to begin the day. He stepped through the front door, mindful to close it softly, and traipsed to the bathroom. He grabbed a towel from the linen closet and placed it on the toilet lid, undressed and entered the shower. As the beads of water hit his body, he noticed the difference in water quality from Amsdale to Pemkey. Amsdale water was harsh and hard as he lathered his body. The soap's foam grew thick and coated. Feeling unclean from the shower, he washed quickly and toweled dry then grabbed a clean pair of shorts and a red tank top from his backpack.

As soon as he was dressed, he opened the bathroom door, and the sounds of his parents in the kitchen greeted him. He walked through the doorway from the dining room into the kitchen.

His parents were examining a rabbit in the back yard from the kitchen window.

"He's a brave little bastard, isn't he, Kayla?" Terrence spoke softly.

Kayla poured a cup of coffee and resumed looking toward the back yard. "I just hope the fucker doesn't tear up my flower garden. I wish we had a pellet gun or something, then we could ping his ass from the back door."

"If I had a pellet gun, I'd shoot that little sonofabitch right through the lungs." Terrence whistled through his teeth and poked Kayla on the side to illustrate where he would aim.

"You could shoot the little asshole in the head for all I care, as long as it would stop him from chewing up my goddamn flowers."

Nik erupted with laughter from the macabre descriptions, and his parents turned to greet their son with warmth. "Oh, there's the kid. Did you have a good night's sleep?"

"Come on, Mom and Dad. Don't you think it's a little hard to go from speaking gruesome murder to acting like Mike and Carol Brady? Especially just how Dad explained the motive of how and where he would aim on Mr. Hoppy Bunny?"

Terrence and Kayla laughed.

"Well, it doesn't really matter anyway. As soon as Dad could shoot the little cocksucker, ten more would replace him. Fucking rabbits are horny little bastards," Kayla responded.

Nik and his parents had a different dynamic than the locals. While it was true that most of his peers in Amsdale had grown up watching family sitcoms and had acted like butter did not melt in their mouths, he and his family had enjoyed watching horror movies and dark comedies. While other families had enveloped themselves with a falsehood of outward ideal family practices, he knew they were privately corrupt and judgmental over him and his family for indulging into shows and movies that embraced the darker side of life.

As he pondered this thought, he extended gratitude to his parents for enriching him and felt it was perhaps an avenue where he had developed his unbridled talents. They had bestowed their shared dark sense of humor. Plus, he realized through this truth that unconditional love and compassion existed between them, mostly with a sense of integrity his peers and their parents only displayed in public to put on heirs. The paradigm truth was that Nik and his parents were all artist. His father was an accomplished bassist in his former band, and his mother proved a talented seamstress and a person of arts and crafts. Unlike his childhood Amsdale peers, lying did not exist in his loving, nurturing family. Despite acquaintances considering their tastes as deviant, they were a tribe of loyalty, love, and compassion.

Nik contemplated this deeper, immersing into his childhood. He remembered Halloween time while other kids had dressed as princesses, farmers, and football players, he recalled the later grades of elementary school when he would dress as Alex Delarge from *A Clockwork Orange*. His mother had made the costume in her sewing room. His peers had been oblivious to the character. Some of his peers' parents had made comments and harsh remarks on how Kayla dressed her son in such a manner.

Concluding his childhood memories, he realized he stood in the kitchen with deafening silence.

"Are you doing okay, kid? You look like you were thinking about something really hard there," Terrence asked.

"Yeah, I'm okay. I was just thinking about some stuff from when I was a kid."

The three of them resumed watching the rabbit in the back yard until it lost interest and jumped through the chain-link fence into the next-door neighbor's yard out of their sight.

"You got really quiet there for a second," Nik's mother said. "It looked like you were thinking about something really deep. What's on your mind?"

Nik stretched and yawned. "Oh, I wasn't really thinking about anything. I was just still breaking myself from sleep."

Terrence and Kayla both dismissed Nik's statement. Terrence stared out the window, watching the neighbors' morning activities while Kayla sipped her morning coffee.

After she finished her coffee, she placed the cup into the kitchen sink and faced Nik. "Do you want anything to eat for breakfast?"

Nik told her that he does not eat breakfast; he only eats one meal a day to maintain his weight and size.

She looked at him baffled that he still maintains the same diet. She exhibited concern that eating only once might cause him to feel weak, and he could pass out behind the wheel.

Nik reassured her that he did not feel faint and that his diet system worked well.

Kayla told him that they would be grilling one of their favorite summertime meals this afternoon—Lipton Onion burgers, potato salad, and macaroni salad, as she and his father had bought a new bag of charcoal and a pound of hamburger on the day before he had arrived.

Nik anticipated the afternoon meal with sense of fleeting fear. While he maintained a strict diet, he felt guilty for indulging in unhealthy food and deviating from disciplined work-out practices. He asked his mother if his mats and exercise equipment were still in the garage.

"Yeah, we still have that Cardio Glide machine you would use and that Perfect Pushup thing."

A great sense of relief consumed him that he could indulge in the meal guilt free.

Terrence looked at the kitchen clock—8:52 a.m. He said he wanted to check the TV for any news and weather before he started his yard work. Nik and his parents headed into the living room. Terrence sat on the couch, followed by Kayla, and Nik sat on the recliner. When Terrence turned on the television, Sheriff Mark Washland was discussing his efforts to increase the county's diligence in drug interdiction and to implement DARE education in the public schools.

Terrence glared at the TV with disgust. "Would you look at this cocksucker? What a fucking camera whore. You don't see any of the other local county sheriffs on the news as much as this asshole. Every goddamn election, I vote against this toad. The dickhead never declares a level three in the really bad times of winter when every other sheriff does. I remember two winters back when I got stuck coming home from work, and those cocksuckers didn't let us leave early. Sure, you can leave, but you'll take a point. Easy for them to say when their corporate assess are comfortable and warm at home."

Nik agreed then regarded his mother whose face looked concerned. It was obvious that she was remembering that evening when his father had been stuck on the road, and she was also thinking about Nik driving the straight truck. Nik employed mature judgment and did not respond or add any further statements. Instead, he sat until the weather forecasted today and tomorrow would be warm, calm, and comfortable.

Nik strategically planned the day's course. Being mindful of the upcoming meal, he retrieved his workout clothes from his backpack for a morning workout in the garage. Nik entered the bathroom, set down his backpack and changed into his workout clothes. He returned to the living room and selected Queensryche's *Empire* album from his father's music collection. He located the worn portable CD player from the utility room.

Feeling nostalgic, he studied the cover artwork, realizing this was the first album he had listened to when he began working out. He strolled through the back door from the utility room onto the brick patio and held his head high with esteem. The smell of gasoline and cut grass from the lawnmower greeted him inside the garage. The blended scent was a pleasant and evocative one he always equated as a rewarding odor of summertime.

He placed the portable stereo onto the cement floor and plugged it into the wall outlet. He began with a slow and thorough stretch, enjoying the appearance and feel of his sculpted body. He knew the garage was where his journey had begun. He felt a sense of humbled peace as he was satisfied with what he had accomplished. After stretching, he felt his body was physically awake to workout. He opened the garage window, placed the CD into the player and started his workout on the Cardio Glide bike.

Nik panned the garage, beholding the view and appreciating the rustic ambiance. He had always enjoyed working out in the hot garage and felt it aided him with achieving his physical goals. He did not enjoy the settings of a gym. A peace existed in working out solo.

He completed his session and placed his mat on the floor and concentrated on his core. He remembered a time when his core was bloated and robust. As he lay on the mat, he was thrilled that was no longer the case. In fact, he now had six-pack abs—something he would have never fathomed having earlier in his life. His core was his favorite part of his body, and it was an aspect that he devoted the most attention to developing. Nik dedicated an hour to his rigorous regimen.

He felt renewed closing the window and leaving the garage, where a comfortable cooling breeze greeted him. He looked skyward and noticed its color was a deep azure blue with thick clouds taking the appearance of freshly whipped mashed potatoes. He remembered when he was a child and thought those types of clouds appeared appetizing. He also looked toward the sky above Pemkey and saw a strange atmospheric phenomenon he had never witnessed before. Nik stood struck by the beautiful oddity. It looked like a rip in the sky—a strange formation of a rainbow spectrum with a starburst fire formation. He stood motionless, concentrating on the formation as he could have sworn the starburst's pointed flares swayed.

He could not move, as he was afraid the strange phenomenon would vanish. Fighting the urge to remain motionless, he collected himself, set down his portable stereo and dashed to the back door. He shouted for his parents to come to the back yard.

His mother arrived first with her hands saturated with dishwater, followed by his father who had just completed getting dressed in his work clothes. Both were in a terrified frenzy when they stepped onto the brick patio.

"What the hell is going on? Are you all right, kid?" Terrence questioned, continuing to put on his work shoes.

"Yes, I'm fine. Sorry to scare you, but you have to see this before it goes away." Nik lead them toward the garage door.

"What the hell am I looking for?" Kayla asked.

Nik pointed upward from his original position. The formation in the sky appeared larger to Nik than previously, and the degree of colors seemed brighter and more solid. The starburst had accelerated, swaying.

"Holy shit, I have never seen anything like that before," Kayla said with amazement as she could not take her eyes off the strange object.

Terrence stood for a moment longer before he spoke. "Check it out, kid. That strange-looking thing is right over where you live. I bet if you were home, you'd be getting one hell of a view of that."

Nik remained silent to his father's comment, agreeing with his assessment. Of all the locations where the strange formation could be, it hovered over where Nik lived. "I know what you mean, but I'm glad I'm here with you guys to see it, and I'm also glad I'm not the only one seeing it. I just wish I had a way to take a picture or video of it."

Nik and his parents stood silent as the object became smaller, eventually disappearing.

"Isn't that the way it always goes? You never get a chance to get a picture or video to prove that you've seen some shit."

Nik looked at his parents. "Yeah, but at least now I have witnesses who can back me up on seeing it."

A moment later, Kayla said she was going back inside to finish washing the dishes, and Terrence said he would start the yard work.

Nik, still feeling invigorated from his workout and dazzled from the strange appearance in the sky, offered his father assistance.

"Sounds great to me. I wanted to get a couple of things done today. First thing I want to do is remove that weeping cherry tree in the front yard. That damn thing is not blooming any more, and Mark from work offered me fifteen bucks for the wood, and the other project I want to do is weed whack the edges of the yard and mow. I need help with cutting down the tree and loading it up, but I'll let you pick whether you want to weed whack or mow."

Nik chose to mow the yard instead of weed whack. Mowing the yard was a relaxing task, and it allowed his mind to drift.

Terrence motioned for Nik to follow him to the garage and get the appropriate equipment. Terrence told Nik to find pairs of gloves for the them and collect the orange extension cord. Terrence grabbed the gas can from the other corner of the garage and placed it outside along with the chainsaw. Nik pushed the lawnmower as they exited. After pouring fuel into both the chainsaw and the lawnmower, Terrence returned the gas can to the corner. Before they reached the backyard gate, Terrence placed the weedwhacker next to the lawnmower.

Nik observed his father's calculated and meticulous methods and thought he must have inherited this trait, as he was the same way with tasks. Terrence firmly held the chainsaw as he walked the length of the back yard and through the gate until they arrived in the boulevard of the front yard.

"Between you and me, I can't wait to remove this damn thing. I know your mom likes the tree, but it doesn't bloom right anymore, and it's such a bitch to duck under when I try to mow around it."

Terrence primed the chainsaw and sawed down the tree. Nik and his father cut smaller sections and carried it to the bed of Terrence's truck.

"Well, I'll be loading this up in Mark's truck Monday night after work, but at least I'll get some money from it, and Mark can use the wood."

They chitchatted for a few moments as Nik enjoyed a cigarette, then Terrence operated the weedwhacker, and Nik followed by mowing.

Nik enjoyed mowing the yard on the bright and beautiful day, and, as he had predicted, he relaxed his mind and became enveloped in the task. Once he finished the yard work, Nik joined his parents on the back patio and sat at the umbrella picnic table. They spent time enjoying each other's company, discussing Nik's and Terrence's work.

Nik was apprehensive when they questioned him about his band. He felt nervous when they made crude jokes, revisiting the subject about hooking up with groupies. Nik's body tensed, and he struggled to not display it. He did not want to relive the experience, plus he did not want to worry his parents with the aspect of a husband's anger stemming from Nik sleeping with the man's wife. Instead, Nik concentrated on a happier thought and focused on the upcoming Lipton Onion burgers.

He thought of a tactful way to transition into another subject. "Well, I think I've worked hard enough for the two of you today. Have I earned my delicious Lipton Onion burgers yet?"

His mother broke from her concentration and realized she nearly forgot about preparing the meal. Through her visible embarrassment, Nik was pleased to see the tide of the conversation had shifted from the subject of his band life to her forgetting about the meal.

"Oh, that's right. What time do you guys want to eat today?"

Nik and his father agreed two o'clock would be a good time.

Kayla grabbed the grill and bag of charcoal from the garage and went inside to prepare the meat patties.

"I know you were probably a little uncomfortable with speaking with your mom about this, but *did* you ever have any one-night hook ups?"

Nik did not want to divulge any details and told his father that his music was a creative outlet for him and a means to showcase his talent, and he was not seeking that kind of attention.

Kayla returned after preparing the patties and placed them on the grill. It had been a considerable amount of time since Nik could indulge in his mother's Lipton Onion burgers. When they were ready, he chewed slowly, reintroducing himself to the taste. After finishing, he collected and threw away their paper plates and napkins.

"So, what's the plan for the rest of the weekend? Are you going back home today, or are you staying another night?" Kayla asked.

Nik felt reluctance on returning home; not wishing to appear overly eager employed verbal tact. "Well, Mom, I thought we had discussed this already last night. I figured, if it was okay with you guys, I would stay the weekend. Also, I wanted to walk uptown to the bar tonight and have a drink."

"That sounds good to me and your father. Just don't drink too much, like you used to. I never liked that bar, and I always hated it when you'd get drunk."

Nik regarded his mother with reassurance. "Don't worry about it, Mom. As I said, I'm walking up to the bar, so you don't have to worry about me driving. I guess I just felt nostalgic about being back in town and wanted to partake in a drink. Or five." Nik chuckled.

Nik remembered days like these growing up—being a child during his summer vacation when his father would have days off from work, he and his family would spend large amounts of the day sitting outside. The evening approached, and the sun's brightness diminished. Nik went into the house to get out of his workout clothes and shower.

After he had washed, he studied his reflection before getting dressed. The fading daylight paired with the bathroom's dim light illustrated a new aesthetic. Nik appeared darker than usual, and his body definition was tighter and prominent. A sense of righteous pride entered as he knew that his hard work and discipline paid off. He looked up and nodded toward the ceiling, giving thanks to whatever force had bestowed him the ability to achieve his current state. He dressed and pulled a brush through his wet hair, slicking it back.

When he exited the bathroom, the steam from the hot shower rolled from behind his body, and the cool air from the adjacent room felt crisp. Nik entered the utility room and slid on his shoes before stepping through the back door to join his parents. He retrieved his cellphone from his side pocket, noticing it was 8:30 p.m., and his father headed for the garage.

Kayla studied her son standing on the patio, stretching his arms. "I hope you won't spend too much time at the bar. I always thought the place was scummy. Dad is getting the chiminea, and we were going to burn some old papers and twigs." Knowing her son always enjoyed a night fire, she was sure he would be home promptly.

Nik told his mother that when he returned, he would knock on the back gate. Nik stepped onto the faded pavement of the alley and walked toward Main Street, feeling stillness in the air. The evening was not overtly hot or clammy. He took long strides, eventually arriving at the local bar. The sign above the bar had stood the test of time and remained unchanged; however, it was desperately in need of paint and tender love and care. The sign still displayed, *Amsdale Bar & Grill*, but, as time claimed its appearance, it became hardly legible.

Nik placed his hand on the rusted stained-metal door. He paused as an unpleasant memory flooded his mind—a harsh realization about the transparent nature of people and how they truly are not what they outwardly appeared, along with the memory of the first time he'd unwillingly viewed pornographic material. Shortly after his eighth birthday, at the beginning of his summer vacation, was when the incident had transpired.

He bent down his head, flattening the palm of his hand on the door.

That day had been hot and humid with a blazing sun beaming down on him. He had just returned into town from a strenuous bicycle ride and was parched and arid feeling. Unable to wait until he arrived home, he had been in dire need to quench his thirst and realized he had seventy-five cents in his pocket—the exact amount needed to purchase a can of pop at the local bar. During the early afternoon hours, underage children had been permitted in the bar to purchase food and drinks. When he had arrived at the front of the bar, he kicked his kickstand into place and pulled open the side door ...

Once he opened the entrance, he was greeted with a sight that appalled him. Sitting in the bar was three of Amsdale's most prominent citizens, observing the corner-mounted television. Immediately, he recognized Jerry Schoolcraft—a slender chipmunk-looking man with thinning red hair who was Gary Town's chief constable. He also recognized the minister, Dwight Morris—another older thinning-haired man who resembled Ichabod Crane who lived next door to him in the parsonage house. And finally, he recognized Eldon Feassey, the village postmaster—a bald, rotund man who looked like a New York cab driver. Nik observed what they were watching on the corner-mounted television. Nik, later in life, would describe what he saw on the television as a BDSM porno.

The scene centralized around two older, hairy, bald men pulling at each leg of a full-figured, curvy redhead woman—spread eagle—while fingering both her orifices while leather straps bound and strangulated her large breasts, turning them purple, while a third hairy, bald man whipped her breast with a leather cat-o-nine-tails. Nik remained motionless as Jerry Schoolcraft leaned forward in his bar stool to behold the scene while Pastor Morris sat with his legs crossed and his arms folded, and Eldon Feassey sat drooping in his stool with his legs spread, his thinly and short erect penis periscoping through his pants.

Alarmed by the open door, they turned to him with shock.

Eldon reddened with rage, slamming his meaty fist on the bar counter. "Get out now!"

Jerry Schoolcraft shrieked at Nik with a shrilling burst. "What's wrong with you, kid? Get out of here! This is no place for you!"

Pastor Morris beamed at him with anger. "What the hell is wrong with you? You just get the hell on out of here, boy, or I'll give you a switch you'll never forget!"

Nik struggled in desperation, trying to break his petrified fear, and flee. Eventually, he slammed the door, sprang to his bicycle and raced home. He jumped off his bicycle, letting it fall to the ground and fumbling for the key to his front door. After entering his house, he raced to the refrigerator and grabbed a gallon jug of water, gulping it without breathing. He placed the jug into the refrigerator and ran to the living room, where he trembled on the couch.

His parents entered the house from the back and asked if he wanted to get some barbeque beef sandwiches and an ice cream cone from Dairy Queen.

Nik and his parents ate their barbecue beef sandwiches in the Dairy Queen parking lot before his mother commented on Nik's quietness. He thought quickly and dismissed it as being hungry. When Nik and his parents returned home and parked the car, they saw Pastor Morris leaving the church's office entrance. Nik's heart pounded and sank in his chest while they exited the car.

Pastor Morris strode toward Nik and his parents with a furrowed brow then glanced at Nik with his unwavering expression and broke a friendly smile. "Well, if it isn't my next-door neighbors, the Vanellis, and little Skip."

Nik trembled as he revisited the same degree of fear thrust upon him earlier.

"Are you attending vacation Bible school coming up in a few weeks, bud?" Pastor Morris asked.

Nik shook his head, remaining speechless.

"That is too bad, Skip. I was looking forward to you singing in the chorus."

Nik's mother noticed Nik felt a great disturbance from the interaction and insisted they make their leave.

Pastor Morris wished them a good day and walked onto the parsonage house porch, waving exaggeratedly at Nik to communicate keep his mouth shut.

"I never liked that Ichabod Crane-looking sonofabitch," Kayla remarked inside the front foyer. "I think the old, perverted bastard likes to watch me lay in the sun from his upstairs window."

Terrence laughed. "What's the matter, hon? Don't you feel honored to have Dimwit peeping at you? You must admit, you look way better than what he lays next to every night."

Kayla shot Terrence a sour look and replied with great sarcasm. "Anything would look better than Sylvester. A dog's shitty asshole would look better than her."

Nik's parents always concocted new insulting nicknames for the locals, justifying their behavior by believing the same happened to them behind closed doors. Nik's parents referred to Dwight Morris as *Dimwit* or *Ichabod* due to his foolish actions, and they referred to his fat, toothless blob of a wife, Joyce, as *Sylvester* from *Looney Tunes*, as she constantly spit while she talked.

"I'm glad you chose not to go to vacation Bible school this summer. I always hated getting involved with the snotty, local moms and having them sucker me into watching the nursery school kids."

Nik felt relief the conversation was dropped, and he was glad his mother did not mandate him to attend. Nik never revealed what he had observed at the bar earlier that day to anyone.

Breaking the entrapment of his childhood memories, he surveyed the rusty bar door, returning to reality. Other memories inhabited his mind that served to him as cosmic justice. No real punishment had ever come to them, but they had individually shamed and tarnished their own reputations. A few short years after the incident at the bar and before his retirement, Eldon Feassey had faced embezzlement charges for misappropriation of post office funds; the authorities had accused Jerry Schoolcraft of possessing child pornography, and then-Mayor Frank Parrish had run Pastor Morris out of town for spreading rumors that his wild-child daughter had contracted genital warts from loose moral activities. The district attorney dropped Eldon's and Jerry's charges, and Pastor Morris found a smaller town to become a minister, but at least all these men's names were justly dragged through the mud.

Nik reached his hand from his flattened position on the door and grabbed the handle, pulling it open. When he entered the bar, Nik noted the place's usual stench of aged frying oil and sulfur water seemed more pungent than it had been in the past. Nik squinted to combat the odor but realized he should relax his face and not appear strange looking to the bar patrons who'd become accustomed to the smell.

Nik sat at the far right-corner bar stool, wishing to drink and have the other boisterous patrons who were bellowing about sports and politics leave him alone. He noticed Bev Bahrenson, the high-school secretary, sitting with her two sons, Mitch and Aaron. They glared at Nik as she spoke loudly. Bev had taken an immediate dislike toward Nik from the beginning of his freshmen year, when he had entered her office to collect his class schedule.

Her attitude had always been abrasive and rude. She had felt strongly, with her integration-type attitude, that if a student did not participate in sports or other athletics then the student did not hold merit. Nik ordered a Bud Light and a shot of Jack Daniel's and raised his glass toward her with a nod. Bev sat on her barstool, sour. She appeared as she usually did, with her short bottle-black hair, her canary-shaped nose held high in the air, paired with her deep riveted acne scars.

Nik laughed, as with age, her acne scars appeared deeper. He remembered his mother used to refer to her as *Roxy Poxy*. Kayla had first encountered Bev when she picked him up from school after he had fallen ill one day during freshman year. Bev had been as rude and abrasive to Kayla as she was to Nik. During the ride home, Kayla commented on how foul and ugly she was, inside and out.

Nik knew her sons must have inherited this trait, as Mitch and Aaron mimicked her behavior. Bev talked loudly, questioning her sons about their success as independent insurance agents. Bev and her two princes were as corrupt as the perverts he had encountered in the bar as a child. He recalled a time during the same summer as the bar altercation when he had gone on another bike ride in the alley behind the Bahrenson's house. Mitch and his younger brother Aaron were playing with their father's arrowheads he used for hunting. Aaron, as usual, wanted to play with what his older brother had in his hand and cried out, demanding he relinquish the arrowhead. Nik watched Mitch lose his temper and diagonally slice the arrowhead across

Aaron's forehead. Their alibi at the beginning of the school year was that Aaron had run into a tree playing ball.

As time had passed and years went on, Nik had also heard other stories regarding Mitch and Aaron. When Nik was a freshman at Bateson High School, Mitch was dating a light blond-haired girl with a crescent-moon-shaped face—Amber Rochett, who everyone agreed was attractive. Nik, however, thought she was overly thin and had an unusually mal-shaped face. Nik privately referred to her as *Amber Rottencrotch*.

Everyone pegged Mitch and Amber as the romance story of the century. This banter always nauseated Nik. However, it was post high school when he took a small interest in their story. Mitch and Amber had married after graduation, but the honeymoon was short lived, as Amber indulged in adultery. Not only did she continuously cheat on Mitch, but the same peers heard she would like to entertain multiple men at once. It was common knowledge that Mitch had come home from his insurance firm early one day, as business was exceedingly light, and caught Amber in their bed with three men penetrating every orifice. Mitch broke down in the threshold of their bedroom, weeping like a child.

Stories about his younger brother's romance life existed as well. While working for his independent firm, Aaron had become involved with his own trophy wife. Aaron's approach was fear-inducing, as he would scream death threats to her from his office; if she was not home by a certain time, he would bludgeon her to death. In one well-known story, she had pleaded with him not to murder her as she would be late due to a stopped train. Needless to say, both Mitch and Aaron were currently single.

Despite Bev's deliberate discussion over her sons' successes, Nik knew it was false, and she was playing face value. Nik finished his second shot of Jack Daniel's, chasing it with his beer, and Bev and her sons headed for the exit while she commented on how she and her husband, Dave, would be launching the boat on the lake the following day and the boys should come out. Nik hoped Mitch and Aaron would bring enough condoms for the family orgy. Nik snickered as Bev shuffled her large banana-shaped ass through the bar door.

Turning his attention, he looked to the far-left end of the bar counter and was surprised to see Brandon Gatchell quietly sitting there, wearing a green work uniform. Brandon sported an out-of-date hair style consisting of a flattop with long hair in the back fanning out as it touched the back of his neck. Despite being the same age as Nik, he had large amounts of grey on the shaved sides. Brandon's uniform had a stitched-on tag over his left pocket that stated, *Grabar's Recycling Service*, and his right stitched on name tag had the letters *BJ*.

He remembered Brandon appearing angry and sour during their school years, having a squinted glare plastered on his face. Classmates had constantly tormented him throughout his school life. During middle school, it had leaked that Brandon's middle initial was *J*, and the other students used this information to insinuate a BJ—standing for *blow job*. Pity creeped over Nik while looking at Brandon.

Growing up in Amsdale, he'd heard stories of old man Grabar treating his employees as if they were less than zero. Henry Grabar's recycling shop, located on Harrison Street next to the railroad tracks behind Garfield Street, appeared as a burnt-out dung heap. As a child, it was common knowledge to never ride a bike or walk close to Henry Grabar's facility, as he was known to stand in the front and scream at passing children. Nik recalled being a child and Brandon's grandparents' mobile home being a few lots down from the facility. Brandon would stare at the facility with fear as he listened to other children receive threats. Brandon's mother was stigmatized a drunk and a woman of loose virtue, and his grandparents were strict, frightening religious zealots. His grandfather was said to beat Brandon while quoting scripture, while his grandmother screamed "spare the rod spoil the child" as she gleefully cheered on the lashings as she sat perched on the living room couch.

His grandfather was rumored as being bisexual, and his grandparents would leave for weekend excursions to engage in swinger sex. Whether the gossip of Brandon's mother and grandparents were true or not, Nik did not know for sure. All he did know from Brandon was he had been a poor child his whole life and was terrified of old man Grabar—which surprised Nik that he would work for the man. Old man Grabar insisted that Brandon's name tag state *BJ* instead of *Brandon*, to exhibit an act of cruelness. Nik had only seen Henry Grabar from a distance, but he always thought Brandon and Henry Grabar shared a strong resemblance.

It was a common rumor that Brandon was the product of his mother getting overly drunk one night and Henry Grabar taking liberties with her. The rumors perpetuated that Brandon's grandfather had owed Henry Grabar money, and he furnished his daughter as collateral. With his grandparents being extreme religious zealots, they would have opposed any termination of their daughter's pregnancy and claimed she had a one-night stand with a stranger. Finishing his thoughts of the circumstances, Nik noticed the strange and out-of-place man sitting next to Brandon.

He was shrouded with black attire that seemed to encompass multi-generations in style. He wore a black fedora that resembled the hat of an undertaker from the old West times. The man donned a cloak-type archaic coat from the times of druids. Underneath his cloak was a strange type of black formal wear that resembled a Gestapo uniform.

Nik, knowing his history, practiced being discreet while surveying the strange man and did not discover any insignia to illustrate typical Gestapo affiliation, such as swastikas, the Iron Cross, and the lightning-bolt-shaped SS insignia.

The man's narrow face was structured with highly placed cheek bones and a bony chin. His pointed nose appeared honed to a sharp edge that Nik imagined could pierce a victim, as a war saber would pierce flesh. Dark circles looped around his eyes that rested behind pince-nez-style glasses. When he whispered into Brandon's left ear, he looked around Brandon's head, darting quick glances at Nik and smiling with large horse-like teeth. His gum lines were compounded with decay, and his face looked synthetic, like a wax mannequin in a horror movie exhibit.

Brandon appeared entranced, as if the man was the Devil on Brandon's shoulder, then eventually looked in Nik's direction and gave him a weak wave. He reciprocated the wave, wondering if anyone else in the bar had noticed them. Nik did not want to dedicate any more attention to either and decided to concentrate on drinking.

After sitting quietly for a moment, Nik ordered two more shots of Jack Daniel's and one more Bud Light. Nik paced himself, so he would not get nauseated. He reached into his pocket to pay his bar tab and staggered to the bar entrance. Once he was outside, the night air comforted him, and the stench of the bar had disappeared. Nik enjoyed his walk home. He scanned the night sky, clear and vibrant with moonlight and stars.

Feeling the alcohol's calming effects, his mind was vacant from all concerns. He was grateful for feeling this way, and the drunken walk became more amusing. Within a few minutes, he reached the alley of Main Street, and his parents' house was down the way. He picked up speed and crossed the street then down the alley, where small bellows of smoke rose from the backyard. He smelled the air, realizing his parents had the chiminea going. When he approached the gate, he grabbed it and rattled it loudly, solidifying his presences.

Nik stood quietly before his father spoke. "I think it is the kid, Kayla. Is that you out there, kid?"

Nik responded slowly.

His father approached the fence gate, and it opened stiffly. Nik's parents had a folding chair ready for him., in-between them. When everyone was sitting by the fire, Nik's father commented on the clarity of the sky and how it was a perfect night to have a fire. Kayla agreed then barraged Nik with a line of questions. Nik assured her that he had not drank in excess; he had just wanted to relax. He mentioned the stench in the bar and how he had no further interest in returning.

"I never could understand how you could drink that nasty-tasting shit." Terrence crinkled his face.

"You're right, Dad. It does taste like dog shit, but I don't drink it for the taste. I drink it because of the feeling and to forget my troubles."

Kayla regarded her son with concern. "Is something bothering you? Is that why you went to the bar? Is something going on back home?"

Panic engulfed him, as if his mother could sense the true meaning of his visit. Nik placed his hands over his face and tilted back his head, speaking through his hands. "No. Nothing is going on back home or at work. Nothing more than usual. I just wanted to leave things at work and not think about them for a while." He lowered his hands to his lap, focusing on the fire.

He looked over the garage to the clear starry night, becoming speechless as he observed a strange convergence. Three distinctive white orbs were spaced significantly apart. He dismissed it at first, thinking they were three airplanes in the south sky. He fixed his gaze harder, seeing that the orbs lacked red and blue flashing lights on either side and realizing the orbs were not man-piloted aircrafts. The flying objects projected zero sound, and their white lights were ovular. Their luster appeared as if someone had dotted the sky with liquid paper, as they proved brighter in contrast than any star.

"Mom, Dad, look over there! I think I see three UFOs."

Terrence's and Kayla's expressions illustrated distrust over their son's assessment, dismissing him as being drunk.

Nik desperately gestured to his parents to observe the strange lights, and they eventually relented.

"I think those are just airplanes, kid," Terrence said dryly.

"I don't think so, Terrence," Kayla replied. "I don't see any flashing lights, and the shape is just bizarre."

Everyone agreed they were not airplanes. The objects moved across the sky in close formation, resembling white pearls on a necklace; however, they did not resemble a conventional aircraft's flight pattern as they crossed the sky from the south to the northeast toward Nik's town.

"Holy shit, kid. It looks like those things are traveling toward your house. That is weird, like earlier today when we saw that rainbow burst in the sky."

Nik did not speak. He had nearly forgotten about that strange formation earlier. He also remembered he had been the first one to notice the strange sights.

The objects stopped over Pemkey, and the formation inverted to an upside-down triangle. The three orbs twinkled then dispersed in a different direction. dissipating as they separated.

Nik looked to his mother as she sat in amazement. "I know I've been drinking, but I'm glad you guys saw those weird-looking things too."

Kayla scanned the sky, now void of the objects. "Yes, it's always nice when you can have someone confirm something. I wonder if anyone you know in Pemkey saw any of these strange things today. Do you want to call and ask anybody?"

Nik did not reply. He could only think of his bandmates and how they were likely conspiring against him. He abruptly told his mother they were probably doing other things not watching the sky.

Kayla was taken aback by her son's gruff response.

Nik felt guilty for being sharp. "I'm sorry I was so quick with you, Mom. I think I'm groggy from the heat and tired from the alcohol."

Kayla reassured her son, and they watched the chiminea fire dwindle. Nik bid his parents a good night and stood, feeling as if his head had gained ten pounds, and walked through the back door. He ambled through the house and climbed the staircase until he reached his old bedroom on the left. He closed the door behind him and turned on the air conditioner to a responsible setting and dove into bed.

As soon as he closed his eyes, he succumbed to the realm of sleep and entered a dream state, a formless disembodied mass floating toward a grey dense fog with a multiple light spectrum beaming from behind. While floating, he found he was in an endless void absent from defining barriers. The dream felt as if it had already been in progress, and he was self-aware that he was in a dream, feeling lucid control. Recognizing both advantages, he should vividly remember the dream. Realizing his current state, he decided to take advantage of the experience and floated toward the fog mass. The sensation was a pleasurable experience, like being suspended above ground with absolute freedom in movement.

Arriving at the fog mass, he could not float any farther. He heard what he believed to be a voice with a distorted language that did not sound human; it sounded submerged under water. The voice seemed to surround him, blanketing him, but vocal cords did produce these words. The source of the voice projected to him within his mind. It evolved and gained clarity. The sounds cleared, and the quality became less submerged.

As he concentrated, he understood what it was relaying. "You are absent. You are not where you are required to be. You have failed to complete your objective." The voice became feminine sounding as it spoke in the same loop.

Nik pinpointed the voice, further thinking it sounded like a beautiful woman. As the voice spoke in the looped statement for the fourth time, he shouted from his formless mass. "What? What do you mean I am absent, that I am not where I am required to be? What could I have possibly failed?"

After his numerous attempts for her to hear him and validate his existence, the voice did not answer. It looped in the same pace, tone, and pitch.

Nik approached the matter with another method. He did not have vocal cords; he was still attempting to speak as a human being. Realizing he maintained lucid control of this dream, he became an all-encompassing voice, projecting the question again.

As the omnipresent voice was in mid loop, it broke off and paused for what seemed to be an eternity. The voice spoke again, sounding pleasant with kindness. It directed with less of an intrapersonal tone. "You are not where you were required to be. You have failed your objective, and your time is now over. You must return home. It is essential that you return home."

Nik's shapeless form lost mass and density, and he felt his time in the dream realm was closing to an end. Knowing if he projected one last time, he would fully disappear, so he employed perfect tact with his next question. He gathered all his remaining strength. "What objective could I have possibly failed? No one had given me a task. Where will I return to if I don't know where *it* is?"

The voice spoke again, and he urged himself to pay close attention before he would awake. "Do not worry about the objective now. It was not your fault that you failed. The time for that now has passed. You simply forgot. Do not worry about coming home. You don't have to do anything. The transfer from here to home will be autonomous. You will just go home when the time is right. You will be collected soon enough."

With the final words of the omnipresent voice echoing in his thoughts, he watched the dream state fade as the realm of reality cascaded around him. When he fully awoke in his bed, he felt well rested and energized. He did not have to press his memories to retain the dream; it remained present and clear. He felt a sense of endowment from the dream, as if he was granted a new sense of private knowledge. He looked at the clock—7:39 a.m. He could not remember what time he had gone to bed, but regardless of the length of time he had slept, he felt as if he'd slept a satisfying ten-hour interval.

He sprung from his bed without effort, dressed and strode to the air conditioner to turn it off. He opened the door and descended the steps with a spring of energy. He began his morning rituals, reaching into the bag for a clean pair of clothes.

Before he closed the bathroom door; he heard his mother yell from the kitchen, "I wasn't snooping through your stuff, but I figured I'd grab your dirty laundry from your bag and wash it."

Nik felt embarrassment that his mother went through his bag but relieved he did not have anything that would raise questions. He thought that even though he had moved out some time ago, she was still extending her motherly grasp. Nik yelled back to his mother, thanking her. He closed the door and shaved and brushed his teeth before entering the shower.

He decided to skip his daily workout and make up for it by eating lightly. He usually felt guilty for skipping a workout, but today he felt charged and powerful.

He joined his parents on the living room couch. Nik and his parents spent most of the morning speaking casually. The morning pressed quickly into the afternoon, and Nik's mother asked him what he would like to have for dinner. Nik told her that he was not extremely hungry, so he would settle for a couple of hard-cut salami sandwiches. Kayla flashed a look of sadness and commented that it was his last day with them, and she thought she would make something nice to eat. Nik reassured her that it would not be necessary for her to do that; he just wanted to spend the day with them.

The afternoon sped by faster than the morning, and Nik went to the bathroom to retrieve his overnight backpack. He headed to the utility room to collect his clothes from the dryer then brought them to the living room to fold them on the recliner. He looked at the hanging clock in the living room, surprised to see it was 8:30 p.m. After he had folded his clothes, he went to the kitchen and made a single sandwich topped with mustard. He was surprisingly not that hungry, and eating the sandwich took effort to consume.

Once finished, he looked out the kitchen window, seeing the daylight fleeting. Nik felt sadness and dread envelope him. He knew he had to return to Pemkey and prepare for the upcoming week. He did not relish what he would face upon his return. He reflected on the joy and relaxation he had experienced while visiting his parents. He suppressed his emotions, swallowing hard. He walked from the kitchen into the living room and grabbed his backpack.

He looked at his parents and smiled hard, maintaining composure. "Well, I'm about to take off everybody. I hope you all have a good week, and everything goes smoothly."

"Well, I hope you have a good and safe week too, kid." His father stood from the couch.

"You be careful driving that truck at work. I was never really crazy about the idea of you getting that commercial driver license. You know how I worry," Kayla said.

Nik assured her that he would practice safe operations of the truck.

Terrence and Kayla walked onto the porch with Nik and hugged him goodbye before he crossed the street. Nik entered his truck and started it with a thunderous roar. He placed his bag in the passenger seat and waved to his parents.

Chapter Seven

Nik placed his truck in Reverse and slowly backed out of the parking space. His father signaled to him to turn on his headlights. Nik paused, embarrassed he had not remembered. After turning them on, he approached the intersection of the church parking lot and Garfield Street. He turned right and stopped at the intersection of Garfield Street and Elmbury Street. He turned onto Elmbury Street, waving goodbye one last time before arriving at the intersection of Elmbury and Main Street. He sat in fear, wondering if Ross Delbert had destroyed his house, and he also feared what awaited him at work. He hardened his chin and raised it high, concentrating on the relaxing visit. He made a left turn onto Main Street, proceeding north out of town.

Nik did not concentrate on the landmarks and the scenery as he embarked on his return trip. He could retrace the route from Pemkey to Amsdale with sheer muscle memory. He travelled autonomously until he reached Hoyle. He followed the main drag through the village, ignoring the nauseating formation of the houses. A few residents were walking their dogs and sitting on their porches, but he did not want to make eye contact with them. He just wanted to press through and leave the village as quickly as he had entered it. He passed the Friendship gas station and turned left onto Donaldson Road. Daylight had diminished, and his drive on the quiet country road darkened.

Nik drove with tunnel vision as he pondered the dream he'd had the previous night. He remembered the fog with the multi-light spectrum emitting behind it. He recalled the voice repeating itself in a loop and the odd and out-of-place message it delivered. It was strange that he could have failed an objective that he did not remember anyone assigning him, and he could not fathom being some place he had never been instructed to be at. He dismissed the thought and concentrated solely on driving.

Before he reached the intersection of State Route 14, a deer leapt from the right side of the road. Nik mashed his brake pedal, nearly missing the deer. It stood still in the middle of the lane while Nik furiously blew his horn. "Goddamn it, Bambi! This is the last thing I need tonight." After two blasts from his horn, the deer pranced off from sight. Nik approached the intersection of State Route 14 and Donaldson Road with heightened caution.

He slowed his breathing, voiding his mind from the dream. He must dedicate his concentration to the road. After a few minutes, something drew his attention to the northern sky again. Within seconds, he entered the winding part of Donaldson Road and saw a great flash in the sky similar to the pattern of the rainbow burst. The fire rainbow lasted only a moment, breaking from its nucleus and revealing three triangular formation glowing orbs. The orbs rotated clockwise, bursting then separating in different directions followed by a single electrical bolt striking the road in front of him. A glowing, luminescent oval-shaped object appearing solid, eight feet tall, and four feet wide emerged from the flash. Nik slammed his brake pedal to avoid hitting the object. Nik thrust forward in the truck's cab, but the seatbelt prevented him from striking the top of the steering wheel with his head.

When he came to a complete stop, he pounded the steering wheel with his right fist, shouting in the cab, "Fuck! This has got to be just fantastic for my breaks. Dammit all to hell!"

After sitting for a moment, the oval object turned clear and transparent, fading from the top to the bottom. It revealed a white glowing humanoid figure that gently floated down to the road. Once landed on the road, it bent down on a single knee with its head facing toward the ground.

Nik sat in his truck paralyzed with fear. He was in absolute amazement from almost striking the ovular object that housed the figure. After gaining composure, he exited his truck to investigate the strange phenomena. He did not know whether he was acting on sheer stupidity or if it was some unworldly force controlling him. Regardless, he carefully placed each footstep as he approached the figure. He peered around for a moment, seeing only the surrounding darkness and the glowing humanoid. He remembered the strange atmospheric shapes he had seen while visiting his parents and wished someone else was here to witness what was before him.

While he approached the figure, it maintained its glow and pulsed twice. He stopped a few feet from the humanoid, and it floated a foot into the air, spreading its arms and legs to resemble a starfish. It tilted down its head to face Nik and curled its arms around the side of Nik's head, touching his temples.

Nik leaned backward on his heels with his arms spread and his back arched as memories from his infancy to current time raced through his mind in seconds.

The glowing figure retracted its arms and resumed the starfish formation while descending to the ground.

Nik fell to his knees after his body straightened, sobbing from the cascade of memories. He trembled as he remembered long-forgotten memories with clarity. He felt like his physical body would expire, and death would be imminent. He raised his head from his kneeling, fetal position and regarded the figure with terror.

The figure bent down to touch him again.

Nik thrust backward, landing on his backside. He scrambled to his feet, gaining proper footing as he dashed to his truck. Engulfed with fear, he lacked the coordination to get his truck in gear.

His passenger door flung open by an invisible force, and the glowing figure approached his truck.

Nik shrieked loudly before it darted across the seat, placing its formless hand on Nik's forehead. Nik felt his body go limp, and his vision blackened as he combatively fought off the figure's grasp; to no avail, Nik lost in his struggle, rendered unconscious.

When Nik regained consciousness, he felt rested and disoriented. He forgot where he was, but the memory of the events immediately returned to him. He panicked, flailing his adrenaline-fueled body and darting his head toward the passenger seat.

The figure casually observed him from the passenger seat.

Nik's throat was sore, and he could not scream. He looked around quickly through the windows of the cab and did not see anyone.

The figure stared at him, tilting its head toward one shoulder followed by the other. After a few motions, it straightened its blank head and concentrated on Nik. The figure pulsed brightly twice, metamorphosing from the top of its blank head to its formless feet. The transfiguration was instantaneous; it revealed the image of a woman shrouded in white garments with a strange unworldly metallic appearance that billowed in a windswept manner, like floating cotton hung on a clothesline. Certain areas of the being's garments appeared slightly transparent, revealing its thighs and central core area, while it appeared to be wearing attractive bra and panties. The area the bra and panties covered had a brighter glow, bringing distinctive attention.

Fear had vacated Nik, leaving him with astonishment and an odd attraction.

The being had long dark blond hair and a perfectly structured face and was shapely, toned, and curvy with a perfect body. It boasted the physique of a swimmer or perhaps a ballerina. Its beautiful hands and perfectly formed feet had gained digits from being a formless mass.

Nik beheld its beautiful face and was shocked to see the being donned heterochromatic eyes, displaying a vibrant green eye on its left side and a cooling sapphire-blue eye on its right. Nik gained control of his emotions, and an ironic thought occurred to him. *What kind of luck is this? Who would have imagined I would cross paths with two beautiful women that both had two different-colored eyes?*

The being tilted its head in a manner illustrating that Nik had flirted with it. The being smiled at him, revealing a perfect pearly smile through rouge-colored lips.

My god, she is perfect. I have never seen a woman this perfect in my whole life.

The being leaned toward him, placing its hands on the armrest that separated them, and gazed with adoration and wonder.

A moment passed between them, staring at each other. Then the dash display brightened, and the radio turned on and scanned various radio stations, followed by the horn sounding and the wipers dancing across the windshield with the washer saturating the windshield.

Nik felt overwhelmed and panic stricken and barked at the being to stop.

The being stopped the telekinetic phenomena and leaned back in the passenger seat with fear in its eyes from Nik's scolding.

"Hey, hey, hey. Look, I'm sorry about that. I didn't mean to frighten you. I don't know if you understand this, but we can't just sit here and draw attention to ourselves. We especially can't drive around with you glowing."

The being looked as if she was pondering a deep, difficult thought. She stared forward then faced Nik, illustrating a loving look as she raised her fingertips to her temples and ran them down the length of her body. Her garments dimmed, and her flesh mimicked a natural tanned color yet unblemished.

Nik felt calmer that she could appear more human and suppress her luminescent glow.

The being drew her fingertips to her lips, covering her mouth and silently giggling, as if she found humor in his relief.

He wondered if she was not only reading his mind but his inward emotions too. Nik placed his truck in gear and drove. He paused and regarded the female figure once again with curiosity. "Do you speak? Can you talk? Do you understand language or what I am saying?"

As he spoke, she looked at him deeper with love and kindness.

Nik felt frustrated. He accelerated, and the being grabbed his arm and instantly stopped his truck.

She stared at him wide eyed with her mouth agape. The sound that came from the being did not resemble human language. Multiple syllables emerged from its mouth without it closing or moving in any manner. The haunting sound frightened Nik.

The being fell silent as he drove again, approaching Pemkey. She donned a look of sadness, as if she had disappointed him. They entered the village limit, and she attempted to communicate again once they entered downtown. This time, the being spoke English. It sounded harsh, as if she was first discovering speech. *"Arrrrrre weeeeee gooooooinnnng tooooo yoooouurrrr dommmmmiiicccciiilllle?"*

Nik was surprised that she could form a complex sentence.

Nik turned onto Main Street and continued to drive through Pemkey. He pulled into his driveway, shifted abruptly into Park and pointed to his house. "This. Is. My. Dom-i-ci-le." Nik stared at her as she processed what he had said, then he realized his backpack was nowhere in sight. "Oh, shit!"

The being startled and leaned away.

"I think I must have lost my backpack when you got into my truck. Look, I'm sorry for yelling and frightening you. You didn't do anything wrong. I just think I might have to back track and find my bag. I didn't mean to scare you."

The being tilted her head from her left shoulder to her right then brought her fingertips to her mouth, silently giggling.

Nik looked at her puzzled, wondering if she understood his apology as something funny instead of expressing kindness.

The being reached behind her and retrieved his backpack, displaying it to him with pride and grinning.

Nik thanked her. "Wasn't that uncomfortable for you to ride with that wedged behind your back?"

The being told him, in a strangulated voice, that it had not been. She drew the backpack to her torso and hugged it like a stuffed animal.

Nik surveyed his neighborhood—quiet and still. This proved the appropriate time he and his new guest could leave his truck unnoticed. "Okay, I think we have spent enough time in here, and we should make our way inside." He reached to collect his backpack; she refused to relinquish it. "Okay, that's fine. You can hold onto it for me, if you like. Let's just get inside my domicile quickly. I don't want to arouse any attention."

The being seemed to understand. The passenger door flung open without being touched, and she exited the vehicle, floating with her toes pointing toward the ground. She levitated above the sidewalk and over the porch steps while hugging his backpack.

Nik scrambled to exit his truck, closed both doors and raced to catch up with her.

She stopped on the porch, hovering, and turned to him gently.

With fear racing through his body and his mind, he tried to catch his breath before unlocking the front door. "Look, you have to stop doing that. Normal people do not float. They walk. Do you know how to walk? Can you walk from now on?"

She regarded Nik with concern as she could read and feel the fear in his actions. She acknowledged him by nodding and landed gently, toes first, on the porch.

Nik felt frantic as he reached into his pocket, unable to find his keys. He thought he may have locked them inside his truck when he had raced to close both doors. He was embarrassed to realize he had been holding his keys the entire time and tilted his head backward, annoyed. He nervously guided the key into the lock as the being observed him with affection, running her fingertips across his cheek. Nik extended gratitude to her as he unlocked his front door.

Once they were both through the front door, Nik turned on the living room light, and the still house became alive. Not wanting to draw concern or worry to his new unearthly guest, he carefully panned the house to ensure nothing was out of place or in disorder. Realizing he had not been home in several days, he ushered the being to his couch then checked his mailbox mounted outside the front door. He saw no mail and closed the door, facing the being who sat on his couch with perfect posture and stared intently at him with wonder and affection.

Nik grew uncomfortable with the silence and decided to engage the being again. "So, do you eat? Are you hungry? Do you need to go to the bathroom?"

The being's cheeks reddened, and she laughed. At first, her laughs resembled a screaming banshee before they became traditional-sounding and lady-like. She covered her lips again with her fingertips, concluding chuckling.

Nik was surprised she had evolved so quickly to demonstrate laughter; however, her next action surprised Nik the most.

She spoke again, her voice no longer raspy and strangulated. "No, I do not engage in those bodily functions. I do not consume, nor do I defecate or urinate." The being playfully brought her fingertips to her lips and squinted, looking comically at Nik. "I don't pee and poop." She giggled loudly.

Nik retrieve his cellphone from his pocket to check the time—10:30. He wondered where the time had gone. He recalled leaving his parents' house shortly after 8:30, which would have placed him at the intersection of State Route 14 around 8:55 or perhaps 9:00. He knew the encounter with the being had happened only a few minutes later, and he wondered how long he had been in his trance when he first encountered her.

She remained staring and studying him.

He pushed the idea from his mind and decided to be a more hospitable host to his strange new guest. He stood in his living room, detracting her attention from his thoughts. He realized the venue had remained the same, but the circumstance had shifted extraordinarily. A couple weeks ago, he had brought home a strange woman and had offered her a tour, and now he was in the same situation, offering an even-stranger woman a tour of his house—a woman he thought far exceeded strange, a woman from an unknown origin.

Remaining pleasant and mindful of his thoughts and his non-verbal communications, he employed polite composure toward her, hoping she was not reading. "Well, okay, so we have established you don't pee and poop, as you put it, but why don't I show you my house so you can see how normal people live?" He motioned her to follow him.

She sprung from the couch, releasing his backpack and floating in front of Nik while furrowing her brow at him. Her flesh maintained its human color and appearance, but her garments moved and billowed as if they fought violent storm winds. "You are a pompous and self-righteous person. How dare you make such a crude and judgmental assessment?"

Nik stepped backward, raised his hands to illustrate a physical apology toward her and swallowed hard with fear. "Hey, look. I didn't mean anything by that. I was just nervous and didn't know what to say. I promise, from now on, I'll choose my words wisely. Please, just give me another chance to make it up to you."

The female being maintained her angry float for a moment longer before gently landing on the floor. She no longer appeared offended from his statements and accepted his apology.

Relaxed at her calmer state, he gestured toward the next room.

She grabbed his right hand and yanked him into the kitchen. Her feet pattered, childlike, on the floor with a flash. Once they reached the kitchen, she stopped in the center of the room, and her body wobbled from the sudden stop. "Kitchen …"

She maintained her grip on his hand and pulled him through the kitchen and down the hallway toward the bathroom. Upon entering, the light switch flipped on automatically, and she studied her reflection in the medicine cabinet mirror. "Bathroom …" she said and beheld herself in a vain manner. After her vanity left her face, she illustrated an expression of satisfaction.

This physical gesture struck Nik as he remembered earlier, while visiting his parents, he had given his reflection a similar look. The female being's next action struck him as the most unusual; she faced Nik, demonstrating a look of gratitude as if she appreciated him for being attractive.

She tugged and urged at his hand, pulling him through the doorway and into his bedroom.

He stood in a panic as the memory of he and Samantha went through his mind. He scrambled to purge the thought.

The female being stood staring at his bed. "Bedroom …" she said slowly and seductively. She faced Nik and brightened her eyes at him, pursing her lips. She pulled him through the hallway entrance of the bedroom and into his music room.

The wall light switch flipped on automatically, and she floated once again as her garments pulsed light and billowed. She studied his upright piano in the center of the room and turned to Nik. "This room is where the dream happens."

Nik tugged her hand. He did not want his neighbors to observe a floating figure.

She complied with Nik's gesture, landed softly then stepped elegantly to the piano. The duet bench slid from under the piano, and she sat down without causing a sound. She gestured to Nik to follow her, sliding to the right side and placing her left hand on the bench, making clockwise circular motions.

Nik approached with tender caution, anxious that the female being might deploy some telekinetic activity. She must have sensed his apprehension, because she widened her eyes, offering him sincerity that his joining her was warranted. Feeling relief as he gained proximity, he exhaled softly, positioning his body with tact on the duet bench, and relaxed.

The duet bench raised one inch off the floor, wobbled from side to side four times then returned to the floor. The female being lifted her fingertips to her lips again, giggling.

Nik shot her an unpleased glare.

She lowered her hands to her chest and cusped her left hand with her right, regarding him with apologetic eyes.

Nik felt sick as he realized his look must have appeared angrier than he had anticipated. He had an epiphany that the being had evolved further and had developed a sense of humor. Nik smiled warmly at her and placed his right hand on her left shoulder. "I see you're a fast learner and you've developed your own brand of humor. I think it's safe to determine your brand of comedy is practical jokes. I have nothing against humor. On the contrary, I love humor, but I hope you can realize that jump scares may not be the best kind of humor right now." Nik smiled, imploring his point.

She straightened her torso and nodded a single time to acknowledge.

Nik returned a smile and repeated, "Good," each time he nodded, illustrating a calming tone. He still held her shoulder, thinking how wonderful she felt, as if he was touching perfection. *If just touching her shoulder feels this good, I wonder what touching other areas would feel like.* He scrambled nervously to purge the thought and refocus. "So, I think you have a grasp of humor. Let's see what else you can grasp, especially since it seems you have taken an interest in my piano."

She scanned the piano keys and faced him. "Fifty-two white, thirty-six black."

Puzzled, Nik realized that, with a single glance, she had counted the number of keys. "Oh my god! You looked at that for less than a second, and you could determine that from a single glance?"

Feeling proud of herself, she finished, "Yes. Eighty-eight keys."

Nik, astonished, decided to enlighten her on some of the basics of the piano. He slid left on the bench and motioned her to follow suit. Delicately, he reached for her right hand and placed her thumb on the middle C. He followed by placing her left pinky on the C, one octave lower, to set her up for the C-major formation. He fingered the C-major scale as demonstration.

Without further instruction, she played through the scale with both hands, arriving at the high C and then the low C with a flurried burst. She looked at him nonchalantly, expressing that his request had not been a worthy challenge, and smirked. "The C-major scale was rather simple. Perhaps you would like me to play another scale. I could play its relative minor scale, the A-minor scale, or perhaps you would rather I play the C-minor scale. Please tell me which scale you would like me to play? Also, would you rather I play the harmonic or the melodic scale of your choosing?"

Baffled at her advanced knowledge of music terminology, Nik said it would not be necessary for her to play either the harmonic or melodic C-minor scales.

She panned the room in the same manner Samantha had a few weeks earlier and stopped her gaze at his sheet music shelf.

Nik sat thinking how much her mannerisms and body language were like Samantha's.

She pulsed a single time before the pages of "Laughter in the Rain" by Neil Sedaka floated from the shelf and landed on the music rest. She indicated to Nik that the song was in common time and in F-major key signature. She flawlessly played the song with expression. When she finished, she pulsed again before telekinetically returning the sheet music to its proper place. "Of course, I did not really need the sheet music. I just like to have it there to add to the ambiance."

Nik felt a sharp frightfulness. He looked at her aghast as she said something he previously had felt before. Had she said that deliberately, knowing it would shock him? His intrigue and attraction toward her now blended with fear.

She panned the room and eyed the desk. She stood from the duet bench and slid it back while Nik remained on it.

Nik clumsily scrambled to stand to not be pinched.

She approached the desk; to Nik's relief, she did not float or glow while traveling. She located the manila envelope and drew it to herself. She faced Nik in a grand-gestured movement, cocking her head and giving him a puzzled look. "It is empty. It is not complete. It has not been started."

The degree of intrigue and fear were equal within him.

"What are you waiting for? Where is your inspiration?"

"I don't know. Maybe I'm afraid to start it. Maybe I'm afraid it will be a mediocre piece of shit. I just don't know."

The female being set down the envelope and glanced at Nik with a serious expression. "It will not be a piece of shit. It consumed nothing to cause it to defecate." She raised her fingertips to her lips and giggled.

Nik's fear broke as she laughed. He laughed with her joke on numerous levels. He found it reassuring that she believed in his work. He felt that if an intelligent being from another world, dimension, or a distant place in time held his abilities in strong accord, then he might actually have what it takes to compose a successful composition. He smiled, sure of himself.

Realizing the time was quickly nearing bedtime, he wondered what to do with the female being. The last time he had showed a female visitor his office, they listened to music then went to his bedroom. Nik knew that would not be the case in this scenario and must employ an ideal strategy.

He retrieved his cellphone from his pocket, and the time displayed 11:11 p.m. He must act quickly if he wanted to get any sleep. He told the female being to wait for him by the living room couch, so he could retrieve clean bed linen.

She acknowledged his request and sashayed down the hallway into the living room.

He collected spare pillows, a sheet, and a comforter. He realized he did not know her name and wondered if she even had one. He hadn't offered his name to her either. He smirked sarcastically and mumbled that telling her his name would probably be irrelevant. Still, he wished he knew what to call her.

He slid closed the closet's gliding doors and heard his stereo blare loudly from the living room. In a panicked shock, he dropped the pillows and bedding and raced toward the living room. He saw her floating and her garments glowing as she moved elegantly around his living room. He broke himself from his trance and lowered the stereo's volume.

She turned to him in midair, flashing and pulsing light, and the receiver volume increased again.

Nik settled his nerves as he watched her move deeply in the throes of pleasure then realized she was listening to the CD he had played the other night, and the song she danced to was the last song on the CD—"Mirage" by Eric Troyer. Nik skillfully reduced the volume, not drawing attention to his actions.

She landed softly on the living room floor with her back to him.

It was compelling that two women guests had illustrated a positive reaction to the song. One woman thought the song was romantic and an immediate turn on, and the other floated while entering a state of ecstasy. He thought maybe, just maybe, he might have a chance with her. He felt uncomfortable about that concept and questioned how he could possibly feel that way for something that, at best, he would describe as an alien. Regardless, he knew now was not the time to entertain those thoughts. He needed his sleep to face whatever lay ahead of him. He needed his strength to safely operate his truck.

She slowly turned to him with a serious expression and delicately raised her right arm, craning it like a ballerina.

Nik knew she wanted to tell him something important.

She slid toward him and gently grabbed his wrists, grazing her fingers across his palms and interlocking her fingers with his. She regarded him with purpose, as if she was going to deliver urgent life changing news. "You are correct. I do have you at a disadvantage. You see, I do know your name. You are Nikolas Cameron Vanelli, and I also know you do not know what to call me."

Nik stepped backward, wishing to break from her grasp.

"I will tell you this, Nikolas. I wish for you to call me *Mirage*."

"Mirage. I like the sound of that. It somehow fits you, and it also says you have good taste in music. Besides, it's easier to call you something than nothing at all. I'll be right back to get your pillows and bedding. By the way, please don't turn on anymore appliances or do anything else that may draw attention to the house."

While strolling down the hallway, he felt he was experiencing shared joy with her. He entered his bedroom and retrieved the pillows and bedding lying on the floor.

Mirage sat on the couch with perfect posture, her demeanor exhibiting that of an obedient child.

Mirage was a wonder to Nik. Sometimes she would appear lucid and of high intelligence, while other times she seemed flirtatious and seductive, then she would seem to have the innocence of a child, with every experience being new and wonderous to her. Nik relished the thought of having something to call her and decided to take her variable moods as they arrived.

He placed the pillows and the bedding onto the chair arm and outstretched his hand to get her to stand, so he could turn his couch into a makeshift bed.

She grabbed his hand and sprung up as jauntily as a child and stood with one foot flat on the floor and the other with her toes pointing downward. She folded her hands across her chest as she twisted at her waist.

Nik ignored her playful gestures and continued to make the couch comfortable. He gently guided her down.

Once lying on her back, she looked at him with content. She wriggled softly into position until she found a suitable formation then relaxed.

While looking at her, he recalled the other weekend with Samantha and remembered how eager he had been to kiss her. He thought how eager he was to kiss Mirage. That eagerness came to an apex as his lips buzzed with urgency. With no possible way to slate his desire, he reared back from her placing his right hand over his mouth. It did not suppress his urge to kiss her; it only caused Mirage to regard him with puzzlement.

"Hey, it's getting late, and I really need to get to bed. I have to get to work early tomorrow, and I really need to figure out what to do about everything. I don't know if you are going to sleep, but just promise me a few things. First, don't cause anything strange to happen. Second, try to lay her quietly, and I'll see you in a few hours. Also, if you need anything, I'll leave the hallway light on. Just don't draw any attention to yourself."

Mirage looked at him with kindness, acknowledging his wishes. She could feel that he felt strained.

Nik stood to his feet from leaning over Mirage, lightly placed his index and middle finger on her forehead and wished her a goodnight.

She wished him a goodnight and closed her eyes with satisfaction after he touched her. She knew that was Nik's way of expressing what he truly wanted to do. Before he could retract his hand, she grabbed it and caressed his palm.

Nik felt a strange sense envelope him, as if she was illustrating to him that he should have acted on his desire to kiss her. Regardless, Nik enjoyed Mirages gesture and collected his backpack before he walked to his bedroom feeling fuzzy and fatigued. He entered his room and gently closed the door behind him. He removed his clean clothes, phone charger, and toiletries from the backpack and placed his clothes into the drawer and plugged his charger into the wall outlet. He stored his toiletries in the medicine cabinet and returned to the side of his bed. He stripped off his clothes, removed his cellphone to plug it into the charger and placed it on the nightstand.

He set the alarm for five o'clock and hoped the few hours in-between would be a slow crawl. He also hoped Mirage would behave and not do anything disruptive. He tossed, turned and stirred restlessly for a while, dreading the possibility of Ross Delbert making an unannounced visit to his house. He also dreaded what his coworkers would say and do the following day at work, and he also wondered what kind of load he would have to deliver. He feared that with all his distracting thoughts and the blended fatigue, he might be involved in an accident. His mind exploded with impending doom.

Nik hated when his mind stirred in this manner. He would continue to urge and fight to not borrow worry, and this would sometimes grant him peace, but he was borrowing worry with compounded interest. After tossing and turning for twenty minutes, physical fatigue encompassed him. He was grateful that his nervous system's autonomic centers were now taking precedence, and the scope of sleep relied on forces beyond his control. Void of motion with cold stillness, Nik lay in bed as his body became inanimate.

In the living room, Mirage felt his stillness as she read his movements. She levitated four feet above her resting position on the couch. She paused and straightened from a horizontal position into a vertical position before lowering to float three inches above the floor. She looked down at her body, observing her white garments falling limp. She arched her back while leaning her arms backward and spreading her fingers. She inhaled deeply and manipulated her physical form. Her garments outer layer billowed telekinetically, and her undergarments illuminated, accentuating her figure. She closed her eyes and concentrated on the entirety of her being, pressing all her energy onto her form.

From the center of her chest, three white glowing orbs emanated and expanded through her. Two of the orbs floated one foot from each of her ears while the third floated in front of her feet. An energy pattern swirled behind her back, causing a small-scale fire rainbow that widened past her shoulders, resembling a wing pattern. She floated down the hallway with stillness.

Nik's door opened with a single creak until it thrust the rest of the way then stopped instantly before striking the wall. Nik felt the momentum of the swinging door and sprung into consciousness. He lay on his back, mesmerized with fear as he beheld the figure in his doorway.

Mirage floated with imposing severity. She rose and dipped, holding her position.

Nik watched her as the rainbow burst flared and waved along with the white orbs surrounding her, rotating in the same pattern they had danced in the sky earlier. Through his fear, he wondered what was happening. Why was this happening to him?

Mirage flung herself backward, leaning her arms backward and bending her calves toward the ceiling. Her pulse intensified, and the rainbow burst brightened while the orbs rotated perpetually faster. After three rotations, the orbs were no longer visible; Nik could only see fast streaks of motion. Mirage straightened herself, projecting an opaque emanation of her that hovered over Nik.

He wanted to throw his covers over his head to hide under them, but, with maturity, he knew that would not bring him any security. Through his fear, he found anger encompass his mind. His anger gave him a small amount of control over his situation.

Mirage had promised she would not do anything strange. The horizontal projection of Mirage stared down at Nik, floating atop of him and expressing an apologetic look. The projection descended to Nik and curved her arms around his head to touch his temples. The Mirage Projection changed into a collective fog cloud before disappearing.

Tilting his head toward the doorway, he watched the Mirage Projection follow the same pattern of changing and disappearing. Mirage Projection was gone, and the door slammed shut.

Nik felt an abundance of emotions, including fear, shock, anger, paranoia, and eventually annoyance—the last cascading emotion. He lowered his head to his pillow and looked at the ceiling. "I am so fucking tired of this weird shit. I can't take this bullshit anymore," he grumbled before he fell asleep.

He did not care about the time. He did not want to know how little time he had left before he needed to wake up; he just wanted to sleep for a little while longer.

The alarm clock on the nightstand blared without forgiveness. Nik flung open his eyes with heightened awareness. He sat up effortlessly and kicked his legs outward, planting his feet. He silenced the alarm clock, turned toward his bathroom and marched into it by sheer propulsion. His appearance illustrated a sense of horror as he looked rugged and aged. He attributed his appearance to a lack of sleep. He assured himself that he would look better after a shave.

He collected his razor and applied a generous amount of shaving cream to his face. He cupped cold running water from the faucet into his hands and submerged his face into the small pool. The water felt sharp and heightened his sense of awareness as he spread his fingers and let it fall. He opened his eyes and stared at his image in the mirror until his eyes focused and adjusted to the artificial light.

The shave aided in the reduction of appearing older. While focusing on his appearance, he realized he felt guilty for skipping the workout on the previous day. He placed his towel on the closed lid of the toilet and stepped into the shower. He vowed to make it a strong point to not skip the workout today. Skipping his routine would bring him unbearable discomfort. Exercise would be an excellent reward after the workday, due to the numerous aspects facing him. The water continued to fall on him as he stood under. Before he realized it, he was panic stricken.

He remembered everything but the most important aspect of the events that had unfolded. He remembered his dread about returning to work, feeling apprehension toward his bandmates, the activities that had transpired between him and Ross, but, during his early morning rising, he completely forgot about Mirage. He stood shaking, feeling foolish and questioning how he could have forgotten about that strange being he had encountered.

"My God, what's wrong with me? How could I have remembered everything else but forgotten her?"

He also realized she was still in the house, and he was naked, exposed in the shower while she could roam free. Feeling panic strike through him deeper, he fumbled to turn off the shower and step out with tact. He roughly flurried the towel around his body and placed it on the toilet seat.

He crept into his bedroom, carefully gathering his phone and yesterday's clothes. He collected a clean work uniform and his boots and dashed back into the bathroom. He emptied the contents of his pockets onto the sink, ensuring nothing was missing. He dressed in his work uniform and threw his dirty clothes into his laundry basket. He tied his boots with narrowed concentration.

The time displayed 5:13. He could not believe it was still that early; he felt as if his morning shower had taken longer. He felt an odd sense of relief knowing it was still early, and he had time to investigate his house for strange activities. He stuffed the contents into his pockets and crept from the bathroom, covertly flipping off the light. He slunk down the hallway with readiness.

He drew his attention to his couch. It was absent of the pillows and bedding he had placed on it. He stared at it, baffled, wondering where the items were placed and what had become of Mirage—maybe she had been a bizarre illusion he had self-manifested. He thought deeper on whether he should report to work. He felt that if he could have an illusion of that sort, he was not fit to drive his truck. Not relishing the thought of having to go to work, he decided he was cognitive enough to go in—it would be best to face the music and deal with the drama and the accompanying gossip.

He reached into his pocket and readied his keys while walking out of the front door. He locked the door and headed for his truck. The cab felt cold and crisp and shortened his breath. While starting his truck, the engine roared, feeling the strain of the cool morning.

Anxiety and apprehension about the work week swirled through him. He retrieved his pack of cigarettes and lighter from his pocket. He realized he had not had a cigarette yet and decided a morning cigarette might calm his nerves. He flicked his lighter, and it nauseated him after one drag. The cigarette tasted wrong—old and stale. He also experienced an overbearing head rush. He quickly rolled down his window and tossed out the cigarette. He jettisoned the remainder of his pack, nearly swerving into the next lane.

Darkness painted the sky while he parked at Moline Medical Warehouse. He knew sunlight was eminent, but it felt like the rising sun had been snuffed out. He trudged forward with reluctance upon entering the facility, as the employee's time clock read 5:47.

With shallow breaths, he padded toward the cafeteria. Alex, Andy, and Kenny had congregated at the usual table. As expected, Alex shifted his glance from him, immediately wanting to avoid eye contact. The others looked momentarily shameful and did not express any intention to look at him. Nik shook his head and headed for the farthest, loneliest table. The time read 5:50 on the wall-mounted clock. Kenny appeared pale and, with sternness and caution, unwilling to approach Nik

Nik regarded him without emotion and barked, "Just what the hell do you want, man? I don't want to be bothered right now."

Kenny's dark eyes grew fearful and glossed over with shimmering moisture.

For a moment, Nik felt remorse, but it was quickly extinguished with judgmental thoughts toward Kenny being a traitor.

Kenny, shaken and hurt from Nik's coldness, spoke while his voice cracked. "I came here because the others sent me over. We all need to talk to you after work today. So, if you get done before us, wait for us in the parking lot."

Nik stood with a flash, and Kenny stumbled backward. "Yeah, I figured this was coming. What? Alex was too chickenshit to tell me himself, so they send you? I tell you what. Go ahead and tell them if I get done before you guys today, I'll be waiting in the parking lot. Better yet, I'll tell them." Nik brushed by Kenny, grazing him as he pushed through. He stormed to Alex and Andy's table as their conversation stopped. "Hey, instead of sending the messenger boy over, why don't you tell me yourself? By the way, I'll be waiting for you in the parking lot for the *big* band meeting."

Alex and Andy stared at the table and shook their heads.

While heading to the dock office, Nik could feel the prejudice glares from the warehouse associates. He could only imagine what rumors and ill words were spoken about him.

The associates congregated around Jim Whitman, already standing on the warehouse floor. Jim boomed loudly, briefing the associates on the scope of the week. He declared that production needed to be increased by twenty-five percent while maintaining excellent accuracy. He boasted over a new production plan that would improve work productivity and safety. While Jim Whitman continued, the associates complained that his demands did not make sense. It would be impossible to accomplish these unforeseen goals. Jim concluded the meeting with an attempt to offer a team-building cheer of encouragement, but the associates dispersed toward their departments.

Nik glanced at Alex and Andy standing across from him in the formation. They avoided eye contact and left before the rest of the group. A small part of Nik expected Andy to walk over and comically speculate what caused the sag in Jim Whitman's pants, but he realized that would not be the case. Instead, he followed Alex, like a loyal mongrel dog.

Nik thought how subordinate and pathetic both Kenny and Andy's behavior had been. He entered the dock office, and Darcy was not present. In Darcy's place sat Matt Finster and

Bailey Sigbert. Nik wondered where Darcy had gone and how his day could become worse.

Matt and Bailey greeted him with false pleasantness.

Nik knew these two despicable people were not truly friendly. It was both their way of being patronizing and wicked. Nik nodded to them, acknowledging. Nik detested Matt and Bailey from the beginning of his career. When Nik was first hired, he had worked as a case picker with both of them and thought they were cruel, gossiping, and acted as if they were still in high school with the way they subjugated, sabotaged, and persecuted others. Matt and Bailey were frequent fliers when it came to making numerous trips to the human resource office, regardless of whether they started the altercation or not. Both sniveling cowards, it was their best defense mechanism. If someone asked Bailey to do a task she deemed too physically demanding, she would report to the human resource office and declare that management was mistreating her.

On one occasion, Bailey had taken a liking to a large, heavy-set coworker that Nik referred to simply as The Goon; he did not know the associate's name was Toby until after his termination. Bailey, still maintaining her high-school mentality, often invited coworkers to hang on Friday afternoons out at various local bars for hot wings and pitchers of beer. During one of these times, she had made advances toward The Goon, and he rebuked her in front of everyone, causing her humiliation. Rumors swirled on the following week that Bailey had reported to human resources that The Goon was stalking her, sexual harassing her, and making her feel threatened on the job. Without further investigation, they terminated The Goon. Nik believed this rumor to be true, as he had observed his boss escorting Toby out while Bailey gathered with her friends, giving Toby a snotty smile.

Matt, equally as cruel, was also a frequent visitor to human resources. His motivations lay largely with being a hypocrite and a judgmental zealot. One incident, when he had first started at the warehouse, Matt was bullying another associate—an older man named Blaine. Nik had been sitting at the table across from Matt and Blaine. Matt had snatched Blaine's bottle of pop and shook it before Blaine opened it. Matt had exploded into a loud and boisterous laugh, causing Blaine to fume. Blaine had grabbed Matt's Diet Coke and dumped a generous amount into his food. Matt had stood, stormed away and demanded that Blaine reimburse him for his drink and his lunch. Blaine did not falter. Matt had demanded that Blaine reimbursed him. Matt's face had been smothered in delight and empowerment when the cafeteria manager made Blaine hand over cash. As the events had transpired, he could see Matt's face expressed entitlement, as he had been blessed with a newfound immunity.

Another occasion Nik recalled Matt bullying and taking dominion over people had been regarding a same-sex female couple. Matt had declared that he was Catholic and explained the church does not accept same-sex marriages. He would sit with Bailey and the other members of the gossiping society and, with a pompous tone, would referred to them as *heathens* and make accusations that the two women's marriage was not valid in the eyes of God and their artificially inseminated child was an abomination. After his insults, he would cross himself and raise his hands upward in mocking praise. After passing his cruel judgment, he would conclusively add that "Catholics do not judge, but others judge Catholics." This gesture always infuriated Nik, as this man would berate and insult someone and follow it up with pretentious acts, seeing no fault in his actions.

Matt and Bailey's physical appearances depicted their cruelty. Matt Finster stood 6'2", robust, boasting the face of a bullfrog and the jaw of a bulldog, with a smashed bridged nose and sagging rude eyes. He consistently wore the same highly visible orange shirt with dirty stained blue jean shorts and dated Nike shoes with a red Ohio State Buckeyes baseball hat covering his large, bald gallon-jug-shaped head. Bailey Sigbert was equally large for her size at 5'6", reeking of overpowering, cheap, supermarket perfume. She was equally repulsive with her dark blond, sweaty, unwashed hair pulled into a tight ponytail, exposing her large bulbous forehead. Her eyes bulged, darkened like a raccoon and circled with rings of eyeliner. Her nose was pixy-like and snouted like an angry hog with a dark brown hemispherical mole below her left nostril. She always wore tight company-labeled t-shirts to expose her large chest that Nik found revolting, as she was clearly proud of her large sagging cow utters. Nik privately referred to her as King Hippo, as she reminded him of the character from the Nintendo game, Punch-Out!!. She was oblivious and self-absorbed, wearing tight Capri pants that revealed her lack of posterior and drew attention to her heavily purpled vein calves and ankles. Nik knew they were chummy and in good favor with Desiree. Seeing them in the dock office did not bode well.

Realizing he had spent a considerable amount of time glaring and detesting Matt and Bailey, someone's firm, wide hand touching his shoulder broke his trance. He turned and faced Jim Whitman.

Jim smiled with his aged, sweaty face. "Well, good morning, Nik. You ready for another strong week of deliveries?"

Nik shook his head, affording Jim Whitman any spoken words.

Jim eyed Matt and Bailey, who were playing the part well of engaging in the throes of work. "I'm sure you already know them, but just in case you don't, I would like to introduce you to Matt and Bailey. They will be Darcy's permanent replacements."

Nik became sickened with anger as Jim confirmed what he had assumed. A part of Nik wanted to question Jim's logic and decision on Darcy's termination, but, through better judgment, he decided to stand and remain mute.

"I know you'll have to get used to two new dispatchers, but I think the workload got a bit too much for Darcy, so we decided to replace her. I noticed sometimes you had to correct her manifest as well, but don't worry, I think Matt and Bailey will work out the bugs pretty well."

Matt and Bailey looked at each other and rolled their eyes, as even Jim was patronizing them.

Nik gathered his keys and paperwork from Bailey and scrutinized it, noticing his stops were non-linear, and the order included a large amount of hospital stops, which should be divided amongst all the drivers.

Bailey turned to Nik in her desk chair and crinkled her pixy-like snout at him. "Here is your manifest, Nik."

Nik's blood boiled, and he refused to accept his outlandish work assignment lying down. "This manifest does not make logical sense. You have not given me adequate time, and you have me doing too many hospital stops. These need to be dispersed through the other drivers, not just a single person."

Bailey widened her large, grotesque brown eyes then glared at Nik. Jim turned and stood behind Nik, and she vanquished her expression, as she had one more trick up her sleeve. "Look, I'm your direct supervisor now, and I've made a decision, and I believe in it. I believe in you too, that is why I assigned you this manifest. You're our super-driver, and I know you can handle it."

Matt added insult to injury as he turned in his chair and faced Nik, gesturing a double thumbs up.

Jim turned away, foolishly believing they were building Nik up.

Exiting the dock office, Nik turned back to look at Matt and Bailey.

"I really put the screws to Nik, didn't I, Matt?"

"You are so bad, Bay Bay." Matt raised his fist for a fist bump.

Nik, in a state of malcontent, wished nothing more than the completion of the workday. Feeling as if his newfound superiors were observing him, or perhaps the other fleet drivers were spying on him, he made grand gestures to demonstrate that he was performing a thorough pre-trip inspection. After the completion of his inspection, he was assigned to back into Kenny's door. Nik grumbled and wondered if Kenny would load him in a timely manner. Nik backed to the dock door, pulled his parking brake, and shifted the truck into Neutral. He sat stoic and brooding as he stared forward.

He recalled Mirage and the events that had led to their bizarre introduction. He thought about his couch being vacant earlier, as the extra pillows and bedding were missing. Paranoia reentered his mind as he wondered if the events of Mirage had been an illusion, hallucination, or a crazy, desperate dream. Regardless, if she had been a dream or reality or strange marriage between, she was exquisitely beautiful and bizarre.

The container of Nik's truck rattled abruptly as Kenny's forklift drove over the dock plate. He looked in the left panel mirror and noticed Kenny flashed the green light toward him, signaling that he could go. Nik shifted his truck into gear, released the park brake and pulled ahead. He saw Kenny waving at him through the bay door window. Nik reciprocated with a small, flick of his fingers. He wondered why Kenny was being friendly to him after the events of the morning and what he and the others would tell him later in the afternoon.

Nik exited the facility and embarked on the day's deliveries. He remained diligent and strong through his first deliveries, but, as time went on, he grew exhausted from the nonsensical manifest and the heavy loads. At 12:00, Nik took his lunch break and pulled into a Fuel Mart truck stop he often passed. He was not hungry but felt the need to stretch his legs.

He used the men's room inside the truck stop then walked to the convenience store side for a bottle of Aquafina. He looked at his phone—12:20 p.m. He wondered where twenty minutes of his lunch break had disappeared. Nik made haste toward his truck, as he had two more short stops to make, wanting to ensure he had adequate time to finish the deliveries.

As he opened the truck door, a voice shouted to him, "Hey you, buddy. Yeah you. Is that you, Nik?"

He stopped climbing as he recognized the voice. It had been years since he had heard the voice of an acquaintance he had made during his month of training to earn his commercial driver license.

He stepped down and turned as Jordan Shoemaker greeted him. Jordan stood in front of Nik, taller and thinner than him, with long black hair. Jordan did not resemble Kenny identically, but he reminded Nik of Kenny, with his dark features and pale skin.

"Hey, buddy. I thought it was you from the distance. How you been, bud? I see you're still driving."

Nik said he was doing fine for the most part and that he was surviving.

Jordan could tell Nik was dissatisfied with his current position while he listened to Nik's tone. "Well, my grandfather finally retired from running Shoemaker Logistics in Gibbswood, and now Dad has stepped up to manage the company. We have contracts with some warehouses now, plus we're looking for drivers and dispatchers. I remember when we attended class together, you mentioned you would eventually like to move to a dispatch position. I also remember that I owe you a favor too."

Nik puzzled at Jordan for a moment before the memories flooded back.

Jordan had excelled in maneuverability while attending truck-driving school but fell short with double-clutch shifting the truck and struggled with pre-trip inspections, largely not properly reciting the air-brake system. He recalled how the gruff and abrasive instructors would intimidate and grill Jordan to the point of nervous freezing. He also remembered how he would explain to Jordan to tap the clutch instead of pressing the clutch. They practiced and worked together until he could identify the air-brake system components. Nik felt esteemed that Jordan remembered him and still felt a sense of returning a favor.

Jordan informed him on the type of trucks they employed and the expansion of his family's business. He retrieved a business card from his pocket that advertised his family's company logo and his father's name and contact information. Jordan instructed Nik to contact his father and include his interest in dispatching.

Nik thanked Jordan and shook his hand. He placed the business card in his pocket, climbed into the truck cab and waved to his friend. He pulled through the parking lot toward the direction of his second to last stop.

The duration of the workday passed uneventfully. While he drove, he felt a sense possible exodus, as he might have a new and promising job prospect. He parked his truck in the designated parking space and quickly completed the post-trip inspection. He removed his phone and observed the time—1:56. He strode into the dock office with his keys and his completed paperwork.

Bailey ignored him as she held a conversation on an instant messenger app, not doing any work-related task.

Nik attempted to hand his material to Matt, but he was too busy playing solitaire on his computer.

"Can you please give me a minute?" Matt barked at Nik.

Nik's temperature and rage rose as he plainly saw both fat swine were doing nothing job related, and Jim Whitman was nowhere in sight.

Eventually, Bailey turned to Nik, rolling her eyes at him before collecting his materials.

Nik thanked her dryly and asked if she could sign him out, since the day was completed.

She reached into her pocket for her phone and said it was only 1:58; it was not time for him to sign out. She included that she did not want to violate any rules.

When two o'clock eventually arrived, Bailey continued to concentrate on her social media page while Nik stood behind her and Matt.

Nik cleared his throat to get her attention, and she growled and huffed before she signed him out. Nik stormed from the dock office and slammed the door behind him.

The two commented how he had been impatient and rushing them unfairly while they both worked.

Nik clenched his fist with anger and disbelief, as he could not fathom that they believed their own lies. Nik charged through the warehouse, not exchanging glances with any occupants. He barreled through the associates waiting at the time clock without asking to be excused. *Thank god Monday is finally fucking over.*

He walked to his truck feeling the weight of the day bearing down. His bandmembers exited the facility, with Alex in the lead followed by Andy and Kenny. Nik caught eyes with Alex.

Alex stopped and allowed Andy to take the lead, until Andy drew back, and Kenny eventually led.

Nik was surprised by Alex's and Andy's cowardice. He could not believe how sniveling they were acting. This was the second occasion when they both reinforced the quiet one to take the lead.

Nik studied each of them as they raised their heads one at a time to look at him with deafening silence. "Well, does anyone want to speak up, or are you all going to stand here quietly with your dicks in your hands? Whatever it is you guys have to say, fucking spit it out, because I'm in no damn mood for fucking kid's games."

Kenny stepped to the rear of the group, maintaining silence. His stance exhibited that he did not want to speak on any subject. He had played messenger boy enough today for Alex and Andy and would not bring any further agitation or arguments. It was now their turn to speak.

Andy retreated quickly behind Alex and hid.

Alex brought his gaze to Nik with fear and anger, his face flushed and struggling to speak. "I'm pretty sure you already guessed it, but we had a meeting about the current state of the band."

Nik regarded Alex as if he was a small Napoleonic dog, rousting for dominance. "News flash, asshole. I already guessed as much. I swear to fucking god, you're so predictable and easy to ready. Tell me this. When did you guys have the meeting? Was it directly after our last show, or did you wait for the next day?"

Alex quivered with fear knowing Nik already knew the answer. "When we had the meeting is not relevant, Nik. But if you really must know, we had it on the following day. All you really need to know is we decided to move on without you."

Kenny raised his head and shot a look of anger toward Alex.

Nik looked at Kenny with surprise, as he was unsure why Kenny had made this gesture.

Alex glared at Nik with tunnel vision and was caught by complete surprise when Kenny slapped the back of his head. Alex launched upward with stinging pain. He turned and shot Kenny a hateful glance.

Kenny folded his arms and exhaled a dry, angry breath. "Why don't you tell him the rest, dickhead. I sure as hell am not volunteering for that shit. Come on, man. Don't be chickenshit. You pussies sent me over earlier to be the messenger boy. Nut up, you assholes."

Alex broke out into a profuse sweat and rubbed the back of his head, attempting to relieve his pain. He fanned his hand toward the ground twice in an effort to silence Kenny.

Kenny looked at Nik with compassion, disgusted with Alex. "If you don't fucking tell him, I'll tell him what you and Desiree have planned."

Nik peered at each of them and stopped, with his focus on Alex. "There's more? What else do you bastards have to tell me?"

Alex, stricken with deeper panic, looked between Kenny, Andy, and Nik as he straightened himself. "Fine. Kenny is right. There is more to be said. First of all, Desiree is now managing us, and we replaced you with Mike Balmer on bass guitar, and his cousin, Channing Dodds, will be our lead vocalist. We've had enough of you and your overly structured shit. You are too ridged, and the music is too progressive and artsy. We want to move in a fun, rocker direction. Also, look at reason, man. Look at the drama you caused with that girl and her husband. We don't need that kind of bad press. By the way, we're keeping the name too. It's my place where we practice, and I'm the cofounder, so we have the right to keep the name."

Nik looked at all three of his former bandmates and laughed barbarically. "I'll tell you what, you bastard chickenshits. That's the funniest fucking thing I've heard in a long damn time. I wonder if Alex knows the shit you all talked about his precious Desi behind his back. Especially you, Andy, you quiet fucking pussy. Now you assholes want to deal with her in and out of work? You're the stupidest bastards I've ever met in my entire life. Keep the fucking name. It's my gift to you. While we're talking about bad press, as you put it, have fun running the name Lapis Lazuli into the ground. While you assholes will be busy sounding mediocre, I'll at least be off that sinking ship. Good fucking luck."

Alex stood quivering from the berating. He could not move or say a word.

Nik noticed something strange amongst Kenny and Andy. When he had finished yelling at Alex, Kenny and Andy exchanged a look of concern. They also cringed when he reminded them of the hell of Desiree managing them.

Nik stood bold as he dealt the final blow. "Why don't you all fuck off and get the hell out of my face. Take your two goddamn pussies with you too, Alex. We're done here. I don't want to speak to you bastards ever again. *Piss off!*"

They left, with Andy storming away first followed by Alex mumbling under his breath, sounding shaken.

Kenny stood back as Alex and Andy approached their vehicles. He employed caution and took small steps toward Nik until he stood a foot away.

"What the fuck do you want?" Nik asked. "Your buddies have already left, and there is nothing more to be said."

Kenny stood silent for a moment. "Look, man. I think what went down was dirty. In fact, I think it was dirty as hell, and I wanted to apologize."

Nik relaxed his facial expression. "It is what it is, Kenny. You guys made decisions behind my back, and that is that."

Kenny swallowed hard and timidly darted his dark eyes back and forth. "If you want to form a new band, I'd join you when you get up and running again."

"Oh, I get it. You must have agreed with me when I said you all are on a sinking ship."

Kenny nodded nervously.

"I'll tell you what, you opportunist asshole. You can go fuck yourself. You had your opportunity to have said this either during your little, private meeting a few days ago or when I was giving Alex the business, but you stood silent and said nothing. You had to wait until everyone left. Well, fuck you, Kenny! You don't get the fortune of passively playing both teams! You know, I felt a little bit sorry for you for having to be their messenger boy, but now I can see you're just a pathetic, little shit. Enjoy Lapis Lazuli and the small time it has left. It's my gift to you. Fuck off, you pathetic loser. We are done here."

Kenny exhaled deeply, expressing hurt. He turned from Nik and approached his car while the other former bandmates exited the parking lot. He slammed shut the driver's side door and peeled out recklessly.

Nik opened his truck door and slammed it with equal force as he sat down. He punched the steering wheel before he started the truck. He had been arguing with his former friends longer than he had realized; he was astonished ten minutes had passed. He noticed the business card Jordan had given him was nearly falling out of his pocket. He read the information on it again. Before he could realize it, he was placing a call to Jordan's father's direct office line.

The line rang twice before a man with a crisp and deep voice answered. "Hello, this is Rick Shoemaker Operations manager Shoemaker Logistics. How can I help you?"

Nik was surprised, as he did not expect an immediate answer, and gained composure to speak. "Hello, yes. My name is Nik Vanelli. I'm a friend of Jordan Shoemaker, and he told me to give your office a call."

"Oh, yes. I was waiting for your call, actually. Jordan told me about you earlier and said you might call. I'm surprised to hear from you so soon."

Nik contemplated what to say next without appearing overly eager. "I spoke with Jordan earlier today, and he said you have some dispatch and driving opportunities available."

"We have both available, as we've expanded our operations. Are you available now for an interview?"

Nik smiled and pumped his fist. "I can head there right now. I just finished work a little while ago, so I'm still in my work uniform, but I can be there in ten to fifteen minutes."

"Sounds great. We're located on LeNoya Road just off Gibbswood Road to the east of town. You'll want to make a left on LeNoya Road, and our facility will be on the right. You can't miss it. You'll see our fleet of straight trucks with blue coloring and green lettering. The facility is a brand-new building that was constructed a few months back."

Nik felt another promising sense and extended gratitude toward Rick for his time. He shifted his truck into gear and shredded out of the parking lot. He peeled to the right down Donaldson Road and approached Pemkey in record time. The more Nik drove, the more excited he became. He always had an interest in becoming a dispatcher and climbing the ranks, but his current employer had never followed through with promoting him. They always told him that he was too good of a driver and his talents were best placed on the road.

Gibbswood seemed smaller to Nik as he passed through the town. He scanned the country setting and vigilantly watched the road signs. The first road he passed was White Star Road, and then he found the intersection of Gibbswood Road and LaNoya Road. He turned without activating the signal and saw Shoemaker Logistics sitting on the right a quarter of a mile away. Nik felt his chest lighten, and a new sense of hope and opportunity engulfed him.

Chapter
Eight

Nik sat in his truck reeling and nervous, hoping to make a lasting impression with his interview. He exited his truck to face the building and looked skyward as a cool and refreshing breeze passed by, like unknown and unseen forces were blessing him with calmness and serenity. He panned down and faced the structure ahead. The new-looking building appeared to be a legit business and not some whistle-stop trucking company operating from a worn mobile-home trailer in someone's back yard in the middle of nowhere.

Nik stepped through the glass door into the modern and climate-controlled lobby, and smell of cleaning products and fragrances from a deodorizer greeted him. Instantly, he was impressed and put to ease; however, he did not expect Jordan's family business to appear as modern and advanced. While attending truck driving school, he had always thought of Jordan looking the part of a heavy metal or thrash metal type and did not expect him to come from money.

Nik walked through the lobby and greeted the receptionist—a middle-aged woman with short sculpted hair named Karleen. "Hello, my name is Nik Vanelli, and I have an appointment with Rick Shoemaker."

Karleen peered through her glasses hanging at the end of her nose. She held up her index finger and told him to wait a moment before paging Rick. She instructed Nik to take a seat across from her.

No sooner than Nik sat down, he saw a man approach from the back cubicles. The man stood slightly shorter than Nik, but it took him little time to identify him as Rick Shoemaker, with a striking resemblance to Jordan only shorter and slightly heavier donning manicured black hair with defining streaks of grey.

He extended his hand toward him. "Hello, you must be Nikolas Vanelli. I'm Rick Shoemaker, and I'll be doing your interview."

Nik offered Rick a well-placed, firm handshake.

"Jordan told me I should be expecting you soon. I just didn't expect you this soon. That's a good thing it worked out like this. I had some free time this afternoon to meet with you. He also indicated you have an interest in dispatching. We can review that when we step into my office. By the way, my lead dispatcher will accompany me during the interview process. Is that something you'll be comfortable with? She'll help me decide the scope of my decision."

Nik told Rick that it would be fine and that he'd had previous experience with a panel interviewing him.

Rick led Nik through the row of cubicles to the executive offices at the rear.

Nik entered the office first and was pleasantly surprised to see Darcy Glenn sitting adjacent to Rick's desk. Rick closed the door and walked toward his desk. Darcy looked up from the files in front of her and took notice of Nik, her eyes lighting up with gleaming surprise and joy.

Rick instructed Nik to sit across from him then turned his attention toward Darcy, watching Nik. Rick looked back and forth between them and realized Darcy and Nik had been acquainted.

"It's so good to see you, Nik. I didn't have a chance to say goodbye," Darcy said with her voice nearly breaking.

"It's good to see you too, Darcy. I wondered what happened to you."

Darcy tried to catch up with her friend and object of romantic desire before Rick interrupted to begin the interview process, discussing Nik's background and driving experience.

Nik recounted his years of service and reminded Rick he had attended the same truck-driving school his son, Jordan, had attended.

"That's right! My father, Rick Shoemaker senior, began this company with a single straight truck and a small refurbished mobile-home trailer that used to stand where we are sitting now, but we have grown and expanded from that to this new terminal. My father was a bit of a traditionalist who started with a chauffeur's license and then grandfather into a commercial driver's license when federal motor-carrier regulations changed. It became policy for us now that all new drivers attend an accredited truck-driving school. Despite my father's more traditional and older values, we still required Jordan to attend the school." Rick smiled at Nik with gratitude as he mentioned that Jordan had spoken fondly of Nik with his assistance in earning his commercial driver's license. Rick also told Nik that

Jordan was now the lead driver, holding the position of route trainer.

Waiting for the appropriate time, Nik presented his interest in becoming a dispatcher. Rick asked Nik if he had any prior experience, and he told Rick he did not have any direct experience, but he used to offer Darcy assistance while working as a driver.

Darcy sat on the edge of her seat, eager to add to the conversation. "I think he'd be an excellent addition to the dispatch office. Numerous times he would suggest loading patterns in the dock office so the units would not violate weight regulations, plus he would propose route planning that I would use to assign driver manifest. With his suggestions, route driving time was reduced, safer, and ergonomic for the drivers. He really was a lifesaver. I would support his decision of becoming a dispatcher in an instant."

Rick looked impressed with Nik's abilities and smiled with satisfaction. "Well, it's true that we have openings for both drivers and dispatchers. Are you interested in dispatch? It sounds like you have the qualifications already, even though you did not discuss them with me, and Miss Glenn took the liberty of informing me." Rick looked at Darcy with slight coolness as she lowered her head with embarrassment. "Either way, a driver makes nineteen dollars an hour and our dispatchers make twenty-three dollars an hour. We pay our dispatchers more, because we require keen and sharp-minded associates who can multi-task. Is this a position you think you could handle?"

Nik looked at Darcy glowing and cheering then looked at Rick waiting for his answer. Nik nodded confidently and said, "Yes."

Rick informed Nik to stay there, and he would return shortly.

Nik looked at Darcy, puzzled.

Unable to contain her excitement, she spoke loudly then gained composure and softened her voice. "This is great, Nik! I just can't contain myself, but right now, I bet you, he's getting you an application and the drug screen kit. He's probably putting the blue tape on the unisex toilet tank and bathroom sink right now. I think you're in. Oh my god, I'm so happy right now."

Rick returned with a job application and a plastic specimen cup. He placed them in front of Nik before sitting behind his desk. "I'd like to move forward with the process and offer you dispatching job. Please complete the application and then go down the hallway to the right for the drug screen. Remember, when you complete the drug screen, do not flush or wash your hands and leave the cup on the top of the toilet tank."

Nik thanked Rick for the position and completed the job application. He handed the application to Rick and collected his drug screen cup. Darcy smiled at him with contentment as he exited the office into the unisex restroom. He filled his cup to the specimen line and returned to the office. Rick offered Nik some hand sanitizer, and Nik rubbed it through both hands. As Nik sat down, Karleen entered Rick's office, informing him that the test came back clear.

Rick asked Nik when he could start training.

Nik told him two weeks, firmly shook Rick's hand then extended his hand to Darcy as she gripped it with excitement. Nik bid both a pleasant remainder of their afternoon and left the office. As he approached the front entrance, he wished Karleen a pleasant afternoon as well.

He wanted to shout with excitement but maintained composure. Feeling his new boss may be observing him as he entered his truck, he ensured that he made it visible as he fastened his seatbelt and checked both directions and his mirrors before carefully leaving the facility. He drove toward LeNoya Road and turned left. He rolled down the windows and invited the pleasant country summer air into the cab. He turned onto Gibbswood Road and shouted and whooped with celebration in advancing from driver to dispatcher and absconding from the coworkers he had known for longer than he had personally cared to be around. He could not wait to report to work tomorrow, so he could give his notice to Jim Whitman.

As he reentered the country between Gibbswood and Pemkey, he imagined Jim Whitman's expression when he gave him the news. He knew Whitman would attempt to employ guilt, saying he had promoted Nik personally and the company had paid for his truck-driving school. Nik mentally prepared for Jim's tactic to retain him as an employee. He knew he would counterargue with Whitman not promoting him further into a dispatch position, and he had also dedicated numerous years post graduating truck-driving school. He would add that he more than gave Jim Whitman his money's worth. Regardless, Nik's decision was absolute, and he was ready for a fresh, new start.

As he passed Trixie's Drive Thru, he dialed Pisanello's number to order an Italian sub to celebrate. As the phone rang, he realized he may have made a mistake by calling. He wondered if Savannah would answer, and he would have to face her upon picking up the sub. Before he could cancel the call, Savanah picked up.

She said hello twice before Nik ordered his sub. She asked for the name on the order, and he ended the call. He felt apprehension wondering if she would mention the events of the other night to him or give him a hard time about the coldness he displayed to Kenny. He pushed the thought from his mind as he drove to Pisanello's.

When he arrived, he felt nervous, hoping Savannah would not be the associate waiting on him. He exited the truck and snuck toward the establishment. Feeling foolish for acting in such a manner, he increased his speed and walked through the front door.

Savannah stood behind the counter, making change for some children to insert into the videogame cabinets. She smiled at them and told them to have fun as she watched them walk away. She turned from the young children to Nik. The smile melted from her face, and her expression grew cold as she asked how she could help him.

Nik told her that he was there for the Italian sub order he had placed a few minutes prior.

She barked that it would be done shortly.

Nik nodded without uttering another word.

When the sub was finished in the oven, she added the toppings with agitation. She returned with the sub wrapped loosely and nearly flung it on the counter. She told him that the sub would be $6.99, and Nik reached into his pocket to retrieve the cash. As he handed her the cash, she snatched it from him, pushing the sub toward him.

Nik clenched his sub.

"You know something, Nik? You really upset Kenny with what you said. I don't know if you know this or not, but he really fought for you and thought that the others were out of line. He truly was your only friend in all of this, and you treated him like shit."

Nik looked at her with a relaxed glance. "I honestly didn't know that. All I know is that he sided with them and stayed in the band."

Savannah scoffed and remarked how Kenny had said he would quit if Nik started a new project. Savannah looked at Nik with hatred.

Nik regarded her with humility. "You know something? You are right. Out of everyone involved, Kenny was the most compassionate, and I was pretty hard on him. I'll apologize to him when I see him tomorrow. I didn't realize he had tried to defend me like that. I guess I was just hurt and felt betrayed. You really seem to care about him, don't you?"

"I've had a crush on him for a very long time, and now that we're dating, I'm falling in love with him, but that is none of your business."

"Kenny sure is a lucky guy to have someone in his corner like you, especially after only being together just a short time. Regardless of the band's success, he surely found something good with you. Don't worry, Savannah. I'll straighten it out with Kenny."

Savannah's look softened, and her eyes glistened as she thanked Nik and apologized.

Nik reassured her that it was okay, that she was only defending someone she cared for. He bid her a good day and apologized.

She accepted his apology graciously and wished him a good day.

He stepped onto the sidewalk toward his truck and felt better about the band situation knowing he had someone on his side. He made a definitive decision to not pursue his former bandmates any further, as their friendship and partnership would be forever dissolved. He did, however, feel he should make peace with Kenny, even though he still held a small amount of resentment toward him. He realized that regardless of the future, he would never work with either of his former friends again. He started his truck, shifted it into gear and drove home, hungering for his sub the duration.

He arrived home, parked his truck and grabbed his sub as his stomach rumbled. He realized the stress of the current events have reduced his appetite to nothing. He checked his mailbox on the porch—only junk mail. He unlocked his front door and headed for the kitchen. He fetched a glass from the cabinet and fill it from the faucet. He raised the glass to his lips and felt refreshed from the cold water. He gobbled the sub, as if he had not eaten in a week, and felt foolish for devouring the sandwich so quickly. He threw away the sub wrapper and went his bedroom to change into his workout clothes.

He did not feel the motivation to engage in a full-impact workout but decided to speed walk around the village instead. When he entered his bedroom, he could not fight the urge to check his closet for the bedding and pillows. He opened the door to discover that the pillows and the bedding were neatly stored. He stood fighting his thoughts. A part of him had hoped the bedding and pillows would not be present. It would have been a small iota of proof of his strange alien encounter. However, the cold truth revealed that nothing had been moved. He shut the closet and turned away from the door.

He retrieved his workout clothes from his dresser. He threw his work uniform into the laundry basket in his bathroom. A wicked thought came to him; he wondered whether to wash his work uniforms before returning them or return them in their current wrinkled, unwashed state. He laughed defiantly as he thought it would be a nice *fuck you* to the facility if he left them as is. Regardless, he could not wait to be free of Moline Medical Warehousing.

He speed walked around Pemkey's perimeter, beholding the late afternoon sun as it cooled and dimmed into the early evening. The beauty of the day, accompanied with the smell of lilac, added to his joy. He made two laps around the town and returned home. He had worked up a sweat, and he felt achieved. He turned on his central air-conditioning unit and stood in the living room until he was comfortably cool.

He shed his workout clothes in his bedroom and readied his towel to enter the shower. He turned on the shower to a cool temperature and plunged his head under the steady flow for several seconds with his eyes closed. After comfort relaxed his body, he reemerged his head from the running water and surveyed the water beads on the wall. As he focused, he saw a strange motion from the water beads. They moved from the tub up the wall, defying gravity. He rubbed his eyes to clear any misperceptions, but what he was seeing was the truth.

The beads ascending from the floor collected in mass and intensity as the water formation sprang off the shower wall to form a three-dimensional shape that remained formless as it grew in height. Nik stood with fear. The figure took a similar form of the humanoid being Mirage had first used to appear to him, only transparent and water based. The motion of the water smoothed and took a defined shape. Standing before him was a water effigy of Mirage, shapely and nude.

Nik fell to his knees in the shower and burst into tears. His mind could not conceive rational thought or proper emotion. While being fearful of the bizarre phenomena, he was also ecstatic to see Mirage, regardless of her appearing in a strange water-based form. He could not help but feel a sexual attraction to her perfect, liquid, naked body. He gained composure of his tears and his lust and focused solely on the water projection.

The water-based projection of Mirage floated toward Nik as he remained on his knees. She curved her arms around his head and placed her fingertips on his temples. As soon as she touched him, it felt as if her fingertips became water jets from a Jacuzzi, pulsing water through his temples' soft flesh. After several minutes of remaining on the floor, Mirage retracted her fingertips and floated back from him. Through her water-based appearance, Nik noticed her smile at him. She tilted her head backward, pressing her arms backward, with her fingers pointing to the ground. She arched her back, rising to her tiptoes before she hovered off the shower floor and burst as a firework, spraying him with exploding water. In a panic, Nik scrambled to his feet and clumsily turned off the shower. He grabbed his towel and slipped and slid as he fled to his bedroom.

He reached the dry carpet, fell to the floor and raised his knees to his chest in a fetal position. He trembled with shock, fear, and euphoria. Motionless, the only thing he could do was stare at the bathroom doorway. He rocked back and forth, fighting to calm his mind and body to decide if the interaction was real or another strange hallucination. He rolled to his knees and sat on all fours with his head tucked down. He fought harder to gain his strength to stand.

As he stood, a monstrous headache greeted him then fleeted within seconds. He rubbed his eyes, gaining his composure and balance. After rubbing his forehead, he moved his fingertips to the temples to make similar motions as Mirage. Nik's body thrust backward, and his back arched while his arms stretched behind him, as if an unworldly force was causing him to maintain his stance.

As the invisible force held him, he felt his breathing shallow. His eyes rolled back in his head, and he surrendered to the outer oppressing force as consciousnesses escaped. He entered a state of foggy grayness and felt that his body had lost its form. He was in the endless corridor, approaching the fog that lay before him with the rainbow burst behind. Regardless of his protest and his attempts, he could not help the force of propulsion thrusting him toward the disembodied fog. The mass in front of him pulsed with light with three large thunderous bursts before the mass swirled like a funnel, consuming and blending with the fire rainbow until it was one large entity.

Undecipherable words projected by the swirling mass evolved into recognizable language within seconds. Mirage's voice echoed through the fibers of Nik's disembodied form. "It is imperative that you maintain control here and in your world. If you fail to comply, you'll only fall farther, and I won't have the capability to render you further aide. You must control your rage or you will be completely lost. Swear it to me!"

Nik felt dire desperation to speak and to be understood. He pressed and strained to talk, only to realize that he was again not in human form. He remembered his dream from the other night and focused his strength and his voice from his form. He projected his ethereal voice to Mirage. "What do I need to maintain control over? What will happen to me that I need to maintain control?" Nik felt he was losing mass and control of his shapeless form as he questioned Mirage.

"You need to control your primitive and raw human emotions. They are what lead you here originally, all those years ago. Human emotions were your failing, and recently they have become your failing again."

Despite being a formless mass, Nik felt human again and felt like he had expressed his emotions toward the swirling spectrum, demonstrating body language, which he knew was impossible.

The swirling mass pulsed with heated flares before addressing Nik with agitation. "Your rage! Your primitive, discipled, thoughtless rage! If you act on it with the heart of provocation, you will be subject to punishment in which I cannot intervene. Control yourself at any and all cost!"

Nik floated with fear, struggling to maintain his presence in the realm, and concentrated his strength once again, knowing his next statement would cause him to lose all his mass and disappear. With solid concentration, he spoke again with meaning "I swear it!"

The swirling mass slowed its movements and stopped rotating to reveal a projection of Mirage, as if she was composed by colored stained glass shrouded with multi-colored prisms. As he faded from the endless corridor, he saw her smiling at him with love and affection.

"You will be rewarded soon."

As she dissipated from the corridor, he ascended from the realm. Before he entered reality, he thought the only reward he truly desired would be to see her again, tangible in his own world. Waking from the strange episode, he bent forward and straightened his back to full upright position. He shuttered with fear that he had experienced a seizure or some other cerebral condition. He stood naked, and his towel dropped to the floor. He picked it up, wrapped it around his waist and sat on the bed. He placed his head into his hands and leaned forward, fighting to gain composure and understanding of the strange events.

He worried that he was suffering from a serious physiological or psychological condition. Frightful thoughts entered and raced in his mind. He wondered if he was suffering some sort of post-traumatic stress disorder, mental breakdown, or if his grip on reality was vacating him. He pushed on and wondered if the condition held stronger gravity. His fear increased as he pondered on whether he was epileptic or something far severe such as a brain tumor. He raised his head from his hands and stared directly in front of him at nothing but the void of his bedroom.

He combated his fear with the reassurance of memories. He remembered that, during the weekend after his workout in the garage, he saw the fire burst rainbow along with his parents, and he also recalled that his parents also had seen the white glowing orbs. Further attempting to relax and reassure his mind, he also convinced himself that if he'd had a seizure, he would have awoken on the floor and not standing. Whether or not people fell during or after seizures, he did not know, but he focused on that aspect only to drive him from his fear. He stood and returned to the bathroom to hang his towel on the rack.

Nik transferred the contents of his pockets and placed them into his lounging shorts pockets and staggered with fatigue to the living room couch. Feeling that he needed an escape, turned on the television as he nested inside the corner.

He realized his favorite television show would be starting. He selected channel twenty-four, and the bumper to *Professor Phantasm's Macabre Movies* played. Nik always enjoyed the low-budget and tongue-in-cheek quality of Professor Phantasm's show. The host styled his hair in an elevated fashion, like the bride of Frankenstein, blended with an Eraserhead fashion, while wearing swirly eyed goggles and a deliberately torn white lab coat with blue hospital scrubs splattered in prop blood.

The setting of his show was poorly painted plywood backdrops illustrated to resemble an underground catacomb laboratory. Nik always laughed due to his appearance while trying to employ proper dictation and expanded vocabulary. On this particular episode, Professor Phantasm claimed he had perfected time travel and reached into his pocket to present his time machine, which was simply an old digital alarm clock with white masking tape across the display that read, TIME MACHINE, in black permanent marker. Professor Phantasm continued stating that he had traveled to the 1980s for his Monday double feature. Professor Phantasm announced proudly that he'd released his first movie in the beginning of the 1980s, and he'd premiered the last movie in the later part of the decade.

Nik sat back and relaxed as the first movie showcased was a dreadful movie with a plot revolving around conjoined twins, titled, *Basket Case*. Nik sat through the movie with minimal interest but welcomed the array of bad acting and subpar stop-motion animation. When *Basket Case* concluded, Professor Phantasm apologized to his audience for the terrible movie and promised that his next movie, yet not exactly a priceless gem, still provided more substance than its predecessor. He concluded by joking that, like the Howard Jones song, "Things Can Only Get Better," it surely was proven in the 80s. The next film Professor Phantasm featured was *Waxwork*. Nik agreed with the professor that the film's quality, storyline, and general thesis was worlds better, and he found himself invested and entertained from the movie. Nik checked the time display once again and noticed it was ten minutes from 9:00 p.m.

Nik turned off the TV and sat on the front glider porch to close the evening. He also was not interested in listening to Professor Phantasm's final thoughts and macabre puns after the show concluded. While he did enjoy the show's low budget and delightfully tacky quality, he could only tolerate so much of Professor Phantasm. Besides, the main reason he usually watched the show was for ideas of movies he might want to add to his movie collection. He decided *Waxwork* was the only show worthy enough for a DVD purchase.

An over imposing sense of loneliness engulfed him. He was not yearning for the company of a neighbor to engage in idle conversation, nor was he seeking the company of one of his former friends or bandmates. He was seeking the company of a female. Sexual urges did not necessarily motivate his yearning; however, if the opportunity presented itself, he would be willing, ready, and able to indulge on those sweet fruits, but his motivations of pleasure ran simple and pure. He would have been content to have a soft, beautiful woman curled against him on the glider as they watched the residual daylight fade into the blackness, before retiring to his room for a passionate romp and a romantic spoon afterward. Numerous parts of Nik ached as he focused on this thought, to the point of a hollow and throbbing pain in his chest.

The thought of Mirage entered his mind and he found his fear of going insane or having a physical condition was absent. He could only concentrate on her image. He yearned and ached for her as he pondered all the images she had manifested and the linear events that had followed. "I'm in love with a mirage."

Embarrassed and hoping no one was present, he laughed at the irony of her name. He leaned back in his porch glider to peering around and was relieved no one had heard him. Still, despite her strange and unusual appearance, she was physical perfection, and he wished she could be with him now as a normal woman, so they may be in a relationship together.

He contemplated how it would work. He was not sure if she had the dynamic for a sexual encounter. He remembered how she had first appeared to him—a glowing blank humanoid figure that metamorphosized into a beautiful woman, a woman of absolute physical perfection that would be the object of all that desired her. When she first saw herself in his bathroom mirror, she appeared proud of her appearance and expressed a look of gratitude. Regardless of her origin, whether she was from a distant place in time, an interstellar being, or possibly an interdimensional being, his affections toward her were fixed. To be with her again would be a miracle.

He saw the darkness of the night rapidly approaching and felt the hour growing late. He stood from his porch glider, approached the end of the porch and curled his toes over the edge. He panned the street and the houses before he rested his head forward and glanced into the void. He recounted what he believed was a message from Mirage after he had jumped from the shower and entered the endless corridor. The message urged him to maintain control no matter his impulse.

He also recalled the message said that if he failed to maintain control, she could not intervene. He pondered the possible reward of maintaining control—to have Mirage with him on a physical plain. If that would be the case, he would fight everything and anything to have her with him. He cleared his mind from all thoughts and concerns and filled it with that motivation. He understood challenges would arise and press him around every corner; however, he did have one card up his sleeve that provided him a ray of hope. He knew he would be leaving his current employer soon, and he would be taking both an increase in pay and a promotion.

Smugly grinning to himself, he entered his house with optimum satisfaction. Growing tired, he knew once he entered his bedroom, comfort would greet him. He wondered what dreams would invade his head, whether they would be pleasant or appalling. He was anticipating tomorrow, to deliver his notice to Jim Whitman and begin his new opportunity with a sense of freshness and unbiased thoughts—thoughts surrounded by positivity instead of long loathsome dread. Filled with gumption and excitement as he entered his bedroom, he laid tomorrow's work uniform on the side of the bed.

After what felt like a single blink, Nik awoke promptly at 5:00 a.m. without activating the snooze a single time. He scooped his uniform and placed his keys, wallet, and cellular phone in the pants pockets. Once he was ready, he drove to work, violating speed laws and rolling through stop signs, as his eagerness grew to approach Jim Whitman before the start of the shift. When he arrived and closed the truck door behind him, he found he was nearly running toward the entrance.

The security officer watched him with concern as Nik flashed his badge and entered the building. He navigated through the break room, onto the production floor and to the dock office. He spotted Jim Whitman sitting in the dispatcher station, appearing worried.

Jim faced Nik while Nik smiled wickedly. "You're here early today, Nik. Are you trying to get an early start on the day? You know the early bird gets the worm."

Nik was suspicious of Jim's positive demeanor. He assumed Rick Shoemaker must have contacted Jim for a reference by now. "No, this has nothing to do with an early start"

Jim swallowed hard.

"I'm here to give my two-weeks' notice. I got another job offer."

"What kind of job offer?"

"A dispatcher position at a new facility."

"I figured as much. Can't say that I haven't seen this day coming for a while now. Well, if you stay on with us, I promise we can start the dispatcher cross training immediately."

Empowerment creeped over Nik's body, and he scoffed. "You've dangled that opportunity over my head for numerous years, Jim, and you've failed to deliver. I've already accepted the new position, and there is nothing more to be said."

Jim leaned back in the office chair and sighed.

Nik turned and left the dock office, heading toward the break room.

The dayshift associates and drivers were entering the break room, mingling with their cliques and waiting for the time to gather in front of the dock office.

Nik sat quietly as he watched his former bandmates congregate at their usual table. Kenny looked toward Nik, and Nik maintained his promise to Savannah to ease his tensions towards him. He offered him a neutral glance and a smile. Kenny appeared surprised, followed by a gracious expression of returning the same gesture.

The time had come for the associates to enter the warehouse, and they walked toward the dock office. Jim delivered his morning meeting, still appearing visually shaken and overwhelmed with stress. He did not offer any patronizing words of encouragement or teamwork motivation. He walked to the dock office with his head hung low.

Kenny hung back as the other associates headed toward their workstations and lift equipment. He casually approached Nik, careful not to exert any aggression. "Look, man. Sorry if I said anything off putting the other day. It has just been crazy drama with all this unwarranted shit. It really will be a shit show without you."

Nik was taken aback as he wondered if word had traveled fast about his resignation. Nik's gesture frightened Kenny, and he was taken aback as well. Nik, feeling absentminded, realized Kenny was referring to the band. "You know what, Kenny? It is what it is. You guys made your decisions, and that is that. I don't have any hard feelings toward you. Hell, I might even take you up on the offer to eventually start a side project. That won't happen anytime soon, but I know an accomplished drummer, when that time might present itself. I will say this though, I will never work with Alex or Andy ever again."

Kenny extended his right hand toward Nik, offering a handshake.

Nik accepted and patted Kenny's shoulder

Kenny smiled with ease and headed for his assigned loading doors.

"Hey, Kenny!" Nik shouted. "You have yourself a good, reasonable woman with Savannah. Do yourself a favor and hold on to her as long as you can. She is wise and blessed with rationality."

Kenny smiled with esteem and waved at Nik as he walked away.

Pleased that he had offered Kenny peace and had set a good mood in motion, Nik entered the dock office.

Bailey and Matt were whispering clandestine amongst each other, and Nik broke their conversation as he deliberately slammed the door behind him. They greeted him with false zeal.

"I hear you're leaving us, Nik. I hate to see you go. We'll miss you," Bailey said, overacting and emphasizing her words.

"Bailey's right, you know. We're losing our top-dog driver. It'll be rough around here," Matt patronized.

Nik wanted to tell both to stuff the false act but maintained his composure and asked for his manifest and keys.

Bailey made grand, accentuated gestures, handing over Nik's information.

Nik knew she enjoyed giving him his paperwork, as he figured it would not be an ideal manifest. He scanned his scheduled stops and route information and confirmed what he already knew.

Bailey batted her eyes condescendingly and faced her computer terminal, whipping her unwashed ponytail like a lasso.

Nik headed for the exit in silence. Nik opened the door and heard Bailey and Matt snickering as they conversed softly. Nik fumed, and, within his mind, told them he hoped they had enjoyed their brief time to screw him over. He arrived at his truck and hastily inspected, not employing his usual thorough attention before backing it into Kenny's dock door.

Kenny loaded Nik's vehicle and flashed the dock light when he finished.

As Nik departed from the dock, he pulled his highway horn twice, blasting loud bursts of gratitude, hoping it would also annoy and infuriate Bailey and Matt. To his surprise, the workday and the deliveries went fast, and he finished at 1:50. Checking the fuel gauge, he noticed the truck was low and pulled to the isolated fuel pump at the rear of the truck lot. While pumping fuel into his truck, he reveled in knowing he would be dispatching at a new facility soon, and he would not have to endure the smell of diesel much longer. After holstering the pump and logging the gallons of fuel used, he pulled the truck into the assigned spot and headed for the dock office.

Bailey and Matt were engaged in their usual activities. Matt was playing a puzzle game on his computer, and Bailey was on social media, posting that she was working hard and how her boss underappreciated her.

Nik rolled his eyes as he forced his keys and paperwork toward them.

Bailey grabbed for his paperwork without diverting her attention from her social media page and told him she would sign him off for the day.

Nik silently exited the dock office, wishing to remain unnoticed, and creeped across the warehouse floor and into the parking lot. He started his truck with a single thought. *Just a little over a week and a half and I am out of here and doing something I really want to do.*

While driving, he decided to stop at Frazier's IGA for groceries. He parked in front of the store and made a mental list of provisions. He sat bewildered, as if some unseen guiding force was advising him to make the stop. Feeling famished, he agreed it was a good idea. He entered the store and purchased two-weeks' worth of groceries, feeling that stockpiling would be a wise idea. He was mindful of Mirage's advisement, though vague, during his dream state. Not taking any chances, he decided that a low-hanging head and minimum conversations or eye contact with other customers or store clerks would be optimum. He arrived at the checkout lane, carefully pushing his shopping cart to not collide with fixtures or occupants.

The clerk respected Nik's silent wishes and did not try to converse with him. Nik collected his bags, left the store and entered his truck. He pulled into his driveway and strode to the front door, groceries in hand. He entered his kitchen and placing cold items into the refrigerator and non-perishables in the appropriate cabinets.

He sat on his living room couch with alertness and fine-tuned concentration. He relaxed his mind and his body to gain a meditative state. He spoke internally to Mirage, hoping she would hear his endeavors. He questioned mutely and repetitively a single question of what he needed to control. He tightened and strained as he concentrated his entire body and mind on the inquiry. Through rational judgment, he knew Mirage would not respond to him, but he held hope he was transmitting his message. Feeling the weariness from his mental and physical strain, he relented and collapsed deeply into the couch.

He sat motionless and slothful for two hours before urging himself to the kitchen. He reached into the cabinet for a generic can of IGA-brand ravioli and then into the refrigerator for his bag of iceberg lettuce. He sat at the kitchen table and ate in stillness. After he finished, he cleared the table and washed the small number of soiled dishes. He spent the remaining day pacing the house, pondering his new employment and Mirage.

He had a bizarre and intrusive thought toward Samantha. He remembered how, only a short time ago, he had yearned for her and had eagerly awaited her company. Nik compared the two women—the only aspect Samantha held over Mirage was that she was a tangible human. Besides that, he realized Samantha was truly inferior to Mirage. Even if Mirage was a dream he could not share a physical relationship with, the time spent with her was always golden.

He grinned at his own madness that he was falling deeper in love with something hardly human—if human at all. His brain was now burning the midnight oil, as far as being overworked, so he sat on the porch and watched the day pass into the night.

Nik shuffled through the next two days, as if he was on autopilot. His two cruel dispatchers overworked and overran him. Exhausted, he fell asleep still wearing his work clothes on Thursday night. When Friday morning arrived as quickly as Thursday night had ended, he rose from bed wearing the previous day's uniform and stumbled through the hallway and out toward his truck.

The drive from his home to Moline was clouded and challenging. Exhaustion rested heavy on him as he passed through the chain-link gate. He parked and found that he stammered, fighting the urge to hunker his body forward and rest against the steering wheel. His boots were like cinder blocks as he exited his truck, feeling as if he was a freshly animated corpse. The security officer offered him a warm morning greeting, and Nik merely regarded the officer with mild acknowledgment.

He walked to the dock office to rest, instead of reporting to the break room. He sat in a vacant chair, propping his elbow on the dispatch desk and supporting his head with his hand. He closed his eyes to gather strength, and a hand grasped his shoulder and shook him. He opened his eyes to see Matt's bullfrog face peering at him.

"You're not supposed to be in here. Go outside now, and wait for the others. You're in my way, and I need to start up."

Nik rose with exhaustion, slowly gathering his balance.

"Go on. Git, git, git, git, git!"

Nik faced Matt, saturated with hatred. "Fuck you, hypocrite. Like it's difficult for you to turn on a computer, you fat, lazy shit."

Matt's ugly, drooping eyes widened. "Whitman will hear about this immediately! Your ass is grass now, bud.

Nik flipped him off as he exited the room and spied Matt through the small window after the door closed behind him.

Matt sat down with thunderous ripples, frustrated and huffing from shortness of breath, and mouthed words of anger.

Nik watched the other warehouse associates file from the break room and gather in front of the dock office. Jim Whitman went from his personal office into the dock office, where Matt was throwing a temper tantrum and gesturing toward him. Nik smiled smugly at both men and waved at them teasingly.

Matt's eyes widened and reddened as he mouthed to Jim that Nik was taunting him.

Jim hung his head as he looked toward the floor, rubbing his temples before taking his place on the floor. As Jim exited the dock office, Bailey entered, and Matt was silently mouthing the events of his and Nik's verbal exchange. Bailey looked through the glass window and glared at Nik, mouthing curse words.

Jim addressed the crowd, bleakly informing the associates they must report for a mandatory Saturday shift. He did not offer an apology for the short notice, nor did he require the associates to participate in either of the pre-shift stretches or provide team-building words of encouragement.

Nik enjoyed seeing the revolting slob sweating in such a stressed manner. It was the only method in which he could see the soft-handed, pampered buffoon suffer.

The warehouse associates went in the direction of their workstations, and Jim trudged through the dock office into his personal office, slamming his door.

Nik felt a second surge of energy, as if he was a bloodied and bashed fighter in the fifteenth round of an intense grudge match. His posture straightened, and his head tilted to the heavens as he entered the dock office.

Bailey's and Matt's heads swiveled in his direction as they delivered sharp looks.

Nik approached Matt, who slouched in his office chair, brooding. "Do you have my keys and manifest?"

Matt mumbled something as Bailey glared deeper at Nik.

Nik breathed harder with agitation, wishing to vacate the dock office. "*Well, do you have my fucking keys and manifest?*"

Matt swiveled in his chair and forced Nik's keys and manifest at him, with his face reddening. "Here, take your shit, and *get out!*"

As Nik collected his items, Matt turned toward his computer once again.

"Go, shoo!" Matt raised his hand, gesturing for Nik to skedaddle. "Get out of he—"

Nik threw his items to the ground, grabbed Matt's hand and twisted it, bringing it sharply behind his back.

Stricken with fear, Bailey slid on her office chair away from Nik and Matt, uncontrollably passing gas with distress.

Nik raised Matt's contorted hand deeper and higher along his back as Matt yelped with pain. Nik's vision became rigid and narrowed at the creased fold of fat on the back of Matt's neck. His rage was nearly approaching the point of blackout.

Matt yelped louder with heightened fear before Nik released his grip. He was surprised as his rage dissipated and his temperament cooled.

Jim Whitman's door flung open as he entered the dock office. Jim stood in the doorway, staring at the occupants. His aged faced tightened and bulged. "Just what in the hell is going on here? What is all this yelling about?"

Matt grasped his hand, nurturing it from the straining pain, and regarded Jim with pitiful distress.

Bailey remained silent, reaching behind herself to ensure she did not soil her pants.

Nik retained his inflated aggressive stance, darting hatred at Jim Whitman. "I'll tell you what the fuck happened here! Fat Ass and Pig Face don't want to lift a finger and do their goddamn jobs! When they do assign me my manifest, they give me bullshit routes and peruse social media and play online games. That's only the tip of the iceberg, Whitman. You promoted these to inapt lazy sacks of shit to dispatch, and they do nothing. Look at their goddamn web history. Why don't you see what they really are doing?"

Jim boomed and ordered silence from Nik.

Ignoring the command, he told Jim that they were assigning asinine routing, multiple hospital stops, and overweight loads to him that should be dispersed amongst all the drivers.

Jim attempted to throw the lack of communication on Nik, and he blamed him for the negligence in not reporting the issue.

Nik stormed at Jim, nearly making contact with his face. "You listen to me, you fat sack of shit! Even if I would have mentioned the route issues or the weight issues, all your fat ass wants to do is hide behind your door and do what god knows what! You know what? I'm done! Fuck you, and fuck my notice! I quit. Get Fat Ass or Pig Face here to deliver your fucking product. But hear me now when I say this, you better check their browsing history, just so you can see how hard they really are working! The last week of my notice, I'm using my remaining vacation time. You better damn well pay me for it, because you owe it to me anyway!" Nik stepped backward from Jim Whitman, as he could see fear and surprise occupy his face.

Whitman marched toward Bailey's computer and demanded to view her browser history.

Bailey assured Jim that her use of the company computer was purely for work-related activities.

Jim balled his pudgy fist at his sides. "Move over, *now!*" Jim grasped the back of her office chair and slid her aside. He mashed the keys of her terminal, revealing the entirety of her web history—dating sites, social media, and shopping sites.

Bailey's already bulged eyes protruded farther, followed by black-tinted, spider-webbing tears from her mascara falling onto the desk.

Matt watched in terror as he scrambled in desperation to the keys of his terminal with sweaty fingers resembling miniature basted Thanksgiving turkeys.

Jim nudged Matt, sliding him to the opposite side. Jim exposed Matt's web history—gambling sites, YouTube, and adult video sites. Jim raised his already clutched fists to the sides of his head and shook his meaty paws in fury.

Matt cowered back in his chair, as he knew that Jim's wrath would be upon him.

"These terminals are to be used solely for dispatch and load tasking, and both of you have grossly misused them! What if there had a dispatch error or load error, or even worse, a driver emergency? You've been sitting here each workday dicking off! Bailey, get in my office *right now*!"

Bailey shot from her chair, cupping her mole-covered face in her hands, and charged blindly toward Jim's office, sobbing.

Matt sat paralyzed, enveloped with dire fear as he exchanged glances at Jim and watched Bailey disappear into the office.

Jim turned to Nik, relaxing the rage from his face and instructed him to wait in the dock office. "I'm going to have an in-depth discussion with Bailey, and Matt will be next." He glared at Matt with aggression.

Matt turned pale with his sweaty hands placed flat on the desk.

"I want you to wait here. We have much to discuss once I finish with both." Jim stormed into his office and slammed the door behind him, instantly erupting with shouting anger.

Nik grinned at Matt as the dispatcher sat shuttering with anxiety, hearing screaming and Bailey's braying sobs. "Looks like I got you by the raisins, don't I, fat ass? It's about fucking time that your pompous, self-righteous ass face what's coming to you."

Matt appeared as if his nervous state would best him and he would vomit.

Jim screamed at Bailey that one more incident and he would terminate her.

Nik and Matt knew that Matt's termination would be imminent due to the gravity of his misuse of the company computer viewing pornographic material. Nik smiled at Matt with wicked satisfaction, as he knew when Matt went home that evening, he would have to explain to his wife—his "best friend"—the how he'd lost his job. He knew that if Matt would not tell his large sea-mammal wife the truth, it would eventually be exposed, as no privacy existed at Moline Medical Warehousing. What happened inside the walls was shared outside the facility as well. This place was certainly not Vegas.

Jim's office door flung open, striking the wall and rattling it and nearly falling off the hinges.

Matt slowly uprighted his obese physique, like a condemned inmate on death row rising from prayer for salvation before the warden executed the sentence.

Bailey charged from Jim's office, cupping her hands as streaks of eyeliner bled through her fingers. As she passed Nik, she reeked of her overpowering perfume and abundant body odor. She sat behind her terminal, sobbing and panting.

Matt walked through the threshold of Jim's office with the speed of a decrepit man and closed the door behind him.

Nik watched Bailey sob and gasp for struggled breaths as he listened through the door.

Jim screamed at Matt with more ferocity than he did Bailey. He delivered the same points regarding driver emergency, load, and tasking errors, but his voiced pitched higher as he covered the subject of viewing pornographic material. Jim's voice became calm and controlled when he then terminated Matt and stated he would not have the option of demotion or be granted the opportunity for future rehire.

Matt exploded in a fit of sobs.

Nik danced a morbidly heckling victory dance as Bailey turned to him in horror. Nik smiled at her as her black-streaked streams increased.

Matt slowly opened Jim's office door and pulled the bill of his Ohio State Buckeyes cap over his eyes to shield himself from Nik's taunting glances. He pushed through the exit and walked the length of the warehouse a condemned man.

Nik watched Matt's defeated gait through the window until Jim addressed him. Nik faced Jim with unwavering resolve and intimidation. It was evident that Jim feared Nik and his departure from the company.

Jim snorted, clearing his throat and rubbing the sweat from his bulbous forehead. "Well, conditions should improve for you, Nik. I'm sure you heard through the door that Matt will no longer be with us."

"If you say so. Besides, I'll not be here any longer to see how things will be. I told you that I am done, and I'm using my week's worth of vacation as my last week of notice."

Jim darted his gaze toward the floor, pondering on an ideal response. "I know you have an interest in moving up and learning the operations aspect of logistics. It's now readily available for the taking."

Nik cocked his head toward his right shoulder. "Are you fucking daft? How convenient for you to offer me the job now that you're desperate. Do you really think I want to sit in this office all day, looking at Pig Snout and choking to death from the stench of her cheap, whore perfume? If you thought I'd accept the position, then you're fucked in the head."

Bailey regarded Nik with her wide mouth gaping from the crushing insults.

"That is just fine! Get out of here then! I'll grant you your severance pay and your vacation, but don't you dare think you'll be classified as a rehire. Get out of here now, and don't you ever come back."

Nik reached for the exit door and turned back as he stepped out. "Don't you worry about that, you saggy-assed fuck. I have no intention of ever coming back to this cesspool." Nik walked through the door knowing with absolute satisfaction that not only was he making his leave of the facility permanently, but he had shaken the place up.

His body felt light and liberated as he traversed the warehouse, feeling its binding grasp on him weaken and knowing he had shaken up the place. He left through the employee entrance and approached the security station. He rapped on the tempered glass.

The security officer pressed the intercom button and asked if he could help Nik.

Nik slid his security badge through the slot under the glass and stated that he was no longer with the company.

The security officer acknowledged Nik and thanked him for the notice.

Nik informed the guard that he would be back the following Monday to return his uniforms.

The guard acknowledged Nik again and wished him luck.

Nik looked at the guard puzzled, for he'd never engaged in prior conversations or exchanges with the man. Regardless, he expressed gratitude and strolled to his truck.

Agitated shouting came from the associate lot. He saw Matt sitting in his midnight-blue Chevy Impala, talking on his cell to his wife on speaker phone as her shrilling shrieks drifted from the car. "What the hell will we do now? You know my salary as a receptionist alone will not support both of us. With what you've done, I doubt they'll let you claim unemployment. You promised me that you would stop visiting those pages. It's bad enough you haven't stopped but to do it at work! What is wrong with you?"

Matt sat panting from the scorching heat while he endured his wife's words. "I'm sorry, Tootsie. I thought I had it beat. I just couldn't help myself. I tried. I'm weak, and I need help." He paused, his large lower jaw quivering as he waited for her response.

"Well, you'll just have to beat it alone, because I won't be here when you get home."

Matt pleaded to Tootsie as she ended the call. He placed his phone in the passenger seat and rested his head against the steering wheel.

Nik grinned with deviance and entered his truck. He rammed the gear shift into Reverse, sped backward and straightened the wheel to guide him toward the exit. While pulling through the parking lot, he stopped next to Matt's Impala. Nik blasted his horn.

Matt shot his head upward.

Nik waved at him, smiling as he wiggled his fingers.

Matt watched Nik as he sped through the parking lot, a defeated man.

Nik drove with accomplished ease as he cleared the facility parking lot, heading toward town. Years of malcontent and mistreatment were finally greeted with retribution. Going against his better judgment, he decided to relish the moment with a long country drive then a victory sub from Pisanello's Pizza. He drove around town and the rural country for a few hours before he called the pizza shop.

Savannah answered, and Nik ordered the sub, telling her that he would be in directly to pick it up. He pulled in front of Pisanello's and placed his truck in Park. Glowing from realizing he had a week's worth of vacation before beginning his new job—plus, with his years of service, Moline owed him a severance package—he entered Pisanello's.

"You seem to really like these Italian subs, Nik," Savannah teased.

"Can't get enough of them! And I have something to celebrate."

Savannah smiled and gave him a look of curiosity. "Oh yeah? What's going on?"

Nik looked at the countertop and reached into his wallet to retrieve his money, searching for a diversion. "Oh, did I tell you that I talked with Kenny? After our discussion a little while ago, I realized he didn't mean any harm or ill will toward me."

Savannah collected his money. "Yeah, Kenny texted me and told me all about it. It really was what he needed to hear." She stepped from behind the counter and joined Nik on the opposite side. "That reminds me. I have to tell you something, and it's important you keep it to yourself. If you can't do that, then please do it for Kenny."

Nik nodded.

"A part of me feels that what I'm about to say may be bad news for you, but the other part may prove to be good news. Lapis Lazuli is carrying on without you, but you already knew that. Balmer and his cousin, Channing Dodds, joined the band, and there is already friction. Kenny was never keen on Balmer, and, to add fuel to the fire, Channing tried to put the moves on me when I delivered a pizza to Alex's place. I haven't been dating Kenny that long, but I've never seen him that pissed off before. Plus, those two assholes are trying to take their places as bandleaders. Kenny told me you said this to him while you were fighting, but you're right about what you said. It *is* a sinking ship, and it's sinking fast. Here, look at this. You might get a laugh at the very least." Savannah retrieved a piece of folded paper from the back pocket of her frayed dark blue short shorts and placed it in Nik's hand.

He unfolded the flier and saw a dodgy picture of his former bandmates wearing Hot Topic-esque clothes. He felt Kenny appeared natural, but Alex and Andy looked ridiculous in their new attire; it was evident that Balmer and Channing were imposing the central focus. Balmer and Channing were both equally unkempt in the photo, and Channing, standing a head shorter than the rest of the band, appeared dirtier with his hair matted and caked with locks of filth.

The show was the following Friday at the Cabana Bay Bar in Sandousten at 9:00 p.m. Nik was beside himself with silent satisfaction. The flier's band photo solidified that Balmer and Channing would hijack and ruin what was once a talented collection of musicians. Nik folded the flier and returned it to Savannah.

She returned to the opposite side of the counter and finished making Nik's sub. She handed it to him and wished him a good day.

He smiled as he grabbed his sub. "Tell you what, Savannah. Go ahead and tell Kenny when this falls apart, I'll gladly reinstate him as my drummer. Everyone else can go fuck themselves, but Kenny will be welcomed with open arms, if that day arrives."

Savannah smiled at Nik before saying goodbye.

Nik left the pizza parlor with his sub and placed it in the passenger seat as he entered his truck. Morbid inquisitiveness entered his mind—how would the band sound, what would be on their setlist, and if they would tank completely with a disappointed crowd.

He knew Samantha and her husband lived in Sandousten and wondered if they'd heard that his old band was playing at a local venue and if they would attend to find him. Nik's curiosity was too powerful to care about Samantha and Ross. He had to make an appearance just to see what the remaining members of his old band, along with their new comrades, would do.

He arrived at his house and parked his truck in the driveway. He grabbed his sub and headed for the kitchen. He slowly ate his sub, savoring the taste with each bite.

He stood up, noticing some mayonnaise and Italian dressing had dropped onto his uniform shirt. Normally, he would have raced for the faucet, removed the shirt and dabbed cold water and a few drops of dish soap on the stain. However, he reveled that this was unnecessary, as he was not returning to Moline.

He threw away his sub wrapper in the waste bin, stripped from his uniform and kicked his boots underneath the kitchen table. He placed his keys, wallet, and phone on the kitchen table and retrieved a black garbage bag from underneath the sink. After tossing his work uniform crumpled inside, he marched down the hallway into his bedroom, collected his folded uniforms and threw them into the garbage bag as one unorganized clump. He changed into a pair of clean workout clothes and placed the trash bag by the front door.

He engaged in an intense workout regimen, concentrating on his core and upper-body strength. He finished the high-intensity workout in an hour's time. He cooled down with a brisk thirty-minute walk through town. He passed the IGA and bought a six-pack of Busch Light and indulged with some cool, well-earned beers.

He reached home and placed the cold beers into the refrigerator. Feeling gritty from the summer heat and the physical activity, he wanted to take shower. As the refreshing water rained on his body, he thought selfish thoughts on how the scope of the day had been all for him—he'd fought a grand fight with his abhorrent former coworkers, he'd stood his ground with Jim Whitman, and it was inevitable his former band would fail.

He exited the shower and dried himself. He returned to his living room and surveyed his house. Large amounts of accomplishments resonated with what he had done with his life. He was proud he had pulled himself from the crumbling brink of suicidal depression and left the town that had inflicted a large amount of emotional distress. He also felt triumph with his physical condition and his musical talents. He stood bountiful in his living room, reeling that his life had changed from an overweight frumpy bag of depression to a person of validation.

Nik's thoughts darkened as he remembered how he had taunted Matt during his coworker's time of failure. His urge to hit Matt would have been pure satisfaction, but he was glad he had suppressed the rage to allow the events unfold organically. If he would have struck him, he might have wound up in the county jail on battery charges. Destroying Matt's pride and career proved more satisfying.

No longer wishing to focus on Matt or any other previous associates, he dwelled on pleasant thoughts. He wished he had the company of someone special to indulge in this moment. His minded shifted to Mirage and her beauty and the warning she had beseeched on him during his trance state. Did he control himself enough? Did he avoid the act she had warned him against committing? Who knows? Her methods and randomness of contact were so inconsistent. Nik remembered other women he'd known or had some involvement with and thought they telegraphed their motivations in some manner. With Mirage, it was blindsiding and nearly shocking. Nothing with her was simple clockwork; it was surprising and extraordinary. Still, of all the women he knew, she was the one he wanted with him.

Nik tired of spending time in his mind and decided the cold beer would not drink itself. He strode to his refrigerator and retrieved the beer. He stepped onto the porch and drank the entire six-pack, as if he was consuming water. When finished, he beheld the horizon as he usually did and watched the light vacate from the sky. Feeling tired and drunk, retired to gain an early rise on tomorrow.

Chapter
Nine

While sleeping, he did not dream, nor did he visit the endless corridor; his body spun, and his breathing was shallow. He woke at 2:11 a.m. and guzzled two glasses of water from the kitchen. He knew if he was hydrated, he would not be hung over. He walked with improved coordination toward his bedroom and planted himself face first onto his bed, feeling his head pop before returning to a dreamless sleep.

At 7:40 a.m., groggy from a night of drinking, he heard faint plinking sounds from his adjacent music room. His eyes felt heavy and blinked slowly, like an infant waking from a nap, as he gained momentum to rise. His ears felt submerged in fluid, muffling all sound. He rolled to his back, gazing to the ceiling. The plinking gained clarity as he recognized it was his upright piano.

He raised his head to try to hear the sound better—someone or something was playing "Clair de Lune" on his piano. He bolted upright, wishing he had not. His head felt ten times the normal size. He shambled toward his music room, clinging onto the doorway, panting and staring at his piano.

Mirage sat on the duet bench, wearing a white sundress. Her hair changed from dark blonde to light brown, full with body, resting against her mid back. Her skin was sun-kissed with a healthy tan, and her back and arms were toned with sculpted definition. She spoke with her back turned to Nik. "I've always thought this piece was romantic, that D-flat major was a passionate-sounding key signature." She turned to Nik with warmth and affection, stood from the bench and slid it under the piano.

Nik admired her body—the perfect structure of her face, her sculpted shoulders, the roundness and symmetry of her breasts, and her tan, silky defined legs.

She enjoyed Nik gawking at her and expressed her satisfaction by flaring her eyes at him. As he regarded her with pure happiness, she also appeared more human.

Despite his head swimming with a mild headache and wooziness, he wanted to control the conversation and divert her from noticing him ogling her. "It's not suprising you mentioned that about D-flat major. It's almost as if you knew I've said that before. Not that I'm complaining, but I'm, surprised to see you here. Are you really here, or is this some illusion or psychological trip?"

She delicately grabbed his right wrist and pulled her toward him, handling him with care, as she knew he was hung over. She led him to the left side of his piano, pulled the duet bench from underneath and guided him to a seated position. "Why don't you play something for me? You'll feel better if you do."

"Look, I don't feel like playing a damn thing. I don't feel well, and I want some answers."

She reached from behind, grazing the top of his hands and moving them slowly to the top of his shoulder blades. "Why don't you play 'Time' by Alan Parsons? You used to play that entirely from muscle memory."

Nik protested through his pain and agitation. "I'm hung over. I don't feel like playing music right now. I'm growing tired of this cryptic shit and your random messages. I need to know a few important things right now. Are you real? Can you read my mind? What are you? And why do you keep disappearing on me? This whole crazy thing is driving me to the point of insanity!" Nik shook her fingertips from his shoulder blades.

Mirage remained unshaken and instructed him to play the song.

Nik sighed with aggravation. As he reached the chorus, Mirage's fingertips touched his temples. At the song's conclusion, ran her tongue along his left ear's outer rim. He arched his back with shock and arousal. His head cleared, and his headache vanished. He stood from the piano, slid the duet bench underneath and faced her.

She beheld him with longing and compassion. "I am real, and yes, I could read your mind. I no longer can, though, as I have now become a physical being. I was only reciting thoughts I had already collected. Each time I had touched you, I was establishing a link and physical manifestation of my presences. The process takes time, and I was growing and honing my ability to dwell with you. I cannot tell you what I truly am now; it is still beyond the scope of your understanding, and the reveal may cause you stifling fear. There's an imperative reason for our encounter, and it is intentional we've established contact. To answer your last question, no, I won't disappear anymore. You have earned my presence to remain with you."

"I understand that patience is a virtue—hell, that's a golden rule they teach us from a young age—but what did I do or not do to earn your company?"

Mirage's face tightened, and she exhibited an air of superiority. "You maintained control over the primitive impulses of your human brain. While you did act on your primal rage in a minimal manner, you maintained better judgment and did not complete the act."

"Matt …"

"Correct. While I was monitoring you, I felt your rage culminate as the urge to strike him approached a dangerously imminent point. If you had struck him, the energy of your strikes would have severed his spine, leaving him a quadriplegic. The lawmen would have incarcerated you for aggravated assault."

Nik stepped back from Mirage, fearful of what could have been a potential life-ruining event for both Matt and him. "I remember, during the dream state when you had mentioned for me to control my rage, you also said my raw and primitive emotions had led me here years ago. What did you mean? I don't remember being in that floating corridor at any other time."

Mirage relaxed her face into a look of compassion. "There is no feasible way you could handle the origin of our first encounter in that place nor would you remember it. It is true your first encounter was under grim circumstances. That will be revealed at the appropriate time. The origin of your first encounter was proportionate to a human being born. While it's true some humans can remember as far back as toddlerhood, no human has the capacity to remember their own birth. Your first encounter in the realm would be a similar experience."

"That's fine, as long as you'll explain at some point, but what did you mean about my *recent act*, when we were communicating in the corridor? What did I do to cause our meeting, and what was my failing that you mentioned?"

Mirage resembled a scorned woman. "If you must know, it was your encounter with that deplorable Samantha woman. Unfortunately, you were meant to have that sordid, careless encounter with her, but the night you visited your parents, you were not supposed to leave town. The intended plan was for you to remain at your house instead. That is why I contacted you during your first cognitive dream state and why I appeared to you while driving home. If you just would've stayed home, I would not have had to manifest myself."

"I know you don't have the grasp of human behavior, but we're prone to mistakes. How the hell was I supposed to know whether I was supposed to do something or be somewhere I did not know about? The way you communicated that to me was cryptic. I'm doing my best, and you told me recently that I had controlled my rage, so I at least did something right."

"You're right. I'm sorry, and I've judged you unfairly. It was not of my character, and I did not mean to hurt you, especially since I'm a guest in your home and you've shown me kindness. I feel obligated to make it up to you with something you'd appreciate."

She smiled seductively, grabbed his wrist and wrenched him from the music room. She led him across the hallway into the bathroom. They stood in front of each other, locking gazes. She reached for his hands and gazed at him with vowing concentration. She yanked down his pants then lifted the bottom of his shirt. She undressed in front of him, exposing her body. Her body was as flawless as he had expected.

Aroused, he beheld her from top to bottom. She looked superior to any woman he'd had seen nude; the airbrushed beauties he had pined for in adult magazines paled in comparison.

He was unsure of where this was going, but regardless of what may happen, he was sure no other man had ever had the fortune to see what he saw.

She tugged his wrist, coaxing him into the shower, then turned on the water. It fell and beaded on her perfect form, seeming to purposefully adhere to her shapeliness and accentuate her beauty. She leaned back her head, allowing the water to run through her hair while she arched her back, pushing her breasts toward him.

Nik felt a stirring in his penis and was instantly engorged. He looked at his member, feeling its throb matching the beat of his heart. Urges compelled his mind as he watched the water fall on her. He wanted nothing more than to grab her, spin her around, press her to the opposite side of the shower and penetrate her. Through the falling water, he noticed he was excreting a generous amount of clear pre-ejaculate. He clenched his fist then spread his fingers as wide as nets and approached Mirage.

She straightened her head and grabbed his hands, feeling his approach. She forced his hands backward, and he nearly slipped. "I know what you were about to do, and your urges must feel overpowering, but that is something forbidden we must never partake in."

Nik could only murmur sounds in response.

"I know that is hard for you, both figuratively and literally, but we cannot engage in that act." She smiled at him with pride, knowing he wanted her to the point of needing her. "I did say you had controlled your primitive emotions in respect to your rage, so I think I can allow you the release. I'd be honored and blessed if I could watch you indulge yourself."

Nik could not believe what he'd heard. He felt privileged just to have that involvement.

She positioned herself to deliberately draw attention to her body.

Nik grabbed his member, pulling with vigor as his breathing heightened. Speed and excitement increased as her movements elevated in sensuality, until his load expanded through his shaft. Climaxing, he felt the compelling urge to lunge toward Mirage and kiss her.

She watched him ejaculate a generous amount and sidestepped as he approached for a kiss.

Nik looked at her, winded and panting—his knees weakening and buckling. He slumped to the shower floor.

She reached under his armpits and guided him upright.

He looked at her with bewilderment as he caught his breath. "What's the matter?" He panted. "All I wanted to do was kiss you. I respected your wishes of no sex, but a kiss during an orgasm would have been nice."

Mirage looked at him embarrassed. "I thought you were going to make contact with me while you were climaxing. I cannot have contact with your seed."

"Babe, we are in the shower, and I shot upward. I don't think it would have gotten anywhere near your danger zone."

Mirage regarded him with embarrassment while his breathing resumed normal pace. "I'm sorry. I just panicked. We can never go completely the way you desire."

Nik shook his head, feeling the aftereffects of his strong orgasm.

Mirage blushed. "Wait a minute. Did you just call me *babe*?"

"Yes, I guess I did. I'd be lying if I said I didn't know where it had come from, but the truth is I do know."

Mirage turned to shut off the water.

Nik bit his bottom lip as she bent over to turn the knobs and the residual water glistened on her backside. *My god, I have never seen a finer looking ass in all my life. I've seen some nice asses in my time, but, my god, if this isn't the nicest one.*

She stepped from the shower and toweled her wet body. She handed her towel to him, and he dried off, never taking his gaze off of her. "I want to return to what you said to me earlier regarding you calling me babe. Where did it come from, Nik? I think I know, but I want to hear you say it."

"I called you that because it had felt right, and I know it may be coming from a place too soon, but I can see myself falling in love with you. I know the circumstances we share are unusual, but, when you were gone, all I could think about was you and how much I needed you. I'd be lying if I didn't tell you that I wear my heart on my sleeve and usually jump the gun developing feelings for people, but I have never been that quick with calling someone that, and you are not a normal person. I don't even know if you *are* a person. I'm sorry if I made you feel rushed or uncomfortable, but I could not help the urge."

Mirage gestured to Nik to follow her to the bedroom. Once they stood at the foot of his bed, naked, she sat him down and looked deeply into his eyes as her eyes glossed. Nik had seen numerous people's eyes gloss over with tears during his life, but he'd never seen as bright and brilliant of a shine. They shimmered, as if blessed by sunlight and moonglow.

She reached for his right hand and placed it on her fluttering chest as her heartbeat throbbed faster than a human's. She kissed his fingertips and redirected her attention toward his eyes. "What you just told me was the most beautiful human emotional expression I have ever heard. Nothing was primitive about your declaration. I know you find me to be the most beautiful being, but, at this moment, your beauty far exceeds mine."

Nik swallowed hard. A part of him regretted not shedding a tear.

Mirage leaned onto her side on the bed and patted the mattress, inviting Nik to lay down.

Nik kept looking at her as he rested his head on his pillow. He broke from his gaze and checked the alarm clock—8:45 p.m. He faced Mirage, yawning.

She watched him drift and fight sleep as she grazed his cheek. "If you'd like to lay naked with me and get some more sleep, that would be fine. I only request that you suppress your sexual urges. If you must relieve yourself again, I'll aide you with visual stimulation, but it is imperative that you do not penetrate me."

Nik nodded. He only wanted her touch and her presence. Lying next to her in his bed was an esteeming pleasure. Nik surrendered to sleep as he closed his eyes, with Mirage doing the same, both entering the sleep state unified.

Nik woke as the late-morning sun peeked through his bedroom window. He was reluctant to open his eyes and check the time, as he had not wanted to sleep the morning away. Mirage had promised she would not disappear, but he still felt it could have all been part of his dream state. He knew he could not remain in bed awake with his eyes closed any longer. Despite reality or fantasy, he would have to rise.

He slowly opened his eyes and was blessed that Mirage still lay sleeping tranquilly next to him. The moment felt as if every Christmas, birthday, wondrous surprise, and best day had been compressed into one. He did not want to disturb her with his joy. He just looked at her, falling in love with her beauty all over again.

He stealthily planted his feet on the floor and eased to a standing position. He padded to the bathroom to gather his clothes and her white sundress.

Just as he entered the bathroom, Mirage sprang up, bare-breasted. "Nikolas Vanelli how dare you leave me here without waking me. I might have had the same fear and thought I had only dreamt you were lying beside me." She brought her fingertips to her mouth, giggling.

Nik thought the action was cute but noticed something else; it pressed her breasts firmly together, tightening her cleavage. Nik swallowed, blowing tension as he did not want to become sexually excited. He feared she would feel Nik viewed her solely as a sexual object. "Well, like you do to me, I'm glad I can make you think I can disappear and leave you wanting more."

Mirage reached for Nik, wishing for him to help her from bed.

Nik grabbed both her hands and helped her stand.

She tilted her head. "You're right. I was quite concerned when you were not next to me. I did not like it. I only missed you for a moment, but I now know what you endured, wondering if I was reality or a dream. I never meant to put you through that. I just had to gather my strength and ability to walk in this plane. I know you have so many questions, and I truly want to answer them, but know the overwhelming capacity could have serious repercussions."

"The important thing is you're here with me now. I have absolute faith that all my questions will be answered at the appropriate time. For right, now let's enjoy being together."

Her expression was enough for Nik; it expressed he had said all the right things.

"Well, sleepyhead, we missed a good part of the morning, so the day is pretty well shot, but what would you like to do? I'm open for suggestions."

Mirage smiled. "You're right. We did get a late start to the day, and I think spending time with you around the house would be ideal for me."

He ushered her toward the bathroom to collect their clothes.

Mirage allowed him to watch her get dressed. She enjoyed the attention he dedicated to her body. Once they were both dressed, they walked down the hallway and sat down on the living room couch, pressing their bodies against each other.

Mirage curled herself into Nik's side, reaching her arm around him and resting her head against his chest. Then she reached forward and picked up a pill bottle and Brian Paone's *Yours Truly, 2095* from the coffee table and brought both items closer to her eyes. She recited the name of the prescription, the milligrams, and the dosage.

Nik snatched the bottle and returned it to the coffee table, embarrassed.

She looked at him with hurtful eyes. She brought the book toward her, clutching it deeply into her chest as a shield.

Nik knew he had been harsh with her, but he was embarrassed that his nerves would best him at times as he looked at her curled position. "That book you're holding is actually my favorite book. I stumbled upon the author and the book quite by accident, and I have read it numerous times. I think you might enjoy it. It has a large amount of bizarre circumstances and romance that you could lose yourself in."

Mirage brought the book from her chest and studied the front cover.

Nik told her the book was fiction as he pulled his cellphone from his pocket to check for messages or notifications—none—but the time read, *11:55*. The local news at noon would start in five minutes, and he turned on the television to show Mirage the current state of events.

She startled as she was not expecting the screen to come to life.

Nik tuned to Channel 10—Sandousten's Local News on the Bay—for a breaking story of an office shooting in Sandousten earlier today, as a terminated, disgruntled worker shot fifteen former coworkers. The news broadcast proceeded with a story of a fatal collision involving a tractor trailer blowing through the red lights of a school bus, distracted from texting and driving, striking a kindergartener and a first grader. The weather broadcast began, and the meteorologist predicted that the seven-day forecast was expected to be pleasant, with warm temperatures and only a few days of light overcast.

The final news story was the water advisories in Sandousten. It was advised that the citizens were not to bath, drink, or use the water for cooking, as a result of toxic algae blooms poisoning the water supply. A field reporter stood in front of the Sandousten Wal-Mart, interviewing customers stockpiling bottled water. The reporter interviewed a morbidly obese woman with greasy, matted hair and a ring of embedded filth around her neck sitting in a supermarket scooter. She wore a stained white t-shirt with Garfield on the front stating how much he hated Mondays. The field reporter asked her about her thoughts on the water advisory and how it affected her family. She informed him that she had already purchased adequate amounts of water for her four children, and the water in her basket was for sale, and she intended to sell them for ten dollars each. The field reporter, visibly stunned, asked her how she could do such a thing during a time of emergency. Unfazed, she responded simply saying because she could.

"It's good to see our tax dollars are paying for this goddamn welfare rat to bilk the system further," Nik barked.

Mirage contorted her face in disgust and used the remote to turn off the television off. She slammed the remote onto the coffee table and glared at Nik. "Human beings truly are shit."

Nik leaned back with shock, both with her decisive judgment and her profanity. Nik fought the urge to laugh but failed.

"I'm mortified you can laugh at your world's current state."

Nik composed himself. "I can't argue with what you just saw and said, and I am not laughing at your opinion. It's just funny how your language has evolved into using swear words, and, quite frankly, your ability to use the words correctly."

Mirage sank into the couch.

"You're quite right. Most people are naturally shit. We're shitty to ourselves and to each other. I know this doesn't offer you much comfort, but Sandousten is a larger city than Pemkey. With more people, you find more shit. However, shitty people are everywhere. A good example would be my former friends betraying me and firing me from the band. That is not to the same degree as what you saw on the news, but it's still an example of people being shitty to others. I know it may be hard for you to understand, but, while the news is supposed to deliver accuracy, they also sensationalize stories to attract more viewers. Human beings are imperfect and opportunistic—a sin all people at one time or another are guilty of. It's just some people don't engage in acts as severe as the people on the television. You just have to use good judgment, Mirage, and realize who are normal shits and who are worse shits."

Still feeling that Mirage needed to cool her foul mood, Nik decided to occupy her mind with splendor. Pemkey was a beautiful town, and the occupants seemed friendly enough—a healthy walk and a tour of the town might return her to a state of joy.

He patted her twice on the leg and gained her attention. "I think you could use a walk and take in the sights of the town. When I'm feeling frustrated, I find a walk can burn off the negative emotions. I also think it would do us both some good to do some activities as a couple." Unsure of her reaction to his label of them, Nik regretted his words instantly.

Mirage's eyes brightened with glee. Mirage "I would love to walk around town and see where you call home. Besides, the only aspect that brought any joy from that broadcast was that the weather will be ideal."

Nik sat up from the couch, realizing he was barefoot and unsure where he had placed his shoes. He noticed Mirage did not have any footwear either. He could not have her walk around town barefoot, and he did not want her levitating.

"Do you know where I put my sneakers?"

She looked at him, fighting to conceal a smile. "They were on your side of the bed."

He strolled down the hallway and entered the bedroom toward his side of the bed. He located his sneakers, and they appeared brand new—both in appearance and smell. He looked inside the shoes and saw a pair of pure white new socks. He slid them on and pondered how to solve the issue Mirage's lack of footwear.

Entering the living room, he saw Mirage's feet elevated on the coffee table as she acted casual. "Are you ready to go for that walk now?"

She raised herself lightly and placed his hands behind her back, drawing him close.

He could have stood holding her in that position for hours. He noticed her smell, one of absolute nirvana to his senses, of natural blooming flowers, fresh as if the sun had kissed it. As she swayed, stimulating her aroma more, he thought a cosmetic company would pay top dollar to acquire this scent and replicate it.

Nik let go, and they stepped back from each other. He wondered if he brought her into public, if other people would acknowledge her unavoidable presence. He focused on her beauty, her scent, and her overall display. He shuttered as he thought of other men looking at her with covetous eyes. His mind darkened, preparing for that impending moment. He masked the line of thinking. She had assured him that she was no longer reading his mind, but he feared that if that was not the truth, she would read something dark and selfish. He grabbed her hand, affirming with a gentle grip, and led her out the front door.

They stood on the porch, scanning the neighborhood and watching the sunny day. The clarity of the sun enriched the hues of all the natural colors. Nik looked at Mirage as she beheld the horizon. Her face was innocent with childlike joy. Nik led her off the porch for their walk. They followed Nik's usual route, hand in hand, around the village perimeter.

"I'd like to see the central part of town. I'm interested in seeing the park."

He knew it was inevitable she would be curious about the park. Despite feeling reserve and cautious jealousy, he had to experiment and see how she would act in a populated environment. Nik led her to the park, and they traversed the busy courtyard.

Mirage was jubilant as other couples walked hand in hand. She greeted each of them as they crossed paths, beaming energetic brightness. Some couples acknowledged her cheeriness, others regarded her as if she was stark-raving crazy.

They passed the basketball court while four men played a two-on-two basketball game. The men paused to gawk at Mirage. Mirage paid the men no attention, turning to Nik to silently assure him. After they cleared the basketball court, they arrived at the fountain in the center of the park.

Mirage ran, grasping Nik's hand and charging to the fountain. She removed her sandals and tromped around, splashing and playing.

Nik looked away from her to shield his embarrassment. He bit his bottom lip and waved in a hurried motion for her to get out.

She was disobedient, not minding his request, before she noticed Nik's embarrassment had grown to firm commands. She raised her legs over the ledge and stomped on the ground, one foot after the other.

"That fountain is decorative! It's not for people."

"I'm sorry if I displeased you. I could not help myself. It looked like so much fun."

Nik accepted her apology and realized she was not wearing panties or a bra under her white sundress. He panicked, hoping no one would notice her now-transparent clothes. He sat her on the fountain ledge. She turned to splash in the water as he put on her sandals. He helped her to her feet and led her through the courtyard and away from heavily populated area, shielding her from exposing her body.

They arrived at the park's entrance, and Mirage was completely dry.

He was relieved her body was no longer exposed and decided to introduce her to Savannah, to see how she would fare with others. Savannah was relaxed, open minded, and accepting toward different people—the perfect verbal sparring partner.

Nik checked the traffic, and they raced across the street. As they entered the pizza parlor, Savannah greeted Nik then directed a look of intrigue at Mirage.

Mirage smiled at Savannah then turned toward the arcade cabinets. She walked past each machines, scanning the title screens and brief game demos.

Nik touched her lightly on the shoulder.

"What are these video screens? They do not look like the images on the television."

"Videogames."

"Games?"

"You put coins in them and the control the images on the screen to complete a specific goal, like rescuing a princess or getting to the finish line first or letting the ghosts eat you."

"Or getting hit by that silly monkey's barrels!" She pointed and chuckled.

"Or that too …"

"Well, as fun as they might be to you, I think they're a poor interpretation of reality. I doubt anyone is as perfect-looking as this woman warrior, sparring with the … whatever that is supposed to be."

"You are," he mumbled.

She faced him. "What did you say?"

"Umm … hey, I want you to meet someone!" Nik waved over Samantha.

Savannah introduced herself, extending her hand to Mirage, and Mirage accepted it in a gentle handshake.

Nik nudged Mirage in her ribs for her to engage further.

"My name is Mirage, and I am in a relationship with Nik. We are a couple, and I enjoy spending time with him.

Savannah raised an eyebrow and grinned. "Wow. Mirage. What an interesting name. Your parents must be hippies. I had a friend once, years ago, and her parents named her Moonbeam."

Mirage tapped a finger to her lips. "Yes. Hippies. You could say my parents were hippies."

Nik exhaled in relief that she had formulated an appropriate response.

"So, how did you meet Nik? I didn't realize he was exclusive with anyone now. Are you guys getting serious?"

Mirage paused and tapped her lip again. "We met when he assisted me on the roadside. I was having trouble with my … *vehicle*." She smiled as she emphasized the word.

Nik searched the pizza parlor for any excuse to end the conversation. "Is that bulletin board new?" He tugged Mirage's wrist to signal that she had started to become awkward and to stop talking.

"Kenny helped me hang it. He'd love to see you."

Nik nodded without making eye contact with Savannah. He studied the bulletin board already decorated with fliers— an ad for lawnmowing services, babysitting services, used car parts—then he noticed a fresh flier for the upcoming Lapis Lazuli show placed square in the center, overshadowing all the other ads.

"Kenny put that up earlier today, much to the desire of the *new* bandmembers. I swear they're already treating my man like shit. If you do start another project, please take him under your wing. Those other guys, Balmer and Channing, walk all over the others, and they target Kenny the most."

Nik studied the flier. "I already told you that if or when the day comes, I know where to find a drummer."

Savannah lowered her head and retreated to her side of the counter.

Glaring at the flier, he knew the band had only recently fired him, and they were rushing to perform. Lapis Lazuli had been his brainchild, not these fly-by-night remnants. Sure, it was Alex's facility they used for practices, but they were using Nik's band name and running it through the mud. They disregarded the band's original format, allowing a rival and his scummy cousin to infiltrate with a hostile coup. His former bandmates had referred to him as overly structured and ridged. He might have attempted to instill theory and structure in the band, but he had not run it like a sweat shop or for his own singular glory. The band photo alone illustrated this, as the remaining bandmembers appeared to be background fodder. Nik decided to attend the show to watch what he had built perish.

"Lapis Lazuli was once yours," Mirage said, standing beside him and scrutinizing the flier. "You built them up and sculpted them, now they're a joke. I want to attend the show and watch them fail too."

Nik scoffed and look away from the flier.

Mirage placed a hand over on his forearm. "I'd like to go home."

They approached the front door, and Savannah waved at them. "Have a good day, you two. Congratulations, Nik. You got yourself a real pretty one." She shot a double thumbs up to Nik.

Mirage smiled at Savannah, gleefully feeling complimented.

They remained silent as they walked home. Arriving at the front porch, she marched up the stairs, waiting to be let in with impatience. He unlocked the door, and she strode into the kitchen, pulled out the kitchen chairs and demanded he sit.

He complied, unsure why her mood had soured.

She sat across from him. "I want to start by saying I'm proud of you for controlling your emotions, but I'm concerned about your other emotional responses. You insulted your coworker and grabbed and twisted his arm. Also, you quit your job to take another job you are not one-hundred percent sure of. I'm also fearful of your lust toward me. I know you're human, but you nearly made contact with me earlier with your seed. You know that is forbidden."

He rose in a flash, nearly flinging the chair to the ground. "Didn't we already have a conversation similar to this earlier? I may not be a perfect person, but I maintained control of the situation. I did not strike him. I did accept a new position on a whim, but it's a step up from what I was currently doing. I needed a change."

Nik swallowed hard and thought about his former coworkers' complaints about their spouses or live-in girlfriends; they would refer to them as *ball busting bitches*. His former relationships had been brief and broken. During his days with the band, he would partake in one-night stands, trying to rid the woman as soon as possible, with no meaningful length of time spent between him and other women.

Still frustrated from Mirage's berating, he felt an odd sensation—a thought of clarity that cemented his mind. Mirage was not only the most beautiful woman he'd encountered, but she was the longest-staying female guest.

He reached for her hands, but she did not reciprocate. She folded her hands across her chest, looking to the sliding door.

He pulled her to her feet, locking his gaze with her angry eyes. She panned from the sliding door to the cabinets. He raised his hand to her cheek, and she diverted her head. He attempted again and was successful with grazing her cheek.

"Look, babe. I didn't mean to scare you and get angry. I'm not a perfect person, and I think, as you're evolving, you're understanding that as well. You're right. I could have handled situations better, and I should not have been guided by a selfish whim. I can't be perfect, but I'll be my best for you as long as I can."

Mirage thrust her head backward as Nik embraced her and burst into tears.

"Don't cry, my love, and don't leave. I just couldn't bear it."

Mirage examined the hurt in his eyes then lunged toward him and kissed him.

Nik felt her tears streak down her face onto his. She was skillful with a natural talent for kissing. He had never experienced an open-mouth kiss as satisfying. Her tongue swirls and her mouth movements excited and enticed him with each movement. With growing momentum, he was engorged, pressing his aroused body against hers with soft thrust.

She felt his excitement pressed against and finished the kiss, gently pressing him away. To his surprise, she ogled him with hungry eyes. "I think a shower session would be ideal."

Nik raced from the kitchen and down the hallway charged with unwavering arousal. He removed his clothes, twisted the shower faucet in a flash and stood with painstaking anticipation, waiting her arrival.

She moved with grand gestures, drawing attention to her body, then pressed her full breast against him. She kissed him deeply, enticing his member to throb. She looked at him with dire eyes as she kneeled on the shower floor, sandwiching his upright member between her breasts. "Thrust between me. But please turn it away when you're close to orgasming."

Nik jackhammered with deep lunges through the wet lubrication from water and her perspiration between her tight cleavage. He increased his speed as his excitement heightened. His movements became a driving machine as she pressed tighter. He felt his fluid crawl up, and he turned to finish the act.

She grazed his back with her fingertips and kissed the back of his neck.

He reached for the soap and cleaned his still-erect member. He faced Mirage, but she had already left the shower to towel off. He washed his body and exited so he may join her and observed that she was already dry. This was the second time she had illustrated her ability to dry quickly.

She faced him after offering him a generous amount of time to behold her backside. She grabbed his towel and finished drying his body, beginning at the top of his shoulders and moving to his legs. She rehung the towel on the rack and craned her arms around his neck softly, exercising caution unsure if he still might be post ejaculating. She puffed her lips at him, drawing attention to her mouth. "Did Mirage fix Nik?"

Nik still panting from the intensity of his orgasm. "Oh, yes. Mirage fixed Nik. I can't remember the last time I've been fixed that well."

She reached for his clothes on the bathroom floor and dressed him.

He returned the favor, pulling her sundress over her head.

Mirage led him to the living room and sat on the couch. She rested her head against his shoulder and rolled her eyes toward him. "You said something interesting when we were fighting in the kitchen that stuck with me. Do you know that?"

Nik's chest tightened. He wondered how she could mention something so harsh after the experience they had shared. "I don't want to fight with you, and I don't want to revisit that."

Mirage straddled his lap, placing her arms on his shoulders. "Don't worry. I'm not starting a fight. I just wanted to know if you remember what you said.

"I think if you reminded me, that may be a little helpful."

She straightened her body and looked down at him. "You said, 'Don't cry, my love, and don't leave, I just could not bear it.'"

He gently grabbed her on both sides of her delicate face and peered deeply into her eyes. "Yes, I did call you *my love*, because you *are* my love. I can't fight the urge, and I had to say it, and I'm sorry it came out right after a fight. As time ebbs forward, I can't help but to fall deeper for you. I had been falling for you since the night you floated above me in bed and disappeared. It was painful when you were nowhere to be found. I am in love with you."

Mirage was speechless. Her efforts of peering into his soul were met with confusion.

Nik could not understand the reason for her confusion—maybe no one had ever verbally expressed or shown her love before.

Mirage leaned down and drove her mouth to his and kissed him. This kiss far exceeded deeper meaning than the first one. If Nik chose to push her away from him, he would have failed, as her conveyance was absolute.

Straightening, she traced his jawline with her fingertips, admiring him. "I love you too, Nik Vanelli. You will never know how much I love you. The magnitude of my love for you is immeasurable. I have loved you longer than you could even begin to fathom."

"You're right. I don't understand. How can you have loved me longer than I've known you?"

Mirage grew stiff and scrambled to find the right un-incriminating words. "I guess I was just being poetic. I just meant I must have fallen in love you with you at the same moment you did with me. Maybe my love for you developed sooner during our first contact."

Nik knew she was hiding something, but he knew her declaration of love was true. Two thoughts crossed his mind: a happy wife means a happy life, and a wise man knows all secrets and surprises cannot be contained forever. Mirage had a method of making him wait for what he desired to know, but regardless of how advanced she was in comparison, he would eventually learn the truth.

They spent the remaining day together, loving each other before retiring to his bed and spooning, safely interlaced with affection.

The following morning sun shined through the bedroom window and coated their bodies with light, enticing them to rise. Mirage released her body from Nik's arms and crawled from bed. She approached the bedroom window, staring out.

Nik felt her absent from his side and awoke, observing the time—8:25. He grew uncomfortable as she gazed naked out the window. He feared his neighbors might receive a full-frontal view. He sprang from his side of the bed and urged her to walk away from the window. He cupped his genitals to not expose his nude body.

She turned to Nik, appearing flawless with her hair resting perfectly. "It's a beautiful morning, my love."

"Yes, it does look like a nice day, but we shouldn't show our bodies to the neighbors. Why don't we jump in the shower, wash up and go out to enjoy it, clothed?"

They joined each other in the shower and concentrated on bathing. He did not want her to feel shower time was reserved for sexual gratification or that he had single desires, so, as he washed, his gaze remained on her face.

Mirage finished and exited the shower. "You're so cute when you're in deep concentration. I love seeing that look on your face."

Mirage handed him a towel as he stepped out and wiped the water from his eyes. When he opened his eyes, he discovered that she was dry and wearing a new lavender-colored sundress.

"You know you have a good romantic partner when they can keep surprising you." She brought her fingertips to her lips and giggled. "Come on, hurry up. I want to get a start on the day. I also have a surprise for you."

Nik followed her to the bedroom to see a new set of clothes laying on the foot of the bed—a black tank top with *Roland* scrolled across it in white letters and a new pair of dark brown khaki shorts.

"I figured you'd like the new wardrobe, since you like Roland keyboards."

Nik reached for the clothes and found his keys, phone, and wallet inside the pockets. After he thanked her, he led her to the front door to take her for a drive and show her the local area so she could become familiar with her surroundings and could navigate the area.

He escorted her to the passenger side and opened the door for her. He did not know why he did this, but he did know that if she was any other girl from the past, he would not have been chivalrous. One-night stands were motivated with quick access and entry; love was motivated by making grander gestures.

Nik and Mirage drove for most of the day. He drove around Pemkey, showing her the areas they did not cover during their walk, and drove to Gibbswood to show her the neighboring village. He pointed out landmarks, and, when they passed Jeanelle's Bar, he became morose, realizing his friendship with his former bandmates was over. He would never play at Jeanelle's Bar with them again. Revitalizing his mood, he decided to show her his new employment. Leaving Gibbswood, they entered the country and eventually into the vacant facility lot.

"This place is immaculate," Mirage commented, "and very welcoming."

They turned around in the lot, heading in the direction they had come. Passing Trixie's Drive-Thru, Nik turned to her. "Do you want to continue the drive?"

"I would love to! This is so fascinating."

He took her to the area where he grew up. He wanted her to see his origins and remaining surrounding areas. Arriving in Pemkey, he turned south down Donaldson Road. He did not point out landmarks or provide road names this time. He felt she already knew the landmarks and the stories behind them. This became evident as they approached Paulding Pike and turned toward Hoyle.

She remembered and felt Nik's memories as they approached Bateson School District.

Noticing her mannerisms, he felt warmth from her loyalty. Despite the memories and emotions not belonging to her, it filled him with a connected kindness.

When they passed the Friendship gas station, she turned to him, knowing he had purchased M.D. 20/20 for his marching bandmates.

Nik slouched in his seat, shamed that she knew his mischievous actions.

She redirected her attention to the road ahead entering Hoyle. Mirage found the village's layout was nauseous; she needed to rub her eyes. Exiting the village limit, she dropped her hands from her eyes and resumed surveying the rural setting. She anchored herself as they approached the Paulding Pike curve so she wouldn't shift in the seat, anticipating Nik making a severe turn. She relaxed once the truck straightened.

Passing the Bateson centralized campus, she winced at the horrid-looking structure before they turned onto Amsdale Road. It was ironic she loathed the place. At least she was fortunate enough to not have to attend. She reached for his hand and removed it from the steering wheel, squeezing it hard then interlacing her fingers with his. They arrived at Eagle Trail Road, and Mirage raised her hand while holding Nik's, like someone going down a rollercoaster hill. The view of Amsdale sprawled in front of them.

Approaching Lafferty Road before entering the village limits, Mirage crinkled her nose from the stench of sewer gas and hog farms. She swirled her hands around, and physical circles materialized. The stench of Amsdale no longer bled into the cab; instead, a sweet aroma of botanical flowers encompassed.

They stopped at the three-way intersection of Main Street and Vine, and a village police department car pulled behind them. The officer turned onto Main Street, following them through the intersection, and heading toward the local bar. Nik relaxed, as Mirage did not have identification.

They stopped at the intersection of Cherry and Garfield Street, and Nik pointed. "See that yellow house? That's where I was born and grew up."

Mirage grew excited and looked at the house.

Nik turned right on Garfield Street, passing his childhood home and the church parking lot continuing through the stop sign.

Mirage watched his childhood home fade in the distance behind them and pouted. "Why didn't we stop? Are you ashamed of me?"

"Ashamed of you? God no. There is nothing to be ashamed of at all. You're beauty and perfection rolled into one. I can't introduce you to my parents yet. How would I explain it to them? 'Hi, Mom. Hi, Dad. This is Mirage. She is this beautiful woman who dropped from the sky.' Besides, if I think you're good at reading my thoughts and emotions, I think my mom is just as good as you, if not better. Hell, in that aspect, I think the two of you would get along splendidly. Plus, my dad would take one look at you and be proud that I scored such a beauty. I just need to figure out how to introduce you to them. Believe me, I can't wait for the day to bring you home to them."

She leaned her head onto Nik's shoulder as they followed the route from Amsdale to Pemkey exactly as they had come.

Checking the gas gauge, he saw it was considerably low. He stopped at Friendship station to refuel. He walked to the side of his truck and opened the gas cap. He startled when Mirage cleared her throat next to him, not realizing she had joined him. "This pump is making me pre-pay inside. Come in with me."

She placed her arm around his waist, and he did likewise as they entered the gas station.

"While we are in here," Mirage started, "I was wondering if you could pick me up a bottle of kiwi lemon MD 20/20."

Nik chortled, as she had requested the worst possible flavor. He approached the counter and told the attendant he wanted twenty-five dollars' worth in gas on pump seven.

Mirage stood with Nik as he pumped the gas. He squinted to decipher the fogged display. He felt the pump slow to a crawl and eventually an abrupt stop. He walked Mirage to her side of the truck and guided her into the seat.

She brushed her hand on his face as she fastened her seatbelt. She watched him the entire way until he joinede her in the truck.

He started the truck, and it sprung to life with a roar then they merged onto Paulding Pike.

Mirage placed her head on his shoulder again.

They drove in silent tranquility as the rural setting was calm with a breeze pressing the vegetation in the ditches.

They entered the winding section of Donaldson Road, and Mirage broke the calmness. "*Stop the truck!*"

He shuffled his foot from the accelerator to the brake.

"Stop the truck! *Now!*"

Nik mashed the brake pedal, and the rear of the truck rattled as he was thrust forward. He turned to Mirage as his heart pounded sharp staccato beats.

Mirage pressed her back against the passenger side door and stared at Nik with a multitude of emotions. Her eyes streamed large tears. She lunged at Nik and clutched him, strangling his lungs.

He struggled to free himself from her grasp to place the truck into Park.

She sobbed loudly as her grasp increased, bringing him nearly to the point of passing out.

"You're … hurting me … Mirage. I can't … breathe, babe."

She recoiled from him. "You don't remember? How could you not remember? Get out of the truck and follow me." She flung herself from the passenger door to the front of the truck.

Nik exited the truck, cautiously leaving the engine running and the door open.

Mirage kept her back to him while he walked. She kneeled to the country road and reached upward, grabbing his hand and yanking him to the asphalt.

Nik saw immediately what she was looking at—a black mark on the road five inches by seven inches in size. The pattern resembled the pattern of the fire rainbow. He was looking at the scorch mark left on the asphalt from the crashing bolt on the night they had first met. He pulled himself from his deep concentration to look at Mirage.

She rained tears upon it as she touched it. Her tears did not wash away any of the burn marks. The scorch had permanently tattooed the roadway.

Nik placed his hand on Mirage's shoulder.

She jolted at first with fright from her broken concentration.

"I remember it now. This is where we met, babe."

Mirage smiled through her flowing tears and leaned to embrace Nik.

He nudged her to follow him back to his truck. He was amazed she could pinpoint the exact location. If she could perform such an amazing feat of memory, their tour of the surrounding area was futile.

"Wow, babe, you never cease to amaze or surprise me. I can't believe you remember the exact location."

Mirage chuckled as she controlled her sobs. She dried her eyes, regarding him with love. "I could never forget such a thing like that, Nik. Right on this spot was where the happiest moment of my life happened. I met the love of my life."

Nik felt warmth from her words that he had never felt before. He did not want to spoil the moment, but he noticed someone was observing them from one of the country houses and did not want the occupants to report a possible accident. He shifted the truck into gear and drove home.

Mirage rested her head on his shoulder again as they travelled.

Nik pulled into the driveway and exited the truck.

Mirage waited for him to join her at the passenger door. Her tears were dry, and she had returned to her normal state.

He scooped her from her seat and swung her out of the passenger seat in a lover's embrace. He closed the door behind with his leg and carried her to the top of the porch then softly released her. He ushered his prized beauty inside his home, which was beginning to feel like both of their homes.

The rest of the week followed like a fast and pleasant dream, spending time together in loving fellowship. They walked around the town as dawning lovers and engaged in shower activities, offering Nik sexual release.

Time passed quickly as the weekend approached, and the newly formed Lapis Lazuli show ebbed closer. Nik contemplated not attending, but his curiosity bested him, and he felt cosmic or other guided forces were beckoning his presence. Regardless, he knew he was mandated to attend the show.

Chapter
Ten

On the night before the show, Nik was plagued with nightmares and borrowed worry. The scope of his dreams was encompassed with failure, fear, and death. His failure was based on his new potential job falling through or him unable to fulfill his dispatcher abilities. His fear was his band succeeding to new heights without him. The death aspect encapsulated either the death of him or Mirage—one or the other would meet their end and the other would be plagued to live alone in misery. No matter his strength and efforts to discern that he was dreaming, the images remained. He tussled and thrashed throughout the night while Mirage remained in a motionless, peaceful asleep.

At 7:15 the following morning, his alarm blared. He rose straight up, thankful the alarm was sounding. He did not recall setting the alarm but was grateful he must have subconsciously.

Mirage was breathing peacefully and blissfully. The rising of her chest and her sweet sleeping expression gave him the strength to power forward, breaking the residual unpleasantness of the dreams. He noticed his personal belongings were on the nightstand—he had no recollection of doing that—and his cellphone had been charging throughout the night.

He stepped out of bed and went to the bathroom to relieve his bladder, careful not to wake Mirage. He splashed water on his face, shaved, brushed his teeth and stepped into the shower. He did not maximize the water pressure, as he was still mindful of Mirage sleeping. The shower streamed light and cool water; he desired cold water to break him from the residual spells of lingering nightmares.

As he lathered his hair, he felt a presence enter the shower. Mirage stepped behind him and rubbed his shoulders then continuing to his lower back. Her massage could have lasted an eternity. It was welcomed and needed. She reached around him, gently tugging on his member and making him rise.

"I appreciate what you're trying to do, babe, but I had some of the most horrible nightmares I've had in the longest time. It isn't you, babe. I'm just not feeling it right now."

Mirage did not relent. She kissed the back of his neck and rubbed her breast on his back. Her nipples became erect as he gained full status. "I'm sorry you had a rough night, love, but I really think you need this now, and I think you need to accept it."

He turned to face her, but she was already on her knees and ready to sandwich his penis with her breast. Nik thrust between her as she tightened her cleavage around his shaft and found that, with his thrust, his negativity disappeared.

When he reached climax, he prepared to turn from her and finish. She grabbed his hips and let him finish in-between her wet, bountiful breast. The intensity of his orgasm peeked at a magnificent climax. For a moment, he felt he could not stop the orgasm. When he eventually finished, he drifted backward and nearly fell, until Mirage grabbed his buttocks to steady him.

She stood to rinse off his seed, being mindful to cover her vagina to not allow any of his fluid around her. Nik panted and spun her around to kiss her, and she giggled.

They stood under the water, and he gave her a curious look. "I'm surprised you let me do that. I didn't think you wanted any of my stuff on you."

She brushed her fingers through his wet hair. "You're right. I don't want to take the chance, but I think, with how you were feeling, I wanted to give you something special. Besides, I think you thought it was sexy to cum on my tits. To tell you the truth, I think it turned me on as well."

Nik smiled a little embarrassed. He did not expect Mirage to use provocative and vulgar language. If she would have been talking like that during the act, it may have made his exploding orgasm all the better. Nevertheless, the intensity had been astonishing, and he remained erect, throbbing as she continued to soak her naked body.

Once the shower had concluded, Nik noticed something peculiar. Usually Mirage could completely dry herself after the shower. This time, she remained equally wet. Mirage had a seeming ability to manipulate her environment to bend to her will. He pondered whether she was becoming more human as time passed. Nik chose not question or press the issue.

She led him to the bedroom and faced him with delight at the doorway. "Hey, by the way, I have another surprise for you."

"Oh yeah? What is it?"

She pointed at the foot of the bed, and a different pair of clothes were laid out—a pair of light blue-jean shorts and a red t-shirt with *Rickenbacker* scrolled on it in a sunburst-orange color. "I know you like Rickenbacker guitars, and I also know it was the brand of bass you play, so I figured, if I got you a Roland shirt, then I had to get you a Rickenbacker shirt too."

Nik kissed her warmly on the lips. "Thank you, honey. You really do know me quite well."

"I agree. And I know you better than you realize."

Nik dressed quickly, eager to model his new attire. His personal items were in the appropriate pockets.

A new wardrobe was laying on the bed for her as well. She picked up a red halter neck top and a pair of light blue-short shorts.

Nik examined Mirage's attire. Something about the way she was dressed troubled him. While the color scheme was different, it reminded him of Samantha's clothes. The only difference between Mirage and Samantha was Mirage looked exceedingly better. Nik smiled at her with approval; he would not allow poisonous thoughts to trouble his mind.

Once they were both dressed and ready to embark on the day, he retrieved his wallet from his back pocket. He only had one twenty-dollar bill, not enough for the trip to Sandousten and back—plus he was unsure whether he would need money for other expenses. He remembered Moline Medical Warehousing would be depositing his final check and his severance in his account.

"Wanna take a walk downtown?"

They left his house hand in hand and discussed Nik's upcoming job—she assured him she was proud of him—and the prospect of introducing her to his parents as they walked toward Huntington Bank.

Mirage beamed with excitement. She added that the trip to his town had been nice but meeting the people who'd created him would be a pleasure and honor.

Nik enjoyed seeing her like this. He was not sure how he would pull it off, but he did not care at that moment. Hell, maybe he would tell his parents the truth: he had met some sort of extraterrestrial being, she is hot as hell, and they are both in love. *Meet your future daughter-in-law, Mom and Dad.* The thought excited him.

Approaching the bank, Mirage shifted the subject to a more risqué manner, speaking with new sexual intentions. She retained her resolve with no vaginal contact, but she offered Nik something new to spice up their activities. She told him the next time they showered together she would allow him to place his penis in her mouth while releasing. She took the scope of the conversation as far as even offering to swallow his essence. Nik felt a tingle on the head of his penis as she spoke and grabbed him on the left buttock.

Nik turned to her with eager eyes. "Damn, babe, I didn't realize what kind of a dirty bird you really are. You never cease to amaze me. How did I get to be so lucky?"

Mirage wrapped her arm around his waist and squeezed. "You found me. That is how lucky you are."

They paused for a moment to exchange a delicate kiss before they crossed the street to the bank. Nik opened the door for her.

"Welcome to Huntington Bank," Aileen greeted.

Nik and Mirage returned her greeting and stepped to the counter. Nik filled out a withdrawal for one hundred-fifty dollars.

Aileena smiled at Nik and Mirage and commented how ideal they looked together as she handed Nik his cash.

Nik and Mirage thanked her and turned away.

"Hey!" Aileena called out. "I noticed Lapis Lazuli is playing in Sandousten tonight. There's a flier on the Pisannelo's bulletin board. What's the deal with you not being in the picture? Are you no longer in the band?"

Nik and Mirage looked at each other before returning their gaze at Aileena. "You could say that. You could also say that I am involved with something more important." He smiled at Mirage.

"That's too bad you're not playing with them anymore, but you *do* look happy."

Nik and Mirage waved to Aileena before stepping into the climbing sunlight. They walked home with a spring in their steps.

"You know, I'm glad to not be in the band. I'm happier being with you. However, I feel compelled to attend the show. It's more than just an urge. It's like a requirement that some unseen force is directed me to do—a force I can't contest nor deny."

Mirage's expression became steadfast as she looked toward Nik's house. "You should follow your feelings. If anything, you would gain closure. Plus, there's no possible way they could replace your talent."

Nik appreciated her words, but he wanted to remain humble.

Mirage climbed the steps first, and Nik placed a gentle hand on her exposed back under her halter-top straps. She headed for the music room and beckoned him to join her. Nik pranced down the hallway and into his music room.

She sat on the duet bench with perfect pianist posture. Her bare back looked smooth as silk. It was strange, but Mirage appeared slightly tanner. He considered the length of time his errand had taken and was amazed she could have acquired a darker tan.

She twisted to face him. "Well, aren't you going to sit and play something for me?"

Nik sat with her, easing his body to an upright position. His mind drew a blank; he did not know what to play.

She continued to look at him with anticipation, eagerly pressing him to play.

He felt like an Iditarod sled dog being commanded to pull through thick dunes of snow. Without further provocation from Mirage, he thought of an ideal song to play, since she was a being of unknown origin. He chuckled as he could not believe he did not think of the song earlier.

He placed his hands on the keys and thought maybe his assessment of her had been wrong. Maybe she was neither extraterrestrial nor interdimensional; perhaps she was something else instead—a magical being instead. He was starting to believe that anything was possible, and the scope of possibility could exist across all spectrums of belief.

He rested his left pinky on the bass C-note an octave lower than middle C and formed a root C-chord with his right hand. He fingered the intro to "Can't Get It out of My Head" by Electric Light Orchestra. As he played, he sang along. He had memorized the music and lyrics.

Mirage gazed upon him with indivisible love, knowing he directed the song's meaning toward her.

After he finished the song, he transitioned into another Electric Light Orchestra tune—"Strange Magic." While the song is in a different key signature, moving from C-major to G-major, he found the transition between the two songs was cogent and continued to sing and play for his beautiful love. He did not want to over inundate her with Electric Light Orchestra, so he decided to play Genesis' "Follow You, Follow Me." He felt this was a fluid progression, as both "Strange Magic" and

"Follow You, Follow Me" were both in G-major. After he finished playing, he decided to move to something with a little more brightness—"Laughter in the Rain" by Neil Sedaka.

She reacted playfully while he played and sang along with the warm and silly song. She seemed to enjoy his mannerisms directed at her while he played.

He decided to move toward a different direction and play something more captivating—songs that dwelled in the scope of magic, love, and eternal yearning. He moved down another key signature and began "Without You" in the styling of Harry Nilsson. He regarded the other artists who had attempted to play the song—Mariah Carey and Air Supply—but he felt they were all wrong—including Bad Finger's original version—and the styling of Harry Nilsson was the ideal manner.

He was troubled with the revisiting nightmare on the prospect of death as he began to play the song. He worried about the strife and struggle a visiting being of unknown origin would face if he died. He also contemplated losing her to death, his days long and painful. He fought to suppress the thoughts and concentrated on playing as tears welled in his eyes.

He stopped playing, instantly turning to Mirage and burying his head deep into her chest, sobbing.

She placed her hand under his chin and raised his face to match her eyes.

He wiped his moistened eyes. "I really couldn't live if living would be without you, my love."

"I know." She craned her arms around his waist.

He collected himself and played the song from the beginning. While he played, again, the sobbing from his voice broke, and he was greeted with a newfound clarity as his voice swelled, matching Harry Nillson's. When he concluded the song, he paused, taking deep breaths. His next selection was one where he wanted to showcase his abilities and talent, hoping to impress Miarge further. He decided to play "99" by Toto, shifting the mood from sorrow to devotion. He concluded his session with "Sea of Love" in the style of the Honeydrippers. He felt the ambiance of this version exhibited more devotion and meaning than its original.

As he his fingers danced along the piano keys, all he thought about was his love toward Mirage. As he belted the lyrics, he visualized a sea of love washing over them as the waves ebbed and flowed. The song ended, and he remained looking forward, staring into nothingness as he sat cemented to the duet bench.

Mirage removed her arm around him and placed a single hand on his shoulder to pull him from his distant dreamlike state. A few harsher shakes later, and she brought him brought back to reality. "You are ready, my love."

Nik raised an eyebrow. What could he possibly be ready for? What was she talking about? How long had he been gone in his dream state?

"You are ready, my dearest, to begin and finish your Life's Work. Your passion and your abilities have achieved the apex. You need to create and share your beauty."

He was afraid his abilities would fall short and he would be mediocre. He did not fear this mediocrity from others; he solely felt his mediocrity would be judged from himself.

"You can do it, my love. Your ability to play, your transitions, and ability to command emotion while playing is pure. If I can see it—and I'm not, well, a local product—then you should see it too."

He grabbed her hand from his shoulder and kissed it with a hard press. "It's funny, but the most pertinent point you made was that if my music could move and touch a being such as yourself, then maybe it just might be worthy and the right time to dedicate to its creation."

Mirage's heterochromatic eyes lit up, as if a source of light had been shining behind them, and the duet bench rattled and levitate off the floor. An unseen breeze manifested and seemed to blow and billow through her hair.

Nik, frightful, slid away from her.

The strange phenomena ended, and she appeared flushed and satisfied, as if she achieved great acclaim.

"You're quite the bold one, aren't you? At least when I get caught up in a daydream, I don't cause the earth to rattle like you do."

"I'm sorry I frightened you, Nik. It's just you made me so happy by your decision to create your Life's Work. I've shared many happy moments with you, but this has got to be one of the best, if not *the* best one yet. Don't you get it? It's me who is your inspiration. I am the deep love and romance you needed to create your masterpiece. I'm honored and humbled that I'm the catalyst that sparked you. You are my love eternal. You are my beauty."

Nik stood from his duet bench, and Mirage joined him as they stood in unison. Nik slid the duet bench under the piano and ushered her from his music room. Mirage walked toward the living room. Nik told her he would follow shortly.

She nodded, as she knew what he was about to do and decided to let him have a moment to himself.

He turned to his desk, picked up the manila envelope, brought the envelope to his lips and pressed a hard kiss on it. Nik felt strange about executing a strange action, but Mirage was right. She was the inspiration and the spark he had needed. His perfect love was an extraordinary woman, and he needed that to create an extraordinary piece. He placed the envelope on the desk and scanned his office one last time, drawing inspiration to embark on his passion project.

He looked at his sheet music shelf, and a thought crossed his mind when he canvassed his disc collection. He would introduce Mirage to some of his favorite music and play a few songs on the stereo. He browsed his albums, tapes, and CDs and decided to not play an album by a single artist—a collection of artists would prove best. He grabbed two burnt mixtape disks—one for home listening and another for the trip to Sandousten. He selected one labeled *80's Pop Favorites* and another with *Progressive Rock* scribbled messily in black Sharpie. Tapping the CD cases against his thigh as he walked, he headed down the hallway to join Mirage.

She sat on the edge of the couch, exhibiting perfect posture. "What do you have, my love?"

"These are two of my mix CDs. I figure I will play one for us right now, and I will save the other for our trip to the show, my dearest … dearest … dearest." Nik became distant as he spoke the word *dearest* three times, growing softer each time.

His mind traveled deeper as wonder engulfed him. He stared at her with meaning and deafening silence as he thought, Dearest *and* beauty *are words I never use. I never used them with any of my previous girlfriends, and I sure as hell never used them with Kara. Wow! Do I sound sappy saying these things? Maybe I have never truly felt these emotions before. I thought when I was younger, I felt this way toward Kara, but to think of her and call her* my beauty *and* dearest *would have come out wrong or never felt right. Is this another way I am telling her that I love her? Is this the great love I needed for the inspiration? One thing is for sure, I hope she knows this means I love her. I am truly in love for the first time in my life. This is fucking amazing, and it is happening to me.*

Nik's long stare startled Mirage, and she feared he would zone out to the point of losing consciousness.

He viewed a gray void shattering in front of his eyes as they focused on Mirage.

Her eyes were desperately full of fear once he regained clarity, and her voice became audible as she continued to say his name. "Baby, you scared me. What happened? Where did you go? This is the second time you've done this to me today."

Nik shook his head and rubbed the bridge of his nose. He looked at the CD cases clutched white-knuckled in his hands. "Oh, I, *aww*, was just thinking about how much I am in love with you. Man, it is intoxicating, like a drug."

Mirage leaned back from him with concern smeared on her face. She controlled her fear and returned to a normal position on the couch. She smirked and wrapped her arms around him.

He raised the CDs to her line of sight.

She grabbed the discs and read the handwritten titles on the back of the cases. She recited the song titles and artist from the *80's Pop Favorites* disk. "Lessons in Love," Level 42; "The Sun Always Shines on TV," A-ha; "Liner," The Fixx; "We Close Our Eyes," Go West; "Everlasting Love," Howard Jones; "Is It Love," Mr. Mister; "It's My Life," Talk Talk; "Nobody's Fool," Kenny Loggins; "History Never Repeats," Split Enz; "Human," The Human League; "Emotion in Motion," Ric Ocasek; "Stay the Night," Benjamin Orr; "Too Late to Say Goodbye," Richard Marx; "View to a Kill," Duran Duran, "Major Tom (Coming Home)," Peter Schilling; "Affair of the Heart," Rick Springfield; "Girl Can't Help It," Journey. When she looked at the *Progressive Rock* collection, she did not recite the song titles or the artist. She pushed the *80's Pop Favorites* toward Nik and placed the *Progressive Rock* CD beside her.

Nik took the disc from her and readied the receiver.

"After reading the song titles on both CDs, I think the 80's one is more suiting for the day. It's bright outside, and I'm feeling lively. I think the progressive rock CD should be saved for the drive to Sandousten. We can listen to something with more substance then. I think you already know your former bandmates and their new members will not be providing us with any depth. Besides, progressive rock is best enjoyed in the evening time."

Nik turned from his entertainment center with a profound look on his face. He was impressed with her assessment and thoughts toward the flow of the day and how to incorporate the appropriate mood and ambiance. "How did you get to be so perfect, and how did I get to be so lucky?"

The CD player displayed the track numbers; he pressed Play and returned to her posthaste. Nik reclined into the couch and felt his body turn into gelatin as the speakers played his burnt CD.

Mirage curled up to him in a fetal position and fell into a state of relaxation. They listened to the music and exchanged silent affection as the tracks progressed and then finished.

Nik's stomach grumbled.

She regarded him with surprise and chuckled, thinking the sounds were amusing.

He stood to eject the CD from the player, turned off the unit off and reduced the volume on the stereo. He went to the kitchen to make himself a sandwich and sat at the kitchen table.

Mirage sat across from him while he ate.

Nik tilted the sandwich toward her, offering her a taste.

She shrugged away and raised her hands. "You know I don't eat, babe."

"You don't pee or poop either," he said with crumbs falling from his mouth as he chewed.

Mirage placed her fingertips to her lips and chuckled. Her expression and tone grew serious as she reached across the table and grabbed his hands. "You know, we really don't have to go to the show tonight. We both know they will be terrible, and I think you should rest in the satisfaction of that alone."

"You're right. They probably will suck tonight, but I need that closure of watching them crash and burn. I built this thing from the ground up, honed and ushered these guys with me, but I need to see them fail. I know it's immature, but I need that experience."

"We should just stay here and relax for the rest of the weekend."

Nik stood from the table. "Sorry, babe. My mind is made up."

Nik checked his cellphone and saw it was 6:45 p.m. "Hey, we've got to get going. It's about an hour and a half drive to Sandousten. Is there anything you need to do to prepare for the trip?"

Mirage shook her head no and stood from her chair.

"Are you wearing the same outfit you have on now?"

Mirage nodded.

Nik crackled a wicked smile. He figured if the other guys saw her with him, they would beam with jealousy. "Great! You'll look excellent."

Nik walked through the house to double check that he had everything and to use the toilet; he did not want to be forced to use the dirty bar restroom. He walked down the hallway and studied Mirage sitting on the couch.

Mirage looked a million miles away, entranced with deep thought.

He sat beside her and gently kissed her bottom lip. When he opened his eyes, Mirage looked at him, shimmering with love. "Hi there, welcome back. Where did you go?"

Mirage wiped the residual trance from her face. "I think I must have trailed off."

"I wish you had broken me from my trances like I did yours."

"Thinking back, I wish I had too. Your method was a far better approach."

Nik stood from the couch and helped Mirage to her feet. She leaned over to grab the *Progressive Rock* CD.

Nik couldn't help but to ogle her while she bent over. He studied her legs and her rear as she exceeded far than necessary time to collect the disc. He knew she was doing this for his visual pleasure alone. The urge to advance behind her to grind and thrust on her overwhelmed him as she remained in the position. Slight arousal pulsed through his member. He knew he did not want to start something they would not have time to finish, so he diverted his gaze and surveyed the front door.

The same feelings of dread from the night Samantha's husband had confronted him came rushing back. He did not want Mirage to see his distress, so he forced himself to relax his face.

Mirage stood from her position and turned to him with a smile, knowing he was observing her. "Are we all set to go, babe?"

"Why don't you wait for me by the truck. I want to do a once-over of the house to make sure all the appliances are off and the lamp timer set correctly. It's just my OCD."

She grazed his cheek with her hand before heading toward his truck.

He scurried through his house ensuring all he had mentioned was secure, but he also confirmed the windows were shut and locked. Then he had the idea to make sure there was no tooling or signs of forced entry. It was something he did not think of when he had returned from his parents' house—he had been too occupied with his strange new houseguest to perform such a thorough inspection.

Once everything appeared normal and his sense of security was satisfied, he locked the front door behind him. He tugged the handle three times to assure the door was locked before walking toward his truck.

Mirage was studying the back of the CD case and reciting the song titles and did not acknowledge his presence as he went to the driver side door. "'Silent Running,' Mike + the Mechanics; 'Three of a Perfect Pair' and 'Sleepless,' King Crimson; 'In the Cage' and 'Trick of the Tail,' Genesis; 'Prime Time' and 'Don't Answer Me,' Alan Parson's Project; 'Wildest Dreams,' Asia; 'This Morning,' Justin Hayward & John Lodge; 'Why Me,' 'To Live Forever,' 'What I See,' 'Planet P Project,' 'Spirits in the Night,' and 'Runner,' Manfred Mann; 'Airwaves Extended,' Thomas Dolby; 'A Dream Goes on Forever,'" Todd Rundgren; and 'True Companion,' Donald Fagen." She raised her head from the back of the case and looked around for Nik in surprise.

He let her search for him in silence. He could tell she felt apprehensive that he was nowhere in sight. He enjoyed that she was expressing concern over being unable to locate him. It made him feel desired and depended on. He caught her attention with a few knocks on the top of his truck cab.

She startled then turned to face him. She opened the passenger side door and climbed inside.

Nik removed his hand from the gear shift before he shifted into Reverse. "Fuck! I just remembered something. They'll never let you into the bar. You don't have an ID."

Mirage grinned smugly and raised her left hand. She flattened her hand, with her palm pointing upward, and a small fire-burst rainbow formed. Three rotating white orbs circled into a triangular formation, and a small rectangular bar formed, glowing bright, burning white. The object dimmed and flattened, and she handed it to Nik.

Nik reluctantly grabbed the object. "You created a driver's license?" He studied the ID for flaws, and it appeared authentic.

The card stated that her name was Mirage Vanelli, height 5'9", weight 125 pounds, hair color brown, eye color blue, and date of birth June 1, 1981. It even included the faux pas driver license number, YT209581.

Nik snickered. "It seems we share the same last name. Does that mean we're married? I also couldn't help but to notice that you were born a year before me. Do you like your men a little younger? You are such a little cougar, aren't you?"

Mirage tilted her head down with shyness. "My age is without a true numeric variable, and, as far as the last name goes, I guess you could assume it is just wishful thinking on my part."

His heart felt as if it had physically grown in his chest and swelled with increased heart beats. Nobody had ever expressed a desire to be his bride. A feeling of nervousness shot through, but then it was overcast with blissful joy.

He checked his mirrors and placed the truck into Reverse. Mirage slid the CD into the player, and they listened to the music. When they turned onto Cedar Mill Road, Mirage's eyes filled with wonder and excitement as they passed the miniature golf courses with waterfalls, windmills, and giant sandcastles. Next was a small recreational area that featured go-carts that zipped by as she perched herself in her seat to watch. The left side of the street boasted the 3D simulator theater that also housed a roller rink and a haunted house attraction.

"An amusement park called Cedar Point is further down the road. At nighttime, the rides have lights that travel the length of the tracks. We'll be able to see the lights from where we'll park at the show. I promise to take you to the park for your first rollercoaster ride."

Mirage could not contain her excitement, and her flesh illuminated.

Nik panicked and urged her to control her impulse as they passed Swirly Dipp ice cream parlor and approached the parking entrance to the Cabana Bay bar. He feared other people would see his passenger glowing.

They looked ahead at the elongated venue structure lined with fake palm trees strung with white Christmas lights. They kissed passionately before leaving his truck. They met each other at the front of his truck and walked with their arms locked around each other's waist.

Nik noticed his former bandmates carrying in their gear and equipment with their heads hung low. They looked like soulless golems animated by a dark necromancer commanding them to do his bidding. Nik stepped onto the sidewalk without them noticing him traversed the length of the building, watching his reflection from the dark-tinted windows.

He saw Mike Balmer and Channing talking to two skanky barflies while Channing incessantly huffed on a cigarette and heard Balmer's voice. "Yeah, I play guitar in one band, and now I play bass with these guys. Me and my cousin replaced the last dude. I guess he was a bossy know-it-all. The other dudes say he was a real cocky prick. I met him a time before, and I wasn't impressed." Balmer snickered as Channing smoked his cigarette.

Nik stormed up to Balmer and jabbed his fingers twice against Balmer's shoulder blades.

Balmer spun around. "Oh … hey, bro. What's up? How's it going?"

Nik did not respond; he only wanted Balmer to see him and know he had heard what was said.

Balmer extended a hand to shake hands. Seeing Nik would not return the gesture, he attempted to fist bump him. Balmer's gaze panned from Nik to Mirage. "Well, who's this lovely lady you have with you? I'm Mike Balmer, and I'm with the band tonight."

Mirage glared at him.

Balmer extended his hand toward Mirage and grabbed it as she stepped backward. She withdrew it before he could press her hand to his cold sore-covered lips.

Nik exploded, jabbing Balmer in the sternum.

Balmer stumbled backward.

Nik grabbed his black t-shirt's collar and slammed him against the tinted window with enough force to crack the glass. He balled his right fist. "Now, you listen to me, shit bag! If you ever touch her—let alone look at her again—I will blast you in your dirty fucking cold sore! Do you understand me? Do you know how fucking serious I am?"

After Nik mentioned Balmer's cold sores, the barflies examined his face and grimaced.

From the corner of his eye, Nik saw Channing puff his chest and advance on him. Nik tightened his grip on Balmer, severing his air flow, and thrusted him upward. "You just back the fuck off, Tiny Tim! Because once I'm done with Mr. Cold Sores here, you'll be lucky if the only thing you can do on that stage is rock back and forth and drool. From the looks of it, I would say that's all you can do anyway!"

Channing receded immediately, dropping the cigarette from his mouth.

Nik darted his gaze from Channing to Balmer as his face purpled. Nik slammed Balmer against the tinted window to solidify his point.

The crack expanded, and Balmer slid down the glass, landing on his rear. He trembled as Channing stood back.

The skanky barflies parted as Nik and Mirage passed between them. They walked the rest of the length of the building until they arrived at the main entrance where Roger the bouncer greeted them. "Nicky, buddy. What the hell are you doing at the main entrance? The band uses the side entrance. You know that."

"Hey, Rog. How's it going?

Nik and Roger conversed for a while, both reminiscing over previous shows he played with Lapis Lazuli along with other acts that played at the venue. Roger gave a thorough critique of the other acts providing praise and harsh words before concluding the conversation.

Roger turned his attention to Mirage. "Who's this lovely young lady with you here, Nicky? Is she your date for this disaster of a show?"

Nik introduced Mirage to Roger, and he shook her hand respectfully and gently.

"Well, bud. I can vouch for you, since you've played here before, but I don't know her. Does she have an ID?"

Mirage handed Roger her identification, and he inspected the front and back. He raised his eyebrows as he flipped it to the front once more with surprise. "Holy shit, Nik! I didn't know you tied the knot. Congratulations, buddy! You weren't married the last time you were here."

"Yeah ... you could say we just eloped recently. You know, man, when its right, its right, and you just go for it."

Roger boomed with laughter. "You ain't shittin' there, bud. It was like that with me and Beth. We rolled up to the courthouse on my bike, got hitched and busted the shit out of the bed in the motel room on our wedding night. Every now and then, we still bustin' beds when she's in the mood for it and she lets me."

"I appreciate your praise and approval, bud, but I have something I have to tell you, and I think it'll piss you off."

Roger's expression hardened.

"Look, man. I had a bit of a situation with Balmer before we got to the entrance, and I bashed his back against the window and cracked it. I promise you though, the motherfucker had it coming."

Roger's face reddened as he murmured and cussed under his breath before shaking it off. "Goddamn it, motherfucker! I knew those assholes would make me work for my money tonight. I'll tell you this, it's coming out of their asses for the damages."

Bewildered, Nik was sure Roger would have been angry toward him.

"Where did this happen again?"

Nik pointed in the general direction.

Roger cracked a smile. "Did you scare the piss out of the skuzzy bastard?"

"I certainly did. You should have seen his face. Well, *after* it had turned purple."

Roger chuckled, handed Mirage's identification to her and ushered them through the door. "I tell you what, the window damage is definitely coming out of the band's ass, and you and your new bride's cover charge is coming out of Balmer's ass. I have a feeling he didn't learn his lesson and will keep macking on other men's women tonight. You folks try to enjoy the show if you can. You hold on to that beautiful woman you got there, and you, miss, you got one hell of a talented guy there with you. It should be his ass on stage with the others, not them dirty bastards. Have a good one, y'all."

Nik and Mirage thanked Roger for the gesture and proceeded to squeeze into the packed establishment as the lingering heat suffocated them. They panned the crowd, noticing the clientele was not at the level Nik used to play for. A few sophisticated and hygienic loyal Lapis Lazuli fans remained, but the majority of the bar population were trashy and unkempt—sub-creatures who had crawled from some centralized manhole from the foulest of cities, like the creature from *C.H.U.D.* Nik regarded them with disgust and muttered, "Troglodytes."

They maneuvered to the front of the stage and turned and surveyed the audience with a better view. He recognized his more cultured fans clustered together, avoiding the general populous. He could read their lips as they looked upon him with surprise. *"What is he doing on the dance floor? He should be coming out with the band. What is going on here?"* Feeling remorse that they had come to see him and did not know he was no longer in the band, he hoped they could leave early enough to find a more engaging activity to do. Nik grabbed Mirage's hand and lead her from the dance floor toward the bar counter.

Alex stepped onto the stage first, followed by Andy and Kenny. The loyal fans cheered lightly as three familiar faces appeared on the stage, but they noticed how somber and stoic the band appeared. Moments later, Mike Balmer and Channing took the stage. The fans grew quiet and shocked. The other patrons hollered and whooped obnoxiously. The fans who'd come to see Nik and Lapis Lazuli illustrated disheartened looks at Nik as he and Mirage approached the bar counter.

Nik and Mirage passed Desiree sitting on a bar stool, oozing over the sides as she had appeared to increase in size from the last time. Desiree did not notice them pass, as she was too busy boasting and bragging about her position as band manager. "These guys were okay before, but now they play rock. They are much better now," she bellowed to the patron sitting next to her already drunk not wishing to be bothered.

Listening to the fat, obnoxious buffoon praise the band, a comical thought crossed his mind. *No wonder you're so fucking fat. You have taste for absolute shit.*

Nik and Mirage navigated through the crowd before they found two vacant seats at the opposite end of the bar from Desiree. Nik was pleased that Desiree or none of the other bandmembers had noticed him. He was sure they knew he was there, because Balmer and Channing would have told his former friends about the fight.

Nik noticed that Savannah and Rebecca were not there. Savannah probably chose not to attend in fear of Balmer or Channing's advances, while Andy surely had blown his relationship with Rebecca.

The stench of body odor and stagnant beer enveloped them at their seats. The odor permeated no matter how much they fanned their faces. The imposing odor embarrassed Nik. He felt ashamed for the establishment and for himself as he used to play the venue. His humiliation lay largely with Mirage—that he took his beautiful companion to such a depreciated place. He shuttered then forced at smile at Mirage, grabbing her hand.

Channing approached the microphone, attempting to placate the audience with light banter. He asked them how they were feeling tonight and if they were ready to party then introduced *his* band, Lapis Lazuli.

The former lineup devotees erupted and shouted rude, condescending remarks. "Where's Nik Vanelli? You aren't Lapis Lazuli. You're a bunch of assholes! That's ten dollars I won't ever get back! Get off the fucking stage!"

The three original bandmembers retained their soullessness. Balmer stood shielding himself with his beaten Ibanez knockoff bass, appearing rattled from the altercation before. His arrogant swagger was absent from his face. Channing fumed as the crowd flung off-color remarks from every corner of the venue. Even the trashy, dodgy-looking patrons joined the onslaught of jeering remarks. He fought with every fiber of his being to sustain from exploding with prideful, short-man's rage.

Channing bent his head upward and tilted down the microphone and counted, "One, two, three, four!"

The band began with a cover of Godsmack's "Voodoo." While Kenny kept proper time playing the drums, Balmer struggled with the bass line, failing to achieve any kind of proper rhythm. The band played on, sounding like an early teenager's garage band. After they finished "Voodoo," they played a Limp Bizkit cover of "Nookie."

Channing marched and flailed around the stage as if he was a larger-than-life star. The crowd erupted with laughter.

Nik had a moment of clarity when he realized the gravity of his dislike toward him. Channing reminded Nik of someone from his past who carried the same deplorable traits—a carbon copy of a guy he knew from high school. Mason Allen had been a senior during Nik's freshmen year. Mason was a short, insecure poser, much in the fashion of Channing. Mason also had a younger brother, Shane, who was in the same grade as Nik. Mason emotionally and verbally tormented Shane due to him being on the spectrum, having a high-functioning case of Asperger's Syndrome and social anxiety disorder.

The catalyst that sparked Mason's hatred for his younger brother was based largely that Shane was nearly a full head taller than Mason, and despite his mental disorders, he was also better looking. When the girls from the high school would comment that Shane was attractive despite his disorders, Mason would feel insecure. It would only fuel his motivation to torment Shane further.

He would berate and insult his brother by any means possible. He would refer to him as Rain Man or Gump. He would feed off the laughter of others at his younger brother's expense. However, during the last month of Mason's senior year—Shane's and Nik's freshmen year—Shane delivered a perfect moment of justice and retribution. The cafeteria had served breakfast for lunch one day—French toast sticks, sausage links, and scrambled eggs on white Styrofoam lunch trays.

Nik sat at the table behind Shane as he ate alone while Mason sat with his entourage at the other end of the lunch table. Earlier in the school year, Mason had tormented Shane by threatening to pick his nose while he slept and put a booger in his belly button. This caused Shane numerous sleepless nights, as there were times when Shane appeared withdrawn and lethargic.

Shane looked up from his meal and saw Mason pretending to pick his nose and rub his finger on one of his friend's naval. Their laughter increased as Shane finished his last bite of food. He collected his tray and strutted the length of the cafeteria tables toward his older brother. Without warning and with precise swiftness, Shane grabbed the back of Mason's neck, smashed his face twice into his tray and pushed his mouth and nose into his heaping pile of scalding French toast and scrambled eggs—with melted cheddar. As Mason's body flailed for air, Shane snatched a tray from another table and walloped his brother's face with it.

Mason screeched with fear and embarrassment at his brother, threatening him that he will get him in his sleep. Shane leaned toward his brother, now dripping with blood and scrambled eggs, and shouted, "I can stay awake longer then you! I will kill you if I have to!"

The vice principal intercepted both brothers and led them down the row of tables. Shane turned toward Nik as they passed, and Nik offered him a smile and quick thumbs up. Shane smiled at Nik with accomplishment despite facing disciplinary repercussions.

Nik reentered the scope of reality, watching Channing and the rest of the band finish their rendition of "Nookie." Mason and Channing were two peas in a pod. Guys like Mason and Channing truly do grow on trees.

Nik scanned the crowd, realizing the loyal fans had all but disappeared. Channing tried to play to the crowd with continued banter and failing humor as the band was constantly tuning their guitars between songs. The crowd only rebutted with rude remarks, that they had stolen the name Lapis Lazuli and should pack it up.

Once the band tuned their instruments, they continued with "One" by Creed. They followed the song with another

Creed song—"Higher." At this point, more bar patrons left the venue as the band played. After doing the two Creed covers, the band played Nickelback's "How You Remind Me."

"If I wanted to see fucking Hexed, I would have seen Hexed," one bar patron shouted.

"I paid for Lapis Lazuli, not goddamn Hexed," another shouted with more resolve.

While the band played sloppily, Channing struggled for his voice, sounding gritty and strangulated. The only surmountable respect Nik could afford them was that they played through the insults and the jeering.

"Oh my God," someone behind Nik said. "The lead vocalist sounds like every word he attempts to sing is painful agony. Shit the hard turd or pass the kidney stone already, then sing the song. Am I right or what? To tell you the truth, I came to see you on stage, not these unwashed ass wipes."

Nik and Mirage spun in their bar stools to face a man they had not noticed in the bar. He stood the same height as Nik, with the same build, and was dressed in a similar fashion, wearing a solid sapphire-blue-colored tank top, white khaki shorts, and black Nike shoes with an orange swoosh. Nik regarded what appeared to be his doppelgänger—just slightly more attractive, Nik thought—with curiosity and wonder.

The man flashed a smile of kindness and joy at Nik and Mirage, as if he had not seen them in a long time and they were near and dear to him.

"Hey, friend. I'm Nik, and this is my wife, Mirage. And you are?"

The strange man eagerly extended his hand toward Nik. "Oh, I'm Gi— John. My name is John. You can call me Johnny, if you'd like."

Nik, Mirage, and Johnny—who Nik now thought of as his faux pas twin brother—conversed as Lapis Lazuli continued to mercilessly slaughter cover songs.

Johnny's body language became awkward and uncomfortable. "I'm embarrassed to say this, but I'm a huge fan of yours. I saw you the last time you played here. You were phenomenal. I wish you were playing with them tonight. The whole reason I came was in hopes to see you. I know it sounds weird, but I think I'm your biggest fan," Johnny said sheepishly.

At first Nik was unsure of what Johnny was conveying—or if he was sincere or a deranged lunatic. "Thank you. I appreciate the kind words, bud. I'm working on a solo project right now, and it does not involve those guys up there. Quite, in fact, I refuse to work with them anymore. As far as biggest fans goes, well, I think you might have to take a number, because my true biggest fan is sitting with me right now." Nik lovingly squeezed Mirage's hand.

Johnny's eyes shot wide open, and he glowed with uncontrollable excitement. "Really? Wow! That is amazing. I'm glad you're still pursuing your music, and oh, of course I'm sure your wife is your biggest fan. I'm a writer myself, much to my dad's strong protest. He wanted me to be an athlete all throughout school, but that is not what is truly in my heart."

"You know something, man? Maybe, just maybe, your father is wrong. I don't want to get too personal, but I lucked out. My father was a musician, and it was passed down to me, and he nurtured me with my endeavors. I don't want to trash your father, but the dreams of being an athlete sound like his dreams and not yours. Go out there and write the best damn thing you can and aspire to great heights, my friend."

Johnny stepped backward, and his eyes moistened as he swallowed the growing bulge in his throat. "Thank you so much, man. I'd love to chat some more, but I really must go." He extended his hand to Mirage and shook it. When he turned to Nik, he looked as if he wanted to hug him instead of shake his hand. He reached out his hand and told him goodbye.

Nik and Mirage watched Johnny cross the nearly empty barroom floor.

He turned around one last time and waved, smiling as if he was holding back tears, then disappeared through the entrance.

Nik nodded toward the door, expressing that it was time to leave. Nik's curiosity had been satisfied with how bad they had performed. This was clearly evident with the other bar patrons as well. Most of them had left, with only five remaining on the floor while Desiree sat at the far end of the bar, swishing her robust body to the lousy music.

Channing announced this was their last song for the evening, and the band followed his lead with Disturb's "Down with the Sickness." Channing began the song with the signature "*Ooooh, aaahhh, aaahhh, aaahh, aaahhh,*" failing to sound hardcore.

Mirage and Nik snickered before traipsing across the bar floor. Nik regarded his former band and knew this night would be their swansong. If any of them attempted to contact him to rejoin, he was solid in his resolve that he would rebuke them. He just needed to see them fail and fall hard.

While walking from the bar to the front entrance, Nik halted as a single tear fell and rolled down his cheek from each eye.

Mirage grabbed his face, cupping it with both hands, and rubbed away his tears with her thumbs. "What's the matter, babe? Was it seeing the guys playing without you?"

Nik cleared his throat. "Those guys? Fuck no. They had nothing to do with it. I was just thinking about Johnny.

Something about him and the way he acted just got to me. I don't know why. It just felt like he needed to spend more time with us. I don't know why I feel this way. It's kind of embarrassing, but I really hope he follows through with his dream." Nik's voice cracked.

Mirage squeezed him and kissed him on the cheek. "You really are a beautiful man. I'm not the only one who sees it."

Nik swallowed the lump in his throat and continued to exit the bar.

Roger was standing at the entrance as Nik and Mirage left. "Hey, kids. You all have a goodnight."

Nik extended him one last bro-handshake then headed to his truck.

"Hey, Nicky! It's always best to be standing on the dock to watch the ship sink than it is to be on the tub. If you know what I mean, kid."

Nik turned and waved at Roger, acknowledging his metaphor.

Mirage approached the driver's side door. "I want to drive home tonight."

Nik raised one eyebrow.

"Come on, babe. Don't you trust me?"

Nik fondled his keys and looked at the ground while tapping his foot. "Eh … what the hell. Go for it. I'm tired anyway."

Nik tossed her the keys, and she opened the driver's side door. He climbed into the passenger seat for the first time. He fastened his seatbelt and watched Mirage do likewise before inserting the key into the ignition.

As Mirage merged onto the divided highway, she lifted her feet from the floorboard and sat cross-legged. She removed her hands from the wheel and lowered them to her sides.

Nik fumbled for the wheel. "What the fuck are you doing? You'll kill us both."

Mirage grabbed Nik's hand and flung it back. She glowed lightly, breathing deeply. "Don't disturb me, babe. I need total concentration."

Nik leaned back in his seat, watching Mirage control the truck with her mind. The instrument panel lights flickered a strange pattern as the truck reached the appropriate speed.

As soon as they crossed the Pemkey village limit, she uncrossed her legs and resumed a normal driving position. She made their final turn onto Caulenberg Street and parked the truck with ease. "See, babe? I got us home safe."

"Why don't we go inside and relax? I think I've had enough activities for one evening."

Mirage leaned over and kissed him passionately for affording her the opportunity to drive. "Sure thing, babe. Let's get inside."

They exited the truck and closed the doors behind them. He located his key to unlock the front door and entered the house.

Mirage gently touched his shoulder and spun him. "You know something, babe? I don't think we're done for the night. In fact, I think it's time you follow your own advice. You told Johnny he should be the best writer that he can be. Well, I think tonight is the night you begin to create."

Nik realized he should not be a hypocrite and should start. They closed the front door behind them and strode to his music room. He grabbed the Life's Work envelope and placed it on the sheet music rest.

Chapter Eleven

Nik turned on the light. His eyes strained to adjust as he approached his piano. He sat on the duet bench with a *thud*, nearly missing the bench. He checked the time on his cellphone—11:50. He felt tired fighting to hold up his head. He slouched toward the piano keys.

Mirage's footsteps approached from behind him. Her soft lips grazed his left ear, and she grazed her tongue along the outer rim of his ear.

He sat up with surprise, as he was not expecting her to do so.

She placed her hands under his armpits and raised him up. She knelt behind him and placed her hands on top of his knees. She ran her hands into his inner thighs and massaged his testicles, bringing his shaft to full erection.

He perked up from his near sleep state.

"Do I have your attention now?"

Nik straightened his neck and back to gain perfect posture. "Yes, you have my full attention, and, might I add, you have one hell of a way of gaining my attention."

"Good. I need you fully awake and aware. I'll help you create. Just relax, my love, and I will guide you."

Nik acknowledged her as she stood. He raised his tired arms and placed his hands on the C-major keys. The room shook, and the lights flickered. Before he could question her on what was happening, her fingertips touched the sides of his temples, making contact with his mind and soul. Nik's eyes grew heavy and rolled back into his head. As his eyes closed gently, he entered a color-spectrum realm of bliss. His once-tired arms were enriched with strength and felt blessed with newfound ability to carry on.

He saw a marriage between magic and futuristic apparatuses. In the distant sky, he saw flying orblike objects without definable shapes hovering around a grand citadel that appeared to be a city and centralized hall. He entered a land of magic where nothing was everything and everything was nothing. He was traversing in a riddle, a realm where the sky was the deepest of azure blue, and the vegetation was emerald green.

Blackbirds turned blue as they sang on distant hills, calling to the wild as if they were the students or children of wise men waiting to be endowed with instruction. The air smelled as if Mirage was near and around him all at once. A tree to his left produced life by a river that roared with clear, pristine water.

A hole in the ground near the river swirled a fierce vortex, switching colors between black and white. Forcing his gaze from the concentration of the swirling vortex, he noticed a strange, old man who had not been there before, kneeling on a single knee and observing the whirlpool. The old man was shrouded in a brown hooded robe that resembled the garments of a wizard from a magical fairy tale.

Nik approached the old man slowly not to interrupt his observations.

The old man eyed Nik with a gruff, aged face.

Nik thought the old man might be a wizard, with his pure snow-white beard and ragged-resting hair.

"Well, are you going to introduce yourself, or are you going to stand there all day spying on an old man?"

Nik was taken aback, not expecting the old man to acknowledge him. "I, uh um … sorry. My name is Nik Vanelli. I am not sure how I got here or what I am doing here. It was by accident, I guess."

The old man stood, rising to Nik's height. "You're a rude person, Nik Vanelli, to spy on an old man. I'm working on something of a magnitude you could not possibly understand. You're trespassing, whether you have chosen to or not."

Nik's bliss turned to paranoia as the old man was course with him.

"Nevertheless, you are here now, and I will be a generous host." The old man kneeled again to peer into the swirling hole.

Nik gazed into the swirling vortex and watched the black and white colors twist in an endless motion. "What is this I am looking at? Also, what is your name? I told you mine. Will you tell me yours?"

The old man huffed and regarded Nik. "You are gazing upon the very essence of this realm. For, you see, I am the beacon of this wondrous place you are standing in, or so you *think* you are standing in. I am under the employment of the wise men—the keepers of Eenyl. I am observing the sins and false alarms and the wrong and the right. Don't you understand anything? If names and titles are so important to you, then you may call me Aran.

Does that slate your appetite for knowledge? My work is of the utmost importance. It will lead to a promotion to the status of *wise man*, if my monitoring and predictions are sound. I think you humans—let alone a brave American—can understand the importance and desire to be promoted. If anything, it is one of the few concepts your simple kind can grasp."

Nik reflected on Aran's comments and remembered a lesson during high-school science class to fundamental niches and keystone species. He could relate to his science teacher's lecture of finding his fundamental niche raising the ranks becoming a keystone species.

Aran glanced at Nik before returning to the swirling hole. "See, boy? You understand it rather well already. Despite your analogy being something you learned in a rudimentary high-school class, you learned the basic concept and retained it splendidly. I must ask you to leave now. I must finish my important work. You're impeding my efforts."

Nik surveyed surroundings, finding no way to return. All he saw were thick trees and bushes. "Aran, I don't know how to get back from here. I think I'm stuck."

Aran groaned and pointed to the clearing behind them.

Nik noticed an empty corridor resembling the place he had first encountered Mirage.

"Go beyond those trees to the black void. You will find your way back. Once you enter, close your eyes and place yourself in the exact state you were when you arrived. Must I explain everything to you? It is really quite simple."

Nik approached the open bushes and trees that formed a shape like a church archway. He turned back and thanked Aran.

Aran waved at him in a dismissive manner.

As he reached the pointed archway, he heard Aran's voice shout with urgency. "*Boy! Boy! Boooooy!*"

Nik turned instantly, surprised that Aran stood next to him. "What're you, some kind of track star?"

"This is no time for trivial jokes boy," Aran said, panting. "Before you go, you heed my warning. Be vigilante of the veil of the night when you return. It has a strange kind of fashion over you humans. If the veiled illusion deceives you, you will return here under unpleasant circumstances and tried for your violations. I believe in your innocence, but, if you do violate the law, I will never—and I mean *never*—fight over you disrupting my chances to walk amongst the wise men."

Nik felt a pull drag him into the corridor. He reached for Aran's hand, but Aran did not extended or offer any further words.

"What do you mean? What is the deception of the veil of the night? What should I do or avoid doing? Aran, help me please!"

A force pulled Nik into the corridor of his dreams as he watched the trees and bushes swing back to their original location.

Aran lowered his head and turn away from him.

The image of the strange realm was gone, and his body levitated to the top. Remembering Aran's instructions, he closed his eyes as he became lighter. Nik felt his mouth move with a tongue inside swirling in the same fashion as the hole in the strange realm. He opened his eyes and was thrust back into his own realm, where the strange phenomena stopped and all his items were in their normal place.

Mirage withdrew her lips from him and backed away. She sat beside him on the duet bench and wrapped her arms around him. "You did it, babe. You not only started it, but you finished." Her warm tears fell on his shoulder.

"That's great. I'm happy I did it, but I don't know what I've done, and I don't know why you're crying. What did I do, my love?"

She grabbed the music sheet from the stand and placed the pages on his lap.

Nik was mystified and surprised as he examined the first page. The words *Mirage/Dream* were across the header. In the top right corner, he saw *Music by Nikolas C. Vanelli*. Under the title "Mirage/Dream" was the sub header, *A Symphony of Love & Passion*, encased with parenthesis. He was amazed as he perused through the once-empty pages now filled with intricate key signatures, time signatures, chord structures, and dynamic values. This was not the work of some dodgy amateur writing chords and lyrics on notebook paper; this was the work of a master of the craft.

He noticed the accompanying string and brass ensembles and the different clefs. Along with treble and bass clef, he identified tenor and percussion clefs. He continued to study the sheet music as he advanced to the end of the pages where he found something captivating. The last page was a dedication.

He fixated on the last page as he read the statement scribed in his own handwriting. *For GLP. We did not have more than a blink of an eye together, but I want you to know I love you, and you are and always will be in my heart through time and time until time has ended. My love for you is eternal and beyond. I dedicate this work to you solely.*

After Nik read the dedication to whomever GLP is, a single tear fell from each eye. He dried his face and turned to Mirage to find her tears as well. "I don't understand. Who is GLP? I've never met anyone with those initials. Why wouldn't I dedicate this work to you or my parents? It's hard enough to believe this came from me but to dedicate it to someone I don't know, nor have I ever met, is truly perplexing. Is it someone who has any merit to us?"

Mirage remained silent as she brought the sheet music to her lips then turned to retrieve the manila envelope. With the delicateness of soothing a newborn before placing them into a crib, she slid the sheet music inside the envelope. She stood from the bench, carefully placing the Life's Work envelope on his desk then straddled the bench sideways.

Nik maneuvered his body to match hers and faced her.

She leaned forward. "I cannot tell you who GLP is right now. But know this, GLP is deeply loved and cherished. This work is to express our unending love for GLP."

A strange feeling consumed Nik as he felt love for this unknown variable, unsure if GLP was a person or something else. He closed his eyes as he engaged Mirage in a passionate kiss. He grabbed her hand and led her to the threshold. "I've got plans for us."

He escorted her to the foot of his bed and reached to remove her halter-neck shirt. After they were both naked, they fell onto their sides on his bed and gently explored the curves and contours of their bodies.

Mirage placed her hands on Nik's chest and gently lowered him onto his back. She mounted him and slid down his torso, laying a breadcrumb trail of kisses, until she arrived at his fully erect shaft and encompassed his entire unit in her mouth. She pressed her breast upward, cupping his penis between her firmness.

Nik tilted his head to watch.

She squeezed him harder then received him in her mouth again, deeper.

He watched her body rock and move as the hallway light shined on her curves. He felt the urge to release but suppressed it as he was seeking more than a means to arrive. He wanted to experience Mirage totally. He pulled her toward him, nearly jolting her headfirst into the headboard. Nik kissed her with purpose before laying her gently on her back. Nik climbed on top of her, spreading her legs.

A look of fear revisited her face. Her chest rose with deep breathes and reverberating heartbeats.

While on top of her, he guided into her.

She placed her hands on his chest and reared back slightly. "Nik, we mustn't go any further. We're playing on dangerous grounds. There might be a chance that something comes from this, along with other repercussions—repercussions that neither of us could return from once we've started." She trembled with arousal and fear.

Nik looked down at her as he remained mounting her, stricken with deep thought. If this would have been any other occasion with an end-of-show conquest, he would have continued the seduction; however, he just leaned down and kissed her once more and rose from her body to behold her beautiful bright face.

"If something comes of this, then something comes of this. If there are any repercussions, then I am ready to face them with you, side by side. I don't know if we can ever legally get married, but I choose you to be my bride. I have waited for you all my life. I know that you are different, but maybe just maybe that is what I need. I love you, Mirage, deeply and truly. Nobody has ever made me feel as I feel with you."

Mirage brought her hands to her eyes and sobbed.

Nik wrapped his arms around her back.

"I love you too, Nik, and I know what you're feeling is true. I'm ready for you, my dearest. I'm ready to face the consequences and the future with you. I want to give myself to you, and I want you to give yourself to me. Whatever happens, know that, from this day of all days, our love will be eternal."

He positioned his body and guided inside of her with care.

As he made first contact while entering her, she moaned with anticipation and grinded against his pelvis, contouring herself for his initial entry. His first thrust was an overeager rushed plunge, and she writhed, arching her back with pain. Nik apologized and decreased his speed and intensity.

Mirage welcomed him despite her pain.

Once he was completely inside her, he withdrew and was surprised to see no blood. This time, his thrusts were careful and loving. He persisted as he watched her face and body change from writhing pain to pleasurable motions.

She craned her arms around his back and tucked her knees to her body, wrapping her legs around his back to allow him to plunge deeper as he drove with increased stamina, then she rolled Nik to his back. "If we're doing this all the way, I want to experience it with as many positions as possible." She smiled with fire and conviction in her eyes.

After the longest romp he's ever endured with a female in his life—including a record-breaking number of positions and angles—he didn't think he could last much longer. He wiped a puddle of sweat from his eyebrow to glimpse at the clock on the wall just to get a reference point of time. How had almost three hours passed since they started? Refocusing on Mirage's figure, he drove his member in her with a solid thrust, wondering if she had the capability to orgasm or should he just release and be done with it; he didn't think he had much stamina left, if she did have the ability to finish.

Mirage's eyes widened, and her mouth gaped open as Nik realized he couldn't stop the imminent storm from erupting from his loins—was she close too?

Then, as if on cue—and through her panting—she mustered, "Nik, I'm feeling a sensation growing in me. I think I'll burst. I don't know, but I think I might be coming soon. Are you close, my love? If you are, please, babe, release in me. I want to feel your beautiful release inside me."

He closed his eyes, gritted his teeth and thought about baseball—isn't that what the old advice said would work?—to buy his climax a little more time now that he knew she was close too.

After only a few more thrusts, Mirage screamed shrilling words. "I'm almost there! Come with me. Come in me now!"

He tightly pulled her to him and released inside her, a wave of shivers rippling across her body.

She cried out with ecstasy with each pulsing blast.

He collapsed on top of Mirage with exhaustion and elation, panting and feeling his pulse pound throughout his body. He struggled to place his shaking hands on the mattress to rise up. Gaining his strength, he stabilized his position and rose with exhaustion to look down on her.

Mirage cried and smiled with love and sorrow.

Nik's face became saturated with confusion as Mirage's smile faded, along with her body. Fear overwhelmed Nik as he watched Mirage vanish. Her physical body grew transparent as the seconds flashed by. When her physical form had disappeared, all that remained was a flicker of a fire burst rainbow and her three glowing orbs that flickered once before they grew dim, blinking out of existence.

He felt a force lift him toward the ceiling. He flailed, struggling to grab hold of for his mattress. The walls of reality and bedroom became paper thin, fading in the same degree as Mirage. His vision clouded, and his body became limp and fatigued. His eyes rolled back in his head as he continued to ascend.

He was sure the ceiling would stop him; however, he rose farther and faster upward. Nik's breathing shallowed, and consciousness and the real world dissolved around him as the realm of dreams inhabited his physical body.

He opened his eyes once he felt himself stop, finding himself in the endless corridor. His body rematerialize from his head to his feet, and an archway appeared in front of him. He moved cautiously through the archway into the strange realm again. The sights were the same as before, only this time the realm seemed to have a more realistic quality. He vividly saw the azure sky; he smelled the thriving life of botanical flowers; he heard the birds sing; and he felt the environment around his flesh truly without the interpretation of dream sensations. This time he knew he was truly in the realm and not dreaming.

He looked to his left and saw the life-producing tree by the once-roaring river now a calm stream. He approached the tree, and it reacted with a defensive retraction. He stepped backward, and the life-producing tree returned to its normal position. He located the hole that had contained the black-and-white swirl. The vortex was now inverted and cone like. He watched the swirl as it gained intensity with speed and degree of point.

He was shaken from the concentration when he heard a familiar voice. "You failed, boy. You failed in every manner possible. I warned you not to fall to the deception of the veil of the night. You could not control your primitive urges. You could not help yourself but to violate her. Oh, for anything but light. You chose to do all that you wanted and refused your purpose. Take her hand. She will lead you to the citadel for your trial and judgment."

Nik turned swiftly and saw Mirage levitating next to him. She wore her white billowing garments with the fire rainbow shimmering behind, along with the inverted triangular formation of glowing orbs floating. She appeared to Nik as she had when she first assumed human form.

Nik leapt with joy as he looked at Mirage. He tried to grab her hand and squeeze it, but it fell limp and dropped to her side as he urged her to acknowledge him.

Her gaze was locked in front of her, expressionless. She was cold to the touch and lifeless.

After Nik tried a few more urgent tries to break her from her trance, she clenched his hand without affection and propelled him forward.

He quickened his pace to maintain her speed. "Babe, what the hell is going on? Where are you taking me? What is the matter with you? I don't know what is happening, and I am scared. Talk to me, *please!*"

Mirage did not look at Nik as she spoke to him in an eerie manner, like she had reverted to a stage of basic robotic function. "You are being led to the citadel for trial and judgment."

Nik became desperate as she pulled him through the foliage surrounding them.

They cleared the foliage, arriving at a clearing in front of a moat.

Mirage stopped as they surveyed the monolith structure. The citadel looked like a spire of gold as it stood proud in front of them.

"You are being led to the citadel for trial and judgment."

Nik puzzled at the moat, as he could not discern whether the moat was water or a view from above the clouds. He felt nearing the point of nausea as he studied the strange fluid or air mass.

Mirage firmed her grip and pulled with greater speed.

Nik panicked and planted his heals, fighting being dragged into the mysterious mass. As his right foot hovered over the mass, a small rectangular panel materialized under his foot. Once his foot was securely on the panel, he placed his other foot on top of it. The panel glistened and shot golden rays of light. It changed color, cycling all the represented colors of the rainbow.

Mirage pulled him faster. She did not make contact with the color-changing panels; she floated without the need to plant her feet.

As they continued toward the citadel, the panels became random as the path curved and winded without logic or sense. Eventually Mirage and Nik reached the citadel's grand entrance and stood before the reddened door with solid iron hinges.

Nik turned to Mirage to question her on the imminent situation but knew it was futile. He studied her beautiful profile, committing her image to memory. He panned down her shapely body and stopped at her once flat and toned core. She bulged, appearing maternal. Nik's desperation exploded, and he shook Mirage's hand, pleading her to acknowledge him. He knew what resided in the bulge. He knew what she was carrying belonged to him. When he reached to feel her pregnant belly, an unseen force pushed him backward.

Mirage spoke in a different language with an unnatural voice. Her voice was no longer sweet and kind nor did it sound human or with gender. Nik could understand the syntax was a command or an announcement to let them through the doors.

The doors creaked as they slowly swung inward then flung open with a vacuum force, sucking Nik through the entrance. He straightened his body and observed the structure's glossy golden bricks and the spectrum-colored lights as they shined through the stained-glass windows.

He and Mirage traveled down the citadel's great hallway. Occupants shrouded with brown-hooded robes regarded them slyly as they neared the end of the hallway. The brown-robed occupants appeared to be cleaning and maintaining the structure and stopped once they passed. Nik could not understand their words, but he could feel their judgment and contempt not just for himself but toward Mirage.

They stopped in front of the door, and Mirage opened her mouth to speak. Nik could not understand her words, but he recognized what she had spoken at the entrance was the same that she had spoken to announce their entrance. The door opened inward in the same fashion as the citadel entrance. She floated through the threshold, and he stepped into the cold central chamber. The hexagon-shaped room's entrance was the base of the shape.

He noticed a wall on the left housing a bookshelf full of old books. The immediate right wall was also inhabited by old books. He thought the books resembled old spell books in a wizard's private library. Gloss-coated and rainbow-colored bricks adorned the diagonal left and right walls with a church archway-shaped window allowing light to shine through a stained-glassed window.

At the center of the hexagon room sat seven robed men positioned higher in elevation than Nik and resembled Aran, with their white hair and white beards. While they were not identical to Aran, all the robed men looked identical, as if they were clones. They sat in a shelved manner, each wearing a robe that represented a solid color of the rainbow. A seat was vacant at the rear right side of the congregation.

Mirage released her grasp on Nik's hand and floated toward the robed men, turning her back to them once she reached the wall. She stared at Nik blankly as she landed gently on the cold, glossed, golden brick floor.

The robed men stood in unison once her back was against the wall and raised their arms to the ceiling. The same fire-burst-rainbow phenomena projected from behind their backs, along with glowing orbs that rotated clockwise from inverted triangular formations to equilateral formations. They spoke in unison in the same language as Mirage, harmonizing together as a collective hive mind. As they continued to chant with their arms raised, their strange phenomena intensified with a blinding glow, and their orbs rotated, leaving only light streaks as their pace, tone, and pitch increased in their voices.

Nik gazed to the ceiling and saw an awesome sight. At the center of the ceiling, a large fire rainbow manifest with three glowing triangular formation orbs appeared, each three different colors—blue, purple, and green. The fire rainbow and the orbs lowered to project a large holographic face identical to the seven robed men. Through his fear, Nik knelt as the face hovered above him and spoke with a booming and echoing voice in the same language. Nik felt his heart blast through his chest and wondered if what he was seeing was their god.

"Foolish primate, I am not a god! I am everything you see in this realm! You have entered the central core of Fantopia! I am the marriage of fantasy and dreams united in perfect utopia! You have disrupted my order and committed a great atrocity against me, along with the perversion of the gift I have given you!"

Nik trembled as the superior scolded him. He stood slowly, wavering to his feet to look upon the large holographic projection. "Who are you? What atrocity have I committed? What gift have I perverted? I don't know what I have done, and I don't know what is happening to me."

The holographic projection glared at him with anger flashing and flickering to accentuate his point. *"I am Eenyl I manifested when humans began to have the capacity to have dreams and fantasies. I am becoming lost to your primitive kind, as your kind only has the depth of dreaming of material and physical worth, with seasons of gasoline and gold currency and self-indulgence. You primates are growing distant from me as your time progresses forward. With your abundance of self-indulged progression, you do not realize that you are, in fact, regressing and burning my history!"*

Nik felt inferior and sadly agreed with Eenyl as he assessed humankind, knowing he was guilty of being materialistic and desiring more as well. Reviewing his own acts self-indulgence, he realized that questions still remained unanswered as to why he had been brought before Eenyl and his council.

"You wasted your life away, Nikolas Vanelli, and the gift and second chance I have given you. If I were human, I would say that you pissed away *your life. You still do not realize the gravity of the situation. You died, you foolish primate, when you committed suicide those years back. I retrieved your soul as you descended into eternal hellfire and brought you here from the brink. I allowed you to retain your life's memories and your identity, but I enhanced you and endowed you with tenacity and conviction. You were charged with writing my song, my opus, my magnificent symphony. With your second chance, you became arrogant, vain, and self-indulged, like every other primate. You squandered my gift to you, and you never dedicated to your purpose."*

Nik stepped forward, refraining from exhibiting any aggressive demeanor in fear that Eenyl could strike him down without effort. "I did write your piece. It may have taken me years to start and finish it, but I did complete what you asked of me."

Eenyl furrowed his brow. *"Your foolishness is exceeding, even for you. You're a failed and broken human soul who I reconstructed from my design. It was not you who completed my work alone. Mirage aided you. She has also committed grave violations against me. You truly are a failed experiment proving to be more of a primate than an enhancement. You could have been a testament to your kind with the blessed evolution of your soul, but you are entirely and utterly oblivious. You honestly do not know the truth of Mirage's involvement to you, do you? Mirage is a pure construct, unlike yourself, who I charged to Aran with her design and creation. You were merely the prototype, and she was the final product, despite her failing. Your world and your kind is nothing more than pure corruption, and her time spent in your world with you only solidified the matter. Her purpose was to intercept you without your knowledge and bring you back here. You were supposed to have died from Samantha's husband's hands the night he confronted you, and your soul was meant to be returned here for deletion, not to be delivered to Heaven or Hell. If you think she is your great love and inspiration, it only proves how fundamentally stupid you truly are. I grew impatient after seven years of waiting with no productivity from you, so, upon completion, I allowed her to reveal herself to you while you visited your parents. Hence why you saw the unnatural events in your Earth sky before you returned home and she contacted you in your dream. Her pity and love for you poisoned and ruined her. The only surmountable aspect from this whole masquerade is that you have completed both objectives. My eternal anthem to restore my history is now complete, and you are here for your final disposal. I will also dispose of Mirage and the abominable hybrid growing in her womb. There will be no continuation or evidence of your utter and absolute failing. Once you have been declared dead in your world, the only remnants of you will be your name on the sheet music. That is the only honor I will afford you, for I have deemed you a failure. Prepare to be deleted, Nikolas Vanelli!"*

The holographic projection of Eenyl expanded to tower over Nik as he stood watching Eenyl's eyes burn red. Nik's body felt engulfed with heated pain from the center of his chest, extending through his extremities. He wished and pleaded silently for any deity to hear him to grant him mercy or the ability to scream, but the pain was far beyond the scope of allowing him to produce sound. He knew the hellish pain of being deleted and fading from existence from this realm and his world. Nik was nearly burnt out of existence when the chamber doors flung open.

Aran ran in, dashing to the center of the room then kneeling before his master and staring upward with desperation. "Wait, my lord! You must stop this now. We are in dire circumstances, and you mustn't continue with this final act. You will destroy not only him but yourself and all of Fantopia if you continue!"

"Insolent servant! How dare you oppose my will and actions? What is the meaning of your intrusion?"

Aran panted and struggled to stand, showing his age. "The vortex, my lord … The vortex has completely inverted and revealed his coming. The swirl has become pitch black—black as midnight, black as the lurking shadows. Your brother, the Dark One, has gained our knowledge of enhancing and evolving human souls. As we speak, he is grooming and preparing a dark human soul to declare his war against us. This *dark warrior* is embracing his promises and his ideals to bring his own retribution upon humankind and ours so he may rule both realities. You must not destroy Nikolas Vanelli. We need him!"

Eenyl's grasp of destruction on Nik ended, and he collapsed to the floor, gasping for breaths. Eenyl's size returned to his rested state as he eyed Aran with grave concern. *"Are you sure of this, servant? Or are you just trying to protect your creation? You know that once Nikolas Vanelli is deleted, Mirage will follow shortly thereafter."*

Aran urged and pleaded that his visions were true and pure, imploring that his master look for himself.

"I will return shortly to confirm what you have seen. If you are wrong or you are trying to deceive me, you will join Nikolas and Mirage in the deletion. Know this; if you are deceiving me, your deletion will be far more excruciating than theirs." Eenyl rose to the ceiling, disappearing instantly.

Aran knelt beside Nik, who quivered with residual pain and shock from the onslaught of pain. Aran rolled Nik to his back and placed his hand under his head to support him. "I think I have bought you a short amount of time. It is true the vortex revealed to me that his brother, the Dark One, is mounting an offense against us. I don't know what will happen to you, but you may be spared, and the master might have a further use for you yet. Just remain silent and rest. He will be back shortly to confirm the vision." Aran placed Nik's head on the floor.

Eenyl returned just as Aran stood from his kneeling position. *"Your observation was correct, Aran. My brother's plans are absolute, and the totality of the circumstance dictates that we must act. We just might have a use after all for your creation and this reconstructed soul. We need someone with equal capacity to combat my brother's dark prodigy, who is someone from your age and time, Nikolas. You must go back to combat him. If you are successful, you will have earned redemption in my eyes."*

Nik rose to his feet, free from pain, and gained his strength. "I will go back, and I will fight him to the end, just don't hurt Mirage or our child. I beg of you, regardless if she was sent to kill or intercept me. We truly have fallen in love. I will return and fight your enemy, just don't hurt her."

Eenyl smiled at Nik, acknowledging his pleas for his love. His holographic face resumed its normal stern expression as he looked through Nik and studied the magnitude of his soul. *"I don't think you understand completely what you have agreed to. When I said you are going back, I meant to the beginning. In this case, a new beginning free of corruption and memories of your life as Nikolas Vanelli. You will be born during the same year as your natural life, but you will be someone else devoid of this life and past. You will live a life blind and unaware of this knowledge until I call upon you to take up arms and engage my brother's prodigy. In your new life, you will not know Mirage or who you once were. You will only know when it is time to answer your call. It will be the only way to save your love, your Mirage. When you return to Earth, your physical body will die there, as it was intended to do. Your time was ending anyways, but now you can fulfill a greater purpose anew."*

Nik eyed Aran staring up at his master and then turned to Mirage standing against the wall, frozen in deep trance. He regarded Eenyl and nodded a single solid time, accepting his task. "Before all of this becomes unknown to me and my memories and my life are truly gone and I fulfill your task, I have one final request."

Eenyl floated above Nik, delivering a look of kindness and compassion for the first time since they had met. *"You have only but to ask, Nikolas Vanelli."*

"I need you to release Mirage from her trance so I can tell her goodbye and that I deeply love her."

Eenyl floated over the seven robed men, and his words grew distant before his holographic image vanished. *"I will grant your last request, Nikolas. After you finish your declaration, you will be returned. Make your declaration to Mirage with the entirety of your heart and soul."*

After Eenyl evaporated with his fading words, Mirage was broken from her entangled trance. She raced to join Nik in the center of the chamber, wrapping her arms around him.

He struggled to free his arms so he could embrace her. He held her deeply, feeling her body and her maternal hump pressed against him. He did not want to release her, and he could feel that she did not want to release him. They continued to hold each other as the council of the seven robed men and Aran looked on. Nik pried his body away from her to look upon her face one last time. He admired and adored his beautiful Mirage as she looked with the same admiration.

Nik's expression deepened as he beheld Mirage and felt something was incomplete about his time with her. He focused on the memory of her license. He remembered it stated that her last name was the same as his. He also remembered how Roger had congratulated them on their recent marriage. It was strange that a small thing crossed Nik's mind in his last fleeting moments with Mirage. Nik smiled at her with full realization knowing what must be done to complete his final moments with her.

Nik nodded warmly with conviction before he dropped to his knees. He embraced her snuggly around the waist, pressing his head against her belly to feel the product of their love move and respond. He began to cry, thinking his child could feel and know that his father was embracing both his mother and him. He pressed his face against Mirage's maternal belly and planted a kiss. "I love you, my son. You are the perfect part of me that will live on and represent what your mother and I shared together. Regardless of how brief the time together, you and your mother are both the love of my life."

She extended both of her soft, delicate hands to him.

"We both know our time together is short. It's growing shorter as we speak, but I need to do something before our time together and my time is done. We could never have done this in my world, but maybe we can do it here. My question will hopefully be the last memory that fades from my mind and existence before I drift into nothingness. Mirage, my dearest, my beauty, would you do me the honor of becoming my wife?"

Mirage hoisted him to his feet, and they pressed against each other in a deep kiss, tears streaking their faces.

Mirage looked at him and softly squeezed his hands. "Yes."

They approached the council of the seven robed wise men, hand in hand.

Aran padded behind them as they stood in front of the council looking at them. "I advocate the marriage of these two. As Mirage's creator, I offer her hand to this human man in the ceremony of eternal wedlock. I ask of you, council of wise men, to validate their marriage and allow them to devote their fleeting remaining time they have left as husband and wife."

The council of the seven wise men looked amongst their collective group and murmured quietly. They turned to Nik and Mirage, sharply gazing at them. In one collective unison voice, the council addressed them. "No, we do not recognize or validate their union or marriage. However, he recognizes and validates their union and marriage." The council of seven raised their hands to the ceiling and beckoned the return of Eenyl to preside their union.

Eenyl floated above them in a different form—a human man with a robe decorated in a fashion that represented all the colors of the council of sevens robes. *"Nikolas Vanelli, I ask you to join hands with Mirage."*

Nik and Mirage faced each other, interlocking their hands.

Eenyl placed his hands on theirs. *"As the ruler and the overseer of the kingdom and realm of Fantopia, I declare the bond and validation of Nikolas Vanelli's and Mirage Vanelli's marriage. Shall their song be sung throughout the land and occupants of this realm. Nikolas Vanelli, you may kiss your bride."*

Without further provocation, Nik leaned toward Mirage and kissed her in front of the council and Eenyl, solidifying their union.

Aran clapped and cheered as their marriage became official. He continued to cheer with intoxicating enthusiasm as the chamber grew silent.

Nik and Mirage watched Aran wipe a single tear from his eye, quickly attempting to not be noticed. Nik and Mirage smiled at each other with laughter over Aran's actions.

The newlyweds faced Eenyl one last time as he delivered his final words to them. *"Nikolas, your final request is now complete. You know what time it is, and you know what you must do now."*

Nik nodded, silently wishing this beautiful moment would never end, then looked at Mirage one last time. "I love you, Mirage. My lovely Mirage, I love you now and always. Goodbye, my love. I hope, in some time, we will find each other. I love you. Goodbye, my wife."

"I love you too, my—"

Nik's body rose from the chamber floor and became light and limber. His eyes grew heavy and his body transparent. He beheld Mirage as she stood watching him elevate. Nik felt a pleasant heat caress his back and protrude behind him as he grew in height and his eyes became heavier. He turned his gaze from Mirage to the heat flares that a fire rainbow was emitting from his body.

He felt his body disappear and separate as he morphed into three different collective parts. He realized the same phenomena he had seen with Mirage and this realm's other inhabitants were now happening to him. Unable to smile, as his physical form was gone, he felt overwhelming joy as his ascension quickened. He knew that more than his marriage and union with her was validated, he was accepted as one of their kind.

His vision blackened as he entered the void of darkness, racing back to his world without slowing. In a flash, he was returned to his bedroom in the waking light of the morning.

He lay naked in bed, still feeling Fantopia all around and through his body. He checked the alarm clock—7:00 a.m. He sat up in bed and threw his legs over the side. He knew that time was not on his side, and he must make the most of his last conscious day on Earth.

He grabbed his clothes lying on the floor next to the nightstand and raced to the bathroom. He climbed into the shower, and a burning question raced through his mind. "How do I begin to live the last day of my known life? What do I do?"

Chapter
Twelve

He washed quickly, scrubbing erratically without concentration. He wanted to be clean for his last day on Earth, but he did not want to afford an extended amount of time in the shower. He felt as if the minutes were already speeding by like seconds. He turned off the water and left the shower drenching wet. He shimmied his towel around his body and dashed to his medicine cabinet to brush his teeth. He brushed quickly and clumsily placed his toothbrush back inside. Once he was ready to face the day, he dressed in the clothes Mirage had given him. As he pulled the shirt over his head, he brought it to his nose to smell her scent; it helped him feel that her presence was still around him. He left the bathroom and entered his music room.

He removed the sheet music from the manila envelope and viewed the piece with clear eyes and studied his and Mirage's beautiful masterpiece. The work may have listed Nik as the composer, but Mirage was instrumental in its creation. He returned the music into the manila envelope and laid it on his desk and thought about something else he and Mirage had created—his child growing in her womb, a child he had declared his eternal love to, along to his mother.

His own mother and father were oblivious to the fact that they were now grandparents and, despite it not being valid on Earth, that he was now a married man. He laughed as he realized they would never know they had just gained two new family members—and those new family members were not entirely human. He reflected on how the harshness of future events would bring his parents sadness and sorrow as they would be burying their son soon.

He pushed the thought from his mind and left the music room, his objective completed. He pulled his cellphone from his pocket to check the time—8:05 a.m.. He knew his parents were early birds on Saturday mornings, so he decided to call them.

After ringing twice, his mother answered the phone with, "Hi, kid. How are you doing?" His mother yawned, breaking the sleep from her voice.

"I am doing okay. I just wanted to call and say hi and see if you and Dad were busy today."

Nik heard Kayla ask Terrence if they were busy today. "No, we're not busy today. What's up? Did you need something?"

Nik did need something; he needed to see them one last time before his death. "No, I don't really need anything. I just wanted to stop by for a visit. I'm going to walk around town and head over, if that's okay with you and Dad."

Kayla told Nik that they would be expecting him and looked forward to his visit.

Nik told his mother that he loved her and said goodbye. He placed his cellphone in his pocket and locked the front door behind him. The morning sunlight warmed his skin and conjured the distinction of Mirage's scent again. He walked the entire town twice, thinking about Mirage and the time he had spent with her. He reflected on their first encounter on Donaldson Road to his last encounter when he devoted his love to her for the last time. He welcomed these memories as he sauntered to the village park.

He headed toward the fountain she had climbed into only a short while ago and played in the water. For a moment, as he watched the movement of the water, he felt he caught a glimpse of her. He knew it was wishful thinking, but maybe she was trying to communicate with him from beyond, wherever or whenever she might be. He stood in silence to honor her.

He felt the morning sunlight shift to late-morning sunlight and strode toward his house. He hustled to his truck with his keys already in hand. He drove through downtown Pemkey, waving goodbye to it as he passed each structure. He left the village limit and passed Moline Medical Warehousing without affording the place a single glance. He drove from Pemkey to Amsdale in his usual route, purging all thoughts from his mind except Mirage.

As he approached Amsdale's village limit, he was stricken with regret as he remembered he had promised Mirage he would introduce her to his parents the last time they were here, and the promise fell short. He projected her image in his mind, hoping she was with him in spirit to meet her new in-laws.

He parked his truck in the church parking lot and crossed the street to his parents' porch. The front door opened, and his mother and father greeted him.

He spent most of the afternoon listening to them discuss their day-to-day lives and the local neighborhood gossip. He wanted to tell them this would be the last time he would see them, wanted to express his love and admiration for them as parents, but mostly, he wanted to tell them about his marriage to Mirage and their new grandbaby. It took every inch of restraint to control his urges as he sat in the recliner, listening to them gab.

Nik's mother told him she was cooking a pork roast for dinner. Nik thought a pork roast sounded delicious and would be a fitting last meal, but he declined and told his mother that he was not hungry. Knowing he would die soon was an appetizer killer and would have been futile anyway.

He sat with them as they ate dinner on TV trays in the living room. He watched the news with his parents as his father cussed at the TV in usual fashion. They sat in the living room, continuing to talk as the sunlight grew dim through the windows. Nik knew he had an impending appointment waiting for him at his home and decided it was time to say goodbye.

He rose from the recliner, and his parents followed him to the front door. His mother and father stood next to each other in the same manner he and Mirage had in the Fantopia realm. He wished he and Mirage could be standing together in front of his parents. He also wished he and Mirage could have had the same amount of time together that his parents have had. He stepped forward, wrapping an arm around each of his parents and telling them that he loved them.

When he stepped backward, they eyed him with concern. Nik swallowed the urge to cry as he beheld his parents for the last time. They followed him onto the porch as he crossed the street to his truck. He looked back at them and waved goodbye. He started his truck, placed it in Reverse and turned right on Garfield Street, waving goodbye to them. He turned right onto Elmbury Street and saw them still standing on the porch, waving at him.

He drove home in silence, feeling his heartbeat pound from behind his chest. As he grew closer to Pemkey, he knew he was on borrowed time. He said a silent prayer as he approached the village limit sign. He did not know who would hear his prayer, but he continued to pray regardless. He prayed for his mother and father, along with Mirage and his unborn child. He concluded his prayer as he entered downtown Pemkey and turned left on his street.

He fixed his vision on his dark house as it stood haunting to him for the first time since he had lived there. He crept into his driveway and turned off his truck. A morbid case of curiosity engulfed him. He wanted to know what the time was now. He wanted to know what time he would die. He exited his truck and retrieved his cellphone—9:12 p.m.

He walked with as much bravery as he could muster to the front porch. He looked at the glider swing and remembered Samantha drinking beer on the swing the night they had first met. He cursed her name quietly as he felt his impending death was her fault. He did not want to fixate on a bitter thought as his last. He pushed it from his mind and replaced the thought that his death was a necessity; it was part of a grand design.

As soon as he approached the front door, he noticed it looked tooled open by force. He inhaled deeply and stepped inside, slowly turning on his light.

Ross Delbert stood in front of him, fuming with rage. "I hope my wife's pussy was good enough to die for, you sonofabitch." Ross raised his pistol at Nik's chest and shot twice—one struck Nik just below the sternum, the other struck him center mass.

Nik landed on his knees then fell forward. He rolled over with his last fleeting strength, writhing in excruciating pain as he watched Ross step over him.

"See you in Hell, boy," Ross barked and left Nik's house.

Nik grew weak, and his vision narrowed as he gasped his last breaths and stared at the ceiling pattern. His body became limber and light, and his eyelids grew heavy. The pain subsided, and he felt the same way he felt when he had entered Fantopia. He closed his eyes and embraced the next stage with bravery.

He felt his body floating in the darkness in an unusual manner; he could not tell whether he was falling, floating upward, or moving to his left or right. He looked into the distance and saw a flicker of light pulsate. It grew closer and larger and intensified. Nik identified a fire rainbow approaching him with three traveling triangular orb formations. The figure of a woman emitted in front of the phenomena as it grew closer.

"Mirage! I never thought I'd see you again. If it took me to die to see you again, it was worth it."

Mirage remained silent until she was directly in front of him. She spread her arms, smiling with welcoming love. "You must start over, my love. You must start anew without your memories. Only as a new person can you save our world and yours. If you succeed, we will be joined again for eternity in our beautiful union. I love you too, Nik."

Mirage tightly embraced Nik. He felt as if he was being sucked into a vortex created by Mirage. His body was pulled and pressed against hers until he was completely absorbed by her. Nik closed his eyes as he surrendered to the vortex, and the last thought to cross his mind was his wedding in the central chamber of the citadel.

Nik Vanelli was gone.

Rain fell hard from above and blew sideways, stinging Mirage's soft flesh as she hobbled with piercing pain on the side of a country road. The rain gained icy substance as she surveyed the dark isolated setting. She did not know where she was or if anyone was around to render her aid. She looked around desperately as she felt her child would emerge into the world soon. She trudged onward, urging her child to hold on until she found a safe and warm place to deliver.

Her white garments clung to her body as the icy rain intensified. She looked down to see her garments were transparent, and her maternal belly was visible. She covered her belly with her arms and walked for what seemed to be an eternity before she encountered a green rural road sign stating Swanta was ten miles in the opposite direction. She knew she could not make a ten-mile walk on the cold, rainy night, and no vehicles were in sight to stop and assist her. She agonized more as the temperature dropped into a bitter sleet, and the labor pains increased.

She discovered a house across the road to her right. She saw a single mailbox—*2317 State Route 74*—with the name *Porcaro*. She crossed the country road and grasped the mailbox to support her weight as the blustering winds increased. She knew she could not rest for long, as she was about to deliver the child.

She traversed the freezing gravel driveway, which pierced her tender frozen feet, and passed a white Chevy C-10 pickup and a brown Dodge van. The soles of her feet bleed warm stinging blood. She saw a two-story white country house with black shutters. She stepped off the gravel driveway onto a narrow sidewalk, clutching her maternal belly. She followed the curved sidewalk and climbed the porch with maximum effort. When she reached the front door, she nearly collapsed to her knees, catching herself and saving her from the fall. She pounded on the door, hoping the occupants of the isolated country house would help her. After pounding on the door several times, the front door flung open, and a large man stood in front of her.

The overweight man stood taller than Nik and wore a green John Deere cap with a red pocket t-shirt and dirty Wrangler blue jeans. "What is going on, girl? What do you want this time of night?" His reddish-brown beard vibrated with his words.

"I'm scared, and I am in labor. I need help."

The man turned to his left and hollered, "Linda, we got a girl out her who's going to have a baby! Help me get her into the house!"

Mirage rested her hand on the doorway as she looked into the house and saw a large woman with curly hair pry herself off a vinyl recliner. Mirage looked down and noticed she was beginning to hemorrhage. She nearly fainted from the sight of her own blood and began to fall forward until the man caught her.

He righted her on her feet and scooped her up. He carried her into the living room and placed her on the floor.

Mirage screamed from labor pains as the child was urging more to enter the world.

Linda knelt beside Mirage and offered her hand.

Mirage took her hand and squeezed it with pulsing agony.

"What's your name, girl? Where's the father of this baby?"

Mirage scanned the living room and realized the structure of the place looked old in comparison to Nik's house. The furniture and the décor revealed to her that she was not in Nik's time but in the past. "My name is Mirage. What day is it? What month is it? What year is it?"

"Honey, that is not important right now. Where is this baby's father?"

Mirage struggled to breathe. "My baby's father is dead. What day is it? What month is it? What year is it?"

Linda turned to the rotund man standing back between the living room and the adjacent kitchen. "JD, get me some blankets and towels, and bring a washtub with warm water. This girl is in trouble, and her baby is coming soon."

JD disappeared through the doorway and behind the wall to fetch the items.

"You hold on, honey. JD will be right back with what we need. To answer your question, it is March thirteenth, nineteen eighty-two. That is today's date, and it will be your baby's birthday. You need to hold on and breathe and make sure this baby comes out safe. Do you hear me, girl?"

Mirage nodded. As JD reentered the room with the requested items, she felt her baby crown.

Linda maneuvered her large body down the length of Mirage's torso and instructed her to push.

Mirage strained and pushed. She felt herself expand as the baby passed through her. Her breathing intensified and sharpened with each push. After the last push, she heard the first cries of her child as he entered the world.

"It's a boy. It's a boy. You got yourself a big baby boy." Linda turned from Mirage to wash the newborn in the tub of warm water then gently dried his body with the towel. Linda wrapped the baby in the blanket and placed the baby in Mirage's arms.

Mirage beheld her beautiful baby and smiled at him dearly. The infant was indeed a large baby boy and donned a full head of black full-bodied hair. She looked at her child with absolute love in her heart. The baby was the spitting image of Nik, exhibiting his features and physical traits.

Mirage turned her attention from her newborn son to the ceiling. She convulsed, and her breathing became rapid and strangulated.

With her last fleeting amount of strength, she handed the infant to Linda. "I won't make it. I need you to promise me two things before I pass. Take care of my baby for me."

Linda held the newborn with one arm and extended her other hand to Mirage. "Yes, honey, I promise me and JD will take good care of your boy. We always wanted a little boy of our own anyway."

Mirage shook her head, gaining the momentum to speak her second and final request. "I want you to name my baby Giovanni Lukather V—" Mirage's strength left her body. In one last attempt to speak, she uttered her last words. "His father would have wanted him to have that name." Mirage trailed off in a distant stare.

Linda placed Giovanni on Mirage's chest to feel his mother's heartbeat slow and fade as she exhaled her last breath in the Earth world.